Praise for *New York Times* bestselling author Cathy McDavid

"McDavid's characters are wonderful, and her story really showcases the hardships and love it takes to blend families."
—*RT Book Reviews* on *Cowboy for Keeps*

"McDavid does a fine job portraying a complex heroine dealing with immense guilt and self-doubt. This romantic story has some beautifully crafted, tender moments."
—*RT Book Reviews* on *Come Home, Cowboy*, Top Pick

"The dynamics of the Beckett family saga intertwine with a second-chance romance offering an emotional look at love, loss and learning to forgive."
—*RT Book Reviews* on *Her Rodeo Man*

"If you want a deep and emotional read, don't miss *More Than a Cowboy* by Cathy McDavid."
—*HarlequinJunkie.com*

Since 2006, *New York Times* bestselling author **Cathy McDavid** has been happily penning contemporary Westerns for Harlequin. Every day she gets to write about handsome cowboys riding the range or busting a bronc. It's a tough job, but she's willing to make the sacrifice. Cathy shares her Arizona home with her own real-life sweetheart and a trio of odd pets. Her grown twins have left to embark on lives of their own, and she couldn't be prouder of their accomplishments.

Books by Cathy McDavid

Harlequin Western Romance

Mustang Valley

Last Chance Cowboy
Her Cowboy's Christmas Wish
Baby's First Homecoming
Cowboy for Keeps
Her Holiday Rancher
Come Home, Cowboy
Having the Rancher's Baby
Rescuing the Cowboy

Harlequin American Romance

Reckless, Arizona

More Than a Cowboy
Her Rodeo Man
The Bull Rider's Son

Visit the Author Profile page at Harlequin.com for more titles.

HOME ON THE RANCH:
RODEO
VOLUME 2

NEW YORK TIMES **BESTSELLING AUTHOR**

CATHY McDAVID

HARLEQUIN® HOME ON THE RANCH

ISBN-13: 978-1-335-00503-8

First published as Dusty: Wild Cowboy
by Harlequin Books in 2010 and Aidan: Loyal Cowboy
by Harlequin Books in 2012.

Home on the Ranch: Rodeo Volume 2

Copyright © 2017 by Harlequin Books S.A.

The publisher acknowledges the copyright holder of the individual works as follows:

Dusty: Wild Cowboy
© 2010 by Cathy McDavid

Aidan: Loyal Cowboy
Copyright © 2012 by Cathy McDavid

Recycling programs
for this product may
not exist in your area.

Printed in U.S.A.

www.Harlequin.com

CONTENTS

DUSTY: WILD COWBOY

To Kevin, the best-looking, hardest-riding cowboy I know. Thanks for all your help with the research for this book and for giving me two beautiful and wonderful (if occasionally recalcitrant) children.

CHAPTER ONE

THE BIG BLACK horse skidded to a stop, rose high on its rear legs and dumped its rider headfirst onto the arena ground. He landed with a dense thud and a loud "Oomph."

"Daddy!"

Terrified, Maryanne Devonshire flew toward the open gate, silently cursing her Gucci heels, which sank like lead weights into the soft dirt. Frustrated, she kicked off the shoes and ran barefoot the rest of the way. She reached her father just as he was pushing himself to a sitting position with the help of a tall, lanky cowboy.

"You're not dead," she blurted.

"Not yet." Gil Devonshire dusted off his pant legs and stood with a grunt. "I don't think dead people hurt this much."

"Is anything broken?" She inspected him closely, touching his arms and shoulders. Not that she had the first clue what fractured bones looked or felt like.

"Just my pride." He rubbed the back of his neck and his left side. "But only in one or two places."

The horse, the devil incarnate as far as Maryanne was concerned, stood nearby, quietly chewing on the metal thingie in its mouth. A bit, right? And the leather straps attached to it were called...reins. Yes. Three days at Cowboy College, and she'd learned two whole new vocabulary words. Maybe by next week she wouldn't feel like everyone was speaking a foreign language.

Maybe by next week her father would come to his senses, and they could leave this place. He had no business whatsoever tie-down roping, a rodeo sport dominated by men decades younger than him. And with good reason. Rodeoing was intended for individuals *with* youth, not those trying to recapture their *lost* youth.

"Daddy, you have to quit this nonsense before you really do kill yourself."

"Thanks for the vote of confidence, Cookie."

She sighed. Asking her father not to use her childhood nickname did no good. He'd only apologize, then turn right around and use it again. Her mother, on the other hand, had always called her Maryanne. Except once three years ago—on the day she died. Her last words to Maryanne's father had been, "Take care of Cookie."

Funny, it had turned out to be the other way around. Maryanne was always taking care of her father. Like now.

"I think you should have a doctor check your neck. You could have whiplash."

He laughed. "I was thrown by a horse, not rear-ended by a car."

A pair of cowboys at the other end of the arena herded the loose calf her father had been attempting to rope into a pen with other calves. Flapping their arms, waving their hats and shouting, the cowboys reminded Maryanne of squawking hens. Probably not the image they were trying to convey.

"Go on, walk it off." The lanky cowboy clapped

Maryanne's father good-naturedly on the back. "You'll be fine."

Walk it off? What kind of insane advice was that? Did he not realize her father was pushing sixty-three? Not to mention his high-blood pressure, high cholesterol and increasingly frequent gout attacks.

She turned to stare down the cowboy and give him a piece of her—okay, sometimes very opinionated— mind. Instead, she was rendered momentarily dumb. The guy was gorgeous. Blue eyes, dark blond hair to his shirt collar, killer smile, kind of gorgeous.

Where had he come from?

Not that Maryanne paid much attention to the staff at Cowboy College. No, wait, what were they called? Wranglers. Or hands. That was it.

"Hi." The cowboy extended his hand to shake hers. "I'm Dusty." His warm, strong fingers swallowed hers. The sensation was pleasant despite his calluses.

Men in L.A. didn't have hands like this, and Maryanne found herself intrigued on yet another level. He'd make a great model, and inspiration for an ad campaign popped into her head. She filed it away for later in the day when she could make notes.

"This is Track." He motioned to a black and white dog sitting obediently at his heels, its tongue lolling to one side.

Maryanne hadn't noticed the dog before then.

"Do you work here?" she asked. Dumb question, of course he did.

"I'm from the neighboring ranch. I drop by sometimes to teach classes on nonsense."

"Nonsense?"

"You were saying earlier that your dad needed to quit

this nonsense." His smile widened, revealing a dimple in his right cheek and a flirty twinkle in his eyes.

Maryanne wasn't normally so captivated by a man's looks, even one resembling a young Brad Pitt. Working as a junior marketing executive for an eco-friendly cosmetic company, she was surrounded by good-looking people all day, every day, and had grown immune. But it was hard not to be affected by Dusty.

Must have something to do with being plunked down in the middle of nowhere. Okay, Markton, Wyoming wasn't exactly nowhere. Still, it was a long, long way from L.A., in distance, culture and scenery. Maryanne couldn't remember the last time she'd seen clear blue skies and unending miles of rugged, breathtaking countryside, except as backdrop for a magazine layout.

"He's the best there is," her father interjected. He'd been taking his instructor's advice and walking in small circles. To Maryanne's relief, he appeared unscathed. "Two-time world tie-down roping champion."

"I've won once. I still have to qualify for this year." Dusty's confidence indicated the technicality was a foregone conclusion. "You got a bit dirty."

She followed the direction of his gaze to her bare feet. They were filthy. So were the bottoms of her Vera Wang slacks. Did Markton even have a dry cleaner? All she'd seen on her short, uneventful drive down the main street was a feed store, drugstore, tackle shop, a handful of churches and The Spotted Horse Saloon, an establishment she'd likely not visit the entire month she and her father were spending at Cowboy College.

"What happened to your shoes, Cookie?" Her father stopped pacing.

"Cookie?"

Maryanne tried to ignore the amusement in Dusty's voice. She managed, but the appreciative glint in his expression proved harder.

Being appraised by men was a common occurrence for her. Working in a competitive industry and in a city overrun with glamorous people, she needed to do her best to stand out or, at least, not go unnoticed.

Dusty was definitely noticing her. Though he seemed more focused on her filthy feet than her meticulously coordinated designer ensemble.

"It's a nickname," she said. "One my father gave me, which gives him exclusive rights to it." She sent her dad a loving smile.

He returned it tenfold.

"Seeing as you're okay—" Dusty gave Maryanne's father a once-over "—you need to get back on that horse and give it another try. Next time, don't pull so hard on the reins. That's why Tiny Dancer dumped you."

He took hold of Maryanne's arm and led her back a few cautionary steps while her father mounted and trotted off. "Come on, unless you want to get stomped."

"Tiny Dancer?" Maryanne had to practically jog to keep up with Dusty's much longer strides. His dog followed with considerably more ease.

"The horse."

"Oh."

"Something wrong?"

"It's kind of a girly name for a big, um, horse." She almost added, "mean."

"Tiny Dancer *is* a girl and not very big compared to the rest of the riding stock around here. But she's fast."

Showed how little Maryanne knew.

"She's a good horse for beginner ropers like your dad," Dusty continued. "I trained her myself."

"Is that what you do for a living? Train roping horses?"

"When I'm not practicing or competing or on location."

"Location?"

"I help my brother manage our family's ranch stock. But I also provide specially trained horses for film work. Been in a few myself, too. Nothing big. Mostly walk-on roles. A couple speaking parts."

"No kidding?" Maryanne was admittedly fascinated. Having had an actress for a mother, she'd grown up on the fringes of Hollywood and was familiar with the industry and its people.

"What did you say your name was?"

"Dusty Cody." He opened the gate, and she preceded him through it.

"And you're from next door?"

"Uh-huh."

All at once, the pieces fell into place. This man was no ordinary cowboy. She and her father had heard all about the Cody family and their six hundred thousand acre ranch just outside Markton across the way during a tour of Cowboy College on their first day there.

The family's ancestor, Mark Cody, had not only started the ranch, he'd founded the town, named Markton after him. In those days, cattle had been the main source of revenue for the ranch. In recent years, their operation had expanded to include riding stock, rodeo stock and, apparently, specially trained horses. It was natural gas, however, that accounted for the present-day

Codys' vast fortune. They were a modern-day dynasty and the town's most prominent citizens.

According to Adele Donnelly, manager of Cowboy College, Dusty Cody was the wayward son, more interested in having fun and appearing in movies than being part of the family business along with his sister and three brothers.

She needed only to gaze into Dusty's incredible blue eyes to know the rumor was true.

"Well, it's nice to meet you," she said, drawing on her vast schmoozing experience to smooth out the awkward moment.

Hopping over obstacles in her path, most of which consisted of horse and calf droppings, Maryanne wondered what in the world had possessed her to kick off her shoes. She could only imagine the thoughts running through the heads of the two dozen or so students and wranglers milling about—not to mention Dusty.

He stopped suddenly and bent to pick up her shoes. He didn't seem to mind that they were covered in muck. "Here you go."

She took them gingerly, loath to put them back on and yet loath to remain barefoot. Then there were her pants. She'd probably wind up tossing them out. Well, her friends back home had warned her to take more than a single pair of jeans.

At least the shoes weren't a total loss, she thought upon inspecting them. With some cleaning and polishing and a weeklong airing out, they'd be good as new.

"You can wash up over there if you want." Dusty pointed to a big metal tub the horses drank out of.

Lovely. Used horse water. "Maybe I should go back to the cabin."

"You'll miss your dad."

Considering the fall he'd just taken, Maryanne decided she should probably stick around. If only to call 9-1-1 in case of an emergency. Removing her cell phone from her pocket, she checked the screen. Service at the college was sketchy at best. Finding two bars, she relaxed…for about a second.

Markton didn't have a hospital. How long would it take for an ambulance to arrive from the next closest town?

"Here. You can use this to wash up." Dusty removed a faded red bandanna from his back pocket and gave it to Maryanne. Not something she imagined the heir to a vast fortune using.

"Thank you."

"You've got time. Debbie and Tamara are up before your dad."

It still amazed Maryanne that women participated in tie-down roping. They weren't allowed to compete in sanctioned rodeo events but apparently did on local levels. Some of them were very good. The girl Debbie weighed no more than a hundred pounds, yet she kept up with men twice her size.

While washing her shoes in the trough, Maryanne observed Dusty meander over to the fence. In classic cowboy stance, he pushed back his hat, hooked a boot on the bottom fence rail and rested his forearms on the top. The dog sat close to his side, ears twitching with interest each time his owner spoke. She could easily picture the pair of them on a billboard advertising men's cologne or western wear and winning the hearts of millions of women.

With a heavy sigh, she returned to her task and submerged the bandanna he'd given her in the murky water.

"Oh, gross," she murmured.

Wringing out the bandanna, she wiped away the worst of the dirt on her shoes. Her feet were next. Holding on to a pole, she balanced on one leg. When she was done, she slid her marginally cleaner feet into her shoes. More than once she caught Dusty and the others watching her. Wonderful. Afterward, she draped the bandanna over the side of the trough to dry.

Soaking for an hour in warm bubble bath was definitely on her agenda when she returned to the cabin.

Feeling slightly better, she joined Dusty at the fence to watch her father, ignoring how her feet slipped around inside the damp shoes.

"Hi." He winked and gave her another drop-dead gorgeous smile.

Her heart immediately performed a somersault.

How ridiculous was that? The guy was obviously no amateur when it came to flirting. She should know, she encountered players every day in L.A. and recognized them a mile away.

Feeling a cold nose pressing into her palm, she looked down to see the dog nudging close to her.

"Hey, fellow." She patted his head. "What kind of dog is he?"

"Border collie."

"They're herding dogs, right?" Maryanne liked dogs, though she hadn't owned one in years.

"Yeah." The look Dusty gave her said he was surprised she knew that.

"We used some once in an ad campaign."

"Was it successful?"

"As a matter of fact, it was." She smiled. "Nothing sells like a cute dog."

"Nothing?" He flashed her another killer sexy grin.

Though totally unnecessary, Maryanne reminded herself that she was leaving Wyoming in a month and not interested in a short-term, doomed-from-the-start relationship with a notorious, albeit wickedly handsome, player. She also reminded herself that she hadn't always chosen wisely when it came to men. Twice she'd attempted long-distance relationships, and twice they'd ended badly. Maryanne had learned her lesson.

And Dusty, for all his kindness toward her father and friendly charm, was exactly the kind of guy she should avoid at all costs.

Dusty watched Gil Devonshire ride to the end of the arena and line up Tiny Dancer in the box. Everyone grew quiet as he checked his lasso one last time, placed the pigging string between his teeth and straightened himself in the saddle. When he was ready, he gave a quick, short nod to the wrangler.

With a whoosh, the chute gate flew open. The calf bolted for freedom and his buddies at the other end of the arena. Tiny Dancer gave chase, going from a standstill to full gallop in the blink of an eye. Clumps of dirt exploded from her hooves as she anticipated the calf's next move, changing direction on a dime. Gil didn't have to worry about anything except roping the calf. The horse knew what to do even if he didn't.

With his left hand on the reins, he raised his right arm and swung the lasso high over his head. Then, with a flick of his arm, he sent the lasso sailing into the air and toward the running calf. Dusty saw Gil's left hand pull back on the reins and knew the outcome before it happened. The horse hopped, then slowed, almost unbalancing Gil. Maryanne let out a gasp. Fortunately, her father managed to stay seated this time. When the lasso finally fell, it missed the calf by a good three feet, dropping limply to the ground.

"Aw, shoot," said one of the other participants sitting on the fence near Dusty and Maryanne. "He's got to quit yanking on that mare."

The bellowing calf was herded into the pen to await his next turn. Dusty waved Gil over. The older man nudged Tiny Dancer into a trot.

"What do you think happened?" Dusty asked.

"I pulled back on the reins again."

"I know it's instinctual to hang on but you've got to learn to trust your horse."

"That calf was getting squirrelly on me."

"Next time, give Tiny Dancer her head and lean into the direction she turns rather than sawing on her mouth."

Dusty had been briefed on each rider's previous experience before taking over the class. Though Gil was raised in rural Ohio, he hadn't ridden in years. Dusty was sure the older man would be fine—he just needed more practice. What he did have in abundance was determination, a trait Dusty admired. It had gotten him and his siblings far on the rodeo circuit and what kept him continually pursuing a writing career after countless rejections and years of disappointments.

"Appreciate the advice." Gil rubbed a shoulder, his fingers digging into the flesh.

"You all right, Daddy?" Maryanne asked, clutching the top fence railing.

Another woman might have needed to stand on tip-toes to see over the railing. Not Maryanne, who was probably five-eight without those silly, inappropriate and—he admitted it—sexy high heels.

Watching her clean them in the trough had been entertaining and enjoyable. Her outfit was completely ill-suited for her surroundings yet fit nicely and showed off a figure that would do a pair of Wrangler jeans proud. Most of the ladies Dusty came in contact with wore boots, even if they weren't real cowgirls and were simply wannabes. Or, wannabe-*with*-a-cowboy as his older brother Jesse called them.

"I'm fine, Cookie." Gil brushed aside her concerns with a chuckle. "Quit being such a mother hen."

Dusty liked the nickname. It was a stark contrast to her starchy personality. He couldn't help wondering if she had another side she revealed only to those people she cared about. The nickname also made him think of things sweet and chewy and chocolaty, all of which he liked. He liked Maryanne, too, though she wasn't his usual type. Despite his reputation with buckle bunnies, he preferred down-home country girls such as his old girlfriend Josie who just last week had married his brother Dex.

It should have been weird seeing them together but somehow wasn't. During the wedding, Dusty realized he was jealous of his twin—which wasn't anything new. What was surprising was he discovered that he wanted the same kind of contentment Dex had found for himself.

Maryanne was clearly the wrong candidate but he couldn't help feeling a strong attraction to her. Brown eyes were his weakness, as was blond hair. Her hair, however, was cut in one of those short, jagged styles meant to appear messy. On her, it looked good and incredibly soft. The color was natural, too, and the makeup on her nearly flawless complexion minimal. He wouldn't have expected that from her. Gil had mentioned his daughter worked for a cosmetic company. Dusty had assumed she'd be a walking advertisement for the company's products. Then again, maybe she was, and the products were that good.

Another student shot from the box. Leaping from his horse even before it came to a stop, he ran toward the roped calf. His horse backed up, keeping the rope taut. When the calf was down and its legs tied, the man threw up his arms to signal he was done. One of the wranglers called out the man's time, which was improved from before but still nothing to brag about. Dusty had his work cut out for him with this beginner class.

"I'd better get back," Gil said. "I'm up again."

"Are you sure, Daddy?" Maryanne shaded her eyes but her hand didn't hide her worried expression.

"I'm fine. And besides, the health insurance is paid up."

"Don't make jokes."

Dusty might have laughed if she wasn't so serious. He had to admit, her devotion to her father was touching. While he had his share of run-ins with his family, hard not to with five kids, all of them stubborn in their own right just like their father, they were also tight-knit and fiercely loyal. Even when the road was rocky, like it had been a few months ago when his older brother Walker returned from the service with post-traumatic stress syndrome. He'd eventually gotten back to his old self and was also newly married.

Dusty began to think there was a trend going on with the Cody siblings. He looked over at Maryanne, and his heartbeat momentarily quickened.

Naw. Who was he kidding? She was a city girl, born and raised. He was… Dusty Cody. Fun-loving. Easygoing. Ladies' man. Unambitious, except when it came to roping and writing. The kid who couldn't be serious for one lousy minute, as his father often said, usually in a raised voice. J. W. Cody wanted nothing more than for his youngest son to assume a greater role in the family's various businesses.

Dusty thought about the two screenplays and four manuscripts saved in a file on his laptop, the hard copies buried in the bottom of a cedar trunk in the back of his closet. He didn't dare mention them to any of his family, least of all his father. Supplying trained horses for films and occasionally appearing in small roles was bad enough. If they knew his true ambition, they'd…well, maybe not disown him but they certainly wouldn't understand.

They'd also try and force him to quit, especially if they learned about the subject matter of his latest screenplay.

Dusty wasn't ready to give up writing and, frankly, didn't know if he'd ever be. It wasn't merely a hobby, it was his passion. Like rodeoing. And this latest screenplay, well, it was really good if he did say so himself. Now if he could only convince a producer to read it.

"I can't believe he's doing it again," Maryanne muttered beside him, her tone ripe with disgust. "He's too old."

"My grandfather rode every day until he was seventy-six."

"But did he rope?"

Dusty smiled.

She rolled her eyes. "Of course he did. Who here doesn't?"

"Besides you?"

"I realize I'm a little out of my element."

That was an understatement. "You work for a cosmetic company?"

She raised her brows in surprise. "How do you know?"

"Your father mentioned it." If he'd realized how attractive Maryanne was, he'd have paid more attention when Gil talked. "But not what you do for them."

"I'm a junior marketing executive."

"Not a model?" Okay, it was a line. An obvious one. But some habits were hard to break.

She gave him a tired look that said his technique was wasted on her.

"What does a junior marketing executive do?"

"Sales. Mostly I assist the senior exec," she said distractedly, keeping her attention focused on her father.

"With what?"

"Advertising campaigns and viral marketing. Our goal is to expand our direct-purchase market as well as recruit retail chains to stock and sell our products."

Selling a product.

Before trying to get published, Dusty had no idea how much selling was involved. Not just his manuscript but himself, as well. One of the reasons for his failure to make any headway thus far was his lack of poise and professionalism. No one took him seriously.

Maryanne clearly possessed those skills.

Maybe she could give him some advice.

As the minutes passed, the idea took hold and grew.

When would he have another opportunity to tap the brain of someone with the skills he himself desperately needed? Of course, he'd have to offer her something in return. While it might be enough for other women, he doubted Maryanne would settle for the simple pleasure of his company.

"Careful, Daddy," Maryanne called as Gil lined up Tiny Dancer in the box.

A second later, the calf was running, Tiny Dancer and Gil in hot pursuit. The horse did everything she'd been trained to do and then some. Gil didn't, and the calf made good its escape. Again. Gil might need more practice than was available to him from the instructors at Cowboy College.

Maryanne groaned. "I wish he'd come to his senses so we could go home."

"I might have another solution," Dusty heard himself say. "If you're willing to negotiate."

"Negotiate what?"

"A deal. My services in exchange for yours."

She turned her large, inquisitive brown eyes on him. "This I have to hear."

CHAPTER TWO

DUSTY WAS A writer. Maryanne tried hard to wrap her brain around that astounding bit of information and couldn't. Not quite.

"What do you write?"

"Novels and, lately, screenplays."

"Wow." If he had said cowboy poetry or roping articles, she might have less trouble believing him. "That's great." Years of working in marketing enabled her to sound enthused when she wasn't.

"I could use your advice."

"Um…well, my experience is limited to composing advertising text. I'm afraid I don't know much about novels or screenplays."

They'd left the arena after her father had taken his last turn and were strolling through a large open area in front of a row of barns. The mid-morning sun beat down on them but a cool breeze from the west chased away the worst of the heat. Still, Maryanne regretted wearing a vest over her blouse. In L.A., dressing in layers during the summer didn't matter because people were continuously blasted by air-conditioning units set on High, be they indoors or riding in vehicles.

Then again, if she were in L.A., she wouldn't be walking next to a cowboy. The genuine article, too, not some imitation. Same for his dog—Track?—who periodically trotted off to investigate an interesting smell or chase a lizard, only to return to Dusty's side. No purse or lap dogs wearing overpriced canine accessories in Wyoming.

"I was thinking more along the lines of tips on how to pitch my current screenplay to producers," Dusty said with a charming dash of sheepishness. "So far, they aren't too receptive."

His use of the word *pitch* gave Maryanne reason to suspect he was a little more serious about his writing than she first thought. It wasn't typical cowboy vernacular. But then, Dusty wasn't a typical cowboy. If the stories she'd heard about the Codys' affluence were true, he was likely well-educated.

"Who have you approached so far?"

He recited a list of names, mostly independent film companies.

"What have they told you?"

"Well, there's the rub. I usually don't get past the receptionist."

"It isn't easy. Even for established screenwriters. You've chosen a cutthroat business."

"I'm not scared. Competing's in my blood."

She remembered how assured he was he'd qualify for the National Finals Rodeo. "I imagine it is."

"I thought I was close with Tierra Buena Productions. I met the head producer last month on a shoot in Calgary. He liked my work, and I figured that would give me an in. He listened to me for about twelve seconds then said while my story concept had broad appeal, it lacked originality."

"Does it lack originality?"

"Hell no."

She smiled. He really was brimming with confidence. That alone should get him a foot in the door. As far as his screenplay went, she had her doubts.

Whatever his educational background and resources, he came across as a good ol' boy out for a good ol' time, which was probably his problem. No one took him seriously. His easy, aw-shucks mannerisms and shameless flirting didn't help.

"I like that."

"What?" she asked.

"When you smile." He flashed his own lazy grin at her, proving her point about the shameless flirting. "Haven't seen you do it since we met."

"I tend to be serious."

"So I noticed." His dimple deepened. "I myself have the opposite problem."

"So *I* noticed." Maryanne's guard fell slightly, and they shared a laugh. "If you want a career in Hollywood, you might have more success in front of the camera. You already have a good start and the connections."

"Naw. It's fun, don't get me wrong. Who wouldn't get a kick out of seeing themselves on the big screen?"

They came to a central area outside the main building and dining hall. Across the way was a hotel-like building with nine rooms. Behind them, down a quaint country road, were the cabins where Maryanne and her father were staying. Dusty motioned to a wagon-wheel bench beneath a sprawling aspen tree.

He waited for her to sit down first. The bench had appeared large enough to accommodate them both until he lowered himself beside her. Then, it magically shrunk so small their thighs brushed lightly against each other. Maryanne's breath hitched. To distract herself from the sudden rush of heat, she patted Track's head. He responded by licking her hand.

"My mother never liked watching herself on screen. She hated attending premieres for that reason."

"She was an actress?"

"A good one."

"Famous?"

"Not exactly, though she was in a lot of movies. Character roles mostly. Her professional name was Dee Devon. You'd probably recognize her face if you saw a photograph of her."

Maryanne was proud of her mother's career, which had spanned well over three decades. She may never have won an Oscar or Emmy but she'd worked steadily, was well liked and respected, and avoided ridiculous scandals that plagued so many celebrities.

"She was in one television sitcom during the late eighties and early nineties. *Family Fortune.* She played the secretary, Wanda Winsome."

"I remember that show." Dusty's face brightened. "My parents loved it." He studied her face, the twinkle never leaving his eyes. "You remind me of her. You have the same smile."

"Thank you." People often commented on her resemblance to her mother, which had pleased her parents enormously. "I consider that a compliment."

"You should, she was an attractive woman." The warm quality in Dusty's voice told her he considered Maryanne attractive, too.

He really did have flirting down to a science.

Not normally shy and with a high tolerance for come-ons, Maryanne felt herself blush. Perhaps because of that, she blurted, "It is kind of amazing we look so much alike. I'm adopted."

"Your dad mentioned it."

Dusty knew! And yet he'd said she reminded him of her mother. More flustered than before, Maryanne stumbled over her reply.

"I don't normally tell people. Neither does my father."

"It came up yesterday. He was talking about your mother. How much he misses her."

"So do I." The pain in her chest, with her always in the three years since she'd lost her mother, swelled.

"I'm sorry. My grandparents both passed some years back. It's not quite the same as a parent but still…"

"The death of any loved one is always hard." Some worse than others. Her mother had fought valiantly but in the end, the cancer had won. The sick, frail, eighty-five-pound woman in the hospital bed had in no way resembled the vivacious, sharp-tongued, larger than life Wanda Winsome—or any of the multitude of other characters Maryanne's mother had played.

"She was lucky to have you. Your dad, too."

"No, I was lucky to have them as my parents. They tried for over ten years to have a child of their own before deciding to adopt."

Maryanne was well aware of how different her life might have been if her parents had chosen an infant rather than a withdrawn three-year-old whose birth mother had dropped her off in front of the Social Services offices in the middle of January, jacketless and with a note pinned to her T-shirt.

She also knew with utmost certainty that the right people had raised her and thanked God every day of her life for them. That didn't stop her from reliving a profound sense of abandonment every time she recalled her birth mother leaving her on those cold, hard steps or her birth father disappearing from the face of the earth a few weeks earlier.

"My mother's the reason my father came to Cowboy College." The same easy charm that made Dusty so likable also encouraged confiding. "He gave up a lot to be with her when they were first married. Not many men would follow their wife to Hollywood and support her while she pursued an acting career."

"Did he act, too?"

Maryanne laughed. "No way. He's a supervisor for a manufacturing plant. This is his first vacation in two years."

"He mentioned growing up in rural Ohio."

"If not for my mom, he'd still be living on the family farm. It's why he's so happy here."

"We country folk always find our way back eventually."

Had Dusty gone somewhere? Spent a long time away from home? She didn't quite know how to ask so let the moment pass.

"Right before Mom died, she made Dad promise that he would live life to the fullest. Do all the things he gave up in order to be with her."

"Like roping?"

"Dad rodeoed some as a teenager. Guess he was pretty good but he didn't get far. Not enough time or money."

"He definitely has the ability and the will. If he keeps after it, he'll do okay."

Maryanne's concerns for he father came rushing

back. "He's too old and has too many health problems to take up roping."

"He doesn't think so."

"He'll wind up hurt."

"Sooner or later."

"And you think that's okay?"

"I think it's his decision."

"And if I love him, I'll support him?"

"You do, and you are. It's why you're here with him."

True on both counts.

Maryanne exhaled. The timing of her father's trip stank. She and the senior exec she currently assisted were "this close" to landing a new account that was sure to gain her company-wide recognition if not another promotion. Not only that, her real estate agent had called the day before with good news. Maryanne was next on the list for Westwind. She'd been waiting over two years to buy a condo in the trendy, exclusive green community. If one came up for sale, she'd have mere days to finalize the deal.

How could she accomplish all that with her father in the hospital?

She refused to lose another parent. Not to something completely avoidable.

"I might be able to help." Dusty's voice penetrated her thoughts.

"How?"

"I can teach your father, not only how to rope but rope smarter and safer. There are no guarantees, of course. Accidents happen. But the more he knows, the more proficient he becomes, the less likely he is to be injured."

Maryanne wasn't sure what to make of his offer.

"Tiny Dancer is a good horse," Dusty continued. "I have better ones at my place. And I can give your dad one-on-one training. We have all the same equipment there as here."

"In exchange for my help with your pitch?"

"Right." He gave her a dazzling grin.

Maryanne once again fell victim to a small, electric thrill coursing up her spine.

"You can be my image consultant," he went on. "A good pitch can't be much different than a good advertising campaign."

"Dad may not like the idea."

"If he's against it, then you're off the hook."

"Spoken like a man who's certain of the outcome."

"Your dad is determined."

"And then some." She chewed her bottom lip. "He'll think I'm being overprotective again."

"I'll talk to him. Convince him I came up with the idea."

She still hesitated.

"Take a day or two to decide. There's no hurry."

No? What if her father fell again? This morning wasn't the first time. She really didn't want him roping but since she obviously couldn't stop him, she might as well see to it he got the best training available. Dusty talked the talk, and her instincts also told her he could walk the walk. Her father probably couldn't be in better or more capable hands.

Besides, it might be fun working with Dusty and beneficial to her, as well. She needed something productive to occupy her many free hours and keep her from worrying about her father.

"I don't need a few days," she said with sudden certainty. "We have an agreement."

Track perked up and gave a small yip.

"Good. I'll tell your dad to come by in the morning."

For a second time in an hour, Maryanne shook Dusty's hand. He held on marginally longer than before.

Track yipped again, his wagging tail hitting the wooden bench.

Maryanne was beginning to suspect the dog possessed an uncanny ability to understand human language when she realized his excitement was due to the approach of a striking middle-aged couple and a tow-headed boy.

Unable to contain himself, Track whined excitedly.

"Go on, buddy," Dusty said.

The dog sprinted off and greeted the boy with an enthusiasm that went both ways.

"Here you are," the man boomed once they were within earshot. Despite his vigor, he walked with a pronounced limp and the assistance of a cane. "We've been looking everywhere for you. Don't you answer that cell phone of yours?" There was an unmistakable reprimand in his voice.

"Sorry, the battery died earlier."

Maryanne stole a glance at Dusty. His expression, usually so open, was unreadable. The trademark grin was there but not the twinkle in his eyes. Except when he gazed at the boy. Dusty liked children, at least this one.

"Careful, Matt," he warned. "That dog will lick the hide clean off your face if you let him."

That got a laugh.

He stood as the couple neared. Maryanne did likewise, expecting and receiving an introduction.

"Mom, Dad, this is Maryanne Devonshire. She and her father are guests at Cowboy College."

She should have guessed the couple's identity. Dusty was a mixture of both his parents. He had his father's build and his mother's eyes, though the color varied slightly.

"Very nice to meet you, Mr. and Mrs. Cody."

"We don't stand on ceremony around here. Call me J.W. And this is Anne."

"Welcome to Markton." Anne's smile was also like Dusty's, only toned down about a hundred watts. "Matthew, come over here, honey."

The boy reluctantly separated himself from the dog. He stopped in front of Dusty and gazed up at him expectantly. No, uncertainly, Maryanne decided. Dusty put a hand out and smoothed the boy's unruly hair. He was rewarded with a shy, awkward smile.

"You want to take Track for a walk?" he asked.

"Can I?" The boy turned to Anne.

She didn't look happy but answered, "A short one."

The Codys seemed past the age to have a child so young, though it wasn't impossible. Matthew, or Matt as Dusty had called him, couldn't be more than four or five.

"He's adorable," she said to Anne, who beamed at the compliment.

"Just like his father."

Maryanne's glance automatically went to J.W.

She felt Dusty's hand touch hers.

"Matt's my son."

His son!

Maryanne promptly closed her gaping mouth, hoping no one had noticed.

"I TAKE IT your father and not you is the roper in the family," Dusty's mother asked Maryanne.

"Yes. I'm afraid I haven't been on a horse since I was twelve or thirteen." She'd visibly composed herself before answering. Learning Matt was Dusty's son must have come as a surprise to her.

It had come as a surprise to Dusty, too. Until two months ago, he had no idea Matt existed.

"We can fix that," he offered, only half kidding. He'd like to take Maryanne riding. Especially up to his favorite spot on Stony Creek.

She shook her head. "I'm not ready for that. Besides, I didn't bring any boots."

Like that, the awkward moment was behind them, and everyone relaxed. Dusty appreciated Maryanne's poise all the more. She would be a good mentor for him. It also helped that Matt was a short distance away playing fetch with Track.

Dusty hadn't quite come to terms with his and Matt's relationship. The news that had rocked his world a few weeks ago was still sinking in. His parents, overjoyed at becoming instant grandparents, had adjusted quickly. As had Dusty's twin brother, Dex, who'd assumed the role of stepfather with no problem when he married Matt's mother. Dusty seemed to be the sole exception, and *he* was the boy's father.

It wasn't that he didn't have feelings for Matt. He liked the boy enormously. Every time he looked at him, he experienced a surge of paternal pride. He also felt responsible and had committed himself to providing for Matt, and not just financially.

What he and his son didn't have yet was an emotional bond. He reminded himself that these things take time.

The situation was further complicated by Matt gaining a new set of grandparents and a stepfather in addition to a father, all in the same month. Not to mention a couple of aunts and several uncles. No one could fault him for being overwhelmed.

"I thought maybe Dusty was giving you roping pointers." His mother delivered her remark innocently enough.

Dusty knew better. She was fishing, bent on discovering what he and Maryanne were doing together. His mother not-so-secretly hoped he'd get serious and settle down one of these days. Like his two brothers.

"Hardly." Maryanne laughed again. "We were actually discussing my father. Dusty's agreed to give him private lessons which, I'm afraid, he desperately needs."

"Awfully nice of him." J.W. shot Dusty a look that shouted he'd rather his son spent his time engaged in more productive endeavors.

If Maryanne noticed the tense exchange, she ignored it. "Very nice. Though he strikes a hard bargain. In return for helping my dad, I have to—"

"She has to have dinner with me," Dusty interrupted, narrowly averting disaster.

Maryanne gave Dusty a blank stare, then understanding apparently dawned for she said, "Yes. He's promised to show me around town."

"Markton is small but picturesque. I'm sure you'll enjoy yourself."

Maryanne's gaze found Dusty's. "I'm looking forward to it."

Was she serious? He decided then and there to keep the dinner date, owing her that much for going along with him.

"I should get back to my father," she said politely.

"Stay," his mother insisted. "We were just leaving. We only came by to find Dusty and tell him dinner's in an hour." She turned to him. "You will be there?"

"I'll try."

"I'd appreciate it. This is our last dinner alone with Matthew. His parents are still on their honeymoon," she explained to Maryanne, "and are coming home tomorrow."

His parents? Dusty's teeth involuntarily ground together. Wasn't he Matt's father?

Dex conveniently hadn't mentioned the arrangement for Matt's care during their absence to Dusty until after the plans were set, saying he and Josie wanted to give the boy an opportunity to spend time with his grandparents.

Dusty remained unconvinced of his brother's motives. They could be genuine, an attempt to please their parents and consideration for Dusty's erratic work schedule. Or not genuine. Josie had once been Dusty's girlfriend, and he was the father of her child. That was a lot for any man to handle.

Matt came running, the dog nipping at his heel. "Can Track go with me to Grandma and Grandpa's?" he asked Dusty.

"I have a better idea. You can stick with me for a while."

"Really?"

Matt's enthusiasm pleased Dusty. "Sure. We can fix something to eat at my place." His three-room apartment above the main horse barn at Cottonwood Ranch wasn't large but then he often traveled for weeks at a stretch and didn't need much space. "What's your favorite food?"

"Hot dogs!"

"Dang it. I ate the last one yesterday. What's your second favorite food?"

"Spaghetti."

"Mine, too." Maybe they weren't so different after all. "And I just happen to have all the fixings."

"Dusty." His mother's voice contained a mild warning.

"He'll be fine. I'll bring him up to your house after we eat. In one piece, I promise."

"His bedtime's eight o'clock."

"I'll have him there at seven-thirty sharp."

She clearly wasn't happy but didn't push the issue.

"Don't disappoint your mother." His father leveled a finger at him.

Dusty's hackles instantly rose, the result of years of conditioning and endless testosterone-infused battles. He kept his cool, however. The fewer witnesses to his confrontations with his father, the better.

During all this, Maryanne had stood discreetly to the side. Now, as they walked back to the arena after his parents left, she chatted amiably with Matt about nothing in particular, which went a long way in restoring Dusty's previously good mood.

At the arena, Matt became instantly enthralled with the task of herding calves from the holding pen to the shoot.

"Can I help?"

"Sure."

The boy ran off to join the wranglers. Track wanted in on the action, too. Dusty signaled the men to keep an eye on Matt. Satisfied that he was in capable hands, Dusty and Maryanne resumed their former place along the railing. Her father waved from where he sat astride his horse.

"Thanks for not giving me away," he said. "My parents don't know about my writing and wouldn't approve if they did."

"I think it goes with the territory. My grandparents were completely against my mother wanting to be an actress. Until she became successful. Then, they couldn't brag about her enough." Maryanne smiled encouragingly. "Your parents will be the same."

When hell froze over. Changing subjects, he said, "Matt's mother and I dated off and on in high school and college. After graduation, she left for the west coast."

"You don't have to explain to me."

"I want to."

They watched the last two students rope. Matt, a born cowboy, appeared to be having the time of his life, which made Dusty glad he'd insisted on bringing him along.

"I ran into Josie about five years ago when I was on my first film shoot. We spent the night together, probably more for old times' sake than anything else. In the morning, it was pretty obvious whatever we once had was over, and we parted friends. I didn't see or hear from her until recently." Dusty paused, his emotions were still raw and close to the surface. "If she hadn't come home to take care of her dad after his heart attack, I might never have found out I had a kid."

Josie's reasons for not telling him about Matt made sense, and Dusty could see why she'd chosen the course she had. The Codys, his father in particular, were a lot for anyone to handle, and Josie, with her gentle ways, was no match for them. They'd have tried to dictate her life—and his—and not quit until they'd succeeded.

Trouble was, Dusty couldn't get past his anger and resentment. It had been wrong of Josie to keep Matt from him and deny him his rights. But for the sake of his brother, his family and Matt, Dusty was attempting to put his feelings aside.

Easier said than done.

"That's a lot to deal with all at once. For everyone."

Maryanne's observation roused him from his mental woolgathering. "It gets even more complicated. Josie married my brother Dex last week."

"Wow!"

"But it's okay. They love each other, and Dex is good to Matt." At least, that was what Dusty kept telling himself. Across the arena, Matt and Track chased down the last errant calf—from a safe distance, thanks to the wranglers. "I've been thinking I should step back for a while. Give Dex and Matt some space to settle in and get to know each other. My mother actually suggested it."

"Are you serious?" Maryanne drew back. Not an easy feat in those ridiculous high heels of hers. She nearly lost her balance. "He's your son, and it's obvious you care about him."

"I don't want to confuse him." More of his mother's words pouring from his mouth.

"He's young, he'll adapt. I did, and I was younger than him."

"But your biological father didn't live next door to your adoptive father."

"I wish he had. You have no idea how much." Her

voice cracked. "I love my parents with all my heart, but I've never forgotten that my birth parents didn't want me. Matt doesn't deserve that, especially because it isn't true."

No, it wasn't. "He'll be living with Dex." Dusty continued trying to rationalize a situation that deep down felt wrong.

"And what's stopping you from visiting him every day?"

Nothing, he thought. What he said was, "My parents would rather I didn't rock the boat."

"Isn't that what you did by insisting Matt have dinner with you?"

"I got mad. It was a knee-jerk reaction."

Maryanne touched his arm. Her fingers were warm and smooth. "I owe you another apology. This is a sensitive subject for me. I have no right forcing my opinions on you."

"I don't want to hurt my brother. He's been through enough."

"Are you worried Matt might come to care more for him than you?"

Dusty didn't answer. He was too busy waiting for his heart to start beating again. Maryanne couldn't be more on target.

He might not be slipping comfortably into fatherhood but that didn't mean he wanted another man—even his own brother—taking that privilege away from him.

CHAPTER THREE

"Q̲ᴜɪᴛᴇ ᴀ ᴛʜʀᴇᴇ-ʀɪɴɢ circus you've got going on."

Hearing his oldest brother's voice, Dusty looked away from the line of horses tied to the hitching rail. "Hey, what are you doing here?"

Jesse passed Dusty one of the travel mugs he'd been carrying. The coffee was hot and black, just how Dusty liked it. The inadequate kick from the cup of instant he'd chugged down at four-thirty when he woke up had faded in the two hours since.

"Figured you could use some backup."

"Thanks, but everything's under control."

"That depends on who you talk to." Jesse kept a straight face until a hearty laugh broke free.

"Dex needs to mind his new wife and quit worrying about me." Dusty signaled for one of the other horses to be brought out. "Did he send you?"

"Naw."

"Dad?"

"Nobody did."

"Liar."

Jesse laughed again. When they weren't arguing, which was often, they got along well. Better sometimes than Dusty did with his twin. "Actually, it was Mom."

Dusty doubted that. If she had asked Jesse it was because their father had asked her. "You can tell her

I'm not such a screwup I can't oversee a few head getting shoed."

A few head was really about forty. With several hundred horses on the Cody ranch at any given time, shoeing took place on an ongoing basis. In addition to the regular riding stock and Dusty's specially trained horses, there was the rodeo stock—a lucrative side business, brood mares, their offspring, many of them for sale, four donkeys, two mules and the family's personal horses. The job of caring for such a large number was more than two men could handle, and Dusty was gone much of the time, leaving Dex to manage alone.

Okay, not alone. They had plenty of hands to help. But Dex liked to complain and give Dusty grief. In that respect, he took after their father.

"New guy?" Jesse asked.

He must have noticed Dusty watching the farrier's every move. While young, the man had come highly recommended. Seven of their best riding stock were tied to the hitching post in front of the main horse barn, their swishing tails chasing away flies. The stout bay gelding on the end was Uno, Dusty's favorite horse and the one he was counting on to take him all the way to the NFR in Vegas this December.

This year, if he was lucky and worked hard, he could be a double World Champion—in tie-down roping, his event, and also team roping. He and Dex weren't just twins, they competed together. And were doing well in the standings.

Bending over at the waist, the farrier braced Uno's right rear hoof between his knees. Pieces of hoof dropped onto the ground as he trimmed and shaped. One miscalculation, one slip of the trimming knife, would result in a sore hoof, not unlike a fingernail being cut to the quick. If serious enough, an abscess could form, putting Uno out of commission for days if not weeks. Time Dusty could ill afford to lose. He and Uno needed to be in top shape for the upcoming Professional Cowboy Association rodeo in Albuquerque. A win would bring Dusty that much closer to qualifying.

Uno snorted, out of boredom at having to stand in one place and not, Dusty was glad to see, pain.

Moving closer, he asked, "How's it going?"

"Fine." The young farrier let Uno's hoof go and straightened. It might only be early in the morning but sweat poured down the sides of his face. He wiped it away with the sleeve of his shirt then rested a gloved hand on Uno's solid rump. "He's no trouble."

"Any problems?"

"Nope. Got a nice healthy hoof."

While they discussed the merits of changing to a lighter weight shoe, with Jesse contributing his opinion, Uno drifted off to sleep.

The stout quarter horse had originally come to the ranch as a green three-year-old with more guts than brains. Dusty had immediately seen the horse's potential and began training him for roping. Uno didn't disappoint even if he did relish engaging Dusty in a periodic contest of wills. Eventually, the two of them came to an understanding about who was in charge, and their partnership thrived.

An inability to stay focused was the only possible glitch to Dusty qualifying for Nationals. Not easy with thoughts of Matt constantly running through his head. Dinner last night in his apartment had been fun. Matt seemed to relax with Dusty for the first time since they met. But the evening also left Dusty at odds with himself. Maryanne had been right. About a lot of things. She'd voiced not only his biggest fears but his deepest desires. He just wished the two weren't in opposition.

A minor commotion distracted Dusty. He and Jesse glanced over their shoulders to see Dex striding toward the line of horses, a scowl on his face. The brothers hadn't seen each other since the wedding reception.

"I guess the honeymoon is over."

"What's he mad about?" Dusty muttered, but was pretty sure he already knew.

"Here comes the groom," Jesse said when Dex got closer. "Good to see you up and around." He socked Dex in the upper arm. "How's the bride?"

A smile replaced the scowl. "Good. She and Matt are unpacking." Josie's parents had given the newlyweds a hundred acres on which to build a home. During the interim, they were staying with Anne and J.W. in their house.

"Back to work so soon?"

"I need to talk to Dusty."

"So talk." Dusty had returned to scrutinizing the farrier who was almost done with Uno.

"Alone."

"Give me a minute."

The two other farriers, one a woman, were also diligently working. As each horse was done, it was led away and replaced with a new one. A six-month-old foal was receiving its first hoof trimming and was not happy. Two men were trying to hold him still. His fussing and high-pitched nickering upset his dam. She twisted her head, pulling on the lead rope. Suddenly, the knot came undone.

"Great. Just great." Dex started toward the loose mare.

Jesse hummed an off-key rendition of a military revelry, ending with, "Charge!"

Dusty wasn't amused.

Dex went three steps and came to a sudden halt. The mare had traveled no farther than her baby's side and was easily caught by one of the hands. With the crisis resolved, Dex returned, looking more put out than before.

Dusty made a mental note to thank the man who'd caught the mare.

Giving Uno one last inspection, he told the farrier, "Good job," untied the lead rope and headed for the barn. His escape was short-lived.

Dex fell into step beside him. "You brought Matt home late last night."

"I see Mom squealed."

"She didn't have to. Matt hasn't stopped talking about you since he woke up this morning."

Dusty's enjoyment of his son's antics lasted only until Dex started lecturing him.

"You got him home forty-five minutes late."

"We were watching the Cartoon Network." Turned out he and Matt had more than favorite foods in common. Their taste in television shows also ran the same. Dusty had been enjoying himself so much, he'd lost track of the time. "I called Mom and let her know we were going to be late."

"He's not allowed to watch Spider-Man."

"Josie didn't mention that." There was a lot about Matt she'd failed to tell Dusty, including the boy's existence.

"We didn't think you'd be babysitting him."

"I can understand. I'm only his father. No reason to assume I'd be spending any time with him while you were away."

"Okay, that was unfair," Dex conceded then came back twice as hard. "You let him chase calves. He's only four."

"We were chasing calves at that age and a whole lot more."

Horses whinnied and bobbed their heads as Dusty, with Uno in tow, and Dex walked down the long aisle. A few banged their stall doors in a bid for attention. Dusty put Uno in his stall and latched the door behind him. The big horse immediately buried his head in the feed bin in search of leftover breakfast.

"We grew up here." Dex wasn't ready to drop the subject of Dusty's shortcomings.

"So will Matt."

"He hasn't learned how to be safe around animals yet."

"No time like the present."

"He could have been kicked."

"I never let him out of my sight the whole time."

"Josie would rather she supervise him on the ranch. Until he's older."

Dusty stopped. "Are you sure it's not you wanting me to spend less time with my son?"

He half expected his brother to take a swing at him. He'd certainly done it often enough in the past—as kids and adults. Dex didn't, however. Apparently marriage had sucked the ornery out of him.

Too bad.

"This is a period of adjustment for all of us. We'd like your cooperation."

"I won't be denied time with my son." Until that moment, Dusty hadn't realized how strongly he felt. What he wasn't sure of was how far he'd press the matter.

"No one's doing that."

"Then back off." Dusty didn't like the idea of involving attorneys, not so soon after Dex and Josie's wedding, but it might come down to that. "So I was forty-five minutes late bringing him home. Not the end of the world."

"Kids have schedules. So do Josie and I. You disrupted them."

"Fine. Next time Matt can just spend the night with me. Then nobody's schedules are disrupted."

That shut Dex up, for the moment, anyway.

Outside the barn, Jesse rejoined them. His horse, Sundae, was next up to be shoed by the young farrier, which explained why he'd snuck away from the ranch office to annoy Dusty. Unlike him, Jesse was toeing their father's line by managing the ranch's day-to-day operations. In fact, all the Cody siblings had jobs. Even their sister, Elly, who was in charge of their website and marketing. Dusty was the only one unable to find his place.

"We got company," Jesse commented, craning his neck. "Isn't that one of Adele's trucks?"

If the old pickup's odometer had rolled over once, it had rolled over three times. Gears grinding, it came to a stop beside Jesse's brand-spanking-new F-350 truck. The engine choked noisily before gasping for its last breath and dying.

"I'll lay you ten to one it doesn't start again," Jesse said.

The pickup's doors creaked open and two pairs of

feet hit the ground. The driver wore old boots. The passenger, a pair of delicate red flats.

Dusty's heart hammered in anticipation. During the heated conversation with his brother, he'd forgotten about inviting Maryanne and her dad over this morning.

"Who's that?" Jesse asked.

Dusty didn't much care for the appreciative glint in his brother's eyes. "Gil Devonshire. He's a student at Cowboy College."

"Not him. Her."

Dusty had no claim on Maryanne whatsoever, unless meeting her first counted. Still, he felt a sudden urgency to assert his position. "His daughter."

"You've met her?"

"Yesterday."

Maryanne and her father spotted Dusty and waved. He waved back but didn't start toward them, hoping first to figure out a way to lose his brothers.

"Friends already, I see." Jesse chuckled.

"Why are they here?" Dex asked.

"I promised to give Gil some pointers."

"Mighty neighborly of you." Jesse removed his hat and combed his fingers through his hair. "I can give pointers, too."

Dusty elbowed him out of the way. "Not on your life."

"Where you going?" Dex demanded.

"The practice arena. I'll be back in an hour. Two tops."

"The hell you will! There are twenty-five more head to shoe."

"You're here. No need for both of us to stick around."

"Damn it, Dusty." Dex charged after him.

"Let him go." Jesse grabbed Dex's arm in a surprising show of support.

Dex wrenched free of his brother's grasp but didn't follow. His glare, however, burned a sizable hole in the back of Dusty's head.

He'd just committed what Dex considered a cardinal sin; walking out in the middle of a job. But right now, Dusty was too mad at his brother and too excited at seeing Maryanne to care.

"Morning, Dusty."

"Gil. How you doing?" The two men shook hands vigorously.

"Can't tell you how much I appreciate you doing this."

If Maryanne had harbored any doubts about her father's willingness to go along with her and Dusty's plan, they vanished in that moment.

The realization gave her pause.

This was more than a passing lark or seeing through the promise he'd made to her mother before she died. He fully intended to rope competitively.

Oh, dear. Her internal worry meter shot up another notch. Maybe she'd been wrong to cut a deal with Dusty. The lessons would only encourage her father to continue on this foolish course of action.

In the next instant, she changed her mind. If he was going to rope, better he learn from one of the best.

"Morning, Maryanne."

Dusty was talking to her. She shook her head to clear it. "Hi."

"Hope you don't mind that she came along," her father said. "She likes to watch me practice."

Dusty didn't let on that he knew the real reason for her presence. The details of their agreement needed ironing out.

"Well, it's not like I have much else to do." She smiled weakly.

"Don't let her kid you," her dad said. "She was up at five-thirty and on the phone by six."

Dusty's brows rose. "I'm impressed."

"We're close to landing a new client."

"That company of hers is always close to something." Her father tugged on his belt, adjusting it to a more comfortable position around his generous middle. "Fact is, her boss couldn't tie his own shoelaces without her."

"He's exaggerating."

"Not by much."

It was true, she did juggle the workload of two people. But she liked being busy and being useful and coming through on a project when others faltered.

"The man almost didn't let her take the whole month off. He only agreed when she promised to fly back for a few days every other week." Teasing aside, pride filled her father's voice.

Maryanne went soft inside. She was lucky to have a parent who endorsed her career choice. Her mother hadn't had her grandparents' support, not at first, and according to Dusty, his parents disapproved of him.

"Ready to get started?" he asked her father.

"You bet!"

The two men walked ahead.

Maryanne brought up the rear. "Is it far?"

"Depends."

"On what?"

Dusty glanced down and grinned. "What shoes you're wearing."

She sighed. Her feet were more comfortable than in yesterday's heels but the flats, a gift to herself after her last promotion, would never be the same again. She really should investigate the town and see if one of the stores sold athletic shoes. If not, she'd bring back a pair on her first trip home.

Maryanne suffered a nostalgic pang. She did appreciate the beauty and splendor of Wyoming, particularly the Cody ranch, which was like nothing she'd ever seen. But she also missed L.A. and the energy and excitement which, in her mind, couldn't be found anywhere else.

Face it, she told herself, you're a city girl through and through.

And Dusty was pure country, from the top of his battered felt cowboy hat to the tips of his scuffed boots. Everything else in between was country, too, she mused as she studied his broad shoulders and decidedly male swagger. Impossible not to stare when he was walking three feet in front of her.

Maryanne promptly tripped on a rock and stumbled. That should teach her to pay better attention.

"You okay, Cookie?" Her father and Dusty stopped.

"Fine." She brushed aside a stray lock of hair in an attempt to hide her embarrassment.

Dusty took her arm and drew her up beside him. "The stable's just over there."

She imagined hearing a silent "if you can make it" tagged on the end, and her determination doubled. It was further aided by his hand, which remained on her arm, strong and steady and…nice. He knew just the right amount of pressure to apply. Enough so she felt secure, not so much she felt uncomfortable.

With his other hand, he pointed to a long, narrow, modern-looking barn painted a deep red. "That's our mare barn."

"Mare barn?"

"When the mares come in season, they're brought here."

"Why?"

Dusty cleared his throat. Her father just laughed.

"What?" Her gaze darted from one to the other.

"The mares are introduced to the stud horses."

It took several seconds but Maryanne finally got Dusty's drift, and her cheeks flushed. Would she ever stop showing her ignorance?

"We breed our own horses but we also provide stud services to other ranches and private individuals. Mom's in charge of the operation."

Maryanne's father proceeded to ask detailed questions, which Dusty answered. She winced inwardly. Apparently the more graphic details of horse breeding were openly discussed on ranches.

She couldn't have been happier when the stables came into sight and the conversation went in a new direction.

They spent twenty minutes selecting the best horse for Maryanne's father to ride and saddling it. She added several new words to her growing cowboy vocabulary. The horse was a friendly sort, and more than once she reached out to pet its soft nose.

When they were done, they went next door to the practice arena.

"This is some fine place you got here!" Her father stopped for a moment to take it all in.

She found herself agreeing with him. Even her novice eye recognized the sophistication of the facility. If this was any indication, the Codys were serious indeed about the sport of rodeo.

Dusty removed his cell phone from his belt. It had been housed in a hand-tooled leather case trimmed with silver. She also noticed his watch, a Cartier if she wasn't mistaken. Apparently not everything about Dusty was well-worn and practical.

"I'm going to round up some help," he said and placed a call. "Unless you're willing to chase calves." He winked at Maryanne.

"Very funny."

While they waited, her father mounted the horse and circled the arena a few times. Their help arrived soon after, riding an ATV. Big Ben, as he was introduced, was older even than Maryanne's father and, according to Dusty, had worked for the Codys nearly his entire adult life.

Practice got underway and for a good half hour, Dusty was either in the arena or sitting atop the fence near the box, giving her father constant instructions. Maryanne sat in the bleachers and was so caught up in watching him, she didn't realize Dusty had come over to join her until she felt the planks vibrate beneath her feet.

He sat down next to her. "How about dinner tomorrow night?"

The remark caught her off guard. "I thought that was just a ruse to distract your parents."

"We have to meet somewhere." He shrugged. "And I'd rather not raise anyone's suspicions."

His idea made sense in a twisted logic sort of way. If he really was the player she suspected him of being, no one would raise an eyebrow at him dating a guest from Cowboy College. "It might be difficult to do more than cover the basics in a public setting."

He grinned. "I'll make sure we have some privacy."

Shame on her for walking into that one. "Are there any restaurants in Markton?"

"I have a place in mind."

Why had she even asked?

"I'll pick you up about six."

"Dressy or casual attire?"

That got a reaction in the form of a widening grin. "Whatever's comfortable."

Maryanne fidgeted. Strange how this Wyoming cowboy unsettled her far more than the worldly men in L.A. did.

"See you then." He climbed down the bleachers to the ground.

"Wait. Don't you need the number of my cabin?"

"I'll find you."

Maryanne didn't doubt that one bit.

CHAPTER FOUR

MARYANNE OPENED THE door to her cabin. "Hi."

Whatever else she'd been planning to say to Dusty was promptly forgotten. He certainly cleaned up nice. Not that she'd had any doubts. Real life, however, exceeded her expectations.

His jeans, though blue and basic, were washed and pressed. His simple and understated shirt, on the other hand, bore a designer label, and the boots he wore were custom-made. His hat probably wasn't purchased at the local feed store, either. She immediately began envisioning another advertising campaign featuring Dusty in a whole new way.

"Hi." He studied her appearance with the same subdued scrutiny she had his. The corners of his mouth curved into what she already recognized as his trademark sexy smile. "You look nice."

"Not too out of place?" Having nothing in her wardrobe that spoke small-town Wyoming, she'd gone in the opposite direction: casual-chic.

"Definitely out of place. Be ready to get stared at."

Maryanne was already thinking the same thing about him.

"Dusty! Come on in." Gil entered the cabin's small living room from the kitchen, a beer in his hand. He held it up. "Can I get you one?"

"No thank you, sir. I'm driving."

"Glad to see you're taking care of Cookie. She's all I've got." He bent and kissed Maryanne's cheek. "Would I be out of line if I told you to have her back at a decent hour?"

"Daddy!"

"Not a minute past ten." Dusty took Maryanne's arm. "I promise."

"Sorry about that," Maryanne said when they were out the door and walking down the cabin steps. "Five days living with my father, and he's back to treating me like I'm fifteen."

"He loves you." Dusty's incredibly blue eyes twinkled.

"You think I'm just as bad. That I mother him unnecessarily."

"You love him, too."

"There's a big difference between risking life and limb and going out to—" For the second time in ten minutes, the words she was about to utter vanished in a small poof. "Is that yours?"

"Like it?"

"You've got to be kidding." She approached the deep green Jaguar almost reverently. "It's gorgeous." And the very last thing she'd expected him to be driving.

"I bought it last year on something of a whim." Pride and pleasure tinged his voice.

"I bought a new sofa on a whim once." She released a long breath. "Not quite the same thing."

He reached into his pocket for the keys. "Want to drive?"

She gulped. "I can't."

"Why not?"

"It has a standard transmission." She ran her fingers lightly along the highly polished fender. "But I'd love to go for a ride," she said with a grin.

Dusty opened the door for her. "Hop in."

"Where are we going?" She sank into the plush leather passenger seat. "Nowhere close, I hope."

"The Spotted Horse Saloon."

"Oh." She tried to hide her disappointment.

Dusty climbed in behind the steering wheel. "We'll take the long route."

They did, turning a fifteen-minute ride into a forty-five-minute adventure. Maryanne didn't talk much. She was too busy having her breath stolen at every hairpin turn Dusty took with race-car driver precision. The scenery, she noticed, appeared entirely different when viewed as an endless blur.

"How come you didn't tell me you like sports cars?" he asked when they pulled up near the honky-tonk and parked.

"Shh." She placed a finger on her lips. "It's a secret."

By the time she opened her door, he was already there, taking her arm and helping her out of the car. Good thing, the bones in her legs had apparently dissolved into putty during the constant adrenaline rush. Without meaning to, she leaned heavily on his arm until she regained her land legs. He didn't seem to mind.

"Why a secret?"

"I drive a hybrid. I work for an eco-friendly cosmetic company. I'm on the waiting list for a condo in the most sought after green community in L.A. County."

"What?" he said with a hearty laugh. "Will loving fossil fuel vehicles get you fired from your job or your name scratched from the condo waiting list?"

"Not if you don't tell."

"You're not joking."

"I do have a reputation to maintain."

"And being with me will tarnish it?"

"Only driving in your Jag."

They entered The Spotted Horse Saloon which was hopping despite being a weekday evening.

Maryanne tilted her head toward Dusty to be better heard over the band and rowdy patrons. "We might have trouble finding a table."

"I have a reservation."

Naturally he did. "This might not be the most conducive atmosphere for your first lesson in selling yourself."

"Just wait. You'll see."

His arm slid from her elbow to her hand, which he clasped firmly in his as he led her on a winding path through the crowd.

"Hey, Dusty."

"How's it going, buddy?"

Friendly greetings were shouted from every corner of the large room. As predicted, they drew a lot of attention. Most of it appeared directed at Maryanne. Several women were quite blatant in their interest. Maryanne couldn't tell if their expressions were curious or mildly hostile. Considering Dusty was one of the most eligible bachelors around and a hometown boy, they may think they had a prior claim on him. Unfortunately there was no way to convey to them that her and Dusty's dinner meeting was strictly business.

"This way."

"Behind the bar?" Maryanne came to a stop. Dusty just smiled.

"Hey, Dusty." A waitress in cutoff jeans and a tank top stood at the drink station waiting on her order. "How's it going?" Her tone more than her generous smile conveyed an intimacy to their relationship that went beyond casual.

"Hey, Mindy Sue."

The bartender barely acknowledged them as he passed Dusty a set of keys.

"Thanks, buddy." He led Maryanne down the hall and to a door marked Staff Only.

The bartender may be ignoring them but Maryanne could feel Mindy Sue's eyes following their every step. "Old girlfriend of yours?" she asked Dusty when they were on the other side of the door.

"Yeah." He flipped on a light and gave her fingers a squeeze. "From second grade."

They faced a narrow wooden staircase.

"Where are we going?"

"The roof." He preceded her up the steps, still holding her hand. "About four years ago, the kitchen caught fire. When the renovations were being done, the manager added an outdoor dining area on the roof for special events and private parties."

At the top of the stairs was another door on which was posted a sign that read Keep Locked at All Times When Not in Use. Dusty used the keys to open the door. A gust of cool, fresh air immediately rushed in to fill the small enclosed space. In the next instant, Maryanne was stepping onto the rooftop. Above them stretched the most stunning starscape she'd ever seen, in the center of which hung a shimmering half moon.

"Oh, wow!" She turned in a slow circle, her head

tilted back as far as it would go. "I'm definitely not in L.A. anymore."

"Quiet enough for you?"

The noisy commotion beneath them was a dull, distant hum.

She smiled broadly, she couldn't help it. "I should say so." Walking to the edge, she exclaimed, "Look at the view." Beneath them, the small town with its quaint buildings and charming storefronts resembled an illustration from a children's storybook.

"Over here." Dusty led Maryanne to a candlelit table set with delicate china, silver flatware and crystal goblets. Beside the table, a bottle of wine waited in an ice bucket.

She took it all in, admittedly overwhelmed. "Something tells me this isn't usual service for the Spotted Horse."

"I called in a couple favors."

Was she the first woman Dusty had brought up to the saloon's rooftop?

Who cares? She reminded herself. This wasn't a date, they were here for a meeting.

But as she sat down in the chair he pulled out for her, it felt very much like a date, complete with wine, candles and romantic view.

Maryanne had to wonder just what she'd gotten herself into.

"YOU SAID THAT producer only gave you a few seconds to tell him about your screenplay before he cut you off." Maryanne sipped at her wine, which was quite good. It complemented her grilled fish. The staff at The Spotted Horse had certainly outdone themselves.

So had Dusty. They'd only met a few days ago yet he'd correctly anticipated her taste in cuisine right down to the rice pilaf and vinaigrette dressing on her salad.

Was she that easy to read or was he particularly astute? Both, she supposed. Her father had blabbed a great deal about her to Dusty, and he was an aspiring writer, or so he said.

"Twelve seconds if that." Dusty cut into his steak. "What you need is a good tagline."

"I had one, just not good I guess."

So, he knew another common writer's term. Maybe he really was serious. "What is it? Do you mind telling me?"

He grinned sheepishly. Maryanne sat back in her chair, a little surprised. In their short acquaintance, Dusty had oozed confidence at every turn. To see him struggle with embarrassment was…interesting to say the least. And, okay she had to admit, a little appealing.

He lifted his head to meet her gaze and cleared his throat. "Secrets threaten to destroy a wealthy ranching family and the people in the small Wyoming town where they reside."

Wealthy ranching family? Small town in Wyoming? Was the similarity to Dusty's life merely a coincidence?

"Not terrible." She lifted a shoulder. "On the one hand, it says it all. On the other, it's, well, kind of boring. You need to punch it up."

"How?"

She finished off the last of her fish. "Tell me a little about the family. Are they normal? Dysfunctional?"

"I thought all families were dysfunctional to a degree."

"Probably." Maryanne laughed. She certainly saw her share of them in L.A. "Not mine."

"You're lucky." Dusty's mood shifted slightly, though Maryanne couldn't quite put her finger on what was different.

"Correction," she said. "My adoptive family isn't dysfunctional. My biological family? That's another story altogether."

"The Weavers are more dysfunctional than most." Dusty polished off his wine and made no move to refill his glass.

"Your fictional family?"

"Yeah."

"Like the Carmichaels in *Family Fortune*," Maryanne said, naming the sitcom in which her mother had starred.

"Only not funny."

"The Ewings on *Dallas*?"

"Closer."

"What distinguishes the Weavers from the Ewings besides the setting?"

"They make their money in cattle, not oil."

"Are they as ruthless and devious?"

"No." He pondered her question. "More like ordinary people."

"Even the secrets?"

"It's not the secrets, rather what they do to the characters' lives when they're revealed."

"There you go." Maryanne smiled. "The Ewings of *Dallas* meet *Brothers and Sisters*."

"Okay."

"When dark secrets are revealed, lives and the happiness of everyone around them hinges on the brink of ruin." Maryanne laughed again. "Might be a little over the top, but do you see what I'm going for?"

"I do." His smile was soft, gentle and genuine. Not at all like the megawatt one he usually flashed. It was also far more potent.

Maryanne reminded herself to stay focused. "Try tweaking it a little. When you've got something good, tell me. I know one or two people in the industry I can bounce it off and get their reaction."

"Thanks." Finishing his meal, he set his fork down and leaned back in his chair. "So let's say I get the chance to talk to some producer and impress him enough with my tagline that he gives me twelve more seconds of his time. What then?"

The door opened and Mindy Sue emerged carrying a tray. "How is everything?" She began clearing empty dishes.

"Delicious."

"Can I get you some coffee with your dessert?"

"Do you have any organic blends?" Maryanne asked.

"Just plain old ground coffee, I'm afraid." Mindy Sue readjusted the tray. "But it's fresh."

Dusty raised a brow at Maryanne. "You could make an exception."

"Two in one night?" She sighed heavily. "You're corrupting me."

"He does that a lot," Mindy Sue said, affecting a knowing air.

Maryanne had no right and no reason whatsoever but she couldn't help feeling irritated. At Mindy Sue for whatever ploy she was attempting to execute *and* at herself for letting it get to her.

"Plain coffee's fine," Maryanne said smoothly. "Cream and sugar please."

"Be back in a jiffy," Mindy Sue chimed and left.

Maryanne removed her wrap from the back of her chair and slid it over her shoulders.

"Cold?" Dusty asked. "We can go inside."

"No, I'm fine." The night air was cool but not unbearable. A nice change from the warm days. Realizing that donning the wrap had been an unconscious gesture to shield herself from unwelcome feelings, she relaxed her arms. "Where were we?" she asked, trying to remember the last thing said before Mindy Sue had appeared.

"What do I say to a producer after delivering my tagline."

Their conversation continued at a lively pace with Maryanne giving Dusty a few basic pointers on how to sell himself and his product to a prospective client. To Maryanne's relief, Mindy Sue didn't deliver any more subtle reminders of her and Dusty's long-standing friendship when she delivered dessert.

"You ready?" he asked twenty minutes later.

"Thank you again for dinner. It was lovely." The temperature had continued to drop. This time when Maryanne pulled her wrap more closely around her, it really was to ward off the cold.

"My pleasure."

They walked toward the door. Dusty hadn't been presented with a bill. She assumed he'd taken care of all the arrangements beforehand.

"You didn't have to go through all the trouble."

"It wasn't any."

He held the door for her and waited for her to start down the stairs ahead of him. At the bottom, he again took her hand and led her through the honky-tonk, which was still crowded and noisier than ever. Then again, nine o'clock was probably when the place really took off.

The double doors at the main entrance stood open, accommodating the constant stream of people coming and going. Dusty and Maryanne were halfway out when they came face-to-face with another tall, good-looking cowboy with a face that looked vaguely familiar to her. Both men stopped suddenly. Maryanne expected them to give each other a friendly greeting. She was wrong.

"Dusty."

"Mark. How's it going?"

"Fine."

Clipped, curt and reserved. Maryanne had felt more warmth up on the roof. He definitely wasn't one of the wranglers as she'd first suspected.

The man touched the brim of his worn Stetson hat and spared her a fleeting glance. "Ma'am."

"Hello." She kept her reply short, not sure what else to say.

"Congratulations on winning at Missoula," Dusty said, his tone neutral.

"Thanks."

"See you in Albuquerque?"

"Count on it." Gruff. Very gruff. The animosity was clearly more one-sided.

The moment stretched on. Neither one stepped back to give the other room. Maryanne thought she might drown in an overabundance of male posturing. Finally, Dusty took her arm and eased her forward. The man—Mark?—moved to let her and then Dusty by.

"Good night," she said.

He nodded stiffly before entering the saloon without so much as a parting glance.

Not that she was egotistical or anything but he was the first person she'd met in Markton who didn't appear at all curious about her. She couldn't say the same in return. Her curiosity about him was piqued and then some. Whatever relationship Dusty and this Mark guy had, it wasn't exactly good.

Then it hit her.

"Is he a rival of yours?"

"Sort of." Dusty's attention had turned inward, though he continued to hold her hand with no obvious intention of letting go. "He's a bull rider. Like my brother Jesse."

"So, *they're* rivals?"

"Since grade school."

There was clearly more going on than Dusty was admitting.

"When I first saw him, I was sure I'd met him somewhere. At Cowboy College or your family's ranch."

"Trust me, hell would freeze over before he set foot on either of those places."

Lights from the storefront windows illuminated their walk to the car. At the corner, they turned down the side street where Dusty had parked. He flipped the remote door lock attached to his key. In response, the Jag beeped hello and the dome light illuminated. He opened the passenger door for her.

"Then I figured it out," Maryanne said, sliding onto the seat. "For some silly reason, he reminds me of your father."

Dusty didn't move. She was about to ask what was wrong when he abruptly shut the door and came around to the driver's side. One look at the ruthless set of his jaw and Maryanne knew that whatever she'd said, it had been the wrong thing.

DUSTY GAVE UNO'S NECK a last pat before moving on. He was checking on the horses for no reason other than to procrastinate. He wasn't ready to head upstairs to his apartment. Not until his head cleared. Maryanne's comment about Mark's resemblance to his father had stirred too many thoughts—most of them confusing and disturbing—for him to consider going to bed.

How was it that she, a complete stranger, could see the resemblance between Mark and J.W. when no one else did? Or, was it that others did see the resemblance and refused to say anything?

Few people had the gumption to intentionally rile J. W. Cody and even fewer got away with it.

Dusty was among those willing but before he confronted his father on this issue, he needed more substantive evidence than an observation made by a visitor to town.

"What are you doing down here?" Dex approached from the other end of the barn aisle. "I figured you'd be holed up going over your new contract."

Dusty and his brother might be twins, but they couldn't be more different. In looks or personality. Like their father, Dex didn't approve of Dusty's sideline business of providing specially trained horses for film work. Just that morning he'd agreed to supply two horses and a donkey for a documentary being filmed in Yellowstone.

"I went out to dinner. Just got back."

When Dex got close, he stopped to give Dusty a lengthy inspection. "Who is she?"

"What?"

"The girl you were with."

"I wasn't on a date."

"Right."

"It was a business meeting."

"Not ranch business, I assume."

"I'm a little tired, Dex, and could do without a lecture tonight."

"What's with you?"

"The lady I was with—"

"So it was a date."

"For the last time—" he snarled.

"Okay, okay." Dex motioned Dusty to follow. "Come on, I'll buy you a beer."

They walked toward the center of the barn. On one side was a large tack room and adjoining storage room. On the other, a small office complete with battered desk, file cabinet and a couple of chairs. He and his brother both had considerably fancier offices at the ranch's administrative office but used this one just as frequently. Unlocking the office door, Dex went straight to the closet and the small refrigerator kept there. He removed two beers and handed one to Dusty before sitting in the chair behind the desk. Dusty took the vacant chair nearest the door. The significance of their chosen positions wasn't lost on him. He popped the top on his beer and took a long swig.

"What brings you here besides the chance to ride me about my new contract?" he asked.

"Do I need a reason?"

"I can't imagine you leaving your new bride at nine-thirty at night for anything that wasn't important."

Dex set his half-finished beer on the desk. "Josie wants to enroll Matt in preschool."

"You came all the way here at night to tell me that? I have a cell phone."

"She needs you to sign the papers."

"Fine."

Dex visibly relaxed.

"I'll talk to her about it tomorrow. And Matt."

"What's to talk about?" Dex straightened.

"I'm not signing any papers until I know more about what's going on."

"It's preschool."

"I want to talk to Josie and Matt first. What if the kid doesn't want to go?"

"He's four. We make the decisions at this age, not him."

"That's right. *We.* Matt's my son, and I have a right to be involved."

Dusty didn't object to the idea of sending Matt to preschool. He knew almost nothing about raising kids but figured parents did it all the time. Plus Matt needed friends his own age to play with. There weren't any to speak of on the ranch. The employees with spouses and children lived in town. But since talking with Maryanne about his role in Matt's life, Dusty wanted a greater one, and that included making important decisions with the boy's mother. Dex would simply have to accept it.

"Tell Josie I'll call her tomorrow."

Rather than jump all over him, Dex took another swallow of his beer. "The three of us need to compromise. For Matt's sake."

"I agree. But it isn't always going to be what you and Josie want just because Matt lives with you."

"Fair enough," Dex said, his tone conciliatory. After a moment, he added, "I shouldn't have gotten so mad at you about Matt having dinner with you the other night."

"Thanks." Dusty was impressed. His brother didn't often admit he was wrong.

"But for the record, if you and Josie disagree on something, I'm going to side with her."

His answer was just as conciliatory. "I wouldn't expect anything different."

"We can make this work."

"We will." Dusty believed what he said but neither was he fooling himself. It wouldn't always be easy. Not with two hotheaded Cody brothers who seldom saw eye to eye.

"So you going to tell me what's really bothering you?"

Dusty deliberated. As far as he knew, none of his siblings had ever discussed the long-standing rumors concerning Mark and their father. Maybe it was about time. And if he was going to choose someone to confide in, it would be Dex.

"The lady I was with tonight—"

"Your date."

"My associate." Dusty wouldn't have minded if his dinner with Maryanne had been more social. He'd even considered the possibility after their semiwild ride in his Jag. But she'd made it crystal clear from the beginning her purpose for going out with him was to keep her end of their bargain. Nothing more.

Too bad.

"What about her?" Dex asked.

"We ran into Mark on our way out of The Spotted Horse."

Dex waited for Dusty to continue. Mark Hansen was a sore subject with most of the Codys, especially Jesse. His and Mark's rivalry was pushing twenty years and showed no signs of abating.

"Maryanne made an interesting remark about him. Especially interesting, considering she saw him for maybe a minute."

"What?"

"She said he reminded her of Dad."

Both men drained the last of their beer then looked at each other. Dex exhaled.

Dusty was about to speak when his brother beat him to the punch, echoing his thoughts exactly in a slow, carefully worded admission.

"I've been thinking the same thing myself for a long time now."

"Me, too. So what are we going to do about it?"

"Why do anything?"

Dex's question was a good one. They'd ignored the rumors for years. No reason not to continue. Except Dusty had recently found out he was a father, and his perspective had changed.

"If Mark really is…" the words didn't come easy "…a Cody, then don't you think Dad owes him?"

"What? Money?"

"Not just that. A place in the family?"

Dex looked uneasy if not downright aghast. "I don't know."

Neither did Dusty. His feelings about parenthood were new, and he was still coming to terms with them. "When I found out about Matt, I did the right thing by him. Am doing it. Trying to. Dad should have done the same."

"I think he would have. Which is a good argument against Mark being...related to us."

"You could be right." He let his voice trail off.

"Except for what?"

"Don't take this wrong but Josie hid Matt from me for years. I'm not angry anymore, though I do wish I'd been there from the beginning. Seen him born. Watched him take his first step. Thrown him his first baseball."

"I know Josie feels bad."

"Yeah, and it's okay." He rubbed his forehead, trying to put his thoughts in order. "The thing is, if Mark's a Cody, we've lost all those years with him and him with us. His life could have been different. Better. All of our lives. I don't understand our parents, how they could have done that to us."

"Are you going to make it your mission to find out?"

"I wouldn't call it a mission exactly." He crunched his empty beer can, compressing it to half its original size. "I'm just done tiptoeing around the issue."

"That's not going to go over very well."

Dex sure wasn't kidding.

CHAPTER FIVE

DUSTY STOMPED THE dust off his boots and entered the mudroom at his parents' house. Thinking his efforts might not be sufficient to satisfy his finicky mother, he grabbed one of the cloths left by the side of the sink and reached down to give his boots a more thorough wiping.

"Track, you're going to have to wait here."

The Border collie didn't look happy but settled on a mat in the corner. Dusty's mother loved animals but not their dirty paw prints trailing across her polished hardwood floors or Persian rugs.

Tossing the cloth into a hamper, he headed down the hall to his mother's pride and joy—a big, brightly lit kitchen with floor to ceiling windows. His father had the windows specially designed so his mother could enjoy the sight of the morning sun rising over the mountains as she ate her breakfast. Barbara, the family's housekeeper, was bent over the dishwasher fiddling with the controls. As usual, her wiry brown hair was tamed with a simple headband. She straightened and smiled as she'd done a thousand times in the many years she'd spent in his parents' employ.

"Hi there. Want some lunch? There's leftover tuna sandwiches and fruit salad in the fridge."

He half expected her to demand he take off those spurs before he scratched the floors, leave that darned lariat in the mudroom where it belonged and to not even think about eating until he'd washed his hands.

"No, thanks. I had something already." When he didn't fix his own meals in his apartment or eat out, Dusty dined with the men in the bunkhouse. "Where's Mom?"

"In her study."

"Not resting? I heard she was sick with the flu." His sister, Elly, had called to tell him earlier.

"She's feeling better this afternoon. I guess it was one of those twenty-four-hour bugs."

"Good. I'm going to check on her anyway."

"She'll appreciate the company, I'm sure." Barbara picked up a heavy platter to wash, then hesitated. "Did you bring that mangy mutt with you?"

"He's hiding under the raincoats."

She nodded approvingly.

Dusty turned away and grinned to himself. The housekeeper's intolerance of animals was a long-standing pretense. Track would be given a doggie treat and some ear scratching three seconds after Dusty left the kitchen.

At the door to his mother's study, he paused. She reclined on a delicate ivory chaise longue that his father had fussed about acquiring because it would break in two if he tried to sit on it but purchased nonetheless. John Walker Cody rarely denied his wife anything. On the floor were several old storage boxes, their lids propped open. His mother balanced a large leather-bound photo album on her lap. Two more were stacked beside her. She slowly turned the pages of the album in her lap, studying the photos intently.

Dusty stepped quietly into the room. "Hey, Mom, how you feeling?"

Her face lit up at his approach. "Much better now!"

"What's all this?" He leaned down to give her a peck on the cheek.

She patted his in return. "I got to thinking of Matthew and how much he looks like you at his age." She tapped a picture, and her expression gentled. It was a candid family portrait taken during a long-ago holiday. "See?"

Dusty gazed at the photograph and his own toothless, dimpled grin. While his brothers had stood quietly as they were told to, he'd been cutting up. What else was new? Put him and his siblings in a room together today, and the results would be the same. He had to agree Matt's resemblance to him was strong. It was easy to see how Dex had first figured out the boy was Dusty's son.

"I'm thinking of having copies made of some of these pictures for Josie and Paula," his mother said, naming her two new daughters-in-law.

"I'm sure they'll like that."

His mother's voice warmed. "Your sister was such a little angel."

Elly, the youngest of the Cody siblings, wore a frilly dress and sat in her mother's lap. Dusty remembered pulling the bow out of her hair right after the picture had been snapped and making her cry. He also remembered the reprimand that had followed and the loss of privileges, doubly hard to take on Christmas Day. Even so, the lesson hadn't sunk in.

His eyes traveled next to his father, standing behind his mother, his hand resting affectionately on her shoulder.

Dusty went rigid.

The dark-haired, dark-complexioned face staring back at him was the image of Mark Hansen.

"Are you all right, honey?" his mother asked.

"Fine." He moved away, not wanting to look at the picture anymore.

Did she really not suspect or was she in denial of the obvious? Dusty couldn't tell. His mother was a strong, capable woman when it came to running the family's horse breeding business but there had always been a certain fragility beneath the competent exterior she put forth.

He pointed to a framed picture of his parents on the corner of the side table. It was taken several years earlier on their thirtieth anniversary.

"Dad's sure changed a lot."

His mother drew back, clearly affronted. "He has not. He's still handsome as ever."

"I heard something interesting in town the other day." Dusty pulled a footstool over and sat down across from his mother.

"You did?" She absently flipped to another page in the album and as her eyes lighted on the pictures, her mouth curved into a smile.

He hesitated, doubting his reasons and yet compelled to continue on the path he'd chosen. Would dredging up the past really make any difference when all was said and done?

Yes. If the rumors were true. Certainly to Dusty, his brothers and sister. They had a right to know if Mark

Hansen was somehow related to them and why his parents had kept the secret all these years.

His mother tilted her head inquiringly. "Well? What was it you heard?"

He could, he realized, tear his family's world apart with one simple question...or, possibly, bring them closer together. Dex and he had both agreed the risk was worth it. What they hadn't agreed on was how to approach their parents.

Dusty had decided to take matters into his own hands.

He swallowed, then asked, "Did you and Dad separate for a while before Jesse was born?"

She flinched as if he'd pulled a glass of ice water from behind his back and thrown the contents in her face.

"Who told you that?"

"Does it matter?"

"Of course. This person could have an ax to grind against us."

"They don't."

"Are you positive? Who was it?"

"Which time?"

Her features, stoic until that moment, crumbled. She didn't, however, cry. His mother simply didn't break down in public, unless her tears were those of joy.

"It's all right, Mom. Lots of couples have problems." Now that Dusty had asked the question, he was almost sorry he did. He hadn't fully considered the pain revealing the truth might bring his mother, only the pain their covering it up had caused. "What matters is that you and Dad worked them out."

"I don't know what those people told you," she

sniffed delicately, "but I can assure you they don't know the entire story."

"What is the entire story?"

She shook her head vehemently. "This is not the time or place."

"When will it be?"

She spoke so quietly, he barely heard her. "Your father would never forgive me if I told you."

"Dad has no right," he ground out. "This affects all of us. More than all of us. What about—"

"Don't jump to conclusions."

"I wouldn't have to if you and Dad had been honest with us from the start." Dusty wasn't aware his voice had risen until his father hobbled through the study door as fast as his bum leg would allow.

"What's going on here?" he demanded, his cheeks flushed a brilliant red. "I can hear you all the way from the stairs."

"It's all right," Dusty's mother reassured him, instantly composed.

"The hell it is." He crossed the room and loomed over Dusty. "You don't ever speak to your mother like that. You hear me? I don't care how old you are, I won't tolerate it."

Dusty stood and addressed his mother. "I apologize. I shouldn't have hollered. I let my anger get the best of me."

"If there's something bothering you," J.W. told him, "take it up with me."

"All right, I will." Dusty pivoted to face him.

He'd stopped being intimidated by his father years ago; however, he still respected him. For that reason, he lowered his voice. Barbara and the other household staff didn't need to overhear them.

"Is Mark Hansen your son?"

J.W.'s dark eyes burned with a fury like Dusty had never seen before. "How dare you," he snapped.

"How dare I what? Accuse you of having an affair and fathering a child with another woman? Or insist you level with us for once in your life?"

"How dare you upset your mother like this."

Dusty looked over at her. At some point she'd pushed to her feet. Her hand gripped the back of the chaise as if without its support, she might collapse.

"I am sorry," he apologized again. "But I'm tired of being lied to. Tired of being the brunt of gossip. Tired of looking at Mark Hansen and wondering if he's my brother."

"We're not discussing this ever again." J.W.'s eyes, burning mere seconds ago, went icy cold. "And if you bring it up, I won't hesitate to throw you out of this house and off this ranch. For good."

"J.W.!" his mother gasped.

"You don't have to throw me out," Dusty said. "I'll leave."

This wasn't how he'd wanted the discussion with his mother to go, though in hindsight, it really couldn't have ended any other way. Not once his father became involved.

At least he had his answer.

Neither of his parents had admitted as much but it was clear to Dusty by their reactions that the rumors circulating about his father's affair with Abigail Hansen were true.

A jolt, swift and painful, shot through him.

Barbara gave no indication of anything being amiss as Dusty all but tore through the kitchen on his way back to the mudroom. Track, overjoyed to see his master, followed Dusty outside, his tail wagging.

Dusty debated his next move. His instinct was to locate Dex and recount what had happened. If his twin was busy, he'd find Walker. Not Jesse or Elly. His oldest brother adamantly claimed not to believe the rumors, though Dusty had his doubts. He'd often speculated if the possibility that Mark might be their brother was at the root of Jesse's rivalry with him. And Elly…well, he wasn't entirely sure how much she knew and wasn't ready to involve her.

When Dex didn't answer his cell phone, Dusty got in his truck and drove to Cowboy College. He was almost as familiar with the layout there as the Cody ranch and chose a secluded place behind the equipment barn. Thirty minutes. That was all he needed to get his head on straight. Grabbing one of the lariats he always kept in the back of his truck and a practice dummy, he began roping. One throw. Then another. The constant repetitive motion slowly worked its magic, eventually putting his thoughts in order. Until a brand-new one crept into his mind.

Did Mark know Tomas Hansen wasn't his father?

Dusty had been so busy thinking only of himself and his own family, he'd failed to consider the other person directly involved.

MARYANNE POWERED OFF the digital camera. She actually preferred a plain old 35-millimeter but those weren't so common anymore. And besides, the digital was all Adele Donnelly had available.

"I really appreciate the opportunity," Maryanne informed the manager of Cowboy College while slipping the camera into its zippered pouch. "You have no idea how bored I've been this last week." Too late, she realized her error and gushed, "I didn't mean that the way it sounded."

Adele dismissed Maryanne's concerns with a good-natured laugh. "Don't worry. I know how tedious it can be around here for someone who doesn't eat, sleep and breathe the cowboy lifestyle."

"Really, it's not that bad."

"Nice try." Adele laughed again, proving what a good sport she was.

Her casually delivered request over breakfast that Maryanne help with updating Cowboy College's website and sales brochure promised to provide a welcome diversion. Maryanne's days had begun to drag. The first couple hours she spent telecommuting with her office flew by but after that, there wasn't much else for her to do except hang around the arena watching her dad and waiting for him to fall and break his neck.

Dinner with Dusty had also been a welcome diversion—or was that an unwelcome distraction?

As if reading her mind, Adele said, "I heard you had a little excitement last night."

"Last night?"

"Your dinner with Dusty."

"You know about that?"

"Markton's a very small town. News travels fast."

"We had a business dinner."

"Ah." Adele's eyes twinkled. "I'm not your first local client then."

Was she also personally acquainted with Dusty like

that waitress from The Spotted Horse Saloon? Possibly. Maryanne guessed the manager of Cowboy College to be around her own age of twenty-eight, and she was certainly attractive enough to catch the attention of any man.

It was on the tip of Maryanne's tongue to explain that Dusty was mentoring her father but she stopped herself in the nick of time. Adele might think the arrangement was taking away from the classes offered at Cowboy College. Guilt ate at Maryanne, and she vowed to made amends.

"No, I guess you're not my first." She provided no further explanation and, to her relief, none was asked for.

"It's certainly none of my business, and please don't take this wrong…" Adele hesitated.

"What?"

"Dusty's a great guy but a bit wild, if you catch my drift."

"Meaning he's a player, and I should be careful?"

"Not a player as much as not serious."

"He is about rodeoing." And his writing, Maryanne added silently.

"That's the one exception."

"No worries. I'm leaving at the end of the month." She repeated what she'd been telling herself since meeting Dusty.

Adele motioned to the camera in Maryanne's hand. "I insist on paying you. What are your rates?"

"Don't worry about that just yet. Let me take some photos of the place first and draft my ideas. If you like what I've done, then we can discuss the cost." It would be minimal, Maryanne had already decided.

"Fair enough."

The two women left the main building together through the front entrance and ventured out onto the sprawling porch. On the expansive grounds in front of them, wranglers, guests and horses milled about. Like everyone and everything Maryanne had thus far encountered in Markton, their pace was relaxed and unhurried. She was reminded again of the difference between country life and the hustle and bustle of L.A.

"Come on." Adele led Maryanne down the steps. "Let me introduce you to Jet."

"Jet?"

"Your mode of transportation."

Maryanne's stomach twisted into a knot. "I can't ride." Nor was she ready to learn. Yet.

"Jet's plenty easy to handle. I promise." Adele linked arms with Maryanne to hurry her along. "Here we are," she announced when they rounded the corner of the building.

A black golf cart with a white vinyl top and a single bench seat large enough for two people was parked in the shade.

Maryanne bit her bottom lip. "Can't say I've ever driven one of these, either."

"Come on, it's easy. I'll show you."

Five minutes later, Maryanne was handling Jet like a pro and having a blast. Not exactly Dusty's Jaguar but it would get her around the ranch just fine.

"How fast does it go?" she asked Adele, peering over her shoulder and parallel parking one-handed.

"Maybe thirty-five on a full battery."

"Electric powered?"

"Can't you tell?" Adele cupped a hand to her ear to

indicate how quiet the golf cart ran. "That way, you won't spook the horses."

"Cool." Her own little green-mobile. Maryanne was liking Jet more and more.

"Let's park over there."

Adele and Maryanne discussed a few more details regarding shots of the ranch and guests before parting. Maryanne waved to everyone she passed as she hummed down the drive. There was a modest hill just beyond the main gate, and she thought she might be able to get some nice shots of the entire facility. While earning her degree at UCLA she'd taken several photography classes and, if she said so herself, wasn't half-bad.

No sooner had she pulled to a stop on the hilltop and begun inspecting the view than her cell phone rang.

"Figures I'd get good reception up here." Recognizing her boss's number, she answered with a bright, "Hello, Jarred."

"I've been calling for hours. Where have you been?"

"Out of range." Unlike usual, she didn't let his nervous anxiety spread to her like a contagious virus. Could it be some of Markton's easygoing pace was wearing off on her? "What's wrong?"

"You've got to fly home. Right away."

"Um…okay." Part of the agreement she'd made with Jarred when he gave her the month's leave of absence was that she return for a few days when needed. "Is there a problem?"

"Hancock has moved the presentation up to the twenty-fourth."

"Wow. So soon?"

"We need you here to help finalize the project and then again to present it. Check your email and call immediately if the e-ticket's not there. Your flight leaves at six p.m."

No staying up late and having dinner with handsome cowboys tonight. Not that Maryanne had any plans, with handsome cowboys or otherwise.

A small part of her felt the disappointment keenly. The larger, more sensible part of her managed to maintain a level head.

"I'll see you in the morning, Jarred."

"I only wish you would stay longer." His heavy sigh of relief sounded in her ear. "It's been total chaos here without you."

"Buck up, pal. Only three more weeks, and then I'll be home for good."

"Three *long* weeks."

They said their goodbyes, and Maryanne disconnected. The prospect of returning home for even two days lifted her spirits, though she'd spend the entire time worrying about her father and—this came as a surprise—missing the people she'd befriended since coming to Wyoming. Like Adele and, okay, it was true, Dusty.

Removing the camera from its pouch, she began taking pictures. As she had nothing to pack for her short trip home, there was no reason she couldn't continue with her plans. When she finished, she drove to the creek where she shot a series of guests fishing. At the horse barn, a baby burro stole her heart. Lastly, she headed for the practice arena but lost her bearings and wound up behind one of the barns.

She was startled to come upon Dusty's truck. At least, it looked like his truck. Cutting Jet's engine, she got out and traveled no more than a few steps when she spotted him. He had his back to her and was throwing a rope at a fake plastic cow head attached to a bale of hay. No sooner did he rope the cow head than he retrieved the lasso and threw it again.

He was beautiful to watch, his movements combining the grace and fluidity of a dancer with the strength and power of an athlete. Maryanne stared, mesmerized. Finally, she roused herself and extracted her camera. She'd never forgive herself for missing such a wonderful photo op.

She inched closer with each shot, too caught up with what she saw through the viewfinder to care if he noticed her or not. Not that she had anything to worry about. He was completely focused on his task and oblivious to the rest of the world. Maryanne circled to the right. When she finally saw his face, her breath caught. His expression wasn't that of someone enjoying himself.

Odd. Dusty was usually so laid-back and affable.

Intrigued by this different side of him, she snapped more pictures. He'd make a perfect cover for Cowboy College's new brochure.

He finally noticed her and for the first time since she'd arrived, his rope missed the plastic cow head.

"Sorry," she called. "I didn't mean to disturb you."

He said nothing, simply collected his rope, wound it into a large coil and prepared for another toss.

"Adele recruited me to take some pictures of the ranch for her." When he still didn't answer, Maryanne fumed. Something might be eating at him but that didn't give him any reason to be rude. "I got a few nice ones of you. Of course, she'll need you to sign a release before she can use them." The silence stretched indefinitely.

She'd about given up when he raised the rope over his head and began twirling it.

Fine. She got the hint. He wasn't in the mood to talk.

She spun on her heel, intent on returning to the golf cart. All at once the rope came out of nowhere and dropped down over her head and shoulders.

"What the—"

He yanked, and the rope tightened. She was forced to walk toward him or pitch forward. He also walked toward her, reeling her in as he did.

"Dusty! What are you doing?"

Her question was answered when he pulled her up against him and brought his mouth down on hers.

CHAPTER SIX

DUSTY'S KISS WAS hot and hungry and bordering on desperate. Even in her semidazed state, Maryanne realized the emotion driving him wasn't lust but something else. Something related to the fierce expression he'd worn when she'd taken his picture. That knowledge didn't stop her weak-kneed response as his tongue parted her lips and delved between them.

Oh, no, not hardly.

Uttering a soft moan, she wriggled against the rope restricting her. He understood her frustration and broke off their kiss—only for as long as it took him to loosen the knot with one quick jerk and lift the rope over her head. Then, he was cupping her cheeks with his hands, murmuring her name and seeking her mouth so they could pick up where they'd left off.

Maryanne's arms, free to do what they wanted, circled his waist and brought their bodies that much closer. Enough of her reasoning remained for her to realize that kissing him wasn't a good idea. She also recognized on a deeper level that he needed this. The connection with her. The intimacy. The release. And she gave it to him without hesitation.

She sensed the change in him a scant second before his mouth relaxed, and his kisses went from demanding to gentle. Until then, she'd been able to maintain a certain amount of control. This tenderness, this vulnerability, was her undoing, and she sank into his embrace, fully aware she would stay right where she was forever if that was what he wanted.

Only he didn't.

Darn it.

Muttering a sound—of regret?—he released her. "I shouldn't have done that."

"It's okay. As you could obviously tell, I didn't exactly mind." She considered asking what had upset him but refrained. It was none of her business even if the effects had spilled over to her.

"Can I give you a ride back?" he said after a moment.

So, things were going to be a little stilted between them. She should have expected as much, given the spontaneity of their kiss and their strictly business relationship up until then.

"No, thanks. Adele let me use Jet."

"Jet?"

"Her golf cart. It's parked by your truck."

Silence followed.

Since he appeared to be at a loss for words, she started to leave. "I'll bring the release this weekend. For the photos I took of you," she said when his eyebrows came together in a deep V.

"Sure. Whatever Adele wants. She's a good neighbor."

"I really think they turned out well. Which reminds me, have you come up with a tagline?"

"Not yet," he said, a muscle working in his jaw.

Well, well. Whatever was bothering him clearly had something to do with his writing. Or, she realized, with whatever was keeping him from his writing.

Work? His family? His son? No, not Matt. Dusty adored the boy. But his issues might be with his brother, the one who'd married his son's mother.

"Take your time. I just thought if you had a tagline, I could try it out on my mother's friends. My boss called. There's a problem with the new account we're trying to land, and I'm flying back to L.A. for a couple of days."

The change in subject must have agreed with him for he perked up. "When do you leave?"

"My flight's at six tonight. But you can call me on my cell if you think of something while I'm gone."

He removed his phone from the case clipped to his belt. "What's your number?"

"Here." She held out her hand. When he placed his phone in it, she programmed her number into his list of contacts. "Maybe later this week we can have another mentoring session." She avoided making any reference to their kiss. "Dad mentioned you're giving him a lesson tomorrow."

"I'll keep an eye on him for you while you're gone."

"I'd appreciate it. And be sure to call me if anything happens, no matter how insignificant. Lord knows he won't." Maryanne reminded herself to secure a similar promise from Adele.

"Look, I'm sorry about…" He didn't finish.

"Don't worry. These things happen." Just not to her. Men didn't haul off and kiss her with no warning. She climbed into the golf cart. "I've practically forgotten about it already." That had to be about the tallest tale she'd ever told.

"Are you referring to our kissing?"

"I…ah—"

"Hell, I'm not sorry about that." He rested a hand on

the bar supporting the canopy roof. "I shouldn't have taken advantage of you but, trust me, I don't regret it. Except maybe for rushing like a stupid fool and not doing it right."

Not doing it right? Was he serious? "Um, okay."

"I'm sorry for being in such a bad mood. I got into an argument with my dad earlier."

"I see." His admission came as no big surprise. She'd sensed an underlying friction between him and his parents on the day she'd met them.

He laughed bitterly. "It's hardly our first one, and I guarantee you it won't be our last. But thanks for caring."

"I do. Care, that is."

"Me, too."

Their gazes connected and held. Maryanne's heart began beating erratically.

Despite all her declarations and intentions to the contrary—not to mention Dusty's excuses—it was clear he was beginning to get to her and that their relationship was *anything* but strictly business.

Maryanne reminded herself to proceed cautiously or risk being hurt.

"See you in a few days." She turned the key, and Jet purred to life.

"Be careful driving back." He removed his hand and retreated a step, looking sorry to see her go.

She decided on the ride back to the main building that it was a good thing she had a plane to catch in a few hours. If not, she might have suffered a lapse in judgment, stayed with Dusty and done something incredibly stupid like kiss him again.

And again.

THE RETURN FLIGHT TO Yellowstone Regional Airport went smoothly except for the last thirty minutes. Maryanne normally didn't mind flying but landing in the middle of a thunderstorm—at night—wasn't her idea of fun. Only when the commuter plane's wheels touched the ground did she release her death grip on the armrests. Once the plane came to a complete stop, the mad race to disembark was on.

It was a tiring end to what had been a physically and emotionally demanding three days. Fortunately, she had only a small carry-on tote and could avoid the cattle call at baggage claim.

She expected to find her father waiting for her at the entrance to the gates as was their prearranged agreement. Instead, it was Dusty waving at her, his grin stretching from ear to ear and as potent as ever. Her pulse involuntarily skipped. So much for getting her emotions under control during her absence.

All at once a new worry popped into her head, and she hurried her pace, cutting through and around people to reach him.

He met her on the other side of security.

"Is Dad all right?" she asked, frantic at this point.

"He's fine."

"Why didn't he meet me?"

"I asked him if I could. I was hoping you could fill me in on what your contacts said."

"Oh." Relief swept over her, leaving her unsteady.

Dusty had wound up calling Maryanne the day after she arrived in L.A. As promised, she'd gotten in touch with a couple of industry professionals, friends of her late mother, and tested his revised tagline on them.

"Let's wait till we reach the car to talk." He took

hold of her elbow and guided her through the terminal. "This place is a zoo." Ten minutes later they were outside and crossing the street to the parking garage. "I had to bribe your dad into letting me pick you up. He's missed you. We all did."

Maryanne tried not to read anything into the casual remark.

"I forgot to ask, how was your trip?"

"Crazy busy," she said. "I feel like I've been running an endurance race."

"Accomplish everything you wanted to?"

"Pretty much."

He'd brought the Jag, which pleased her. It was a nice ending to an otherwise long, tedious and, at one point, harrowing plane trip. So, she reluctantly admitted, was being with him.

Nice, that was, not harrowing.

"Did the new client like your presentation?" he asked, merging onto the highway that would take them to Markton.

They'd already discussed his son, who was excited about starting preschool, and her father, who was surviving, if not excelling at, his lessons. Maryanne purposely didn't inquire after Dusty's family and whether or not he and his father had resolved their disagreement.

The small reminder of that day was enough to catapult her back in time to their kiss. Of course, it didn't take much. During her entire stay in L.A., whenever her mind wasn't fully engaged with work or some task, she was thinking about Dusty and his mouth on hers, eliciting feelings she was better off without but having nonetheless.

"The client's not new yet." She rested an elbow on

the armrest and stretched out her legs. It felt good to relax. "They're supposed to let us know by the end of the week whether or not they'll sign with us. But the presentation went well, in spite of a half-dozen last-minute disasters."

"Your boss should be happy."

"He is. For now. But that won't last."

"Then you'll be flying back again?"

"Definitely."

He hadn't mentioned her contact with her mother's friends since picking her up but she knew he was anxious to hear what they'd said. It must be hard for him, she thought, having to wait. Dusty Cody was far more used to getting what he wanted *when* he wanted it. She decided to cut him a break.

"I spoke to Herb Machol. Have you heard of him?"

"No."

"He was my mother's agent."

"Yeah?"

"He's…let me see, how did he say it? Mildly intrigued by your screenplay premise."

"Mildly?" Dusty's expression was priceless. "That doesn't sound good."

Tired as she was, she laughed out loud. "Don't worry, it's good. Herb's usual response is an obscene sound."

Dusty took his eyes off the road long enough to gape at her. "Really?"

"Seriously."

His face split into a ridiculously wide grin, reminding her a lot of Matt when Dusty had given him permission to play fetch with Track.

"Unfortunately, there's bad news, too. The other two people I called didn't have the slightest interest."

His grin turned philosophical. "Win some, lose some."

"That's not all."

"I'm not sure I can take more bad news."

"This isn't bad. Herb says he'll read your screenplay."

"He did?"

"Keep in mind, he doesn't rep writers, only actors. But he said if it knocks his socks off, he'll pass it on to a few of his associates."

"I wish to heck I wasn't driving right now."

"Why?" she asked.

"Because I'd kiss you."

Her insides fluttered. She tried to cover her reaction with a snappy comeback. "A handshake will do."

"Yeah, but not nearly as much fun."

Not nearly as risky, either.

The trip home had reminded her how futile any relationship with Dusty would be. Her life was firmly planted in L.A., and his in Markton.

"Would you do me a favor?" he asked when they turned onto the long drive leading into Cowboy College.

"What's that?"

"Read my screenplay before I send it to your mother's agent. No one's ever read it, and I'd like another opinion."

"Not even a friend?"

"Writing's my deep, dark secret, remember?"

There was that tiny bit of hesitancy again. The one that showed he wasn't nearly as confident as he pretended to be. Maryanne instantly relented.

"Sure, I'll read it."

"Thanks. I'll print it out and drop it off in a day or two."

At the door to her cabin, she got her handshake…

and a kiss. On the cheek—which left her walking only a few inches off the ground and not ten feet.

"Hi, Cookie." Her father was waiting up for her. "How was your trip?"

They chatted for half an hour, him over a nightcap and her over a cup of hot tea, before he yawned noisily, stood and headed off to bed with a spring in his step, the first one she'd seen in the three years since her mother had died. Inconveniences aside, she was glad they'd come to Wyoming. She was also looking forward to them returning home and getting back to their regular routines.

Except for leaving Dusty.

She chewed on her bottom lip, annoyed with herself. That thought had no business rolling around inside her head and needed to go back to wherever it came from.

Another equally disconcerting one promptly occurred to her. What if Dusty's screenplay was bad? How could she tell him without hurting his feelings? Maybe she'd been wrong to agree to read it.

Too late now, she'd already committed.

Her father, dressed in his pajamas, came out to find her sitting on the couch, her legs tucked up under her.

"I can't believe you're still up. You must be exhausted."

"I am but my mind won't shut off enough for me to sleep."

"Well, I'm glad because I forgot to tell you the big news."

"What's that?"

"There's a rodeo in Albuquerque this weekend. Dusty's competing. So are his brothers and sister."

Funny, he hadn't mentioned anything about a rodeo during their ride home from the airport.

"He's invited me to go along with him and his family."

"He did?"

"You, too." Her father beamed. "Isn't that great?"

"Yeah, great," Maryanne said weakly and waited for her father to leave the room before she let out an expansive sigh.

DUSTY DISMOUNTED AND TIED Uno's lead rope to the hitching post. The horse raised his head and whinnied loudly.

"Hold on, big boy. Your turn's coming."

He gave the horse a pat then strode over to join his family who'd gathered to watch the morning practice. Climbing the arena fence, he straddled the railing next to Jesse.

"About time you showed up. Dex had to practice with Len."

They both knew having to use a substitute didn't make their brother happy. To get really good, team ropers had to practice endless hours together.

"Better late than never."

Dusty had actually risen early. Over a quick breakfast, he'd printed out his screenplay then left to drop it off at Maryanne's cabin. Only she wasn't there. Considering how late she'd gotten home the previous night, he'd assumed she'd be taking it easy. After knocking twice, he left the manila envelope containing his screenplay near the front door. On the return trip to Cottonwood Ranch he'd dialed her number but disconnected before the call went through. Better not to appear too eager.

"Late night?" Elly asked.

"No later than usual."

She rolled her eyes as if to say "typical." Only the night hadn't been typical, for that wasn't how he'd describe Maryanne or his growing attraction to her.

"That city girl again?" This question from Walker. When had his other brother found out?

"Can't blame him," Jesse said with far too much leering for Dusty's liking. "She's easy on the eye."

"And off-limits to you," Dusty said irritably.

That got a laugh.

"Good morning, son." His mother ignored the bickering amongst her offspring and smiled in his direction.

"Morning, Mom."

Unlike his father, he and his mother *had* spoken regularly since the argument in her study. Also unlike his father, his mother pretended nothing was out of the ordinary. Had she also pretended nothing was out of the ordinary after finding out about his father's affair with Mark Hansen's mother?

"Aren't you heading over there?" Jesse asked.

"Let Dex take another turn with Len. That way, he'll appreciate me more."

A small commotion at the box drew everyone's attention. Dex's horse, spooking at who knew what, had reared. Pulling on the reins and sitting low in the saddle, he fought to bring the skittish animal under control.

"Let's see what's going on." Jesse nudged Walker with his elbow.

Dusty knew from personal experience that "see what's going on" really meant "give our unsolicited advice."

His two brothers hopped off the fence and crossed

the arena to stand on the railing around the box with their father and three other wranglers.

"Aren't you going, too?" his mother asked.

"If the six of them can't figure out what's spooking Dex's horse," Dusty said, "I sure as heck can't."

Elly laughed and punched him lightly on the arm.

For a family that lived within a few miles of each other and worked at the same place, the entire Cody clan didn't get together more than two or three times a month, and that included holidays. There was, of course, one exception: rodeos. The event itself along with practicing for them. Then, nothing could keep them apart. Not even an argument between father and son.

J.W. offered Dex his opinion on what he was doing wrong with his horse, his booming voice carrying across the arena.

"Go," Len called, when he and Dex were ready to try again.

In the next instant, the chute opened, and a calf bolted. Len, in the header position, went first, his horse flying. Dex, in the heeler position, came second. Ropes circled high in the air and then were tossed at the fleeing calf, one at its head, one at its rear legs. Debates over which position in team roping required more talent and skill were generally heated. The fact was, both men and their horses needed to be good. Damn good. Dex and Len weren't half-bad as the stopwatch proved.

"If they keep that up," Dusty said when the calf had been released and rounded up, "Dex might have himself a new partner for Albuquerque."

Elly clapped her hands as the two men rode by. "Awesome job, guys." An exceptional barrel racer herself, she was well on her way to qualifying for Nationals.

In Dex's and Walker's defense, they'd been distracted by their respective recent weddings. Temporarily. Dex was clearly back in the game.

"Think you can do as good as them?" Elly challenged.

"Hell, yeah," Dusty answered with more confidence than he felt.

He'd had his own share of distractions. Finding out about Matt, for starters, and the impact of having a son in his life. The recent argument with his father, for another. And then there was Maryanne. She'd laid out the ground rules for their relationship, clearly and succinctly. Dusty, however, was inclined to break them.

On the surface, she didn't appear to be his type. Cool, sophisticated and career-driven. Underneath was a different story. She was everything he liked in a woman. Warm, caring, compassionate, bright, a phenomenal kisser—the list went on and on. Too bad she lived hundreds of miles away. He'd sensed without having to ask that she wasn't one to engage in flings. Neither was he, though most people would be surprised to hear that.

Dusty's reputation might have been well-deserved at one time in his life but not for the past year or two. The more serious he'd become about his writing, the more he'd come to believe the rumors regarding his father's infidelity, the less interested he'd become in…socializing. Unfortunately, no one, not even his family, had noticed the change in him.

Jesse cupped his hands to his mouth and hollered, "Your turn."

Dusty started to swing his leg over the fence but stopped when his cell phone rang. The number flashing on the small screen was a surprise. Josie hadn't contacted him directly since before her wedding to Dex.

"Hello—" He stopped himself before saying her name. For some reason, he didn't want his family to know the identity of his caller.

"Hi, Dusty. Sorry to bother you."

"It's all right. I'm not busy."

"I know it's a last-minute imposition but is there any way you can pick up Matt from preschool? I'm stuck at an appointment and can't get away for another hour."

"Sure." He tucked the phone between his ear and shoulder and climbed down the fence.

"I tried calling Dex but he's not answering his phone."

Dusty's gaze automatically darted to the other side of the arena where his brother sat astride his horse talking to their father.

"I'd rather you called me first anyway." He walked farther out of earshot.

He didn't press the issue. She was walking a narrow line between duty to her child's father and loyalty to her new husband. It was enough that she'd called him today and for that, he was grateful.

"Is there a problem? I thought his preschool didn't get out until eleven."

"Oh...maybe. Hard to tell yet. One of the students at the preschool has apparently come down with that new strain of flu, the one in the news these last few weeks. As a precaution, they've closed their doors until next Monday. I don't know what I'm going to do the rest of the week." Josie worked part-time for an attorney in town. Another benefit of Matt attending preschool was that it freed up her mornings.

"I'll watch him."

"But you have your job, and you're getting ready for the rodeo."

"Matt's more important. Besides, I'm ready as I'll ever be."

She breathed a sigh of relief. "Thank you."

"No, thank you, Josie."

After disconnecting, he made straight for Uno and mounted. Instead of heading into the arena, he turned the big horse's head in the direction of the barn.

"Hey! Where you off to?" Elly called.

"I have an emergency."

"You're up next."

"Not anymore." Dusty nudged Uno into a fast trot.

He sensed his brothers' and father's eyes tracking him from their places by the box. They were undoubtedly annoyed, thinking he was once again being selfish and irresponsible. Dex would be more annoyed than any of them if he knew the reason for Dusty's abrupt departure.

Half an hour later, he pulled into the church parking lot where Matt attended preschool. Several parents were leading their children to their parked vehicles. Dusty had heard about the new strain of flu but hadn't really paid much attention. Entering the wrought iron gate, he followed the walkway to the classrooms, remembering which one was Matt's from when they'd registered him the other day.

Besides Matt, only three other children were waiting to be picked up.

"Hi, buddy."

Matt bounded over to greet Dusty. "Where's Mommy?"

"She had an appointment so she sent me."

"Cool. Did you bring Track?"

"Not today."

Matt's face fell.

Dusty ruffled the boy's hair. "Next time, I promise."

A young teacher approached him. "If I can get you to sign Matt out, you two can leave." She pointed to a table near the door where a three-ring binder lay open.

As he signed his name, Dusty noted with a small amount of satisfaction that he was the only one besides Josie to drop off or pick up Matt.

"Are we going to my house or your house?" Matt asked as Dusty helped him into the rear seat of his truck and fastened the seat belt.

He wanted Matt to think of his place as home, too. An apartment over the horse barn probably didn't feel permanent, even to a four-year-old. Now might be a good time to consider building a house of his own on that piece of land his parents had deeded him near Stony Creek.

"Neither." Dusty shut the rear passenger door and went around to the driver's side. Climbing in, he said, "I was thinking we might stop by the Bush General Store for an ice cream."

"Yippee!"

Dusty concurred.

After selecting their ice cream bars from the large reach-in freezer, he and Matt went out onto the store's large front porch to eat them. Dusty walked in a straight line while Matt took the crooked route, stopping at various shelves and displays to check out the merchandise. Outside, they plunked down at one of three small tables and chairs set up for customers.

"Good?" Dusty asked, trying to remember the last time he'd eaten an ice cream bar.

"Yep." Chocolate dripped down Matt's chin.

Dusty handed him a napkin, wondering when that particular action had become second nature.

Matt scrubbed his chin then beamed up at Dusty. "All gone?"

"Most of it." He didn't mention the dribble on Matt's T-shirt.

"Look, Daddy."

Dusty was so taken aback by Matt calling him daddy, he didn't immediately realize what Matt was trying to show him. His chest constricted with an emotion new to him and one he never wanted to lose.

For the first time, he truly felt like a father.

"What, son?" Talking wasn't easy.

"Isn't that Grandpa?"

"Grandpa?" Dusty had to force his gaze away from Matt and across the street. He assumed the boy had spotted Josie's father.

"Over there."

He looked in the direction Matt indicated. The scene before him took a moment to fully sink in.

It wasn't Matt's maternal grandfather but J.W. standing in front of Markton Feed and Grain store. That alone wasn't any big deal. It was the person he was talking to—in an obviously heated discussion—that had Dusty battling to contain his shock and anger in front of his son.

Abigail Hansen.

Mark Hansen's mother.

MARYANNE HADN'T EXPECTED her meeting with Adele Donnelly to finalize the brochure and website updates for Cowboy College to take such a large part of her day. But it had. After the frantic pace of her trip to L.A. and her restless night, she was ready to drop. The short walk from the main building to her cabin felt more like the last mile of an all-day hike.

Stepping into the small living room, she spotted her father snoozing in the oversized recliner. He'd been getting up at five and putting in long hours with both his regular classes and then his extracurricular lessons with Dusty. She envied her father's ability to nap so soundly and considered following suit. A large manila envelope on the kitchenette counter stopped her.

There was nothing on the outside other than her name written in bold strokes. She didn't need a return address to know the envelope was from Dusty and, judging by the heft and thickness, it contained his screenplay.

She hesitated only a fraction of a second before undoing the clasp. Glancing at the living room to make sure her father was still asleep, she slid out the stack of bound papers. She'd seen countless screenplays and scripts while growing up with her mother and for a brief moment, she relived fond childhood memories.

Nostalgia mingled with curiosity. She took the script and the envelope with her to her bedroom, reading as she walked, and shut the door behind her. She had promised Dusty she'd keep his secret and didn't want her father to wake up suddenly and catch her with the screenplay.

Thinking she'd read for a few minutes until she fell asleep, she lay on the bed, stuffing pillows behind her back. Only she didn't fall asleep.

She read until her father knocked softly on her door an hour later.

"Cookie, you hungry?"

"Not yet. Are you?"

"I could eat something. Think I'll heat up some of that leftover chili from yesterday."

"Go ahead. I'll be out later."

Only she didn't emerge for quite some time. Her weariness long gone, she continued reading straight through until she turned the last page, her eyes damp with tears.

The screenplay was that good.

CHAPTER SEVEN

MARYANNE DIDN'T CONSIDER herself a morning person, but she could rise at the crack of dawn when necessary. Before the crack of dawn? That was something else entirely. The coffee she chugged down helped only marginally. Her eyelids were heavy and her feet felt as if she was trudging through deep snow. Maybe when the sun came out—another hour according to her watch!—she'd finally wake up enough to function normally.

She leaned against the side of the horse trailer. Drifting off wasn't likely. The humongous truck pulling the trailer was idling loudly. In addition to the horrific noise, it emitted a strong diesel fuel odor. Maryanne wrinkled her nose, hating to imagine what the fumes were doing to the air.

All around her, people hurried by, preparing to leave for the rodeo in Albuquerque. Dusty was among them though they'd had little opportunity to speak other than a quick good morning. His sister, Elly, was the one who'd distributed the coffee. Maryanne hadn't bothered to ask if it was organic. She hadn't cared. Let the ecology police find and arrest her.

"Be patient, Cookie," her father said. "We'll be leaving soon." He carried a bucket in each hand, lugging them to the front of the trailer.

"I'm fine." She refastened the top button of her

jacket. The weather had turned considerably cooler over the past couple of days. "Just wish I could help."

"Don't worry, everything's under control."

After her father left, Maryanne continued leaning against the side of the trailer, feeling like an alien from a distant galaxy observing life on Earth. She understood very little of what was going on around her.

Dusty's brother Dex and another man were lugging trunks but what those trunks contained was a mystery to her. Elly kept going in and out of the front of the horse trailer, toting boxes and bundles with each trip. At one point Maryanne had walked by the open door and was surprised to see what resembled a cozy and comfortable motor home interior, complete with a tiny kitchen, sleeping bunk and a sitting area. Dusty and his other brother Walker were doing something with the lights on the back of the trailer, which didn't appear to be working correctly. She'd heard Walker, Elly and their parents would be flying to the rodeo later in the day and that Dusty's oldest brother, Jesse, a pilot, would be taking them in the family's private plane.

Seeing Dusty and his brother working side by side, she found it hard to believe they were twins, even fraternal twins. The differences in looks and personalities were almost startling.

At a shrill whinnying, Maryanne craned her neck and spied a wrangler approaching the trailer leading a pair of horses. Behind him were two more wranglers, also leading horses.

Good heavens! Were all these people going? Where would they fit?

"The horses are the last to be loaded," said an unfamiliar voice behind her. "Which means we're about ready to leave."

Maryanne turned, and her eyes immediately went to the woman and young boy whose hand she held tightly. Matt. Dusty's son. She barely had time to make the connection when the woman introduced herself.

"Hi, I'm Josie Cody. Dex's wife."

"I'm Maryanne Devonshire."

"And this is our son, Matt."

"I remember you," Matt said. His attention remained on Maryanne for about one second. After that, it traveled back and forth between the hundred and one far more interesting activities.

"When did you two meet?" Josie asked.

"I guess it's been about a week and a half now. Over at Cowboy College."

"She was with Daddy," Matt supplied.

Josie didn't quite hide her startled reaction. It pleased Maryanne to see that Matt was calling Dusty *Daddy*. His mother evidently had mixed emotions. Or maybe she was still getting accustomed to Matt's father being involved in his life.

"You and Dusty are friends?"

"My father's one of his students."

"Ah. You're here to help load and see him off?"

"Actually, we're going to Albuquerque, too."

"Really!" Josie's face lit up. "Are you and Dusty dating?"

His sister-in-law definitely cut to the chase.

"No, no." Maryanne waved a hand in front of her to emphasize her denial. "He invited my father. I'm just tagging along to keep Dad company."

"Right."

"It's true."

"Of course." Josie smiled knowingly.

Maryanne bit her tongue. She didn't like being thought of as one of Dusty's conquests.

"Mommy, can I go help Daddy?" Matt tugged on his mother's arm.

"No, sweetie. You need to stay with me."

"Please." He tugged harder.

She shook her head. "There's too much going on, and you'll be in the way."

Matt relented. Maryanne suspected only temporarily. He had his father's penchant for pushing boundaries.

Josie turned back to her. "We'll be traveling with you. Well, not with you. In another vehicle." She spoke behind the shield of her hand so Matt couldn't hear. "Jesse offered to fly us. Matt would probably leap at the chance but I'm not ready for a small plane trip yet. He's still so young."

"I understand."

A horn beeped.

"We should probably get going. We'll see you on the road, I'm sure," Josie said brightly. "It's a long drive and, with this group, we'll be making quite a few pit stops."

"I'd like that." Now that they were past their initial awkwardness, Maryanne was sure she and Josie would be friends.

Matt abruptly broke free of his mother's grasp and darted off straight for Dusty and Dex.

"Matt!"

Josie was too late. Dusty caught the boy and swung him up in a big hug.

"Boys." She blew out an exasperated breath. "I don't

know how Anne raised four of them." She took a few steps, then hesitated. "If you and Dusty *are* dating—"

"We're not," Maryanne insisted. "Honestly."

"Then, just in case you're thinking about it, there's something you should know. His reputation isn't completely deserved."

"Reputation?"

"As a player. At one time it was true. And he's still a notorious flirt, which I'm sure you've figured out already. But he's settled down the last couple of years. The rest of the world still believes the worst of him, and he hasn't done anything to change their opinion."

"I appreciate the advice but it isn't necessary. My father and I are leaving in a couple weeks."

"Too bad. I think you'd be good for him." With that, she left to collect her son.

Maryanne didn't know what to make of the observation.

There was a definite attraction between her and Dusty, going both ways. It was hardly enough to base a relationship on, however. Especially for two people with as many challenges as they had to overcome—distance and lifestyle being just two.

She knew from personal experience the strain a lengthy separation put on a couple. Maryanne wanted and needed a man she could trust. One who wouldn't ask her to wait for him and then leave her or find someone new. Been there, done that—twice—and didn't plan on a third time.

"Come on, Cookie," her father called. "We're ready to roll."

Maryanne walked alongside the horse trailer to the truck, disposing of her empty paper coffee cup in a trash barrel. Her father, Dusty and another man she'd noticed earlier were gathered, their voices booming in order to be heard over the chugging of the engine.

"We've decided I'm riding with Boyd here," her father said. "You can go with Dusty in his truck."

Maryanne swallowed her surprise. "I thought I'd be riding with you." She peered at the truck. It resembled a small semi, complete with two chrome steps for climbing up into the cab.

"You're more than welcome to," Dusty said with a glint in his eyes. "There's only two seats, however."

"Oh."

"Boyd'll enjoy having you along, won't you, buddy?"

The man flashed a wide, crooked-tooth grin. "You bet."

"And your dad can ride with me."

"I…ah…" Great. She'd dug herself into a big hole with no means of crawling out.

"Go with Dusty, Cookie." Her dad put an arm around her shoulders. "He'll take better care of you than that rascal will."

Boyd chuckled robustly. "You're smart not to trust me with her, Gil. Then again, I'm not so sure you should trust Dusty, either."

"Let's get a move on," Dex shouted from across the way. He was helping Josie load Matt into his truck. "At this rate, it'll be midnight before we arrive in Albuquerque."

Dusty took hold of Maryanne's hand much like he had the night they went to The Spotted Horse Saloon.

She told herself she had nothing to worry about being stuck alone with him in such close proximity for hours on end. That didn't stop the butterflies inside her stomach from banging into one another.

His truck was parked behind Dex's. Josie waved as they walked by, and Maryanne felt her cheeks burn. All that insisting she and Dusty weren't dating...for what? Josie was no doubt drawing a different conclusion.

He opened the front passenger door for Maryanne. Track suddenly popped up from where he'd been sleeping in the backseat next to Dusty's suitcase.

"Hey, boy. I didn't see you back there." Once seated, she reached over the seat and patted the dog's head. He responded by licking her hand. "You brought your dog," she said when Dusty had settled in behind the steering wheel.

"I always do if I'm driving somewhere. He has to stay with a friend, though, once we arrive. Dogs aren't allowed on the event grounds."

"Poor Track."

"Trust me, he doesn't mind. She spoils him." Dusty started the truck and pulled into line behind Dex. With the huge truck and trailer, the three vehicles made an impressive convoy.

Maryanne should have kept her mouth shut but she didn't. "Another old girlfriend from grade school?" Thank goodness Josie wasn't there to hear.

"High school, as a matter of fact. Though I don't think my crush was reciprocated."

"That's hard to believe."

"Mrs. Leonhart." Dusty's grin grew. "She was my English teacher for two years. I wouldn't have passed my college entrance exams without her help. Heck, I might not have even graduated. She's the only person who ever encouraged me to write. A few years ago her husband's company transferred him to Albuquerque. I visit every time I'm there."

Their slow-moving caravan reached the main road. One by one, each vehicle turned onto it, with the huge truck and trailer taking the longest time and greatest effort.

"She was right to encourage you," Maryanne said. "I read your screenplay last night."

"You did?"

"It's good. Very good."

He didn't speak right away.

"I'm serious, Dusty. I'm not just saying that to be nice or because you're helping my father."

"I thought it was good, but it's hard to be critical of your own writing."

"I can't imagine a producer not being interested if you can just get it in front of them."

"I'm glad to hear you say that. A production intern I've worked with in a couple films called me last night. Sundown Pictures is going to be at the Albuquerque rodeo scouting locations for a new film. They're a small independent outfit, but have put out some quality films in recent years."

"Are you going to try and meet with the producer?" Maryanne sensed Dusty's excitement. Hers soared right along with his.

"Damn straight I am. This is the break I've been waiting for." He reached across the seat for her hand again and clasped it tightly. "I really need your help."

"With what?"

"I'm going to have only one chance to sell myself to this guy. I need you to teach me what to say and how to act so I don't blow it."

"Okay, let's go over the list one more time."

"Image," Dusty said, watching the road.

He and Maryanne were leading the caravan, ahead of the truck and trailer. Dex, Josie and Matt brought up the rear. They kept in constant contact by cell phone. So far, three hundred miles into the trip, the arrangement was working.

Dusty and Maryanne hadn't spent the entire time grooming him for his meeting with Sundown Pictures. They'd veered off topic frequently. Their conversation, however, had remained general in nature rather than personal. Neither of them brought up their kiss. Except for the memory forever seared in Dusty's mind, it might not have happened.

"And what about your image?" Maryanne prompted.

"I need to look the part. It raises my perceived value."

"Right. Dress similar to what you wore the night we went to dinner."

So, she'd noticed. And wasn't nearly as immune to him as she pretended to be.

"What next?"

"A good opening line."

"Which includes…?"

"Putting my hand out to shake his. And I do this because," he answered before she could ask, "it subconsciously sets him up to follow my lead."

"Right. And don't forget eye contact. It will get you further than that smile you're always flashing."

She'd noticed that, too.

Dusty promptly slammed the door on his thoughts. They weren't doing him any good. Maryanne had no interest in him. Wait, that wasn't entirely accurate. She'd kissed him back plenty, and it had been great. She just wasn't willing to act on that interest.

"Sure you don't want to be my wingman?" he asked, only half joking.

"You don't need any help."

"Really? Isn't that what you're giving me now?"

"I'm teaching. It's up to you to put the lessons to good use in the field. And you will, I have no doubt."

"Thanks." The vote of confidence affected Dusty more than he would have guessed. Very few people had given him one outside of the rodeo arena. Certainly not his father.

His cell phone abruptly rang. "Yeah, Dex," he said.

"There's a rest stop a mile ahead. We need to pull in."

"Okay."

"Another break?" Maryanne inquired after he'd disconnected.

"Dex didn't say but I'm sure Matt is getting restless again."

"Maybe a change of vehicles would help," she offered.

"You'd be okay if he rode with us for a ways?"

"Of course. Matt's a sweet kid."

"And a handful." Dusty signaled to turn into the rest stop. "You could ride with Dex and Josie if you wanted."

"What?" She smiled. "And miss all the fun? Besides, Track will keep him busy."

At the mention of his name, the dog lifted his head from where he'd been snoozing in the backseat.

"I miss having a dog." Maryanne scratched his ears affectionately. "We had two while I was growing up. Popeye and Munchkin."

She liked kids *and* dogs. What more could a guy

ask for in a woman? If only she weren't leaving in a couple of weeks.

"You can borrow Track anytime you want."

It took them a good five minutes to park all the vehicles at the rest stop and climb out. Shortly after they climbed out, Jesse called to let them know he and the rest of the family had landed safely.

"Do you think we're in for trouble?" Dex asked Dusty. They were standing by his truck, giving everyone a chance to stretch their legs.

Dusty followed his brother's gaze to where Maryanne and Josie were sitting at a nearby picnic table, water bottles in their hands and the remnant of a snack in front of them.

"No." He shook his head.

"You positive? Josie's got more than enough dirt on you to ruin your chances with Miss Beverly Hills over there."

"She lives in L.A." Dusty was actually more concerned about the dirt Maryanne had on him. She'd promised not to say anything about his writing, and he believed her, but unintentional slipups happened. "It doesn't matter anyway. Maryanne and I aren't involved." His mind flashed once again on the kiss they'd shared behind the barn. "Not that way."

"Ah, yes." Dex smirked. "The junior marketing exec. She's advising you on how to grow your business, and you're helping her dad rope in exchange."

"There's a real market for trained horses in films." Dusty had decided to give a modified version of the truth for why he'd invited Maryanne and her father along to the rodeo. Less chance for one of those unintentional slipups.

"Don't go too far," Josie hollered at Matt.

He'd taken Track on a short walk along a path that circled the restrooms. The dog evidently listened better than a four-year-old for he pulled on the leash in an attempt to return. Matt would have none of it.

"He's your kid, all right," Dex said. They'd finished checking under the hoods of all three trucks and inspecting the tires. Boyd and Maryanne's father were tending to the horses. So far, everything was in order. "You never listened worth a damn when we were kids, either. Still don't."

Dusty didn't take his eyes off his son. "Maybe between the two of us we can do a better job of instilling some responsibility in him."

"I know it isn't easy for you to have Matt living with me."

"Trust me. I'd rather have you as his stepfather than some other guy."

"Did I tell you what a fool you were to let Josie go?"

"Repeatedly."

"Like I said, you don't listen well."

"She's better off with you. I'd have only made her miserable."

"What about her?" Dex inclined his head at Maryanne.

Dusty shook his head. "'Fraid not."

"Why? She likes you, and from what I can see, the feeling's mutual."

"She'd get fed up with me in three months and leave."

"Maybe not."

"Look at her."

They both studied Maryanne's designer jeans, wool shawl—handmade with naturally processed wool,

Dusty had learned that during one of their earlier conversations—short blond hair and hoop earrings large
enough to wear as bracelets.

"Can you see someone like her fitting in on the ranch?"
Dusty asked.

"It's just clothes and hair."

"Her job and home and family are in California."

"As much as you travel, you could live anywhere. At
least part of the year."

For a few seconds, Dusty imagined just such a sce-
nario. It wasn't hard. He loved his home and would always want to return frequently, especially to visit Matt.
But his writing and film work could allow him to have
a second home on the West Coast.

In the next second, reality returned.

"You're forgetting something, bro," he told Dex with
a harsh laugh. "Dad would disown me if I left."

"Do you care?"

Dusty didn't think twice about his answer. "Yeah,
I do."

"You two made up yet?"

He glanced around. Gil was heading to the restroom
while Boyd waited, his back propped against the truck
door. Josie had abandoned calling Matt and was now
chasing after him. Maryanne waited at the picnic table,
a gentle smile on her face. No one was paying any attention to Dex and Dusty.

"We're talking. Barely."

"What does Mom say about the fight?"

"Nothing. Not one word."

"That's not like her."

"Which makes me think she and Dad are hiding
something."

"There could be another explanation."

"Yeah? Then why was Dad outside the feed store the other day talking to Abigail Hansen?"

Dex's eyes narrowed. "You saw them?"

"When Matt and I were having ice cream at the General Store. And whatever they were discussing was pretty heated."

"Matt saw Dad, too?"

"Don't worry. He doesn't have any idea what's going on. I told him the woman was an old friend."

Dex murmured an expletive. "Why didn't you tell me?"

"We've been busy getting ready for this trip. And when you think about it, Dad speaking to Abigail Hansen on the street isn't exactly incriminating evidence. They've lived in the same town their entire lives."

"And would go a mile out of their way to avoid each other."

The feud between their father and Abigail's husband, Tomas, went back decades. It had started over land and continued to this day.

"She didn't look good," Dusty commented, remembering how frail Abigail Hansen had appeared, especially standing next to J.W.

"I hear she'd been sick a while now."

"There's still one thing that doesn't make sense."

"What's that?" Dex asked.

"Let's say Dad did have an affair with Abigail Hansen. Why would Mom have taken him back after that? I think she'd be pretty perturbed with him."

"She may not know."

"Trust me, she does. She told me before Dad's and

my argument that he'd never forgive her if she said anything to me."

"Wow."

"Let's haul out," Boyd called out. "Time's a-wasting."

Everyone started moving toward the parked vehicles.

Dex lowered his voice as he and Dusty walked. "She could have taken him back to keep the family together. Mark's only a few months older than Jesse. What if she didn't find out about Dad's affair until she was already pregnant?"

"It's possible. Or she has some other hold on him."

"Do you think Mom's capable of that?"

"I think," Dusty said with growing certainty, "there's a lot about both our parents we don't know and a lot they're hiding from us."

CHAPTER EIGHT

DUSTY AND WALKER stood on the first rung of the arena
fence, their arms hooked over the top rail, watching the
bull riding event and waiting for Jesse to go. In front
of them, on ground level, the cameraman filmed the
bull's face through the railing. Behind them, a giant
TV screen showed the action in between posting scores.

It was day three, final round of the competition.
Dusty's parents were in the stands along with Dex and
the rest of the family. Maryanne and her father were
also in the stands.

He hadn't seen much of her during the rodeo, and, as
a result, spent too much time dwelling on her and not
enough on competing. Amazingly, he was doing well
in tie-down roping, holding steady in second place. His
event was scheduled to start next, and, unlike usual,
he was a bundle of nerves. He wanted to win. More so
today because Maryanne was watching.

Adding to his anxiety, he'd seen neither hide nor hair
of the producer from Sundown Pictures. In a follow-up
phone call, the production intern had assured Dusty the
producer and a small crew would be in Albuquerque.
Dusty could only conclude whatever locations they were
scouting weren't on the rodeo grounds.

He surveyed the crowd, something he'd been doing
constantly, his hand involuntarily constricting into a fist.

"What's with you?" Walker asked.

"Nothing."

"Not like you to be so damn fidgety. That's my thing."

Dusty's older brother had a tendency to pace restlessly, a symptom of his post-traumatic stress syndrome. He'd improved steadily since his discharge from the army and dramatically in the weeks following his wedding. Paula, his wife, hadn't come along with them to the rodeo, stating she had to work. Dusty's mother speculated Paula was pregnant. Walker wouldn't comment.

"Mark Hansen's up next." Dusty inclined his head toward the far right chute, diverting the subject away from him.

"He's been doing good this weekend."

"Real good."

Jesse and Mark were almost neck and neck with Mark in the lead by the slimmest of margins. Assuming they could hang on, either one of them could—and probably would—win.

The gate swung open, and a contestant astride a bull named Gizmo erupted into the arena. The rider lasted three-point-six seconds before being tossed into the air like a wet dish towel. Gizmo trotted in a victory circle before being rounded up by the bullfighters dressed in their oversize sports jerseys and knee-high athletic socks. By then, the uninjured cowboy was on his feet and accepting the audience's applause.

"I thought Jesse and Hansen would quit their fool rivalry while I was in the service." Walker tugged on the brim of his cowboy hat until it sat low over his eyes.

"If anything, it's gotten worse."

"You think it has to do with Dad and Hansen's father?"

"It could."

"What about Janie?" Walker said, naming Mark Hansen's sister. "Jesse's always had a hankering for her."

None of the gossip about their father and Mark being his son had anything to do with Janie. What, Dusty wondered, did she think of it? He'd always been fond of Janie and respected her for making the best of what had to be a difficult life living with an alcoholic father.

"Speaking of Dad, what's with you and him lately?" Of course Walker had noticed, as did anyone with eyes and ears.

"You know Dad. Same ol', same ol'."

"He's not happy about your latest film job at Yellowstone?"

"Among other things."

Dusty was about to mention his and Dex's recent conversations regarding their father when Walker hitched his chin at the chute.

"Check that out."

Mark Hansen was at that moment lowering himself onto the back of a massive half-Brahma bull. Both Mark and the bull wore the same fierce expression, and the contest between them promised to be a worthy one.

The crowd wasn't disappointed. Mark rode the Brahma-cross the full eight seconds, and his score landed him in first place.

Dusty whooped and hollered. The stern look Walker shot him had no effect.

"Lighten up, will you? He gave a hell of a ride."

Four more contestants took their turns, each one finishing by eating dirt. Dusty continued surveying the stands. He wasn't sure who he wanted to see more, Maryanne or the producer from Sundown Pictures.

The person he did catch sight of was Nicki Sable, Jesse's best friend since high school. Funny, she wasn't watching his brother, who was standing near the chutes. Instead, her gaze was centered on Mark Hansen.

Walker nudged Dusty in the side. "Relax. You're gonna smoke the competition."

Dusty didn't correct his brother's assumption. He wasn't in the mood to explain the reasons for his nerves.

"Here we go."

At the note of excitement in Walker's voice, Dusty peered above the heads of the other cowboys to see Jesse lowering himself onto a plain brown medium-sized bull. Appearances, in this case, were deceiving. Jesse had drawn Willie Wonka, a bull with a reputation of making or breaking cowboys, usually the latter.

Not that eight seconds is long but it was over in a heartbeat. At least for the spectators. Jesse hung on, giving the ride of his life. The buzzer sounded, and the crowd roared, Dusty and Walker right along with them. Moments later, the announcer proclaimed Jesse had moved into first place. Leave it to his oldest brother to pull a rabbit out of a hat.

Turning sideways, Dusty caught sight of Mark Hansen. The other man's face wasn't hard to read. He didn't like coming in second.

"Be right back." Dusty hopped off the fence.

"Where you going?"

He didn't answer his brother. Instead, he walked straight up to Mark. "Good ride earlier."

Mark stared at Dusty's extended hand. "Not good enough."

"There's always next month and Oklahoma City."

After a moment that stretched indefinitely Mark

clasped Dusty's hand and returned the shake with vigor. His respect for his brother's rival grew. If not for the dispute between their fathers, Mark could just as easily have been their friend.

"See ya tonight at the dance." Dusty smiled. Mending fences with Mark didn't feel wrong. Even if it turned out they weren't brothers.

"I'll be there."

So would most of the competitors. The winners would be celebrating and the losers nursing their wounded pride. Liquor and/or women were often the chosen remedy. At one time, they'd been Dusty's remedy, too. Not anymore.

"What's going on here?"

An angry male voice boomed from behind Dusty, and he turned to face Jesse. Nicki stood behind him, her long blond hair tucked under a pale blue cowboy hat. She said nothing, though her eyes appeared to take in every detail.

"Just having a friendly chat with Mark about his ride." Dusty flashed a wide grin.

Jesse's eyes narrowed dangerously—as did Mark's.

Dusty stepped directly in the line of fire. "If not for three points, he'd have won."

"But he didn't," Jesse growled.

"Not this time," Mark fired back.

Walker came over, his features taut, his eyes darting nervously from one man to the next. "Come on, Dusty, you gotta get ready." He didn't acknowledge Mark. "Jesse, you, too. Mom and Dad are waiting to congratulate you."

Neither Jesse nor Mark budged. They were both too

stubborn—which made for some mighty fine entertainment.

"Hey, Dusty." Leroy, another tie-down roper Dusty frequently competed against, rode past them on a high-stepping buckskin gelding. "You ready to have your hide run into the ground?"

Leroy's taunt reminded Dusty that Uno was in the care of one of the hands, waiting for Dusty to warm him up in the smaller practice arena. The last thing he needed was his horse seizing up because his muscles weren't sufficiently limber.

"Let's go, Jesse." He went over to his brother and clapped him on the back.

Jesse acquiesced, albeit reluctantly. His parting glance to Mark contained enough firepower to burn through steel. Mark seemed none the worse for it. Turning on his heel, he went in the opposite direction, joining a group of cowboys eager to offer their congratulations on his placement.

While Jesse and Nicki lagged behind to talk to some buddies, Dusty and Walker cut behind the bleachers and crossed in front of a row of vendors. Suddenly Dusty stopped. The producer from Sundown Pictures stood about thirty feet away, his crew of three surrounding him.

Even if Dusty hadn't remembered the man from their previous meetings, he would have recognized him instantly as someone from the film industry. Despite the chilly air, he wore khaki shorts, hiking boots and toted a backpack. A canvas ball cap covered his shaggy hair. In the next instant, all Dusty saw was the man's back as he and his crew melted into the crowd.

Dusty didn't think. He started forward.

"Where you going?" Walker hollered.

"Be right back."

"Damn it to hell, Dusty!"

"I said I'll be right back."

His mouth had gone bone-dry. For three days he'd been waiting for this moment. Now that it was here, he couldn't think of a single tip Maryanne had given him. Hell, he couldn't remember the name of his screenplay or what it was about.

He caught sight of the producer only to lose him again.

Shit. He was going to screw this up royally if he didn't get his act together. He forced his legs to move faster, still unsure what he was going to say once he caught up with the producer.

From the corner of his eye, he spotted Maryanne. She and her father were brandishing sodas and corn dogs and coming toward him. The ridiculous straw hat she wore sat at a crooked angle and her sunglasses had slid down her nose. His befuddled brain marginally registered her meal choice—junk food? That didn't seem like her. But then, neither had her love of sports cars.

A look of concern crossed her face. "Are you all right?" she asked as she neared.

"Sorry. I can't talk now."

She followed his gaze and understanding dawned on her face. "Go," she urged.

"I… I…"

She placed a hand on his arm. "You'll do fine."

Her encouragement was all he needed. Like that, his brain snapped into sharp focus.

"Dusty!" Walker had caught up with them.

It didn't matter. No way would his brother or anyone else stop him now.

Not caring who saw or what they thought, he swooped

Maryanne into his arms and gave her a sound kiss on the cheek.

"Thanks. For everything. I owe you."

Flustered, she stepped back, barely managing to hold on to her corn dog and soda.

"Good luck." She smiled radiantly.

He took the memory of that smile with him as he sprinted to catch up to the producer.

"Mr. Casey."

The man and his crew came to a halt. None of them were smiling, much less radiantly.

"Yes?" He squinted at Dusty, and his face relaxed. "I know you." He wagged a finger as if to trigger his memory.

"Dusty Cody. I was in *Rio Rojo*."

"That's right." His half smile drooped. "If you're wanting a role in *Five Miles to Purgatory,* the casting call hasn't gone out yet."

"I don't want a role. Well, I do. But that's not why I stopped you."

The producer grimaced.

Not good.

Dusty drew a deep breath, ignored his brother who was bearing down on him, and took the biggest leap he'd ever taken in his entire life.

THE LOCAL ALBUQUERQUE honky-tonk was overflowing with rodeo patrons, participants and personnel. It wasn't that Maryanne didn't like the place. Though lacking the small-town charm of The Spotted Horse, the rustic decor was interesting and the atmosphere definitely fun.

No, her discomfort stemmed from how like a fish out of water she felt—*still* felt. At her father's insistence, she'd purchased a pair of boots from one of the vendors at the rodeo. Rather than help her fit in, the boots made her stand out. She was certain her awkward gait had everyone in the place chuckling at the rookie. Wait, what was the term? *Greenhorn.*

"You having fun, Cookie?" her father asked.

"Sure, Dad." She didn't wish to tarnish his good mood.

"Not to worry." He winked at her. "Dusty'll be here soon."

"Oh, I'm not waiting on him."

Boy, the white lies were just rolling off her tongue.

The one and only reason she'd even agreed to accompany her father tonight was in hopes of seeing Dusty. She was dying to find out how his meeting with the producer had gone but no one had seen him since the end of the tie-down competition. By some miracle, he'd made it in time to compete only to promptly disappear after taking first place.

Except for Dusty and Matt, who was spending the evening with Dusty's former teacher and Track, the entire Cody clan had put in an appearance at the honky-tonk. Josie had explained to Maryanne earlier that J.W. and Anne didn't normally socialize after a rodeo but because all the boys and Elly had done well in their events, celebrating seemed in order.

"I can't imagine what's holding him up," Gil said checking the door again.

"Really, Dad, I don't care about Dusty or where he is."

"Didn't look that way to me when he was kissing you."

"I told you, I have no idea what prompted him to do that."

He set his beer glass down with a resounding thud. "No idea my foot!"

So much for playing innocent.

"Do you mind if we join you?" Dusty's mother appeared at their table, speaking loudly to be heard over the noise and music.

"'Course not." Gil immediately sprang to his feet. "Take my chair."

"Thank you." She sat with practiced grace and poise. "J.W. is on the hunt for more chairs. If anyone can find them in this crowd, it's him." She smiled at Maryanne. "How are you doing tonight?"

"A little tired, and I'm not sure why. I didn't work nearly as hard this weekend as the participants."

"Sitting in the sun all day can wear you out." If Anne was worn out, she hid it well, looking more as if she'd just come from a day at the spa than the rodeo. "Ah, here's J.W., and he's had some success."

"We haven't seen Dusty tonight," Gil said as they rearranged their tiny two-person table to accommodate four chairs.

Maryanne groaned inwardly.

"I imagine he'll be here soon," Anne replied smoothly.

J.W., on the other hand, scowled.

Strange, thought Maryanne.

"Dusty won't miss a chance to congratulate Jesse," Anne added.

"That was a nice ride he had today." Gil's remark appeared to jump-start J.W.

"Hell of a ride."

The two men entered into a lively discussion of the rodeo in general and the merits of various contestants.

"Did you and Dusty enjoy the drive here?"

Anne's casually posed question felt loaded, and Maryanne wavered before responding.

"The scenery was spectacular. I haven't been on many road trips and didn't realize what I was missing. I think I came up with at least a dozen ideas for ad campaigns."

"That's right. You work in advertising."

"A junior marketing executive."

"She's helping Dusty," Gil chimed in.

"Oh?" Anne's eyes widened.

In stark contrast, J.W.'s thinned to slits. "With what?"

Maryanne held herself erect under his withering stare, silently thanking her experience with demanding clients. "With his side business."

"Dusty's giving me roping lessons in exchange." Her father beamed.

"Oh, good God," J.W. spat out.

"Now, honey," Anne soothed. "Watch your blood pressure."

"I have that problem, too," Gil said cheerily. "What do you take? The stuff my doctor has me on gives me the awfulest heartburn."

J.W. grumbled the name of his prescription under his breath.

All Maryanne could think of was how sad for Dusty that he had to hide his writing from his parents. Perhaps if they knew how truly talented he was they'd change their opinions.

"Dusty's lucky to have Cookie's help. She's the best there is at all that marketing stuff."

She returned her father's smile. How could she not?

"We need to go." J.W. pushed his chair back.

Maryanne ignored the slight. Her father, however, appeared stricken.

Anne didn't move from her seat. "Not quite yet."

"Did I say something wrong?" Gil asked.

"Not at all. We're just tired. It's been a long week-end, and we have to get up early tomorrow." The reproving glance she shot her husband dared him to disagree with her.

He didn't. But neither did he return his chair to its original position. "I'm going to the bar for a beer. Anyone want anything?"

His offer was met with a chorus of no-thank-yous.

"I apologize for J.W.," Anne said after he'd left. "Rest assured, his problem isn't with you. He's always wanted his children to follow in his footsteps and work in the family businesses. Dusty is the one holdout."

"I thought he helped Dex with the horses," Maryanne said.

"He has so much more potential than that."

His mother had no clue how much more.

"Sometimes children have to choose their own paths."

"True. But that doesn't stop us from wanting what we think is best for them."

A commotion near the front entrance drew their attention. Dusty emerged from the group of people clustered there.

Maryanne's heart rate immediately quickened. She told herself it was because of her eagerness to hear how his meeting with the producer went. It wasn't a lie. But she also wanted to see him, be close to him, talk to him, touch him. Not good feelings to have considering she was leaving in two weeks.

Managing the ride home might be harder than she'd anticipated.

Anne raised her hand and waved.

Dusty spotted them and strode forward. His progress, however, was impeded by the many people stopping him and congratulating him on his first place in tie-down roping. Maryanne's father had explained to her that the win advanced Dusty to the number one spot in the Mountain States Circuit for tie-down roping and qualified him for the National Finals Rodeo. Unfortunately, he and Dex weren't quite there with team roping.

Several of the people offering Dusty their well wishes were attractive young women. They hugged him, hung onto his arms and kissed him, more than a few aiming for his mouth. Maryanne tried pretending she didn't care but her relief when he deflected their kisses was undeniable.

J.W. wormed his way through the throng to their table. Upon seeing Dusty, his expression changed, first to unabashed gladness, then to annoyance, lastly to—could it be?—regret.

Maryanne had no doubt that Dusty and his father loved each other but their recent rift was growing wider. And all because they disagreed about his chosen occupation.

Or, was there more to it?

Dusty's reputation wasn't the only talk she'd heard concerning the Codys. A particularly chatty server had told Maryanne about J.W. and a woman named Abigail Hansen, the mother of the man Maryanne had met at The Spotted Horse. The man who looked remarkably like J.W.

"Hello, sweetheart." Anne stood and greeted her

son with a kiss on the cheek he didn't deflect. "We've missed you. Where have you been?"

"Sorry. I got detained." His eyes sparked with unsuppressed excitement. When they connected with Maryanne's, she experienced a tingle clear to the toes crammed inside her brand-new boots.

"Congratulations on your win."

"Thanks."

They looked away only when his father cleared his throat.

"You did well today," J.W. said, his comment seeming to temporarily close the gap between father and son.

"I got lucky. I drew a good calf."

"Luck's only part of it. You have yourself a good horse, and you trained hard."

"Lot of guys have good horses and train hard." Dusty's glance found Maryanne again. "Sometimes, everything comes together just right."

"You were great." She didn't mean just at tie-down roping. She was proud of him for seeking out and speaking with the producer, even if nothing came of it.

His smile grew, and her previously guarded heart opened to all sorts of new possibilities. When he came around the table to her side, she rose, already anticipating his invitation.

"Let's dance," he said and took her hand.

CHAPTER NINE

"I'M NOT A very good dancer." Especially not in her new boots which clung to Maryanne's feet like lead weights.

"I don't care." Dusty lowered his head to her ear. "I want to hold you. Right this second."

She knew how he felt and went willingly with him to the dance floor.

"Dusty, come back," his father called after them. "I'm not done talking."

"Later," he hollered over his shoulder, but his voice was drowned out by the band and the rowdy crowd.

At the edge of the dance floor, he pulled Maryanne into his arms. The music called for a lively two-step. They danced instead to their own beat. One considerably slower and requiring their bodies to fuse together and sway as one.

Maryanne's left hand circled Dusty's shoulder. Her right hand fit snugly inside his. She contemplated resting her head on his chest but then she wouldn't be able to gaze into his blue eyes, and that was a sight she refused to miss.

"How'd it go with the producer?" she asked now that it was safe to bring up the subject.

"I just left him."

"You're kidding! You've been with him since the rodeo?"

"No. Only for a few minutes before I competed." Dusty's

hold on her tightened as he maneuvered them to avoid colliding with another couple. He didn't release her even after they were in the clear.

"Where were you the rest of the time?"

"At a business center. And trust me, it wasn't easy finding one open on a Sunday evening."

"Why a business center?"

Dusty's smile practically exploded off his face, and his heart beat so strong, she could feel its echo inside her. "He asked to read my screenplay."

Maryanne squealed. "Oh, Dusty! That's fantastic."

"He listened to my pitch for maybe a minute, then told me to go ahead and send it to his office."

"That was it?"

"Pretty much. I didn't want to take any chances he'd forget about me or change his mind so I found a business center, printed out the screenplay and arranged to have it shipped overnight."

"Clever."

"Desperate. This is the closest I've ever gotten." He twirled her around as the band launched into another number.

"What did he say after he told you to send the screenplay?"

"Nothing. Just goodbye. Then he and his crew left." For the first time that night, Dusty's elation faltered.

"He'll like it. And if he doesn't, you'll pitch it to another producer." She made a mental note to contact her mother's former agent and see if he'd had a chance to read Dusty's screenplay.

"And what if he does like it?"

"You'll be incredibly successful and eventually win an Oscar."

"Will you be my date for the movie premiere?"

She laughed when he abruptly dipped her. "I wouldn't miss it for the world."

He suddenly sobered. "As much as I want to sell my screenplay, I'm worried about the repercussions."

"With your family?"

"The storyline hits close to home."

"I wondered if it was based a little on them."

"A *lot* on them."

Maryanne wasn't sure if she should ask or not, but she did. "You have a half brother?"

"That's just it. I don't know. My parents won't admit anything. But the evidence is mounting."

"That guy we ran into at The Spotted Horse?"

"Yeah, him."

They danced in silence, enjoying the sensation of their bodies perfectly aligned. Dusty would remember this day always, and she was glad to be a part of it.

"Everything will work out."

She began to doubt he'd heard her when he whispered, "I hope so," and brushed a stray lock of hair away from her face.

She sank into his arms, and, changing her mind, laid her head on his chest.

The music came to an end, and they stopped dancing along with everyone else. When the band announced they were taking a break, Dusty guided her off the dance floor. She assumed they'd return to their table, only he took a detour.

"Where are we going?"

"Someplace private."

It would be cold outside, and she'd left her jacket

with her father. Still, she didn't protest. Dusty needed someone to share in his excitement.

He needed her.

She may not want to get romantically involved in what would surely be a short-term relationship but there was no reason they couldn't be friends.

Friends who danced so close a sheet of tissue paper couldn't fit between. Held hands. Kissed behind barns. And followed the other outside without asking questions.

Exactly how long was she going to keep fooling herself?

The honky-tonk was large and packed and not easy to navigate. It became quickly apparent they weren't heading toward the front entrance. Just when Maryanne thought they'd exit by the rear door, Dusty led her down a tiny hall and to a door marked Employees Only—No Admittance.

What was it with him and staff-only doors in the dark recesses of honky-tonks? She had barely enough time to wonder how many women he'd previously kidnapped in the same manner when he pushed open the door and pulled her inside.

It was dark and chilly and very, very quiet.

A soft click signaled the latching of the door. In the next instant, Dusty trapped her against its hard surface, his hands braced on either side of her shoulders.

"Damn, but you look hot in those boots."

"You noticed."

It was such a line. Tired and old and probably used dozens of times.

Regardless, Maryanne tilted her face up to accept Dusty's kiss.

MARYANNE HAD KNOWN from the second she'd seen Dusty across the honky-tonk floor she wanted this and blast the consequences.

Unlike their first kiss, which had been hot and hard and motivated by a surge of anger that had nothing whatsoever to do with her, this one was soft and gentle and achingly tender.

For about five seconds.

Even as Maryanne sank into Dusty's embrace, his mouth became increasingly demanding. She accommodated his advances—no, welcomed them would be a more accurate description—and parted her lips. He let out a desperate groan and fitted his hips snugly to hers.

She couldn't move. Then again, she didn't want to. Looping both her arms around his neck, she hung on, reveling in the pleasure of his tongue tangling with hers and her sensitive breasts pressing flush against his solid chest.

The noise of the honky-tonk was a distant hum, making it easy for her to forget where they were and who was waiting for them. Her mind and all of her senses were focused on Dusty's mouth and the incredibly delightful liberties he was taking.

All at once, he dropped his hands to her waist. She experienced a momentary wave of disorientation when he lifted her off her feet and spun her in a circle, gasping softly when he set her back down. She realized they'd traded places. Dusty now had his back to the door, and she was securely anchored in his arms. The change in position also altered the immediacy of their kiss, increasing it tenfold.

Good thing he held her tight because he was taking her on the wildest ride of her life. The tiny part of her brain that wasn't involved in kissing Dusty realized his shallow breathing and rapidly fluttering heart mirrored hers, and satisfaction at her ability to affect him to such a degree coursed through her.

When his hand moved from her waist to her rib cage, her lost senses returned in a rush. The line they shouldn't cross was suddenly there in front of them, and she had no intention of stepping over it. Putting a few inches of much needed space between them, she inhaled sharply. The blast of oxygen restored her equilibrium.

"Sorry about that," Dusty muttered, also making an effort to pull himself together.

"Don't be. You were hardly acting alone."

"For which I'm very grateful." His voice was like warm honey.

Maryanne automatically straightened her blouse and finger-combed her hair, not that she could see the results of her efforts. "We should probably get back before we're missed."

"Too late for that."

"What will we tell our parents?"

She felt like a sixth grader, sneaking into the house after a forbidden adventure, and she almost giggled. At least they were both finding humor in the situation.

"We got overheated dancing and stepped outside to cool off."

"What!" Her dad was no dummy. Neither were Dusty's parents. "I don't think so."

He was grinning again, she didn't have to see him to know it.

"Relax. My parents won't say anything, not in front of you. And I'm sure your dad won't, either."

"Not now. Later's a different story."

Outside the supply room door, Maryanne paused, her emotions in a whirl. She liked Dusty. A lot. And kissing him…well, it had been earth-shattering. But it was also leading nowhere and potentially setting them both up for disappointment later down the road. "Is something the matter?" he asked.

The hallway itself was empty but just beyond it, the honky-tonk bustled with activity.

"I'm leaving in two weeks."

"Don't remind me."

His expression was so endearing, she found herself wanting to slip back in his arms. She'd miss him, and the sadness washing over her at the prospect of their inevitable parting took her aback. Could she have changed that much in two weeks? Could a mere kiss—well, several—be responsible?

"Maybe we should…" she hesitated, then spoke quickly "…take things a little slower."

"Do you want to see me again?"

"After tonight?"

"After you leave at the end of the month."

She sought his eyes, their color almost black in the poorly lit hallway. After the way they'd kissed, her fervent response to him, she was surprised he'd asked the question. "Of course I do."

"Then I'll fly out to L.A."

"Just like that?"

"It won't be my first trip."

"Your film work?"

"And looking for an agent."

More than one person stared curiously at them as they passed on their way to the bar. Any second either

Maryanne's father or one of Dusty's family members would come searching for them.

"If the producer from Sundown Pictures buys my screenplay, I may have lots of reasons to come to L.A. I could even spend part of the year there."

"True." She smiled. Selling his screenplay was a huge long shot, but she didn't want to burst his bubble just yet.

"Besides, I don't need an excuse." He leaned down and gave her a swift, sweet kiss. "Seeing you is reason enough to hop a plane."

He would come to L.A., she had no doubt. "I'd like that."

No sooner had she uttered the words than she wished she could take them back. If she allowed herself to fall for Dusty, he might unintentionally hurt her if those trips to L.A. didn't materialize. Or, she dreaded considering the possibility, those trips didn't include the promised visit to her.

Maryanne recalled her previous relationships that had gone awry. It hadn't taken long for her boyfriends to lose interest once they weren't seeing each other regularly.

Dusty captured her hand and raised it to his mouth, pressing his lips to her open palm. "I'd also like to see you tomorrow."

A small thrill coursed through her. "You will. We're riding back to Markton together in the truck."

"I can hardly wait." His dimple appeared, cutting deeper into his cheek as his grin expanded.

She laughed, her worries about their uncertain future dissolving—for the moment, anyway.

"But I was talking about after we get back," he clarified.

"I have to fly home midweek for a couple days."

"I'll be gone, too. I'm taking a horse and burro to Yellowstone for a documentary."

Fate, it seemed, was sending them a message. One they should probably heed.

"There's always next week." Perhaps by then they'd cool off and start thinking clearer.

"How about Tuesday before you fly home?"

That caught her off guard.

"Come by the ranch at noon," he said, not giving her the opportunity to object.

"What are we doing?"

"Do you like picnics?"

"I love them." Visions of them sitting on a blanket, her leaning against a sprawling tree with Dusty's head in her lap filled her mind. So much for cooling off.

"Be sure and wear your new boots."

In the main room, the band had returned from their break and was launching into a new song with a pounding beat.

"Why?" Comfy shoes was more of what she'd been thinking.

"We're going riding."

"But I don't ride."

"You'll learn. I'm a great teacher, just ask your dad."

Swell.

The good news was she'd be too busy worrying about her fear of horses to give her feelings for Dusty much thought.

DUSTY CHECKED HIS WATCH and noted the time. Almost noon. Maryanne should be arriving any moment. For a second, he imagined her standing him up, then dismissed the idea. Matt had ridden with them yesterday for most of the drive home from Albuquerque. Maryanne had seemed to really enjoy herself, playing travel games with Matt and chatting comfortably with Dusty when Matt took a nap.

Just maybe he could get used to the idea of settling down.

Who'd have guessed it? Dusty Cody a family man. Stranger things were possible.

He adjusted the cinch, taking it in another notch. Snowball blew out her breath in protest.

"Not my fault you're getting so fat."

He patted the old mare's rump. She'd been a steady working ranch horse for over two decades before being retired the previous year. There wasn't a gentler or quieter or older horse on the place. That along with her small stature made her the perfect mount for Maryanne.

Uno stood tied to the hitching rail beside Snowball, his head bobbing in eagerness to get started on their ride.

"Easy, boy." Dusty moved from Snowball to the big gelding and stroked his sleek neck. "We'll be heading out soon enough."

At least he hoped they'd be heading out and resisted checking his watch again. Maryanne would be here, she'd promised.

The horse reached his head sideways and gave Snowball a friendly sniff. She twitched her ears in response, then nibbled at him playfully.

"Well, you two are pretty cozy. I'm jealous."

Dusty inspected the contents of the saddlebags one last time. Barbara had come through, preparing a picnic lunch to surpass all picnic lunches. Pâté and crackers, fresh sliced fruit, gourmet cheeses, sugared walnuts and homemade chocolate chip cookies for dessert. Dusty had made only one contribution to the fare: a bottle of chilled wine.

Now, if Maryanne would just show.

He'd phoned her this morning to confirm their date and give her directions to the barn. She hadn't sounded particularly enthused but he'd credited her trepidation to riding, not a disinterest in seeing him.

Maybe she was lost. The Cody ranch was big and confusing to someone unfamiliar with it.

He reached for his phone but stopped at the sound of an approaching vehicle. He turned, ready to offer Maryanne a smile. Only it wasn't her. The pickup truck slowing to a stop belonged to his brother Jesse.

"Going on a ride?" Jesse stepped out and slammed the truck door shut behind him.

"As a matter of fact, I am."

"With that gal from over at Adele's place? Maryanne, right?" Jesse lifted the flap on one of the saddlebags and peeked inside. "What's all this?"

"Lunch."

"Mighty fancy lunch." He dropped the flap back down. "Careful your ice packs don't melt and your food spoil."

"I'm not worried."

"Dex has Doc Chester coming out this afternoon to worm the stock."

"Yeah."

"Dex is getting the horses ready now."

"And you think I should be helping him." There wasn't much to get ready other than checking off lists and counting heads. Dex could do it in his sleep.

"It is your job," Jesse reiterated.

"But it's not your job to manage me."

"Maybe you need someone to do just that." Jesse leaned against the hitching rail. Uno paid little attention. He was too busy mooning over Snowball, who'd lost interest in him and was dozing. "Especially since you're leaving in the morning for Yellowstone. How long you going to be gone this time?"

"Three days. Maybe two."

Until his brother had arrived, Dusty couldn't wait for Maryanne to show. Now he was glad she was late and didn't have to witness him and Jesse bickering. The two of them hadn't been getting along well since the rodeo when Dusty had congratulated Mark Hansen.

"What are you going to do when you get back from Yellowstone?" Jesse chewed on a toothpick while Dusty rebuckled the saddlebag flap his brother had left undone.

"About what?"

"Work."

"What I always do."

"You mean a half-ass job?"

Dusty stared down his brother. "Much as I'm sure you're enjoying yourself, you didn't come here to rag on me. What's really on your mind?"

"Let's start with Maryanne. How serious are you about her?"

"I'm not sure yet. What difference does it make?"

Jesse pushed off the hitching post. "You have enough things pulling you in different directions. You don't need another one."

"Don't you mean pulling me away from Cody Enterprises?"

"Same thing."

"Did Dad recruit you to be his helper?"

"I've always been on his side when it comes to the family and running this ranch."

"His side? More like his decree. The one where we all have to work here whether we like it or not? You know, it's possible to still be a Cody and not work for the family."

"What else would you do?"

No one had ever asked Dusty that question. He considered telling Jesse that he wanted to be a writer. In the next instant, sanity returned.

"I like film work."

"That's not a job," Jesse scoffed.

"I work pretty damn hard at it."

"Do you make decent money?"

"Now you do sound like Dad."

"He has a point."

"There's more to job satisfaction than the size of a paycheck."

"You have a duty to him."

"And what about a father's duty to his kid?"

Jesse frowned. "Dad's always been there for us."

"Has he?"

"What are you talking about?"

The words came out before Dusty could stop them. "Did you know he and Mom separated before you were born?"

Jesse exploded. "Bullshit!"

"Mom told me."

"She admitted it?"

"Not exactly. But she didn't deny it."

"You asked her?" Jesse's face flushed a vivid red. "I can't believe you did that."

"Somebody needed to." Dusty defended himself. "There's been talk about him and Mark Hansen for years."

"Rumors. And lies. I wouldn't be surprised if Hansen started them just to cause trouble."

Maryanne chose that moment to show up, the dilapidated pickup truck bumping to a stop beside Jesse's.

Dusty stormed past his brother, his relief that she'd arrived outweighing his anger. "Do me one favor. Ask Dad what he was doing last week talking to Abigail Hansen in front of the feed store."

"He wouldn't talk to her," Jesse spat.

"He did. Matt saw it, too. And judging by how close they stood, I'd say it wasn't their first conversation."

Dusty turned to greet Maryanne. He could tell by her expression she realized she'd walked into an argument. He tried to put her at ease with a smile and a "Hey, you made it."

Jesse didn't stick around. He tipped his hat at Maryanne and muttered, "Nice to see you again," before hopping in his truck and leaving.

The sunglasses he donned didn't hide the hurt and anger in his eyes. Dusty regretted being the cause, but it was past time his oldest brother stopped ignoring the obvious and faced the truth about their parents.

CHAPTER TEN

"Did I interrupt something?" Maryanne asked as Dusty's brother Jesse climbed into his truck after making an abrupt exit. "I can come back."

"Don't think you're getting out of riding that easy." Dusty put her at ease with his supersexy grin.

She couldn't help but wonder how often his charm came to the rescue and about the real man behind it. She'd had a glimpse of that man when she'd read his screenplay, and *he* was the Dusty she wanted to know better.

"Come on," he said, "let me introduce you to Snowball."

The horse appeared gentle enough. Nonetheless, Maryanne approached cautiously.

Dusty came up behind her. "Here." Taking her hand, he placed it on Snowball's neck.

She didn't need any further encouragement and began stroking. The horse dropped her head and snorted.

"I think she likes it."

"'Course she does."

Maryanne combed her fingers through the horse's shaggy mane.

"You'll have no worries with her," Dusty said. "She's bombproof."

"Bombproof?"

"It's an expression. Means a bomb could explode, and the horse won't do anything."

"Are you saying we might encounter bombs on our ride?"

"Anything's possible."

Her hands stilled. "You're kidding, aren't you?"

He laughed, and the strain she'd sensed when she first arrived evaporated. "Trust me. I won't let anything happen to you."

She did trust him with her well-being. Dusty might be reckless and, yes, irresponsible on occasion. When it came to horses and livestock, however, there wasn't anyone more knowledgeable or experienced.

She was less sure about trusting him with her heart.

"So what next?" She smiled through gritted teeth.

"We mount up."

"I was afraid of that."

Placing her foot in the stirrup wasn't the hard part. It was swinging her leg over the saddle without falling. Her recently acquired boots might look hot, but their unfamiliar feel impeded her efforts. By her third attempt, she'd developed a newfound respect for cow folk and their abilities.

Snowball deserved her reputation and then some. She was indeed bombproof. If not, she would have spooked multiple times during the process of Dusty helping Maryanne into the saddle. Both the horse's and Dusty's patience paid off. Eventually, Maryanne sat upright in the saddle, the reins gripped between her fingers and her legs hugging Snowball's sides for dear life.

"Relax." Dusty placed his hand on her knee. "If you're nervous, you'll make her nervous."

How could she even think of relaxing with him constantly touching her?

Snowball shifted her weight causing Maryanne to gasp. "You didn't tell me I was going to be this high off the ground."

"You'll get used to it." He untied Snowball's lead rope from the hitching post. "I'll pony you for a while, until you're more comfortable."

She didn't know what "ponying her" entailed but it sounded better than being left on her own.

With enviable agility, Dusty swung up into the saddle on his horse, easily managing both his reins and Snowball's lead rope. How did he do that? Before Maryanne knew what was happening, they were walking up the road.

Forgetting all about the reins, she held on to the thingie in front of the saddle—a horn?—with both hands. Before long, she adapted to the horse's surprisingly easy rhythm. The ground that had first appeared so far down took on a new and interesting perspective. After going over some basic horsemanship with Dusty, she got up her nerve, let go of the horn and reached down to pat Snowball's neck. When she didn't tumble head over heels, her confidence soared.

"I just realized," she said, looking around. "Where's Track?"

"With my sister, Elly. I asked her to babysit."

"He doesn't like to go on a ride?"

"He likes it too much. I'd be spending the entire time watching out for him. I'd much rather be watching you."

Maryanne tried not to notice how Dusty's voice had dropped at the end.

They stopped at the gate leaving the main complex.

Beyond it, stretched endless miles of rolling green land-scape.

"You ready to fly solo?" Dusty asked.

"What do you think, Snowball?" She craned her neck sideways to peer at the horse's head. "We say yes."

"That's my girl."

His girl?

Dusty surely hadn't meant anything by the remark. A player like him probably called all the women he knew by cute endearments. Still, Maryanne couldn't stop the direction her thoughts took.

What would it be like to really be his girlfriend?

He closed the gate behind her and remounted, then, they were off and running. Walking in Maryanne's case. Slowly. She couldn't have handled anything faster.

They didn't talk a whole lot on the ride, which was nice. It allowed her to fully enjoy the spectacular scenery and abundant wildlife. Dusty was quick to point out anything of interest, which included a small herd of antelope startled into flight at their approach.

"That was amazing," Maryanne gushed as the last antelope sprinted over a hill and vanished. She mentally kicked herself for not bringing her camera. "I've never seen anything like that in the wild."

Neither had she seen bison, elk and hawks, all of which they spotted on their ride. She understood why Dusty loved the ranch. It was just as much a part of him as his family and rodeoing. If he left, it wouldn't be for long, and he'd always return.

"We're here," he suddenly announced, and reined Uno to a stop.

Maryanne didn't have to signal Snowball. The old horse copied whatever Uno did.

"Where's here?" Maryanne looked around. They were atop a gentle hill with stunning views of the distant mountains and a creek running through the valley below. Large trees surrounded by thick foliage grew on the banks of the creek. She suppressed a sudden urge to run barefoot through the high grass.

"My place. Stony Creek. Strange as you may find this, I have no intentions of living in an apartment above the barn for the rest of my life. I've been thinking of one day building a house."

"It's perfect."

"I kind of like it, too." His gaze scanned the horizon. "There's a road on the other side of the hill so access isn't a problem."

Maryanne's earlier observation about Dusty belonging here was further enforced. The raw beauty of the land and sense of freedom it instilled matched the wild side of his personality. He, like the land, wasn't easily tamed.

"I can see why you'd want to build a house here." She envisioned waking up every morning to this spectacular view instead of the dingy one from her apartment window.

While Dusty held Snowball's reins, Maryanne tried to lift her leg over the saddle and dismount. Her limbs, however, refused to function properly. Finally, through sheer force of will, she succeeded and all but fell out of the saddle. Luckily, Dusty caught her and eased her onto the ground.

Pain shot up her calves as her feet made contact, and her fear that she'd lose her balance was realized—only she wasn't in the saddle this time.

Dusty grabbed hold of her arms right before she crumpled. "Hold on, I've got you."

He did have her. In more ways than one. Staring into his tanned and very handsome face, it occurred to her that kissing him would be a simple matter of leaning into him. He must have been thinking along the same lines for his eyes turned dark and smoky.

Danger signals went off in Maryanne's head. He was planning on building a house on the very spot they stood. A house he'd share with his son. She, on the other hand, was returning to L.A., a city she loved. To a job she loved just as much. And if all went well, she'd be closing soon on a new condo in the development of her dreams.

She stepped back, her message subtle but clear. Dusty's disappointment was evident by the slight sag of his shoulders, but he didn't press the issue and let her go. Not for long, however.

Her legs still resembled cooked spaghetti.

"I'm okay," she murmured and took a wobbly step.

"You sure?"

"What was that advice you had for my dad? Walk it off?"

"It only works if you can actually walk."

"Watch me," she said bravely.

The friendly banter had them back to their old selves. Maryanne supposed she should be glad. And she was, or so she told herself repeatedly while she hobbled back and forth. Before long, the pain in her legs decreased and mobility returned.

"Hungry?" Dusty began pulling all sorts of food storage containers from the saddlebags on his horse.

"A little." She hated admitting just how hungry she'd gotten on their hour-long ride.

"Grab that blanket, will you?"

"Where is it?"

"Tied behind your saddle."

All this time she'd been riding with a blanket tied behind her and she hadn't realized it.

Dusty had tethered the horses to the low-hanging branch of a nearby tree. Within a matter of minutes, they'd spread the blanket beneath the shade of another tree and were divvying up the fare.

"Did you fix all this?" she asked, opening a package of gouda cheese.

"As much as I'd like to impress you by taking credit, I have to be honest. My parents' housekeeper is the one to thank." He grinned, and Maryanne's resolve to keep things strictly platonic faltered. "I did pick out the wine," he said producing a corkscrew from his pocket.

It was one of her favorite kinds of wine, too.

He poured two glasses—plastic glasses—and they toasted the success of his screenplay.

"How soon do you think I'll hear from your mother's former agent?"

"It could be tomorrow or not for months. Time in the entertainment industry doesn't move at the same pace as for you and me." She took a bite of pâté and cracker. "I can check with Herb when I fly home tomorrow."

"That'd be great." He ate his pâté and crackers at twice the speed she did. "I'll drive you to the airport."

"You don't have to."

"I want to."

Damn, he was insistent. "We'll see." She deftly

changed the subject. "Have you written any other screenplays?"

"Two. One's completed. My first attempt. It sucks." He refreshed their wineglasses. "I started a new one recently."

"Another family theme?"

He shook his head. "This one's more of a coming-of-age story about a roper who takes his young son on the circuit with him."

"Is that what you'd like to do with Matt?"

"I'd like to take him with me. Not sure I want us to go through the same hell as my characters."

She enjoyed how he talked about the people in his story as if they were real. And how he talked about his son.

"If I was out of line pushing you about Matt when we first met, I'm sorry. I sometimes let my feelings about my birth mother's abandonment get to me."

"If you were out of line, I don't care. I've only known him a few months but already I can't imagine my life without him."

"I'm glad."

"We're still having some difficulties. Bring-your-dad-to-preschool day is coming up soon. None of us can decide who should go."

"What does Matt say?"

"He wants to take both of us." Dusty popped a fresh strawberry in his mouth. "I'm trying not to turn it into a contest."

"Good for you. Hard as that is, it's the right thing to do."

"He's coming over tomorrow to spend the night. Do you think he'll like leftover pâté for dinner?"

She took another bite and eyed the container. "I don't think there'll be any left for him to eat."

"You're right." He scooped the last of the pâté onto two crackers and passed her one. "Fish sticks and tater tots it is."

"Oh, gosh." She made a face. "I haven't eaten fish sticks in years."

"You're not missing anything." Dusty leaned back on one elbow, his expression becoming thoughtful. "I know you've heard a lot about me and the women I've dated."

"Adele says your exploits are legendary."

He chuckled. "They're also exaggerated."

"Ha!" She gave him an arch look.

"What about you? Any men in your life?"

"Not at the moment."

"Ever married?"

"Nope."

"Close?"

"Mmm…" She lifted one shoulder. "A couple of serious relationships but they didn't last."

"You get tired of them?"

She plucked a piece of dried grass from the blanket and flicked it away. "More like they got tired of me."

"I can't imagine that."

She shrugged again. This wasn't a comfortable topic for her.

"What happened?"

"I dated this one guy in college. He got a job offer right after graduation in a town outside of Portland. I still had another year to go. We tried dating long-distance over the summer but we were young, and it didn't work out."

"What about the other one?"

"He was in the military reserves. We'd just moved in together when he got called to active duty."

"You didn't want to wait for him?"

"He didn't want to wait for me. He came back on leave before being shipped overseas, and things were different."

Maryanne let Dusty think she and her former boyfriends had simply drifted apart. Now wasn't the time or place to expound on what had been painful breakups.

"Their loss," he said with a half smile and caressed the back of her hand with his fingers.

"Everything happens for a reason."

Did it? she wondered.

After a leisurely postmeal respite spent lying on their backs and watching the clouds float by, they packed up the empty containers and mounted their horses. Dusty took them on a different route, one with fewer up-and-down trails. Maryanne's sore bum appreciated his consideration, not that she'd admit in a million years what specific part of her body ached.

The closer they got to Cottonwood Ranch, the faster the horses moved—or wanted to move. Dusty held Uno back to accommodate Snowball's shorter legs and instructed her to "give Snowball a nudge." The horse didn't exactly break into a run but she did move out at a more brisk walk.

Maryanne's sore muscles sang in happiness when the main gate appeared ahead. At the hitching post, she again required Dusty's assistance to dismount. Solid ground had never felt so good. While Dusty began the process of unsaddling Uno, she held on to Snowball's neck, still unsteady.

"Thanks, girlie," she cooed to the mare. "I'll tell you a secret if you promise not to repeat it."

Snowball flicked her ears.

"You're only the second horse I've ever ridden."

Snowball turned her head around and looked at Maryanne as if to say she'd figured that out.

"No fooling you, is there?"

One of the wranglers drove up on an ATV. Maryanne recognized him from the night Dusty had given her father his first roping lesson.

"Hi. It's Big Ben, right?"

"Yes, ma'am." He touched the brim of his hat. "Is Dusty around?"

"He took the saddles to the tack room and should be right out."

The older man climbed off the ATV. Apparently, he was in too much of a hurry to wait and started for the barn. Her curiosity spiked, she couldn't help it, and she was tempted to go with him. Just as he reached the entrance to the barn, Dusty emerged. Maryanne was close enough to hear their conversation.

"Hey, Big Ben. What are you doing here?"

"Barbara sent me with a message." He handed Dusty a slip of paper. "Guess this person's been trying to reach you for almost two hours, and you're not answering your cell phone. They finally called the main house. Barbara says it's real important."

Dusty read the note quickly, and a flash of intense emotion crossed his face. Maryanne's stomach knotted. Had something happened to his son? Without thinking, she went to him.

"What's wrong?"

"The message is from Kenneth Casey of Sundown

Pictures." Sweat had formed on his brow, and he wiped it off with the back of his hand. "He wants me to call him right away."

"So soon?" Maryanne asked Dusty. "You just sent the screenplay."

"Would he read it that fast?"

"He could have, I suppose. You won't know till you call."

Dusty turned to Big Ben. "Take care of the horses for me, will you?"

"Sure thing."

"Come with me," Dusty said to Maryanne once Big Ben had left.

She wavered. If the news was bad, Dusty may prefer to be alone until the worst of his disappointment abated. Her mother always had when she'd lost a role she wanted. Then again, if the news turned out to be good, Maryanne was the only person on Cottonwood Ranch, the only person in the world except for a handful in California, who knew about his screenplay and could share in his excitement.

"Are you sure?"

His gaze didn't falter. "Very sure."

Damn warning signals and good sense and guarding against heartache. He'd asked her to be with him during what could be one of the most important—or devastating—phone calls of his life. How could she refuse?

"All right."

They went into the barn. Instantly, the temperature dropped by about ten degrees. Maryanne was overwhelmed by the number of horses in the barn, about seventy by her rough estimation. And there were a half-dozen more barns on the ranch.

Midway down the main aisle they came to an opening and a set of stairs, at the top of which was a landing and a door. He didn't have to tell her his apartment lay on the other side of that door.

What was it with him and long narrow stairways or darkened hallways?

She battled a sudden case of nerves. They'd been alone often, but not *this* alone. There had always been people in the vicinity or riding in vehicles behind them.

He unlocked the door, and they went inside. Considering the apartment had been built above a horse barn, Maryanne expected to find basic accommodations at best and a hovel at worst. To her shock and delight she walked into roomy, spotlessly clean and tastefully appointed living quarters decorated in a striking combination of western and contemporary decor. In hindsight, she should have expected as much, given his tastes.

"Holy cow," she exclaimed.

"You like it?"

"I'm wondering why you want to build a house. This place is great."

"For one thing, I need another bedroom. This has only one, which is fine for me. But there's no place for Matt to bunk when he stays with me except the couch."

"That's true."

"And I'm pretty sure most women wouldn't like living in a barn above a bunch of horses."

"I would." She realized her mistake when Dusty's eyes lit up and mentally kicked herself.

Behind the overstuffed leather couch, afternoon sunlight streamed in through a pair of shutters, creating a criscross shadow pattern on the area rug. The effect was quite lovely.

"Have a seat." He removed his hat and took hers, hanging them both on a coatrack by the door. "Can I get you a cold drink?"

"I'm fine, thanks."

He sat at what was obviously a custom-made mahogany desk in the corner of the living room. This, she thought, was where he wrote and created his characters. Setting the note from Barbara in front of him, he smoothed the paper flat, then picked up the phone beside the computer monitor.

"Here goes," he said and flashed his trademark grin, only it lacked luster.

"Good luck." She returned his grin and gave him a thumbs-up before sinking into the couch.

High tension situations weren't uncommon to Maryanne—at work or personally. She found herself thrown back in time to when her mother had gotten the call from her agent about the role of Wanda in *Family Fortune*. Maryanne had been a child but she remembered the afternoon clearly and how she'd stood by her mother's side while her agent delivered the good news. How odd that Maryanne should find herself in a similar situation here, in Markton, Wyoming. And with Dusty Cody of all people.

"Is Mr. Casey there?" Dusty gave his name. "I have a message to return his call."

Seconds ticked by, accumulating into minutes. It must have felt like a million years to Dusty. Frequently, their gazes connected across the room and more than once she considered going to him and standing by him like she had her mother.

"Yeah, I'm here." Dusty wiped his damp brow again. "How are you doing, Mr. Casey?" After a pause, he said, "Ken."

Maryanne sat with her hands folded in her lap. It was that, or wring them compulsively. Was an invitation to call someone by their first name a good sign? She hoped so.

It was difficult to tell what the producer was saying from Dusty's end of the conversation. Other than answering a few basic questions about his screenplay, he mostly listened and fidgeted, his leg beating an erratic tattoo beneath the desk. All at once, he swallowed and when he said, "Okay, I'll do that," his voice cracked.

With a solemn goodbye, he hung up the phone.

When he didn't speak right away, Maryanne feared the worst and scrambled for the right words to say. Only lame platitudes like "There'll be a next time" came to mind.

Dusty stood slowly and pushed the chair back in under the desk. Its wheels scraped noisily on the hardwood floor, almost like an omen. When he was done, he shoved his hands in his jeans pockets. "He told me he's sorry."

"Oh, Dusty."

One corner of his mouth curved up. "He wishes he could give me more but he just can't."

Maryanne didn't understand. "Give you more?"

"Money." The other side of his mouth curved up, and his dimple appeared. "But they have a standard rate for first-time offers."

"They're buying your screenplay?" she squealed and sat bolt upright, her fingers pressed to her mouth.

Dusty scratched the back of his head, looking every

bit like the lanky cowboy she'd first met and not the talented author she knew him to be who'd just happened to make his first sale!

"Technically, they're optioning it. For five years. Is that too long? Should I ask for less?"

"I have no idea."

"Do you think your mother's agent has the names of those associates?"

"Call him. Right away." She couldn't contain herself. Leaping up from the couch, she raced across the room. He met her halfway. "You sold your screenplay," she repeated.

"Optioned."

"Okay, whatever."

"He wants some changes first."

"No problem. You can do that." She laughed giddily and clamped his hand between hers. "Do you realize they could really make it into a movie?"

"Don't forget, you're my date to the premiere."

Though the odds of such a thing happening were slim, she indulged her imagination for just a moment.

"I'm serious." He abruptly sobered. "I wouldn't want to go with anyone else."

She didn't want him to go with anyone else, either, but saying so would be acknowledging feelings she wasn't ready to deal with just yet.

"Have your people contact my people," she said in a teasing tone to keep the mood light.

His arm circled her waist. "None of this would have happened without your help."

"Yes, it would have. You're pretty determined."

"And you're an excellent coach." He drew her close until their bodies were flush like the other night in the honky-tonk. "We make a good team. And we'll celebrate in style when I fly out to sign my contract."

"That's right."

Maryanne had been so wrapped up in Dusty selling his screenplay, she'd forgotten what his option deal could mean for their relationship. He'd likely visit L.A. regularly over the next few months or even years. And if he sold another screenplay, which wasn't impossible once he established himself, he'd be visiting even more regularly.

Perhaps Markton, Wyoming, wasn't so far away from L.A. after all, and the prospect of them having a future together not so bleak.

"I can't wait." She threw her arms around his neck. "There's so much we can do, so many places I can't wait to show you."

His eyes turned dark and smoky like they had earlier during their picnic. In the next instant, he bent his head and kissed her.

She wasn't prepared for the instantaneous fireworks that followed.

The low groan emanating from Dusty's throat told her neither was he.

CHAPTER ELEVEN

MARYANNE HELD ON to Dusty for without him, she'd be swept away. He wasn't her anchor in the surge of desire overpowering them, he was the source of it. And she was helpless—make that unwilling—to resist its heady pull.

Since their first meeting that day in the practice arena when her father fell, she'd been cautioning herself against becoming involved with Dusty. Not only because she was leaving soon. She also feared he wouldn't return her feelings or return them for long.

Except he did. Even as they kissed, he told her how much he cared for her in sweet, lovely words whispered against her mouth, the hair at her temple, the base of her neck. She arched into him, molding her soft curves to his hard muscles. The sensation sent silky ripples winding through her.

"You're so beautiful," he said in that slight twang of his she found so appealing and slipped his hand under her blouse.

The skin to skin contact was electrifying.

Tugging open the snaps on his Western shirt, she placed her mouth on the patch of bare chest showing above the edge of his undershirt. A whorl of soft brown hair tickled her lips.

He drew back suddenly and covered her hands with his, staying them.

She lifted her face and searched his blue eyes. "Did I do something wrong?"

"Not at all."

"What is it?"

"I want you, Maryanne." He let out a breath. "So much, I can't stand it."

She could tell, and she liked being the reason for his obvious and undeniable arousal. "I want you, too."

"This won't be a one-night stand for me. If it is for you, then we need to stop right now while I still can."

And here she'd been worried all along he didn't share her feelings.

"It's not a one-night stand for me, either." She laid her head on his chest and listened to his pounding heart. *This is for me,* she thought. *For us.* "I want to keep seeing you. For the rest of my stay here and when you come to L.A."

"You don't know how much I was hoping you'd say that."

He set her back from him and promptly unfastened the rest of his shirt. Shrugging out of it, he flung it aside. His undershirt followed. When he was done, he stood before her, bare chested and dangerously sexy. It wasn't his lack of clothes, however, that had warmth curling in her belly. Or the prospect of what was about to transpire. It was the way he looked at her. As if she were everything to him.

And in that moment, she was.

She considered falling back onto the couch and taking him with her. He evidently had other ideas. Maryanne wasn't exactly short but when he lifted her into his arms and carried her across the apartment, she felt tiny and cherished.

In the bedroom, he laid her on the large four-poster bed. She was too preoccupied with her escalating desire for much of anything else about the room to register. Except for the sunlight. Lots and lots of it poured through the open window.

"I'll be right back," he said and kissed her forehead.

She sat up. "Where are you going?"

"Not far."

At the window, he closed the drapes partway. Like that, the room was thrown into semidarkness—the seductive kind that promised myriad delights.

He reached for his belt buckle.

Maryanne scooted to the edge of the bed. "Wait."

"Having second thoughts?"

"Not at all." She rose onto her knees and linked her arms around his neck. "There's only one first time for two people." She smiled coyly and nibbled at his earlobe. "I don't want to hurry."

He made a sound, a low, throaty groan, and lowered her onto the bed. "Oh, baby, we'll take all the time you want."

And they did. Slowly, one piece at a time, the remainder of their clothing came off until they were both naked atop the luxurious down comforter. Pillows surrounded them and, like the closed drapes, cocooned them from the outside world, allowing all of Maryanne's inhibitions to fade away.

Dusty's hands, bold and skilled, roamed her body. He murmured his appreciation at each new discovery. The feminine slope of her hips, the shape and heft of her breasts, the curve of her buttocks, the silky skin between her thighs. She hid nothing from him and when his fingers delved inside her, she sighed contentedly, then moaned with need.

"What do you like best?" he asked.

Because she knew how important it was to him that she be satisfied, she told him.

His sexy smile took on a wicked slant. "I like that, too."

Then he was moving down her body, burning a trail on her fevered flesh with his lips, teeth and tongue. At his urging, she parted her legs, and he placed his mouth where his hand had been moments before.

Liquid heat poured through her, and she moved her hips in response to his expert ministrations. Weeks of fighting her attraction to him gave way, and she began to peak quickly.

"Easy, sweetheart." He blew a cooling breath on her moist skin. "Like you said, we only have one first time together."

She tried to hold off, really she did. But no sooner was his mouth on her again than she began hurtling toward a shattering climax. He stayed with her until the last wave had crashed over her, then retraced the same path up her body that he'd taken down.

When he reached her breasts, he took a pebbled nipple between his lips and flicked his tongue over it. Maryanne squirmed against him. It wouldn't take much to send her over the edge again.

Except that she had her own plans for Dusty.

Pulling him to her, she kissed him, her tongue tasting every corner of his mouth. Instantly, his muscles tensed and his erection pressed firmly into her lower belly.

Her hand snaked between their bodies and closed around him.

He uttered her name on a ragged moan. "Keep that up, and I won't last."

"We can't have that." She smiled and released him. "Besides, I have something else in mind."

"What?"

Actions, she decided, spoke louder than words. Giving him a gentle shove, she rolled him onto his back and straddled his thighs. Once he was sufficiently trapped beneath her, she moistened her palm with her tongue and took his erection in her hand.

"Now it's your turn," she purred, stroking lightly. "Tell me what you like."

Because Dusty wasn't shy, either, he told her, and Maryanne was delighted to accommodate him.

She took great pleasure in watching his response as she dipped her head and slid her tongue along the length of his shaft. The lines around his gorgeous mouth hardened. The color of his blue eyes darkened to an inky black. She was curious just how far she could take him before he passed the point of no return.

Apparently, not much further.

"Wait." He groaned.

"You sure?" she teased.

"There's only one first time for two people, remember?" He reached over with one arm to the nightstand. Opening the drawer, he withdrew a condom. "For us, today, I'm going to be inside you."

Maryanne melted. "That's what I want, too."

Ripping open the packet, he quickly sheathed himself. When he was done, she leaned forward, thinking she would guide him inside her. She was certainly ready. Dusty, however, had other ideas. Before she quite knew what was happening, he flipped her onto her back, pinned her beneath him and parted her legs with his knee.

"I haven't been able to think of anything else except this since Albuquerque."

She lifted her hips in invitation. "Only since then?"

He drove inside her and immediately began moving. Maryanne inhaled sharply at the sudden and powerful sensations their joining evoked. She realized in that instant, no man would ever be like Dusty, no lovemaking like this, and that her life was forever and irrevocably altered.

He showed her with tender caresses and sweet, sweet kisses how much she, and this moment, meant to him. Then he showed her with ever increasing urgency how much she excited him. Cupping her buttocks in his hands, he lifted her to meet his thrusts. The sensation was exquisite. She could only imagine how it must feel to him.

Sifting her fingers through his hair, she drew him down for yet another searing kiss. The contact wasn't enough, and she wrapped her legs around his waist, sealing their physical connection along with their emotional one. After that, maintaining any semblance of control was a lost cause. With a shuddering cry, Dusty came inside her. She didn't let go of him, even when his spasms ceased, and he lay prone on top of her, unmoving except for the steady rise and fall of his chest.

As one moment stretched into two, she shifted to a more comfortable position. When he still said nothing, she began to worry. Did he regret making love with her? Oh, please no. It had been too wonderful, too incredible for stilted conversation and averted gazes. She considered saying something cute or clever, just to break the ice.

"Dusty?" she finally whispered.

"Hmm?"

"Are you…um…is everything okay?"

"Shh. I'm not ready yet."

"For what?"

"This to end." He rolled off of her then and lay beside her, his leg draped over hers with a comfortable familiarity. "But I guess it has to."

Her anxiety instantly vanished. "Somebody's bound to notice. We've been gone a long time."

"We could stay holed up here." He turned and traced his fingertips between her breasts and down to her stomach.

"My father's expecting me."

"When exactly?" He drew invisible circles around her belly button.

"Now, actually."

"You could call him. Tell him you're going to be late."

"I could."

Dusty sat up and swung his legs over the side of the bed. "If you did, that would give us time to talk."

MARYANNE SAT UP, TOO, mildly concerned. She wouldn't have guessed a conversation to be what Dusty had in mind.

"Talk about what?" she asked.

He hooked an arm around her waist. "Plans for my trip to L.A."

So, he was coming. For real. The afternoon became

even more special for it marked the beginning of their relationship, one with an indefinite end.

"When does the producer want to see you?" she asked.

"He's going to send the contract. I'm supposed to call his secretary tomorrow with the address. Once I've reviewed it—"

"You need to contact Herb," she interrupted.

He nodded. "Once my agent and I review it, we'll send it back with any changes. I'm guessing I'll be flying out mid- or late-October."

"That quick!"

"Too quick?" Dusty's brows came together. "You weren't lying about there being no boyfriend?"

"Not at all." She gave him a playful tap on the arm. "If I had a boyfriend, I wouldn't be here now."

"Neither would I if I had a girlfriend." He brushed a lock of hair from her face. "You know that, don't you?"

"Yes."

He linked fingers with her. The simple gesture warmed Maryanne.

"I won't lie, most of what people have told you about me is true. *Was* true. I haven't been with anyone since last year. Like I said, I did ask Josie to marry me a while ago. But that was strictly for Matt's sake. She and I… we didn't. Not even kiss. Not since I saw her in L.A."

She hadn't known Dusty then and had no reason to be jealous yet somehow the knowledge he and Josie hadn't been intimate for five years filled her with relief.

"I'm not assuming that just because I'll be visiting you in L.A. means I can stay with you. I'll get a hotel—"

She covered his lips with her fingers. "You can stay with me. I want you to."

"You sure?"

She brightened. "You've shown me around your home. Now, I'll get to show you mine. You'll love L.A. Yes, it's the most polluted city in the country but it's also fun and exciting, and there's a million things to do and see. Oh, and the food. We have the most fantastic restaurants. Do you like sushi? There's this incredible place near—"

Now it was his turn to silence her. Only he did it with a kiss.

"Speaking of restaurants, have dinner with me tonight."

"I wish I could. I already told Dad we'd go out. Mom's birthday was this week, and he's been a little down."

"He can come with us."

"You wouldn't mind?"

"Not at all. I'll pick the two of you up at six-thirty. How's that?"

She kissed his cheek. "Perfect."

He checked his watch then reached for her, his grin seductive and his eyes brimming with mischief. "Which gives us three-and-a-half hours."

"Uh-uh." She scooted back. "I have to make that call to Dad, tell him I'll be late. And you have to call Herb about repping you or recommending someone who will."

Before she could make her escape, a phone rang from somewhere on the floor.

"Maybe that's your dad," Dusty said. "Calling me to check up on his daughter's whereabouts."

"Don't even joke about that!" The prospect of her father finding out about her and Dusty making love mortified Maryanne. She may be a grown woman but she was still Gil Devonshire's little girl.

Dusty rummaged around on the floor for his jeans. He found them and managed to locate his phone by the fourth ring. Checking the caller ID, he scowled and sat back on the bed.

"Not your dad. It's mine." He placed the phone to his ear. "Hello." A considerable silence followed during which Dusty's scowl deepened. "Yes." More silence. "That's right." He rubbed his forehead. "I can't. I have plans." Still, more silence. "Fine. I'll be there." He disconnected.

Maryanne edged closer and put a hand on his shoulder. "Problems?"

"We're going to have to put a hold on the rest of the afternoon." He started collecting his clothes. "It appears the moment of truth has arrived."

"What happened?" Maryanne found her bra and panties and slipped into them. The turn their conversation had taken called for being dressed.

"The message from Ken Casey's secretary was apparently detailed." Dusty stood and donned his boxer briefs, then his jeans. "Barbara told my dad about it."

"Oh, no."

"Dad wants to know—" Dusty lowered his voice to mimic his father "—just what the hell is going on. He's waiting for me now in his study."

IN THE TIME it took Dusty to dress, walk Maryanne to her vehicle, make sure she got off safe and sound and drive to his parents' house, his father had managed to round up his mother, Dex and Jesse for the meeting.

Dusty recognized a power play when he saw one.

Walker and Elly hadn't been invited not because they were unavailable but because they might possibly understand Dusty's ambition to write or at least not be opposed to it. His father had made sure his camp outnumbered Dusty's.

He didn't care. He'd just received the best news of his life, next to finding out he had a son, and spent the last hour with Maryanne, discovering an intimacy infinitely more special than any previous ones.

Bring it on, Dad, he thought as he walked confidently into his father's study. *I can handle it.*

Dex and Jesse sat on the long cowhide couch which dominated the room, their boots resting on the highly polished coffee table. His mother occupied a matching chair adjacent to the couch, and his father stood at the small wet bar, pouring himself a drink. Irish whiskey over ice, his usual.

"A little early for hard liquor, isn't it, Dad?" Dusty said, taking the offensive. "Not to mention unhealthy. I thought your doctor told you to cut back."

"Don't start with me."

How often had Dusty heard that?

His father gestured toward the door. "Shut that, will you."

So, it was going to be a loud conversation. Dusty shouldn't be surprised. His father seldom took a quiet stand.

He retraced his steps to the door and closed it, his resentment growing. In other families, this gathering would be entirely different. They would be congratulating Dusty on his accomplishment. Not the Codys. He was seen as breaking tradition. Letting the family down. The black sheep.

"Have a seat," his father said.

Someone had brought in a lone dining room chair and positioned it across from the sofa. Dusty had the immediate impression of being on a witness stand. Make that an interrogation.

"No, thanks. I'll stand."

"What the heck's going on?" Jesse demanded, looking first at Dusty then their father. "I've got a pile of work orders to go through at the office."

Dex's expression was similarly perplexed.

Interesting. His father hadn't told his brothers about the screenplay. Did he not have time or was that all part of the plan?

"Dusty received a phone call here today," J.W. started. "From a producer at Sundown Pictures."

"I'll tell them," Dusty said.

His father visibly started at the interruption, then stiffened. He didn't like people stealing his thunder.

"What's going on?" Dex echoed Jesse's question. "Are you leaving again for Canada? Because we've got the Oklahoma City Rodeo coming up next month."

"I will be leaving in a couple weeks, but not for a film shoot. And I won't miss the rodeo."

"Then where?"

"L.A. Sundown Pictures has optioned my screenplay."

"Your *what*?" Dex glanced around as if to confirm he'd heard right.

"My screenplay. It's a script for a movie."

"I know what a screenplay is," he answered sharply.

"I thought you gave up that writing nonsense years ago," Jesse said.

"Nonsense is right," J.W. boomed and slammed his drink down on his desk.

"I didn't give it up." Dusty crossed the room to the wet bar. His throat had become increasingly dry, and he needed a glass of water.

"Are you saying you've written more than this screenplay?" Dex appeared amazed.

"Another screenplay and four books."

"For the love of Mike." J.W. clamped a hand to his head.

The rest of Dusty's family said nothing, apparently stunned into silence.

After a moment, Dex asked, "How's this going to affect your job here?"

"I don't know yet." Dusty drank half his water and refilled his glass.

"But it definitely will."

"To some degree."

Dex made a disgruntled sound, and the look he exchanged with Jesse spoke volumes. They sided with their father and weren't happy with Dusty's announcement.

His chest tightened. He'd expected this reaction from his family but it still hurt.

Why couldn't they be happy for him like Maryanne had been? It was possible she understood more about how hard he'd worked for his success, having had a mother in the entertainment business. More likely, she was a warm and wonderfully supportive person by nature, and he was lucky to have her in his life.

Not that the Codys weren't supportive of each other. But they, and J.W. in particular, had zero tolerance when it came to any of them choosing a path that might lead them away from the family and Cottonwood Ranch.

A thought halted Dusty.

Was his father so intolerant because of his affair with Abigail Hansen? It was the one and only time in his entire life J.W. had turned his back on his family and the moral values he held so high.

Dusty remembered something from a lesson his college psychology instructor had taught in class. Parents disliked seeing their own faults reflected back at them in their children. Maybe his father saw himself reflected in Dusty, which could account for why he'd always ridden Dusty harder than his other children.

"How much does Maryanne have to do with your decision?" Dex asked Dusty.

"Maryanne?" His father came over to stand behind the couch. "The girl from Adele's place?"

"My writing has nothing to do with her."

"But she does live in L.A.?"

"Yeah."

"And you'll see her when you go there?" Dex asked.

"I plan to." Dusty checked his anger. Losing it would serve no purpose.

"Her mother was an actress, right?" Jesse glanced at Dex for confirmation. "Her father mentioned it when we were in Albuquerque."

"Did she help you sell your screenplay?" Dex asked.

"She gave me a few tips on how to pitch it to the producer." The sensation of being cornered intensified, squeezing Dusty's middle.

"This is just like you." J.W. stormed back to the wet bar and tossed the remaining contents of his glass in the sink. "Some woman shows up and the next thing we know, you're leaving the ranch for Hollywood of all places. Have you lost your mind?"

So much for checking his anger. Dusty lashed out, mostly at his father.

"Maryanne isn't just some woman. And I've been writing seriously since college and attempting to sell for years. Six, to be exact."

"Good Lord," J.W. fumed. "I can't believe what I'm hearing."

"You may not like what I do, Dad, but you're not going to stop me."

"You're a member of this family, and you have an obligation to us."

"And you have an obligation to your children to be a good parent."

"I've always been a good parent."

"Really?" Dusty and his father exchanged hard stares. He was certain by the fury building in his father's eyes that he knew Dusty was thinking of Mark Hansen.

"That's enough." Dex stood, interceding. "Let's take a breather here before someone says something they'll regret."

"I agree." Dusty started to leave. He needed time to calm down before seeing Maryanne and her father for dinner.

"Wait," his mother said, rising from her chair. It was the first she'd spoken since Dusty had entered his father's office. "Please don't be mad. We're all just a little surprised. We had no idea you were writing, you didn't tell us."

"That's not true, Mom. I did." At her puzzled look, he clarified. "Back in college. I had some essays published in the campus newspaper. Only Dad didn't like it and insisted I stick to my business classes."

"I remember." She walked toward him. "They were good."

"I'm better now."

"Obviously. You sold a screenplay." She reached up and patted his cheek like when he was a boy. "I'm proud of you."

They were the words he'd been waiting his whole life to hear from one of his family.

"Thank you." He pulled his mother into a hug.

"This is bull crap." J.W. strode forward.

Dusty's mother halted him with a stern, "No, it's not."

"I won't put up—"

"You will." Her gaze encompassed everyone in the room. "For now, we're going to accept that Dusty is a writer. When we find out how much this affects his job at the ranch, if it even does, we'll decide what to do. As a family." She included Dusty in her statement.

The others didn't object, undoubtedly out of respect for her.

"I love you, Mom. And the family. But I have the right to live my life in a way that makes me happy."

"Of course, Dusty. We all do."

Her contemplative expression made Dusty think she was referring to someone else besides him.

"We're not through discussing this," his father said. He always made sure to get the last word in.

Dusty didn't care and let him.

Despite his mother's show of support, he didn't fool himself when it came to the rest of the Codys. They'd be much harder to win over. His father would come around only when hell froze over.

"I'll see you later," he said to his mother and started toward the door.

She came after him. "There is one thing. Can we read your screenplay?"

Dusty stopped. "I'm not sure that's a good idea."

"Why not? You said yourself, you've improved."

Dusty debated. Sooner or later his family was going to find out about the subject of his screenplay. He'd just been hoping for later. Much, much later.

"All right."

His mother's face relaxed.

She wouldn't be so happy once she read the screenplay. And his father's outrage would make today's rant seem like a minor tiff in comparison.

CHAPTER TWELVE

"CAN I DO IT?" Matt asked, his eyes alight.

"Sure, buddy." Dusty ruffled his son's hair.

They were in the main aisle of the south horse barn. Snowball had showed signs of limping after her ride with Maryanne three days ago. Dusty had initially thought the mare to be a little stiff, which, considering her advancing age, was reasonable. But several doses of bute, the equine equivalent of aspirin, hadn't lessened her limp. This morning, he'd decided to have a closer look.

"I'll hold her hoof," he told Matt and nudged the mare, who obediently lifted her right front foot. Bracing it against his knee, Dusty handed Matt the hoof pick. "Take the tip and dig around in there. Gently now, don't hurt her."

Matt followed instructions well. Being so short, he didn't have as far to bend over as Dusty to see. Track sat by Matt's side, a place he stayed whenever the boy was around. Dusty wasn't jealous of the dog's preference. Nothing made him happier than to see how easily and comfortably Matt fit into his life.

Okay, maybe one thing came close. How easily and comfortably Maryanne fit into his life, too. He'd missed her terribly while he was in Yellowstone and she was in L.A. and couldn't wait to see her today.

Snowball suddenly flinched.

"There," Dusty said. "Do you see it?"

Matt scrunched up his face. "No."

"She has a small abscess underneath the shoe." Dusty indicated an inflamed area about the size of a dime.

"How did she get that?"

"Probably from a small rock getting lodged in there."

"Can you fix it?"

"Sure can. I have to remove the shoe, though."

"Will it hurt her?"

"Naw. Hooves are like fingernails."

Matt watched in fascination as Dusty removed the metal nails holding the shoe in place and yanked it free. The new strain of flu going around might have caused problems at the preschool but for Dusty, it had been a gift. He'd been able to spend two mornings this week with his son while Josie worked, giving him and Matt a chance to build on the bond they'd already forged.

"I see you boys are hard at it."

"Mommy!"

Was it twelve-thirty already? Dusty glanced at his watch. The hours with his son had flown by.

"I'm helping Daddy with Snowball. She hurt her foot." Matt hadn't rushed over to greet his mother and instead, stayed beside Dusty.

"Poor Snowball. Is she going to be all right?"

"Daddy says so."

"That's good. You ready to go?"

"Do I have to?" Matt pleaded.

Dusty didn't offer to keep Matt longer, though nothing would have made him happier. He and Josie were still learning how to coparent, and they'd agreed not to engage in tugs-of-war in front of Matt.

"Come on, buddy." He put Snowball's foot down and straightened. "I'll walk with you to your mom's car."

"Can Track stay with me tonight?"

"If your mom doesn't mind."

While they were saying their goodbyes, the old pickup truck from Cowboy College pulled up and parked. Gil Devonshire had arrived for his roping lesson. Despite already knowing Maryanne would be with her father, Dusty experienced a surge of anticipation. They were having dinner again tonight at The Spotted Horse. This outing would definitely *not* be business.

His feelings must have shown on his face for Josie hitched her chin at the truck and said, "I like your new girlfriend."

Luckily, Matt was in the backseat with Track and disinterested in his parents' conversation.

"Me, too."

Josie opened the driver's side door. "It's completely none of my business but do you think she'll be sticking around?"

"No." He shook his head. "But I'll be going to L.A. Frequently, I hope."

"I heard about your screenplay. Congratulations."

Other than his mother, Josie was the only family member to wish him well.

"Unfortunately, you're mostly alone in your sentiment."

"Dex shares it."

Dusty shot her a look. "He wasn't exactly cheering me on the other day in Dad's study."

Josie laughed. "Okay, let me rephrase that. He isn't happy about you having another reason to go gallivanting off as he puts it. But he's impressed with your talent, and your drive to succeed."

"He's like Dad. He thinks I should stay here."

"Markton isn't the entire world. Some people just don't realize that."

"Spoken like someone who left."

Josie had also defied her parents' wishes and moved to the L.A. area soon after high school. If anyone understood his burning desire to make it on his own, she did.

"I did leave, but I also came back. Not that I'm saying you should, too, if you left. Only to keep the option open."

"My family may not want me to come back."

"That will never happen," she said emphatically.

Dusty was less certain. "It really doesn't matter. As long as Matt's here, I'll be around. You can count on that."

"I know." She climbed in behind the wheel. "And so does he."

Maryanne had been waiting by the truck for Dusty to finish talking to Josie.

"I'll be right there," he hollered.

She waved in return and headed to the practice arena. Her father had already made his way to the horse barn to saddle up.

Before meeting him for his lesson, Dusty needed to finish up with Snowball. While shutting the door on her stall, he decided to contact the vet just to be on the safe side.

In the barn office, he quickly placed a call to Doc Chester. Gil wouldn't take long saddling the horse he used at Cottonwood Ranch. After eight lessons, he was getting pretty familiar with the place. A few minutes warming up in the practice arena, and he'd be ready to start.

Maryanne was also getting familiar with the place. Dusty liked seeing her at the ranch. Her clothes and shoes were still completely inappropriate, but her style of dress was a part of her personality, and Dusty wouldn't want her any other way.

At first, he hardly noticed the distant echo of approaching footsteps. Ranch hands were always coming and going. Just as he was finishing his conversation with Doc Chester, the door to the office—already partially open—swung wide.

Dusty's father stepped inside, looking ready to bite off the closest head, that head being Dusty's.

"Thanks, Bill, I'll see you Monday," he said to the vet and hung up the phone. Since a confrontation seemed inevitable, he faced it head-on. "Hey, Dad."

They remained at odds with nothing being resolved during Dusty's trip to Yellowstone. He'd been tempted on numerous occasions in the past weeks to ask his father about his conversation with Abigail Hansen. Dex insisted Dusty refrain until after the National Finals in Las Vegas, contending they all needed to focus if they were going to win.

Dusty was of the opinion that his screenplay had already affected everyone's concentration, but he respected his twin's wishes and had remained mute on the subject of the Hansens.

"We need to talk," J.W. said.

"About what?" Dusty strived to keep his tone neutral.

"Your screenplay. I read it."

"You did?" He leaned back in the chair, hiding his surprise. Considering how much his father abhorred the idea of him writing, he'd figured his father wouldn't touch the screenplay with a ten-foot pole.

"Yes. And I forbid you to sign the contract from that production company."

Dusty couldn't help himself. He burst out laughing. "You're joking."

"Not in the slightest."

His laughter died. "You can't forbid me. Threaten me, sure, which you've already done and will continue to. But you don't control my life."

"I control this ranch and this family and you as long as you remain a part of both."

"I don't understand you, Dad. You've been after me for years to grow up. Well, I have. I took responsibility for my son and am a good father to him. I run my own business separate from Cody Enterprises. And the writing you criticized and told me was a colossal waste of time might actually earn me decent money and make me famous." Okay, the famous part was a stretch but he was on a roll.

"You always did like being the center of attention."

"And you've always approved of that."

"When it comes to rodeoing or your position in this community."

"You think that's what this is all about? Attention?"

"Yes. And you'll realize that eventually."

It hurt Dusty to know his father still thought of him as self-centered and superficial. And the hurt, as it often did with him, morphed into anger. "News flash, Dad. I'm going to make something of myself. Something significant. That has meaning to a lot of people. Though I know you don't believe anything's more important than this ranch."

"Fine." To his surprise, his father didn't explode. "I won't forbid you to sign the contract. But I'm asking you to reconsider."

"*Ask?* That word's not in your vocabulary."

"It is now."

This was a different tactic and one Dusty didn't trust.

"Consider the harm you and your screenplay can do to us, your mother especially, if it's ever made into a movie."

Dusty laughed again, only there was no humor in it. "How's that? You'll be embarrassed because one of your children didn't follow in your footsteps?"

"The whole Hollywood industry is trashy," his father said with disgust.

"And you're above trashiness?"

"We're not talking about me."

"Maybe we should be."

J.W.'s cheeks flushed a dark red but when he spoke, his voice was level. "The characters in your screenplay resemble our family too much."

"The resemblance is minute. The story's pure fiction."

"If it's made into a movie, we'll all be humiliated." It was as if J.W. hadn't heard Dusty.

"Stupid me. And here I thought you might be proud of me."

"Anyone who sees the movie will think it's based on fact and that I have an illegitimate son."

Dusty pushed to his feet. "Do you?"

"That's enough."

"You wouldn't be the first. Not in this town. Not in this family, either." Dusty's words gave him pause. Why hadn't he seen the similarities before? And was it those similarities that made him so intolerant of his father? "I'm no saint myself. Of all of us, I'm the one who'd understand you and what happened the most."

For a moment, he thought he might have cracked open his father's rock hard exterior, but so such luck. The fury in his eyes blazed anew.

"I won't have you destroying people's lives with your accusations."

"It's only an accusation if it's untrue."

"Don't you care about your mother and what this is doing to her?"

"I do care. And I hate seeing her hurt." Some of the fight drained from Dusty. "But I didn't create this situation. You did when you had an affair with Abigail Hansen, and that had to have hurt Mom far worse than my screenplay ever will."

"Don't you ever mention that woman's name again," J.W. said through clenched teeth.

"Why were you talking to her outside the feed store last week?"

"I don't remember."

"It seemed pretty heated."

"I said I don't remember."

"You're lying." Dusty couldn't stay in the same room with his father another minute. He was sick of the secrets, sick of the covering up, sick of the two sets of rules his father lived by, one for him and one for everyone else. "I need to go. Gil's waiting for me."

J.W. remained rooted in front of the office door. "Promise me you'll reconsider selling your screenplay."

"I already told the producer yes."

"I'll call our attorneys and get an injunction."

"Do that, Dad. And everyone's going to realize, just

like me, that you wouldn't give a tinker's damn about my screenplay unless Mark Hansen really is your son."

Dusty's remark struck a visible blow, and his father stumbled backward out the door. He pushed past J.W.—only to come face-to-face with Jesse waiting in the barn aisle.

"What the hell are you doing?" his brother demanded.

"What somebody should have done a long time ago."

"Dad's right. You'll destroy this family."

"Me? What about him? He cheated on Mom. And for all we know Mark Hansen is our brother."

Dusty didn't see Jesse's right hook coming until it was too late but he sure as heck felt it…and the ground when he hit it going a hundred miles an hour.

MARYANNE RAISED HER hand to knock on Dusty's apartment door and hesitated. He'd sounded a little strange when he called her earlier to cancel her father's roping lesson at the last minute and change the location for their date. She'd assumed—actually, counted on—them returning to his place after dinner. The new arrangements shouldn't bother her. For all she knew, he could have a delightful surprise in store for her.

But then, there had been that odd quality in his voice.

Knocking firmly, she waited for him to answer. When he did, her mouth dropped open.

"What happened to you?"

"A slight difference of opinion with Jesse."

"What is it with you Codys and your disagreements?"

"Short tempers run rampant in our gene pool."

She barely had time to examine his swollen eye and

bruised cheek when he pulled her inside and into his arms. Kicking the door shut, he brought his mouth down on hers in a ravenous kiss.

"Shouldn't we talk first?" she asked when they paused to catch their breaths.

"Later."

He pulled at her jacket, slipping it off her shoulders and letting it fall to the floor. Her blouse was next. Then his hands were on her naked flesh, fondling and caressing.

"You're not wearing a bra." A throaty growl escaped his lips.

Her wardrobe choice hadn't been intentional. Now, however, she was glad for it. Like the day of their first kiss, Dusty was being driven by strong emotions and a need to vent them. She could help him. She *wanted* to help him.

Responding to his need with one of her own, she arched into him.

"You're amazing," he said and kissed each breast until she forgot about everything except the maelstrom of feelings he let loose in her.

The rest of their clothes evaporated in a blur, and they dropped to the thick rug. Dusty produced a condom—where had that come from?—and covered himself. Then, without waiting, he pushed inside her.

She wrapped her arms around him and entwined her legs with his. His thrusts increased, becoming faster and harder. Her hands traveled down the slope of his taut back to his buttocks, urging him on. When she lifted her hips to meet his, he lost control.

The storm raging inside him eventually abated, and he raised his head to gaze at her. Not that her heart had any real barriers anymore, but the tenderness and affection in his eyes stole away any last vestiges of them.

He kissed the tip of her nose. "Come on."

"Where to?" She snuggled closer, not ready to leave his embrace.

"The bathroom."

Her eyes widened. "Seriously?"

"I had this idea." Pushing off her, he rose. Night had fallen during their lovemaking, surrounding them in dark shadows. In the dim light, Dusty looked like a silver warrior. "Only we didn't quite make it that far."

She clasped his extended hand. "I'm not sure I'm ready for whatever you have planned."

As it turned out, she was more than ready.

Dusty had filled the spacious tub with warm water, on top of which floated a blanket of frothy bubbles. Lighted votive candles sat on the counter and along the rim of the tub. Also on the counter was a crystal vase containing a dozen red roses and an ice bucket with a bottle of chilled champagne.

"Very nice," she cooed.

While she stepped into the tub, he opened the champagne and poured two glasses. "Here."

She took the glasses and watched in avid anticipation as he joined her in the tub, sitting across from her with his back to the faucet.

"Is the water hot enough?"

"Not bad."

He flipped on the spigot and in a matter of seconds, steam filled the bathroom.

"To family," Maryanne said, and lifted her glass.

Dusty gave her a wry look but returned her toast.

Before she could ask about his fight with his brother, he
shut off the spigot and plucked her glass from her hands.

"Your turn."

"For what?"

"To even things out." Setting their glasses down, he
moved toward her, his hand sliding up her thigh. "Much
as I enjoyed earlier, it was a little one-sided."

"I didn't mind."

"But I do."

Maryanne slid farther beneath the bubbles as his
fingers began their intimate exploration. She could tell
from the determined set of his jaw he intended to pay
back the pleasure she'd given him measure for measure.

Who was she to argue?

"ARE YOU READY to tell me about this?" Maryanne gently
traced the outline of the angry bruise discoloring the
left side of Dusty's face.

He winced slightly, more, she thought, from her
question than pain.

"I told you, my brother and I got into a fight."

"One that involved fists?"

"Boys will be boys."

"Was it about your screenplay?"

"Indirectly."

"You don't have to tell me if you don't want to."

They were still in the tub, still facing each other,
their legs straddling each other's hips. Enough time had
passed that the water had cooled again and the champagne bottle was empty. The candles, however, continued to flicker brightly.

Maryanne thought they should probably get out

before they turned into prunes but was loath to leave Dusty and the small private sanctuary they'd created.

What would it be like when the time came for her to leave Wyoming?

She pushed the question from her mind. Just because her past temporary separations had ended badly was no reason to believe this one would, too.

"I want to tell you what happened," he said, rubbing his foot along her thigh. The bubbles had made her skin slick and slippery. "I'm just afraid it'll sound stupid."

"Two grown men—brothers at that—slugging it out. How is that going to sound stupid?"

"Your sarcasm isn't appreciated," he said jokingly, then sobered. "My father doesn't want me to sign the contract for my screenplay option."

"What!"

"He's afraid that if it's made into a movie, people will jump to the conclusion that the storyline is true."

"Is it? Is Mark Hansen your brother?"

"I still don't know for sure. Other than Dex, nobody in my family is willing to speak Mark Hansen's name much less consider he's related to us. Jesse especially."

"So he punched you?"

"He was mad, and I was handy."

"Your family being tight-lipped about Mark only fuels the rumors." Maryanne twirled a finger in the tepid water. "Are you going to do what you father asks? Not sign the contract?"

"Hell, yes, I'm going to sign the contract."

"I'm glad. You've come too far to give up."

He traced his fingertips along her cheek much like she had his. "Thank you."

"For what?"

"Believing in me. Not many people have."

"Your family will now."

"If they don't disown me."

"You aren't serious, are you?"

His laugh reassured her. "They won't disown me. Not right away. But Thanksgiving and Christmas are probably going to be a little awkward this year."

Maryanne craned her neck to look out the bathroom door. "I just realized, where's Track?"

"Matt's watching him tonight."

"I bet they're both enjoying that."

"And picking Track up tomorrow is a good excuse for me to see Matt again."

"Do you need an excuse?"

"We're still ironing out the wrinkles in our visitation arrangement. It'll be different when I have a house of my own."

"How long until you start construction?"

"I have to hire an architect first."

Maryanne's heart sank at the reminder that Dusty would always make his permanent home in Wyoming. She'd allowed herself to hope he might spend weeks, maybe even months, on end in California.

"Do you think Josie will let me take Matt with me on one of my trips?"

She recalled Josie's refusal to let Matt fly with the family to the rodeo in Albuquerque. "I don't know her well but my gut instinct is no. Not until he's older."

"You're probably right." He picked up Maryanne's hand and brought it to his lips. "I'll just have to depend on you to keep me busy. And Shirley Lowery."

"The agent Herb referred you to?" Her disappointment subsided.

"I signed with her this morning. It's funny how people who wouldn't give me the time of day before I had a contract are now happy to talk to me."

"That's the way it goes in Hollywood." The temperature in the tub had finally gotten too cold for Maryanne to tolerate. Bracing her arms on the sides, she stood, water sliding off her, and grabbed a towel from the rack. "Get used to it."

His eyes traveled the length of her as she dried herself. "I can get used to this, too."

As could she. Maybe *too* used to it.

He stood up quickly, and water sloshed onto the sides of the tub. Stepping out of the tub, he yanked her unceremoniously into his arms, soaking the skin she'd so carefully blotted dry.

"Are you sure? Because I plan on coming to L.A. a lot."

There was more to his question than seeking simple assurance. He was letting her know he was willing to put forth the effort required to make a long-distance relationship work.

It was all she could ask of him.

It was also enough.

"I'm sure."

He grinned. "You hungry?"

In their frantic rush to be together, they'd forgotten all about dinner. "Yes, but I don't want to get dressed and go out."

"I have stuff here we can eat."

"Are you offering to cook?"

"I am. Don't know how organic or natural the food will be."

"Unless you burn everything, I'll suffer through it."

"I'll have you know I'm pretty good with a skillet and spatula."

"You don't say?"

As Maryanne slipped on the terry cloth robe he'd left for her, contentment stole over her. This time would be different. She was older and wiser and going into the relationship with her eyes wide-open. More important, she was less emotionally invested.

Or was she?

As she watched Dusty prepare a simple dinner wearing just a towel, she wasn't so sure.

CHAPTER THIRTEEN

"WHAT'S A JACKPOT?" Maryanne asked her father over lunch in the public dining hall. Their cabin had a kitchen but they often ate meals with the other guests.

"It's a roping competition," he answered her around a spoonful of turkey soup.

Maryanne was enjoying the same soup, only hers was accompanied by a small salad and not a thick ham sandwich topped off with a generous slice of apple pie. Of course, if she worked as physically hard as her father did, she'd be consuming mass quantities of food, too.

"Are you ready for a competition? You've only been roping three-and-a-half weeks." To date, her father had managed to avoid serious injuries, if she didn't count the various sprains, bumps, bruises and contusions he'd sustained.

"Sure I'm ready."

"But you'll be going up against people a lot better than you." The two young women Maryanne frequently watched practice came to mind.

"Not really. You only compete against people who are ranked the same as you so it's fair. I'm a one now."

"That's good! You've gone up a level."

"A one is mediocre." He chuckled robustly. "I'd wanted to be a two before I left."

"You have until Wednesday." As did she. Three more days to be with Dusty.

But it would only be another week or two until he flew to L.A. and she'd see him again. They'd talked at length the previous night, discussing his trip, where they'd go and what they'd do. She wanted most to show him her office and the community of Westwind where she hoped to buy a condo.

"Dusty'll be competing today, too," her father said.

"Oh?" Maryanne pursed her lips.

He hadn't mentioned anything about the jackpot last night. Then again, their conversation had centered on each other and nothing else. When they were talking, that was, and not engaged in other activities of a somewhat decadent nature.

She smiled at the memory.

"What are you thinking about, Cookie?" Her father had finished his soup and sandwich and was starting on his pie.

"Leaving on Wednesday. I can't believe our month here is almost over."

"I'm really glad you came with me. I know it wasn't always fun for you or easy."

"Are you kidding? I've had a great time."

"Because of Dusty?"

She shrugged. "He helped pass the time."

"More than helped, I'd say."

She hadn't discussed her and Dusty's relationship with her father, though she hadn't hidden it from him, either. Merely omitted a few of the more personal and intimate details.

"He's a fine man. I'm glad the two of you found each other." The remainder of her father's pie disappeared in a last forkful. "Are you going to see him when he comes to L.A.?"

"I am."

"I had no idea he was a writer."

"I'm sorry I didn't tell you, Dad. He asked me to keep it confidential."

"I understand. You had an agreement." He patted his belly. "And I got the next World tie-down roping champion to give me lessons."

"If he wins."

"He'll win."

Maryanne didn't doubt it, either.

She'd told her father about Dusty's screenplay option and upcoming meeting with Sundown Pictures only after Dusty gave his permission. Word had evidently spread quickly throughout the small community. From what Maryanne had observed, people's reactions varied. Most didn't believe it. Writing was a serious endeavor that required dedication. Dusty was too irresponsible.

It just went to prove how undeserving his reputation was.

"What are you doing after the jackpot?" her father asked.

"Dusty and I are having dinner." They were going to The Spotted Horse Saloon to make up for missing last night. "Want to come with us?"

"You don't want your old man tagging along. I'd only be in the way."

"You aren't ever in the way, and I know Dusty would love having you along. He considers you his friend."

"We'll see. I could be busy."

There was an elusive, almost mysterious, quality to his demeanor. Was he implying he had a date? He hadn't even remotely considered going out with a woman since her mother's death. But then, it had been three years, and he seemed so much more like his old self these days.

Maryanne might have pressed for more information but he jumped up from his seat and said, "I'd better head out. The jackpot starts in less than an hour. You coming?"

She drained the last of her iced tea and pushed her plate away. "I wouldn't miss it for the world."

Forty-five minutes later, Maryanne was climbing the small row of bleachers alongside the main arena at Cowboy College. The day was pleasant though nippy, making her glad she'd worn her warm jacket. By her estimation every guest in residence was there, along with their family and friends, making it difficult to find a good seat. Trucks and horse trailers crowded the dirt parking lot to the south of the arena with barely any walking room between them. Maryanne had heard the event was open to anyone, not just the students, and the number of unfamiliar faces confirmed that.

"Hi," she said and waved at Dusty's parents and sister sitting several rows over.

Elly returned Maryanne's greeting with a great deal of friendliness, prompting her to wonder how much Dusty's sister knew about her and Dusty. However much or little she knew, she apparently approved. Conversely, his parents were harder to read, and his mother's responding wave lacked enthusiasm.

Maryanne recalled his father's demand that Dusty not sign the contract. Was J.W. aware of her part in mentoring Dusty, and did he blame her for leading his son astray? She suffered mixed feelings of regret and anger. It had never been her intention to contribute to his problems with his family.

As if on cue, the woman next to Maryanne pointed. "Look, here come them Cody boys."

Maryanne had become acquainted with her neighbor during yesterday's practice. The woman and her husband were recent arrivals at Cowboy College, and he appeared to be a skilled roper.

Dusty and Dex rode over to the open area behind the boxes and chutes. They looked tall and handsome astride their horses, though in Maryanne's eyes, Dusty was just a little bit handsomer. Walker and Jesse accompanied them on foot. They didn't rope but as Maryanne had learned, when it came to any rodeo event large or small, the "Cody boys" as her new friend had called them traveled in packs.

It was also why the rest of Dusty's family was there despite his father's anger at him.

The woman bumped shoulders with Maryanne. "If I weren't plumb crazy about my Ernie, I'd take a turn at them. The single ones, that is. What about you?"

At that moment, Dusty spied her across the arena and waved, his face splitting in a wide grin.

"I guess you already did," the woman said with a bawdy laugh.

Maryanne and the woman chatted amiably until the first round of competition started. She easily followed the action, cheering along with the rest of the spectators when someone did well and clapping encouragingly when someone didn't. It pleased her to realize how much knowledge she'd picked up in the past month and gave her hope that while she may not live in Dusty's world, she could at least exist comfortably on the fringes.

"Give that feller a hand," the crackling voice on the one-speaker sound system announced when the competitor's rope missed the calf entirely, "'cuz that's all the money he's gonna take home today."

"How much do the winners get?" Maryanne asked her neighbor during a break.

"It depends on how many people are competing and what the entry fee is. The total money collected is split between the winners. That's why they call it a jackpot."

"I see."

Her father's group was next. She kept her eyes glued to the box, waiting for him to take his turn. It wasn't always easy to see with so many men standing on the fence. She hadn't quite figured out why they did that, assuming they liked to be in the thick of things. Her wariness of horses had diminished since her ride with Dusty, but she was nowhere near ready to stand next to one like those men. Especially roping horses and rodeo stock, which were big and full of unpredictable energy.

Finally, the announcer called her father's name. He was the last to go in his class.

"No one else has done very well," Maryanne's neighbor said. "He could win."

"I hope he does." She leaned forward in her seat. "Then he can retire a champion."

"He's quitting?"

"I...ah...think he is." She'd taken it for granted he would. That roping was a lark, one he'd abandon once he'd realized his ambition.

"That's too bad. He seems to love it, and he's getting really good."

He did love it.

Did they have roping facilities in the L.A. area? She made a mental note to look online later. Then again, he could always come back to Wyoming. And she could come, too—to watch her father rope and see Dusty.

The door to the chute flew open releasing the calf, and her father, riding the horse from Cottonwood Ranch, broke from the box. It was over quickly. Very quickly. As her father knelt in front of the calf and threw his hands up in the air to signal he was done, the announcer called his unofficial time. Eleven-point-two seconds. Not bad for anyone, great for someone ranked a one. As he walked out of his arena, the announcer confirmed the time as official and verified by the judge. Applause broke out. Her father had won his class.

Maryanne was thrilled.

"Excuse me," she said to her neighbor and left the bleachers to find her father and congratulate him. She located him behind the box talking with Adele, their heads bent in an obviously serious conversation. One they immediately ended the moment they spotted her.

"Hi, Cookie! I won."

Her father's exuberant smile and booming laugh didn't quite dispel Maryanne's concern that something was going on. Something her father didn't want her to know about.

"You ready?" Dex asked.

"Yeah." Dusty tugged on a loose glove and, for the fourth time in the past two minutes, checked his rope, rewinding it until it fit exactly right in his hand.

Uno pawed the ground, eager to start. This had been a good season for them so far, and Dusty was confident they could—and would—win the National Finals Rodeo for tie-down roping and perhaps team roping. Not that he needed another belt buckle to add to his collection. But he wanted this one. If only to prove his worth to his family. They didn't appreciate the effort or dedication required to write and sell a screenplay but they did when it came to rodeoing.

Winning would also go a long way in mending his relationship with his father.

For someone who was always bucking J.W.'s authority, Dusty sure seemed anxious to win his approval. The irony didn't escape him.

Cottonwood Ranch was his home, and he loved living there. And while he enjoyed managing the horses, it wasn't his passion. Neither was working in films or providing trained horses, though both were fun and something he'd like to continue.

Writing was what drove him, what fueled his need to succeed, what filled him with a sense of satisfaction and accomplishment. When he thought about what he wanted to do for the rest of his life, what he'd cut off his right arm for rather than give up, it was writing.

He was also starting to have those same feelings for Maryanne, that his days wouldn't be complete without waking up beside her.

Shading his eyes, he searched the bleachers and spotted her sitting about midsection. She was easy to pick out, her clothes were better suited for walking down a city street than perched on some rickety wooden bleachers. He didn't care what she wore. Seeing her, knowing she was there for him, infused him with a confidence that their future, while not guaranteed, was promising. Funny, he never dreamed that first day he saw her running barefoot into this same arena that she'd turn out to be the one woman he'd connect with more than any other.

Could he finally be falling in love after years of diligently avoiding it?

Yes. She was exactly what he needed and everything he wanted. He only hoped he didn't disappoint her. Face it, he had a lousy track record. She'd be taking a big chance on him. Not to mention making room in her heart for his son because Dusty and Matt were a package deal.

Fatherhood had come as a surprise to him but once he embraced it, he wouldn't trade it for anything. Not even, he realized, his writing.

When had that happened?

He didn't need to scan the bleachers to find Matt. His son sat with the rest of Dusty's family. This might only be a local jackpot, just another practice session for him and Dex, but his parents were sitting there watching as if this were indeed the Finals in Vegas.

Like they sat in the stands at every competition.

And regardless of their current differences, Dusty wanted them there.

His throat abruptly tightened. Everything to make his life complete was here today, within his reach. Maryanne. His son. His family. His writing career.

Nothing stopped him from having it all.

And the fight with his father? They'd get past that, too. Somehow. Eventually.

"Pay attention," Dex warned.

"I'm not the one sitting on a train wreck waiting to happen," Dusty shot back.

His brother's horse had started acting up again

shortly after they'd arrived—snorting, crow-hopping and nervously bobbing his head. Dex had managed to bring the animal under control each time but the strain was beginning to wear on him.

"We don't have to do this if you don't want," Dusty suggested.

"Hell, yes, we're doing it." Dex pulled back on the reins, the muscles in his neck standing out.

"Dex, Dusty, on deck," one of the wranglers hollered at them.

They moved closer to the box. Uno, all business now, stopped pawing the ground. Dusty checked his rope for the fifth time. Local jackpot or professional rodeo, competing was encoded into his DNA. Already his nerves were on fire, lit by the adrenaline pumping through his veins.

The team ahead of them went. Most of the competitors today were tie-down ropers. A few, like Dusty and Dex, were team ropers. The two men in the ring were the team to beat, and they finished with a very respectable time. Dusty was already calculating how he and Dex could better that time.

Uno, in his eagerness to go, all but charged into the box, nearly running over a wrangler. The gelding had his eyes glued to the calf. His uncanny ability to sense which direction the calf would bolt had made him an exceptional roping horse.

Dex's horse initially balked but eventually settled into the box beside Dusty and Uno. Dusty glanced one last time over his shoulder at his brother who nodded. Blocking out everyone and everything, he narrowed his world to just his horse, the calf and the rope coiled in his hand.

A curt nod to the man on the ground, the chute door flew open, and the calf leaped out, hitting the ground at a dead run. Uno took off after the calf at a full gallop, turning on a dime as it darted sharply to the right. Dusty's arm was in the air and the rope circling his head before they'd traveled three feet. He could sense Dex right behind him, and for the next several seconds, magic happened.

Dusty's rope sailed out in front of him and landed right where it should, squarely on the calf's horns. Only Dex's rope didn't snake out and circle the calf's rear feet as it should have. Instead, the calf loped off with only Dusty's rope trailing behind him. He reined Uno to a stop and turned around.

What he saw wasn't good.

Dex's horse had acted up again, and his attempts to calm the animal were failing. Dropping his rope, he used both hands to jerk back on the reins. Several wranglers hopped off the fence and approached cautiously. Dusty also moved in closer, thinking a familiar horse might settle the agitated gelding. He thought wrong, unfortunately, and the horse reared on its hind legs.

Dusty didn't immediately panic. His brother could sit a riled horse better than anyone. But then Dex suddenly lost his balance and fell backward over the saddle onto the ground. Dusty jumped down from Uno and ran toward his brother, glad to see Dex roll clear of danger. The riderless horse ran off, bucking his way to the end of the arena where another pair of wranglers caught him. The crowd cheered when Dex staggered to his feet, favoring one leg.

"You okay?" Dusty asked when his brother's face twisted in a severe grimace.

"Yeah." Dex glanced at his horse, now standing quietly for the wrangler holding him. "Son of a bitch." He attempted a step…and went down like he'd been slammed from behind.

The audience's collective gasp drowned out his cry of pain.

CHAPTER FOURTEEN

FOR THE FIRST time in his life, Dusty spent the entire night in a hospital waiting room. The Codys had taken over the area outside the ICU, huddling together as if the sheer force of their prayers would improve Dex's condition.

He'd pulled through his 3 a.m. surgery with no complications and, according to the doctor, was stable. Orders were already in place to move him to a regular room the moment one became available. Josie had been allowed to visit Dex after he was out of recovery but no one else.

The only Cody to leave the hospital and go home was Matt. He'd conked out about ten the previous night. Josie's parents had picked him up and taken him to their house. He was also, according to his grandparents' report, the only Cody to get more than a few snatches of sleep here and there.

As morning dawned, they'd gone in pairs and trios to the hospital cafeteria for a bite to eat. With Dex doing well, there was no reason they couldn't leave and return later but none of them were willing to until they'd seen him and assured themselves he was all right.

Finally, at around seven-thirty, Dex's doctor exited the ICU after checking on him. Everyone sprang from their chairs in unison.

Josie reached the doctor first. "How is he?"

"Good." He addressed the entire group, all eight of them. "You can visit him, two at a time and only for a few minutes. He needs his rest."

"What's his prognosis?" J.W. asked the question on all of their minds.

"His knee is badly damaged and will require at least one additional surgery. Possibly two. We won't know for sure until we run more tests and see how he progresses." He gave a detailed description of Dex's injury which included a dislocated kneecap, ruptured tendons and torn ligaments. "If not treated correctly, he could suffer permanent damage."

Josie bit back a soft sob.

Dusty's stomach clenched as if he'd been kicked in the gut. They'd been riding their whole lives from the time they could walk, competing in rodeos across the country since they were kids and taking ridiculous risks without so much as blinking an eye. That Dex should injure himself during a local jackpot in what appeared to be a minor fall boggled Dusty's mind.

The doctor continued laying out Dex's lengthy and involved rehabilitation program. He was considered to be the best orthopedic surgeon in the state and had been called in by J.W. the previous night to take over Dex's case. When the doctor finished, the family voiced their commitment to ensuring Dex made a full recovery. After shaking J.W.'s hand and promising to speak to them again the following day, the doctor left.

Josie and Dusty's mother couldn't wait any longer and went first to visit Dex. The rest of them resumed waiting.

"One month bed rest." Jesse ran his fingers through his spiky blond hair. "Then another surgery."

"And at least three weeks on crutches after that," Walker added.

"Damn. What rotten timing." Dusty leaned the back of his head against the wall, the long night catching up with him.

"There's another Nationals next year."

"I was talking about him and Josie just getting married."

"Ah." Jesse stuck his hand in the left side of his shirt, lifting the material several times to simulate a beating heart. "I forgot you're the writer in the family and a romantic."

Unlike their father, Dusty's oldest brother didn't hold a grudge. He'd apologized the day after their fight for slugging Dusty, who'd assured him retribution was coming at some unspecified future date.

"Maybe he's just in love." Walker wore the look of a besotted newlywed, which he was.

Dusty picked up a magazine off the nearby table and threw it at him. Walker ducked, and the magazine missed him by a mile.

Elly put down her BlackBerry. "Stop it, you guys," she said in a fair imitation of their mother.

Dusty paid her no heed and reached for a second magazine.

"Enough," J.W. growled. He turned to Dusty. "Have you contacted that production company yet and told them you're refusing their offer?"

The grin he'd been wearing died. "Let's not talk about this now."

"Why not? It's as good a time as any."

Dusty frowned. "I told you, I'm taking the offer."

"What's going on?" Jesse asked.

"Nothing."

"Your brother's laid up and will be for a couple of months." J.W. stood.

So did Dusty. "Which has nothing to do with my screenplay."

A nurse from the nearby station glowered at them.

Walker stepped in. "Maybe we should discuss this at home."

J.W. didn't appear to hear him. "You have to take over for Dex and manage the horses while he's laid up," he told Dusty.

"I can do that."

"Not if you're gone two out of every four weeks."

"We have more than enough experienced hands to pick up the slack."

"They're not family. It's not their duty."

"But it's their job, and they're paid well to do it."

"It's also *your* job. One you don't take seriously."

Dusty thought of Maryanne and the plans they'd made. "I'm signing the contract and going to L.A. The ranch can survive without me for a week."

"One week, sure," Jesse said. "But then you'll have another film job or another meeting with the production company."

"Even one day is too long," J.W. cut in. "We have a crisis on our hands."

The crisis, in Dusty's opinion, was more Dex's and less the rest of theirs. His brother was the one going to be laid up, the one facing a long recovery, extensive physical therapy and considerable pain. The one forced to put his life on hold after just getting married.

Maybe his father had a point. Dex didn't need to be worrying about his job on top of everything else.

"J.W." Dusty's mom entered the waiting area along with Josie. "Don't pressure Dusty into doing something he doesn't want to."

"It's not that I don't want to, Mom." He rubbed the back of his neck, his muscles aching. "I accepted the offer, and I won't back out."

"Because it would damage your career," J.W. scoffed.

"Because a Cody honors their word. You taught me that."

"I also taught you to put family first."

It was on the tip of Dusty's tongue to ask if his father had put family first when he cheated on his wife.

"Will finalizing your contract take an entire week? Heck, we do most of our contracts by email these days."

Dusty sent Jesse a look that warned him to mind his own business.

He immediately defended himself. "I'm just trying to come up with a compromise."

"I also have a meeting with my agent."

"How much of that week will you be spending with Maryanne?"

Dusty didn't answer.

"Let me rephrase the question," Jesse said. "Is she the reason you refuse to take over for Dex?"

"No, and I'm not refusing."

"Just not willing to work any harder or more hours than you already do."

Their argument sounded like all the other ones they'd had since Dusty could remember. They wanted him to toe the line, and he resisted. The older boys behaved, he acted up. Yes, Dex was hurt, but he'd recover in a few months. And even if he couldn't compete in roping again—which Dusty doubted given his brother's iron will—it wouldn't be the end of the world despite what the rest of the family thought.

Dusty's mother dropped wearily into one of the waiting room chairs. "Can we please talk about this later?"

"Sure thing, Mom. Sorry." Jesse sat beside her.

Hadn't Dusty suggested as much? Only no one had listened to him.

"Come with me." J.W. hitched his chin at Dusty.

"Where?"

"To visit your brother."

"Go on," his mother encouraged.

"He asked for you," Josie added.

Dusty had thought he was prepared for the sight of his twin lying prone in a hospital bed. The reality of seeing Dex surrounded by beeping monitors, his bandaged leg the size of an elephant's, his complexion pasty and eyes dull, hit Dusty hard.

"Hey, bro. How you feeling?" Emotion thickened his voice.

Dex groaned and shifted. "I think the surgery hurt worse than the fall."

Dusty didn't mention the doctor's earlier report that there would be another one. "All this to get out of competing at Nationals? I'm thinking you went a little overboard."

Dex gave a weak chuckle. "You'll just have to win for me. Have Len take my place."

"I'm not replacing you." Dusty put a hand on Dex's shoulder.

J.W. moved closer to the bed. Dusty couldn't remember ever seeing his father so tired or so shaken. He'd aged five years during the course of the night and another five since walking into the ICU. Dusty thought of Matt and knew he'd be a mirror image of his dad in the same circumstance. Nothing could be worse than seeing your child injured.

Except losing them.

All at once, Dusty understood why his father pushed him to stay in Wyoming and give up his writing and film work. He loved his children beyond life itself and wanted them near him always. Dusty didn't necessarily agree. Not to mention J.W.'s methods left a lot to be desired. But he meant well.

Perhaps Dusty had been wrong about Mark Hansen. If he was a Cody by birth, surely J.W. would love him as fiercely as he did all his children.

"How you doing, son?"

"Been better." Dex clasped his father's hand.

"I don't want you to worry about anything, you hear me? Just concentrate on getting well."

Dex's gaze went to Dusty. "If Josie needs anything, will you see that she gets it?"

"No problem."

"It could be. A problem, that is."

"Dad," Dusty warned.

"What's wrong?"

"Nothing, Dex. Forget it."

"Your brother won't be around to help Josie or take over management of the horses because he's going to L.A."

Drawing Dex into their battle of wills while he lay in a hospital bed was low even for Dusty's father, and he lost much of the ground he'd gained with Dusty in the past few minutes.

"When are you leaving?" Dex reached for the cup of ice water on his bedside stand and took a sip through the straw.

"A week from Wednesday."

"Good."

"Good?" J.W. gaped at Dex.

"You're signing your contract, right?" Dex asked Dusty.

"Yes."

"Congratulations."

"Thanks." Dusty figured Josie must be having some influence on his brother. That, or the pain meds the doctor had prescribed were doing the talking.

"Dusty *won't* leave," J.W. stated. Make that insisted. "Not while you're laid up."

"It's only for a week."

"His place is here with the family."

"It's okay, Dad." Dex's eyelids drooped. "We'll get along without him."

It felt strange to hear the same words Dusty had been saying coming from someone else.

"I want him to stay."

Dusty couldn't remember ever hearing that much emotion in his father's voice.

"We need him," his father continued. "Big Ben and Len can manage the horses but they can't be a father to Matt, a brother to you and a son to me and your mother."

Dusty's throat tightened. Not once had his father said he needed Dusty or indicated in any way that he made a significant contribution to the family.

Until today, Dusty hadn't realized how desperately he'd wanted to hear that from his father.

"Gee, Dad." Dex yawned. "When did you get so sentimental?"

"Maybe I've always been," he said gruffly.

"Let's go, Dad." Dusty placed a hand on his father's shoulder. "Dex needs to rest."

On the other side of the ICU door, J.W. asked, "What are you going to do?"

"I'm not sure now." Dusty was still grappling with what had transpired. He needed time alone to wrap his brain around it.

"I didn't say what I did in there just to make you stay."

Dusty nodded.

"I'm proud of you, Dusty. You're your own man. I may not always agree with you, hell, I'll probably seldom agree with you, but I respect you."

The surprises just kept coming and coming.

"That means a lot to me, Dad."

In the waiting area, Dusty and his father rejoined the family and gave their report on Dex. Since he was sleeping, they all decided to go home for a while, nap and shower. Then those who wanted to would return in the afternoon or evening when Dex was hopefully more alert and been moved to a regular room.

Dusty had ridden to the hospital with Jesse and Elly. Josie, who'd accompanied Dex in the ambulance, joined them on the drive home, sitting in the back with Elly.

"Dex is going to require a lot of care." Josie leaned her head back and sighed heavily. "I have to find a good babysitter for Matt or make some other daycare arrangements. I can't keep up with a four-year-old and be driving Dex fifty miles round-trip every weekday to doctors' appointments and physical therapy."

"We'll all help," Elly assured her.

Dusty turned around from where he sat in the front passenger seat. "Don't worry. I'll take care of Matt."

"I don't want to impose. You have your work and trips to California coming up."

"I'll do it. I want to. Jesse's right." Dusty cast his brother a look. "I don't need to fly to L.A. I can handle the contract negotiations and signing by phone and email."

"You sure?" Josie's features, weary from stress, brightened. "Matt would love that. And I trust you."

Four small words, but they meant the world to Dusty. He knew in that moment nothing would stop him.

"Way to go, bro." Jesse glanced away from the road to smile at Dusty.

"What about Maryanne?" Elly asked.

"She'll understand."

Jesse harrumphed and his eyebrows shot up.

Dusty pushed all doubts aside. Maryanne had supported him one hundred percent since they'd met. She would about this, too.

"Do you mind dropping me off at Adele's?" he asked as they neared the turnoff to Cowboy College.

"Aren't you tired?" Elly asked.

"I'm beat. But I want to talk to Maryanne." He didn't add how much he wanted to see her. Corny as it sounded, she was his safe harbor in a storm.

Jesse drove straight to the guest cabins. "Which one?"

"There." Dusty pointed to Maryanne's.

She answered his knock right away and after giving him a hug, ushered him inside.

"How's Dex?"

"Not bad, considering."

"You look awful. Why didn't you go home?"

Maryanne led him to the tiny kitchen, sat him at the table, poured him some coffee and proceeded to fuss over him. It was nice. Very nice. Which made having to tell her he wouldn't be coming to L.A. all the more difficult.

"THE DOCTOR SAYS he's going to require at least one more surgery."

"Oh, wow." Maryanne listened intently to Dusty while stirring her coffee. "I didn't think he fell that bad."

"Apparently it was the way he landed."

"How long until he can walk again?"

"Two, maybe three months." He summarized his brother's daunting rehabilitation plan.

"Poor Josie."

"She's already given notice at her job so she can take care of him full-time."

"Is there anything I can do?"

Maryanne and her father were leaving the day after tomorrow. Her boss had been calling practically hourly, giving her extensive and detailed lists. Still, if Dusty needed her help, she'd do it.

"Not at the moment." He fidgeted, which he'd done often since arriving.

She'd initially blamed his restlessness on lack of sleep and stress. Now, however, she began to wonder. "Is something the matter besides Dex?"

Dusty cleared his throat. "I won't be flying out to L.A. Not for a while."

"You're still signing the option contract!"

"Absolutely."

"Then how—"

"We'll handle the negotiations and signing by e-mail."

"Oh." She tried to absorb the full ramifications of what he'd said. "How long's 'a while'?"

"I don't know. I'm taking charge of managing the horses while Dex's laid up. And watching Matt during the day while Josie's busy."

Maryanne didn't like the uncertainty in his voice. Or the sense of déjà vu stealing over her.

"That's going to keep you busy."

He reached across the small table and took her hand. "Just because I can't come to L.A. doesn't mean you can't visit me."

"I've used up all my vacation days. I won't have any time off again until Thanksgiving."

Two-and-a-half months away. Even then, she might not be able to afford another trip. The stay at Cowboy College had used a large chunk out of her savings. The rest was in reserve for a down payment on the condo. She didn't tell Dusty. He'd offer to pay for her plane ticket, and she wouldn't feel right accepting.

"Then stay here," he said.

She gaped at him. "Be serious."

"I am."

"What about my job?"

"Get another one," he said as if marketing jobs grew on trees.

"I've worked hard for this one. And I like it. Besides—" she shook her head "—there's my dad. I won't leave him. We're all each other has since Mom died."

"He can move here with you."

"What if he doesn't want to?"

"You're right." Dusty leaned back in his chair. "I shouldn't be pressuring you."

"Why can't you bring Matt with you to L.A.?"

"I already thought of that. Josie thinks he's too young to fly."

Maryanne remembered. "Your parents could babysit." They had before.

"I don't want to take him anywhere. Not yet. He's had so many changes and disruptions lately, he needs some stability."

"Of course." She lowered her eyes.

"I know you're disappointed." He squeezed her hand. "And I'm sorry."

So was she.

It wasn't that Maryanne didn't appreciate the sacrifices he was making. After all, she'd made a similar one for her father. But not at the expense of someone else's feelings.

Be fair, she chided herself. *He's doing the best he can.*

"If you can be patient," he said, "wait a few months, things will get back to normal."

She'd heard that before. Only her former boyfriends hadn't returned as promised, and nothing was ever normal again.

Would Dusty do the same? Forget about her and turn to another woman the moment she was gone? He'd have plenty of opportunity. And there was his reputation to consider.

Her breath caught. What if she'd been just another of his conquests?

Maryanne didn't like having doubts and insecurities

but she was suddenly filled with them. They pushed against her heart like an oppressive weight.

"I don't want to lose you," she said in a half whisper. "Not after just finding you."

"You won't lose me. As soon as Dex is up and around, I'll be flying out to L.A. so often you'll be sick of me." He smiled and for a fraction of a second, he was the same impossibly charming man she'd met in the arena a month ago. "The time will go quickly. You'll see."

He was wrong. She'd been through this before, with men she'd dated considerably longer than Dusty, and the days and weeks had passed excruciatingly slow. Especially when the phone calls and emails decreased.

"What if you get tired of waiting? What if Dex's recovery takes longer than expected?" Unable to sit any longer, she got up from the table and went to the counter.

"We'll cross that bridge if and when we come to it."

"You make it sound so simple."

Dusty also stood. "There are no guarantees in life. Look at Dex. He didn't think yesterday morning when he woke up he'd be in a hospital that afternoon."

Not exactly the assurance she was hoping for.

When he took a step toward her, she moved back.

Confusion clouded Dusty's features. "You have to know I didn't want this."

"I do." Unshed tears clogged her throat.

"My family comes first right now. They need me." She sniffed. "And I don't."

"Not as much."

True, but hearing it still hurt. Why was she always the last one on everyone's priority list? Even her birth mother had put herself first.

"I guess you're right," she said more testily than necessary.

"This isn't a choice between you and my family."

"Sounds to me like you already picked them."

For the first time, a note of impatience crept into Dusty's voice. "I thought you'd understand."

"Understand or go along?"

"The two aren't that much different."

"They are. And if you can't see that, you can't possibly know how I feel right now."

"I'm not rejecting you."

"Really? Because this sure smacks of being let down easy."

"If you think that then *you* don't know how *I* feel." He reached for his hat, which he'd left on the table. "Maybe I should go."

There was a finality to his statement, as if he wasn't coming back.

She could stop him. Tell him she was sorry and that she'd wait forever if necessary.

Except he hadn't said he'd wait for her, and that was what she'd most needed to hear.

"I'll call you tomorrow." He reached for her, sorrow in his eyes. "We're both tired and not thinking straight."

Or was that thinking straight for the first time? The truth was, their romance had been a whirlwind. Possibly even a fantasy.

She avoided his hand. "Please don't. This is hard enough." If he touched her, took her in his arms, it would be her undoing.

"All right, then." The muscles in his jaw twitched. Whether from anger or some other emotion, it was hard to tell. "Goodbye, Maryanne."

After shutting the door behind him, she hid in her bedroom crying softly and wondering if she'd made a terrible mistake.

What had she been thinking? She and Dusty hardly knew each other. No one fell in love in such a short period of time. Certainly not two people from two entirely different worlds.

Except she *had* fallen in love. How else could she explain the hollow place inside her and the pain rushing in to fill it?

CHAPTER FIFTEEN

"ATTENTION PASSENGERS," A generic male voice boomed over the airport loudspeaker. "Flight 279 for Reno, Nevada, has been delayed and won't be departing until 9:17."

"Isn't that your flight, Cookie?"

"Yes, darn it." Maryanne peered over the heads of fellow passengers to the bank of digital screens behind the ticket counter. According to the flashing numbers, her flight had indeed been delayed. "I'd better talk to an agent." She moved toward the line she'd left mere minutes before. "It's possible I'll miss my connection."

Her father waited with her in the line, chatting about this and that, his mood relatively good considering the circumstances. Her decision to leave a day early had no doubt inconvenienced him. Instead of spending his last morning at Cowboy College roping, he was with her at the regional airport, standing in a slow moving line.

She probably should have toughed it out and waited until tomorrow to leave. But after her conversation with Dusty yesterday—or was it a fight?—Maryanne couldn't bear to stay a moment longer. She wasn't, she told herself for the hundredth time, avoiding Dusty.

"How 'bout another cup of coffee?" Gil suggested once Maryanne finished with the ticket agent.

"Maybe a water. You know, you don't have to hang

around." They'd moved to yet another line, this one at the small café.

"You seem kind of upset. I figured you could use the company." By sheer luck, they found an empty table in the corner. "Is it Dusty? Leaving him has to be hard but you'll see him soon."

"He's not coming to L.A."

"What!"

Maryanne hadn't told her father about her and Dusty. Last night her emotions had been too close to the surface to talk without breaking down. She was only marginally better this morning.

"He's staying to help with Matt and take over for Dex at the ranch." She explained the details while sipping her water. When she finished, her father patted her hand. The paternal gesture caused a painful lump to form in the back of Maryanne's throat, and she wound up pouring her heart out.

"Asking you to wait doesn't seem unreasonable."

"Dad, I've been through this before." Maryanne's defenses rose. "It always ends with me being hurt."

"Do you love Dusty?"

"I... I..." When her voice failed, she nodded.

"I'm guessing he feels the same."

"Then why didn't he find a way to be with me?"

"I could ask you the same question."

"I did find a way."

"On your terms."

Was that true? She averted her eyes to stare at the people hurrying to their gates.

"It takes two to make a relationship work."

"But it seems like I'm always the one compromising." The one forced to wait. *The one left behind.*

"If he won't come to L.A.," her father said, "you could move here."

Dusty had suggested the same thing. "I have my job to consider."

"Telecommute like you're doing now."

"Jarred only tolerated that arrangement because it was temporary and he needed me on the Hamilton project."

Her father scoffed. "He'll put up with it if he wants to keep you. If not, you'll get a job here. Adele will give you a recommendation."

Dusty had also suggested that. What was it with men? Did they think all problems could be solved with a snap of the fingers?

"Even if I wanted to move here, I wouldn't leave you, Dad. I'm all you have."

"Well, ah…" He cleared his throat. "That's the thing. I was going to tell you last night except you were so upset."

"Tell me what?"

"I've been talking to Adele the last couple of days."

Maryanne recalled seeing her father and Adele with their heads together at the jackpot.

"She's offered me a job."

"Doing what?" Maryanne sputtered.

"Wrangling."

"You're too old to be a wrangler!"

Fortunately, her father chuckled rather than taking offense. "I've got a few good years left in the saddle, and I'd like to spend them here."

"But what about your job?"

"I'll take an early retirement."

"And the house?"

"I'll sell it."

"You and Mom lived in that house for almost thirty years!"

"I know. I hate the idea of parting with it. What about you? Do you want it?"

"I... I...no." What she wanted was her dad living there. Forever. "You're staying in Markton," she repeated lamely.

"Well, I'll be back in a few weeks to close up the house and pack the contents."

Mindless of a potential audience, Maryanne promptly burst into tears.

"Oh, Cookie. Don't cry."

"I'll be alone," she blubbered.

"You've been living on your own for years."

"But you and Mom were only forty minutes away. Not hundreds of miles."

"We'll still visit. I'll come home and you can fly here."

Maryanne could hardly hear him over the dull buzzing in her ears, fueled, she was convinced, by the pain exploding in her chest.

"You're leaving me, too." The words were torn from her aching throat.

"I'm not, honey."

"You are. Like everyone else."

The announcement about her flight departing couldn't have come at a better time. She started to rise from the table. Her father stopped her with a hand on her arm.

"Just because Dusty has to stay here and I took a—"

"What about Scott and Ryan?" Maryanne pulled

away and reached for her carry-on luggage. "And my mother."

"She died, honey. It's not the same."

"I was talking about my birth mother."

Giving her father a quick peck on the cheeks, she pivoted and walked quickly to the security area. If she stopped, even for one second, her courage might fail her.

Later, as she sat in her seat and stared out the airplane window at the Wyoming landscape that was both beautiful and primitive, her eyes filled with fresh tears. What was it about her that was so unloveable people were always choosing someone or something else over her?

DUSTY WATCHED THE WRANGLER lope the young mare in slow circles around the arena.

"She can really move out," his companion commented. "Good leg action."

"She's a little small for roping."

"But fast. Just watch. Hey, Joel!" the man, a horse seller from California, called to the rider. "Give her a run."

The wrangler trotted the mare to the far end of the arena, then galloped her across it at full speed. All at once, the wrangler brought the mare to a dirt-flying, bone-rattling stop not twenty feet in front of Dusty and the man.

"Nice, huh?" The man's eyebrows bobbed up and down. "She's got speed *and* stamina. The darn thing's not even breathing hard."

An exaggeration, but Dusty expected the man to

talk up the horse. He was, after all, trying his best to make a sale.

"I don't know. With Dex laid up, we're not really in the market for any roping stock. Especially a horse that's so green."

"How's your brother doing?" For the first time, the man dropped his sales persona.

"Hates being laid up, as everyone within earshot is constantly reminded. He's scheduled for another surgery the first week of October."

"That's got to be tough." The man shook his head sympathetically. "How you managing?"

"I'm doing all right."

And he was doing all right, as far as work and Matt were concerned. The rest of his life, however, was another story. Without Maryanne it was empty and shallow and devoid of satisfaction. She'd only been gone three weeks but if felt like a century. A long, lonely century.

The wrangler loped the mare back across the arena to await his next instructions.

"I'll take her," Dusty said abruptly. "If you come down five thousand on the price."

"Let's talk." The man's perpetual smile widened. "You by chance have a cold drink in that office of yours?"

A half hour later, the man drove his empty horse trailer down the drive, both he and Dusty satisfied. The man because he'd gotten a decent price for the mare, though he'd protested vehemently that wasn't the case, and Dusty because he had one less thought weighing on his mind.

It had been like that ever since Maryanne left. Dusty

made decisions and handled tasks quickly, allowing himself more time to dwell on the month they'd spent together and to regret the circumstances of their breakup.

Given a second chance, he would have started out that last morning telling Maryanne how much he loved her.

Even now it surprised him to realize the speed with which he'd fallen for her. But he had fallen, as his inability to bounce back proved. Not even finalizing the option deal with Sundown Pictures had eased his misery.

"Did we buy a new mare?" Jesse joined Dusty as he was latching the door to the mare's stall. They both rested their forearms on the low wall and watched her cautiously acquaint herself with her neighbors. "A tad on the small side."

"But she's fast," Dusty heard himself repeating the horse seller's words.

"You going to have any spare time to train her?"

"No." His days began at dawn and ended well after dark. "I'm considering sending her over to Adele's."

"Sounds like a plan."

When his brother made no move to leave, Dusty asked, "Something on your mind?"

"No." Jesse pushed back from the wall in order to study Dusty. "But I'd say something's on yours. And has been for weeks."

Dusty's defenses rose. "I'm doing my job."

"Hell, you're doing it and then some. No one in the family can quite believe how dedicated you are. I was going to set them straight, tell them they were wrong, then decided against it."

"Set them straight about what?"

"That you haven't turned over a new leaf, that you're avoiding your problems."

"I don't have any problems."

Jesse laughed, so loud he spooked the already skittish mare.

"I'm a changed man," Dusty said. "Isn't that what everyone wanted?"

"Changed, just not all for the better. None of us likes seeing you so down."

Dusty kneaded the back of his neck, which had been paining him for three solid weeks. "There's just no pleasing you guys."

"Come on, Dusty."

"I did it—I stepped up. Now get your nose the hell out of my business." He started to walk away, wishing there was something—*anything*—in his path he could kick.

Jesse grabbed his arm.

Dusty shook him loose. "Lay off me."

"Go after her."

"What?"

"You're in love with her, right?"

Dusty gaped at his brother. "Why would you suggest I leave when you and everyone else are dead set against it?"

"Not for good. Just long enough to convince her to move here."

"And you think the family would be okay with that?" Dusty scoffed.

"I know they would. They like Maryanne." His brother sobered. "We were wrong about you. Me and Dad, especially. We thought she'd be a distraction. Turns out, she's the reason you've changed. Her and Matt."

Dusty should have been happy. After all these years, his family finally understood and supported him.

Only it didn't make him happy.

Nothing had since Maryanne left.

"I can't go after her."

"Why the hell not?"

"She won't move here." She probably wouldn't even talk to him. Not after the things he'd said to her.

"You won't know for sure unless you try."

Dusty wavered.

"Come on, bro. You're a Cody. We don't quit. Not when we want something like I know you want Maryanne."

"And if she won't agree to come?" Dusty voiced his biggest fear.

"Then you'll just have to fight for her. Like Dex did for Josie."

And like their father fought for their mother. Dusty still wasn't sure what happened all those years ago but if his parents had given up on each other, he and his siblings wouldn't be here now.

"Do it." Jesse slapped him on the back. "I'll even fly you out there."

Dusty made another quick decision. The difference was this one set him free rather than added to his burdens. "All right."

Jesse beamed. "When?"

"Friday. I have to watch Matt tomorrow."

"I'm surprised you can wait that long."

So was Dusty.

MARYANNE PARKED HER CAR in her father's driveway. A wave of acute sadness prevented her from immediately getting out. This could be—and probably was—the last visit she'd ever make to her parents' home. Pulling herself together, she went inside, not bothering to ring the bell.

"Dad, where are you?" she called, her voice echoing in the empty living room.

"Back here."

She found him in the master bedroom, repairing the hinge on the adjoining bathroom door with a Swiss Army knife. The sight of the familiar room stripped of all its furnishings caused a painful lump to form in the back of her throat.

"Where are the movers?" She hugged and kissed her father. Several phone calls and as many apologies had smoothed over their tiff at the Wyoming airport.

"They left about a half hour ago."

"I can't believe you got everything accomplished in one day."

"There wasn't much to pack." It was true. Her father had downsized considerably after her mother died. "Ann and Lou helped."

At the mention of her parents' neighbors of the past fifteen years, the lump in Maryanne's throat doubled in size. Who knew when she'd see them again?

"I'd have been here sooner but Jarred insisted I stay to meet with a new client."

"It's all right. We have the whole evening. I'm not leaving until the morning."

"So soon?" Maryanne let out a small cry. She'd planned for her father to stay with her for at least a few days before he returned to Markton.

"I have to get back to work."

"But you just got here, and you're already leaving?"

Twice in one month was too much for her to take, and she let her emotions overwhelm her—something she'd been doing a lot of since breaking up with Dusty and returning to L.A. Their relationship might have been short-lived, but tell that to her aching heart.

Maryanne had been operating in a blur for three weeks, missing Dusty, her father and—this was a huge surprise—Markton acutely. She had hoped the short visit with her father would alleviate some of her despair. Apparently not. Even the job she'd once loved had lost its appeal, becoming a drudgery.

"Maybe I should go," she muttered and hoisted her purse farther up on her shoulder.

"Stop it."

Maryanne stared at her father, her mouth open. He hadn't raised his voice to her in...well, she couldn't remember when.

He slowly retracted the screwdriver attachment on his Swiss Army knife and returned it to his pocket. When he spoke, his tone had softened.

"I've often wondered why you push people away."

"I don't do that."

"No? What about now? I told you I was leaving in the morning and your first reaction is to hightail it out of here."

Maryanne's lower lip trembled. She *had* been ready to run off and leave her father, even knowing she might not see him again until the holidays.

"I'm sorry, Dad."

"Your mom and I worried that being abandoned at such a young age had affected you," he said in a hoarse voice. "That it was why you tended to bail out of relationships when the going got tough."

A jolt went through her. "I don't bail out." As soon as she spoke the words, she knew her father was right.

"It may not seem that way at first," her father said gently, "but sometimes people aren't leaving us as much as they're leading us to a better place."

"Since when did you become philosophical?"

"My perspective's changed a lot recently. I think yours has, too. You just haven't realized it yet."

She stared out the curtainless window at the backyard of her childhood home. "I know you love it in Wyoming but I wish you weren't going back."

Her father smiled. "Why don't you come with me?"

"What!"

"Just for the weekend. Long enough to talk to Dusty."

"He may not want to see me."

"'Course he will. He's plumb crazy about you."

"You think?" Hoped stirred inside her. Had she been too hasty? Bailed, like her father said, instead of giving her and Dusty's fledgling relationship a fighting chance?

"Dusty's a fine man, Cookie. Solid and dependable."

"He is, isn't he?"

In fact, Dusty Cody wasn't anything like the wild cowboy everyone had described to her when she'd first arrived in Markton. He'd shown admirable responsibility and maturity by stepping up when his family needed him and fully embracing his role as Matt's father.

Wasn't that the kind of man she'd always wanted to find? The kind of man she'd always hoped to marry?

Yes. And just maybe if she tried hard enough, she could be the kind of woman he'd always wanted.

"Come on." She grabbed her father by the arm and

dragged him from the bedroom. "We don't have much time."

"Where are we going?"

"My place to pack. Then to Cottonwood Ranch. I have an apology to make and some convincing to do."

Her father's laugh resounded throughout the house. "That's my Cookie."

MARYANNE AND HER FATHER parked the old truck beside the practice arena at Cottonwood Ranch. Stones crunched noisily beneath their feet as they walked to the fence. Maryanne had worn her new boots, which had finally stretched and were beginning to fit better.

Who'd have guessed she'd ever trade her Guccis for a pair of Tony Lamas?

All at once, her heart tumbled inside her chest.

Dusty stood in the arena with Matt, a practice dummy nearby. Maryanne congratulated herself on remembering what the fake calf head mounted on a metal stand was called. If she could learn the name of that, she could learn anything.

Even how to become a bona fide country girl.

"Hello."

She and her father halted at the female voice hailing them. Maryanne had been so focused on Dusty, she hadn't noticed his parents standing nearby. As desperately as she wanted to see him, it seemed rude not to go over and speak to Anne and J.W.

"Hi. How are you doing?" Concern that Dusty's father would disapprove of her return visit kept her steps slow and measured.

"You've come back." Anne smiled brightly.

"For a little while."

"Howdy, folks. Good to see you again, Maryanne."

She blinked. Was J.W.'s friendliness genuine or feigned because he thought she was leaving soon?

"Hey," Dusty called from the arena. "What are you doing here?"

Even at a distance, she could see his surprise.

"I came with Dad." Yes, she'd stated the obvious but she was suddenly nervous having four pairs of eyes watching her and Dusty's reunion.

"I'm glad." He sent her the same charming smile that had won her over the day they'd met.

Relief made her knees weak. Whatever pushing she'd done hadn't sent him away for good.

"Give us a minute," he said. "I'm just showing Matt a few tricks."

The boy clearly wasn't getting the knack of roping—yet. That didn't, however, affect the fun he and his father were obviously having.

"How's Dex?" Maryanne inquired of Anne.

"Better. His doctor's optimistic."

"That's good news."

"I'm so glad we ran into you before you left again."

"She might be staying for good," Maryanne's father announced.

There went her chance to talk to Dusty first.

"Really?" Anne regarded her curiously.

So did J.W., though his expression was more guarded than curious.

"I'm considering it." Maryanne grimaced, wondering when she'd lost control of the situation.

"I do hope you'll stay." Anne touched her arm. "Dusty's missed you terribly. You've had such a positive effect on him and been a big help with his writing career. I can't tell you how happy and proud he's made us."

Maryanne almost asked Anne to repeat herself.

"You and your father will have to come to dinner one night."

"We'd be delighted," Gil answered for both of them.

"Grandma, Grandpa," Matt hollered. "Watch this!" He executed a wobbly toss at the practice dummy. The rope caught on one of the fake horns.

"Good job," Anne called.

"Remember to keep your elbow up." J.W. demonstrated.

Matt tried again with slightly more success.

"Maryanne." Dusty waved to her. "Come here. We need your help." He bent and whispered in Matt's ear.

"But I don't know the first thing about roping."

"That's okay. You don't have to for this trick."

"Go on," her father urged, also flashing a wide grin. Did he know something she didn't?

Maryanne went through the gate and into the arena, her boots sinking into the soft dirt. No kicking off her shoes anymore. Before she reached Dusty and Matt, the boy broke into hysterical giggles.

"What's going on?" She narrowed her gaze.

"Nothing," Dusty and his little sidekick answered simultaneously.

"You're not playing a joke on me, are you?"

Matt doubled over with laughter. Dusty removed the rope from his son's hands and wound it into a coil, his movements precise and deliberate.

Maryanne's suspicions were confirmed, but she decided to go along for the moment. The glint in his eyes was too endearing to resist, and they could all use a little fun after the emotional roller coaster of the past weeks.

"Stand over there." Dusty pointed to a spot twenty feet away.

Maryanne did as instructed and faced him, her hands at her sides.

"When I say now, you jump."

"Jump?"

"Show her, Matt."

The boy crouched and then hopped in place, putting so much force behind it, he toppled momentarily before regaining his balance.

"Got it?" Dusty asked, raising the rope over his head and twirling it

"Sounds simple enough."

Matt stepped back to give his father room.

Swinging his arm wide, Dusty widened the loop, then let it shimmy down the length of his body. Right before it hit the ground, he flicked his wrist, and the rope climbed back up to his head.

"Woo, hoo!" Maryanne's father cheered from the fence.

Dusty repeated the trick, only this time, he hopped in and out of the loop.

Matt clapped.

Maryanne did, too. "When am I supposed to jump?"

"That part's coming next." Dusty twirled the rope faster and higher. "Get ready." He tossed the rope at her.

She waited for him to say jump. He didn't and, like the day he'd kissed her behind the barn, the rope fell over her. He pulled it tight just as it reached her waist, pinning her arms to her sides. Had she not known what to expect, he might have knocked her off her feet.

Then again, in a way, he already had.

"You didn't say jump," she protested.

"I lied." He reeled her in until she was close enough for him to wrap her in his embrace.

She gazed up into his face and said in a teasing voice, "Aren't you going to remove the rope?"

"That depends."

"On?"

"Your answer. Why did you come back?"

"To apologize."

He nibbled her neck just below her ear. "That's not your only reason."

How did he know?

"Tell me." He nibbled her neck again.

She hesitated, gathering her nerve. "I've been thinking…"

"About?"

Something told her this was the moment she'd been waiting for her entire life.

"Staying in Wyoming a little longer."

"How long?"

She could feel his chest pounding. "That depends."

Yanking on the knot, he loosened the rope and slipped it off her. Before she could speak, his mouth was on hers, hungry and wild just like him. Any similarities to their first kiss ended there. This one, rather than being demanding and greedy, promised a lifetime of love and devotion.

His wicked grin greeted her when they broke apart. She became vaguely aware of Matt's giggles and her father's whoops and whistles. What had they done? What had *she* done? She touched a hand to her burning cheeks.

"Since you're not leaving right away," Dusty linked fingers with her, "that means you'll be able to go with me tomorrow."

"Where?"

"The architect's office. I'm using the option money on my screenplay to have plans drawn up for my house at Stony Creek. I'd like your input."

"I can probably do that. After I call Jarred and present him with my telecommuting proposal."

"Working at home from now on?"

"If he'll agree."

"I have an idea." He raised their joined hands to his lips. "When we're done at the architects, why don't we head to the jewelers?"

"Jewelers?" She dared to hope.

"I can't have my fiancée going around without an engagement ring."

"Fiancée? But you haven't, we haven't."

"You're right." He dropped to one knee. "Better remedy that right away."

Maryanne let out a soft gasp.

"Daddy." Matt came closer. "What are you doing?"

Dusty didn't take his eyes off her. Good thing because without his gaze to steady her, Maryanne might have swayed.

"I'm asking Maryanne to marry me."

"What did she say?"

"Nothing yet." He leaned toward Matt and whispered loudly, "I'm starting to get worried."

"Do you need help?"

"Appears I might."

Matt went down on his knees next to Dusty. "Will you marry my daddy?"

Maryanne laughed, then started to cry. "Yes, I'll marry your daddy."

Matt and Dusty scrambled to their feet with Dusty claiming a quick hug from Maryanne. Matt ran over to deliver the news to his grandparents, but it was Maryanne's father he stopped in front of. "Does this make you my grandpa, too?"

Maryanne's father patted Matt on the head and said in a hoarse voice, "I think it does."

Matt counted on his fingers. "I have three grandpas now."

J.W. pulled Matt to his side. "You're a lucky boy."

Dusty lowered his head until it touched Maryanne's. "I know a house on Stony Creek isn't the same as a condo in Westwind."

"It's better. I've been wanting to live in a totally green community, and nothing is as green as Cottonwood Ranch."

"I'm glad to hear you say that because if you turned down my proposal, I would have hogtied you and kept you against your will."

"Not a chance, cowboy."

"Oh, I'd have done it."

"Not a chance I'd say no." Leaning up, she pressed her lips to his, giving him the first kiss of what promised to be a long and happy life as husband and wife.

"Guess it's not so far between L.A. and Markton," she heard her father say.

No farther, Maryanne thought, than her and Dusty's hearts, joined now together as one.

* * * * *

AIDAN: LOYAL COWBOY

To all the people who made this book possible.

First, the five lovely and talented ladies who are my coauthors in this continuity—C.J. Carmichael, Roz Denny Fox, Shelley Galloway, Marin Thomas and Linda Warren. Your creativity amazes me, and I am truly honored to share this continuity with you.

It's true that behind every good author is a good editor. I've been fortunate to work with Kathleen Scheibling since I started writing for Harlequin. I can't thank you enough, Kathleen, for all the opportunities you've given me and all the faith you've placed in me. Writing books for Harlequin isn't just my job, it's my passion and a dream come true. I'm also delighted to have worked with Johanna Raisanen on this and the previous continuities. There isn't a more conscientious, more charming, more intelligent editor. Just how lucky can an author get?

Last, I must give a nod of appreciation to Walter Farley, author of the Black Stallion and Island Stallion series. The books I discovered in third grade led to a lifelong love affair with horses and, ultimately, *Aidan: Loyal Cowboy*.

CHAPTER ONE

MID-MARCH IN SOUTHEASTERN Montana was no time of year for a bucking horse auction. And yet, better than a hundred people had driven as many miles or more, braved ice-covered highways and trudged across acres of gray-brown slush, all in search of a bargain.

Ace Hart among them.

He stood with seven other potential customers, appraising the coal-black stallion and contemplating his finer qualities, which, at first glance, appeared in short supply.

The horse, slightly underweight for his intended use and a bit on the rangy side, had backed himself into the farthest corner of the pen. Ears flat, head stretched forward and nostrils flaring, he stomped a front hoof in the wet, mucky ground, flinging clumps of mud into the air. The customers took the horse's warning seriously and maintained a respectful distance, some of them scratching notes on the back of their bidding numbers for reference when the auction started.

Normally Ace would pass up a potentially aggressive horse like this one, outstanding bloodlines or not. But the animal's eyes, alert, inquisitive and highly intelligent, told Ace what he needed to know better than the AQHA registration papers taped to the pen railing.

This was no ordinary horse and no ordinary stallion.

The Midnight Express, or just plain Midnight as he was once known on the rodeo circuit, had been born to buck, his purpose in life to unseat any cowboy with nerve enough to ride him into the arena. Most of those rides had ended with the cowboy eating a face full of dirt.

No more.

If Ace purchased Midnight—make that *when,* he'd already decided the horse was his—he'd use Midnight exclusively for breeding purposes. Ace wasn't the kind of business manager or big-animal veterinarian to risk injuring a valuable investment.

"What do you think?" His mother came up beside him, linked an arm through his, then stuck her other hand in the pocket of her sheepskin-lined jacket.

"A little underweight. A little temperamental."

"But a beauty."

Indeed. Despite his ragged appearance, Midnight had all the potential Ace and his mother were seeking in a foundation stallion for their bucking horse breeding operation. He mentally calculated the top price they could afford to pay. With luck, the horse's prickly personality and poor condition would scare off other buyers.

"Howdy, Sarah. Ace." Earl McKinley, the Harts' neighbor and competitor in the bucking stock business, approached and fell in beside Ace's mother.

"Hello, Earl." She returned the greeting. "I didn't think you were coming today."

Neither had Ace. He glanced around, his throat suddenly dry.

Had Flynn accompanied her father to the auction? Told him about her and Ace?

Not likely. If Earl had any idea Ace spent the night

with his daughter three weeks ago, he'd have a lot more to say to Ace than "howdy."

Just when Ace decided Flynn had stayed home, she appeared, casually approaching as if this was just another chance encounter with her neighbors.

"Flynn, good to see you," Ace's mother exclaimed.

"Hi, Sarah, how are you?" Flynn acknowledged Ace with a tilt of her head, the epitome of cool, calm and collected.

Not so Ace.

Sweat promptly broke out on his brow—both at the memory of the incredible night they'd spent together and his disgraceful exit the next morning.

What must she think of him?

Her demeanor gave nothing away.

She appeared to be concentrating on the conversation between his mother and her father.

At one time, the Harts and McKinleys had been fierce rivals. That changed to friendly rivals ten years ago when Ace's father died.

"Rumor has it you might be getting out of the business," his mother said to Earl.

"I haven't decided either way. If I can pick up a few head today at a good price, I may end up adding to my string. If not, I'll probably sell off. It's been a tough go the last few years, what with this economy."

"It certainly has."

"I heard you leased out three thousand acres to a cattle company from Missoula."

"We did. And sold off most of our cattle. We're down to three hundred head."

Earl whistled.

The recent recession and drop in the commodities

market was a frequent topic among ranchers. Ace's mother was counting on the family's expanded bucking contracting business and reduced cattle operation to stabilize the ranch's shaky finances.

"I also hear you're planning to add to your string in a big way," Earl said.

"We are indeed." Her face lit up. "That's what brought us here."

"You thinking of buying this here fellow?"

All eyes went to the big horse in the pen.

"Considering it," Ace's mother answered coyly.

Earl's bucking string had always been significantly larger than the Harts' and included a dozen championship bulls and horses. If Earl retired, that would certainly benefit the Harts and their plans.

From the glimmer of interest in Earl's eyes, he also saw and appreciated Midnight's potential.

Ace momentarily tensed. The old rivalry might just heat up again.

"I didn't know you were wanting a stud horse," he said.

"I like to keep all my options open." Earl's smile remained fixed, much like his daughter's.

She stood across from Ace, looking everywhere else but at him.

Well, he deserved her disdain. He'd messed up pretty bad.

That didn't stop him from missing her and wishing things were different.

"Shame about old Wally," his mother mused. Like most of the rodeo folk at the auction, she'd been acquainted with the late owner of the stock up for sale today. "He was a good man and will be missed."

"His kin must be in a hurry for their share of his money." Earl lifted his foot and examined the muddy water pouring off his galoshes, then stepped sideways to a spot that was only marginally less wet. "Couldn't they have postponed the sale six weeks till the weather improves?"

"They may have debts to pay off. Wally was sick a long time before he passed."

"More likely they didn't want to compete with the Miles City Bucking Horse Sale in May. Those kids of his never gave a flying fig about taking over his string even before he died. A shame, too." Earl shook his head. "He had some quality stock. Whoever those kids hired to care for these horses should be arrested."

"True." Ace's mother's gaze went from Midnight to the other horses on the next aisle over. "Some of them are faring rather badly, I'm afraid."

Earl made a sound of disgust. "I betcha this here horse couldn't buck off a ten-year-old boy."

Ace wouldn't take that bet. Midnight and the rest of Wally's string may have received less than adequate care in the two years since the old man fell ill, but Midnight possessed the heart of a champion and the spirit of a warrior.

He also had impeccable genes.

Earl knew it, too. He intentionally downplayed his interest in purchasing Midnight by finding fault with him and the other horses. Ace's mother employed the same tactics with Earl. They'd been doing it for years, with Earl usually coming out ahead.

"You ready, sweetie?" Earl asked Flynn.

"Let's go."

"I'll be seeing you later when the auction starts."

Earl tipped his hat at Ace's mother, then he and Flynn leapfrogged over wet patches to the double row of pens holding the geldings and mares.

The challenge had been officially issued.

"He's going to bid against us for Midnight," Ace's mother observed.

"He won't be the only one."

Ace watched Flynn go, ashamed at his relief. He should apologize to her. He owed her that much, if not more. But after three weeks without any contact, she'd probably refuse to speak to him, and he wouldn't blame her.

God, he'd been such an idiot.

"Aidan?"

"Yeah." His mother was one of the few people to call him by his given name.

"Are you going to examine that horse or what?" She inclined her head at the pen.

"I will. Eventually." He returned his attention to Midnight, forcing thoughts of Flynn from his mind. It wasn't easy.

It seemed as though the horse ignored everyone else except him. Good. They were of similar minds.

"Too muddy?" his mother asked. "Or is the horse too mean?"

"Unpredictable and wary aren't the same as mean." On the ranch and in his veterinarian practice, Ace had examined his share of mean horses. "He's a stallion standing within fifty feet of twenty mares. *His* mares. Not to mention the geldings. His competition, in his mind. He's in a strange environment, surrounded by strange people and hearing strange noises. He's bound to act a little temperamental."

"No one's been in the pen with him that I've seen."

"Are you challenging me?"

Ace's mother arched a brow at him and smiled. "When have you needed someone to challenge you other than yourself?"

He hadn't, not since his father died.

Eventually, Ace decided both he and Midnight were ready. He slipped the latch and opened the gate. The horse snorted and pawed the muck again, his way of saying, "You sure about this? Because I have a thousand pounds of solid muscle on you."

Ace was sure. He stepped inside the pen, shut the gate behind him and waited. When it came to horses, he had an endless supply of patience.

Now, people? Not so much.

"Easy, boy."

Midnight flicked his ears slightly at the silky smooth tone of Ace's voice but didn't budge.

"That's right."

Minutes ticked by, Ace wasn't sure how many. From the corner of his eye he noticed a small crowd had gathered in front of the pen. A few of the louder comments reached his ears.

"Watch this. You ever seen Hart at work?"

"He's got more nerve than me, climbing in with that brute."

"What is he? Some kind of horse whisperer or something?"

Not exactly, Ace thought. But he did have a knack for reading animals, horses especially, and for getting them to trust him. Enough to earn himself a reputation around the state.

When he sensed the moment was right, he took a

small, slow step forward. Midnight jerked his head, his gaze still fastened on Ace.

"There you go."

Another small step, this one met with an angry snort and a head toss. No problem. As long as the horse didn't show signs of charging him, Ace was okay.

"We'll do this on your terms, buddy."

Finally, Ace was close enough to touch the horse, though he hesitated.

"Good job," he murmured softly.

Midnight's breathing increased as he inhaled Ace's scent, the fine whiskers of his velvety nose brushing Ace's jacket sleeve. He was determined that the horse make the next move.

His patience, as usual, paid off.

Midnight sniffed Ace's hand, drew back and sniffed again.

It was a small but vital victory for Ace. When he reached out to stroke Midnight's neck, the horse flinched. He didn't bolt or rear, however, and after several more long moments, allowed Ace to run a hand along his neck and chest, his hide twitching.

Sadness squeezed Ace's heart. Neglect had scarred this magnificent animal. He just didn't understand some people, which would explain why, other than his family, he'd spent much of his thirty-four years a loner.

His attention wandered, as did his gaze. Flynn had evidently concluded one chance meeting with him was enough, for she was nowhere in sight. When Ace looked back around, Midnight had retreated to his corner and had resumed glaring at people. Ace in particular.

Rather than antagonize the horse unnecessarily, Ace conducted the remainder of his examination visually.

Skittish personality and weight loss aside, the horse appeared in reasonably good health. Ace had no reason to doubt the copy of the medical report, which hung on the pen railing along with Midnight's registration papers.

Ace turned, his movements calm and measured. He was taking a big risk presenting his back to Midnight. He'd once met an old cowboy with a sizable chunk missing from his shoulder after just this sort of move. But Ace had to know for certain if Midnight was wary and not mean.

He walked unscathed to the gate and sighed quietly. On the other side, he paused to look at Midnight.

The horse bobbed his head.

Yeah, I agree. Ace grinned to himself, feeling as if he, too, had passed a test. *You're coming home to Thunder Ranch with me.*

His mother wasn't standing where he'd left her. Ace spotted her several feet away, conversing with his uncle Joshua and cousin Duke who'd accompanied Ace and his mother to the sale.

He'd barely started toward them when Flynn unexpectedly crossed his path. A jolt of alarm brought him to a halt.

"Hi," he muttered, trying to move. The soft ground pulled at him, sucking his boots down into the muck. He was trapped.

Served him right.

She stared at him in silence, tendrils of corn-silk-yellow hair peeking out from under her cowboy hat.

Memories surfaced. Ace had sifted his hands through that hair, watched, mesmerized, as the soft strands coiled around his fingers like spun gold.

Then, not two hours later, he'd abruptly left her bedside, hurting her with his transparent excuses.

No longer calm and collected, she stared at him with the same pained expression she'd worn that morning.

"Flynn, I'm sorry," he offered lamely.

"For what exactly?" She crossed her arms in front of her and glared at him through slitted blue eyes. "Slinking out of my room before my father discovered you spent the night, or acting like it never happened?"

FLYNN THOUGHT SHE'D readied herself for their inevitable confrontation. All the phrases she'd used to bolster her defenses during the drive to the auction suddenly abandoned her, and she was once again an emotional weakling.

What had possessed her to sleep with him?

Easy. Ace had been her first love—unfortunately, a very one-sided first love. She'd invited him home, hoping to ignite that elusive spark with him at long last.

And she did.

For several hours his passion had burned brightly. Beautifully. Flynn had never been loved so intensely, so thoroughly. She'd told herself he must have genuine feelings for her, even if he didn't acknowledge them.

Reality, unfortunately, had returned when the sun crested the horizon, its soft rays breaching the blinds of Flynn's bedroom and vanquishing the cozy cocoon of night. Ace couldn't get dressed fast enough or leave in a bigger hurry. He'd had horses to check at home. A morning surgery scheduled. Then there was the meeting at the bank.

Legitimate excuses, but why hadn't he been able to look her in the face when he gave them? Or do more than kiss her forehead before escaping through the back door, sock-footed and boots in hand?

Because he hadn't wanted to stay with her or make a commitment.

Flynn had heard it all before. From her ex-husband and now Ace. The two men were peas in a pod. Both married to their jobs, both using their jobs as an excuse not to spend time with her.

Damn her foolish heart for always picking the wrong kind of man.

She should walk away from Ace, leave him the way he'd left her.

Instead, she stayed, his expression rooting her in place. If she wasn't still angry at him, she might have been swayed by the regret brimming in his incredibly dark brown eyes.

"Can we talk?" he asked. "I'd like to explain."

"This I have to hear."

"Not now, not here." He glanced over his shoulder at the people milling nearby. "Later. Somewhere less crowded."

That was exactly what had gotten her into bed with him, his suggestion they leave the Number 1 Diner and go somewhere more private to continue their conversation.

Flynn rediscovered the confidence she'd lost upon first spotting Ace. "No, I don't think so."

"You have every right to be angry with me," he began slowly.

She cut him off. "Do you not own a calendar? You've had better than three weeks to explain. I'm either working at the emergency clinic or helping Dad with the horses. Finding me isn't a problem. Heck, I live next door to you."

"I'm a jerk."

His admission didn't soften her resolve. He'd wounded her when he hurried off that morning. Hurt her worse when he didn't call or come see her.

And she'd have walked barefoot across broken glass before calling him. Been there, done that—back when they'd dated briefly in college.

"Aidan!" his mother hollered. "We're heading over to inspect the mares and geldings." She waved and smiled at Flynn. "Don't be a stranger. Come to lunch the next time Dinah's over."

Flynn waved in return. "Thanks." Her father and Ace's father might not have liked each other, but Sarah Hart had always treated Flynn like a second daughter.

And Ace had treated her like another little sister.

A four-year age difference hadn't helped. Not until she was in community college and he in vet school did he finally notice her as someone other than his sister Dinah's school chum.

They'd been careful in those days, keeping their relationship a secret in order to avoid their respective fathers' wrath. It was anyone's guess where things might have led if John Hart hadn't died and Ace's world hadn't crumbled.

"I need to go," he said.

"No one's stopping you."

It would be easier to hate him if he didn't appear contrite and miserable.

She'd seen him steady a full-grown steer as it collapsed to the ground. Cushion the animal with his body in order to spare it injury.

How could a man so big and strong and capable be completely inept when it came to understanding women? No wonder he was still a bachelor.

Who was she to talk? She had one failed marriage behind her. A marriage that was, in all probability, a rebound from Ace.

"Flynn…" He reached for her.

"Forget it." She started toward the horse pens where her father waited, then hesitated. Squaring her shoulders, she turned and faced Ace. "You made a big mistake three weeks ago. You walked out on the best thing to happen to you in a long time."

She expected him to blush and falter and possibly be at a loss for words. That happened to him on occasion.

Today, he surprised her.

He met her stare head-on and said without missing a beat, "You're right."

Then why? her mind cried out.

When he said nothing else, she left, sniffing in an attempt to hold back her tears. She'd given him an opening, a chance to say he wanted to see her again, and he'd refused it.

When would she learn?

She'd come home to Roundup following her divorce, in large part because of Ace and the possibility that they could pick up where they'd left off.

Except they hadn't—a one-night stand years later didn't count—and, after today, it didn't appear as though they ever would.

CHAPTER TWO

"LAST UP, FOLKS, is the horse you've all been waiting for, The Midnight Express." Loud speakers mounted from poles on either side of the ring gave the auctioneer's voice a tinny and abrasive quality. "This here stud's lineage goes all the way back to the great hall-of-fame bucking horse Five Minutes to Midnight. He's won Bucking Horse of the Year twice, competed at the National Finals Rodeo a total of five times and has sired over sixty offspring, seven of which are actively competing on the rodeo circuit and doing well for their owners."

Flynn sat with her father in the aluminum bleachers, listening to the auctioneer recite Midnight's selling points. The horse himself, however, had yet to make an appearance in the ring.

She fingered the flyer in her hand as they waited. Murmurings as to the reason for the holdup traveled through the crowd like a signal zipping along a cable. Her father's boot beat an agitated tattoo on the bleacher floor. He'd shown some interest in a few of the other bucking horses up for sale but let them all go to other bidders.

Ace was the new owner of ten, mostly mares. He and his family sat not far from Flynn, down a couple of rows and one section over. She'd noticed him glancing in her direction now and again, had noticed because her glance was constantly straying to him.

Enough already, she chided herself. *He's not worth it.*

And yet, her insides insisted on fluttering.

"What's taking so dang long?" her father complained to no one in particular.

"Are you going to bid on him?"

"Yep."

"A stud horse, Dad? What happened to retiring?"

"I wouldn't retire if I owned that horse."

He'd been going back and forth for months now. Flynn had, too.

If her father got out of the business and moved to Billings to be near her sister, what would she do?

She regularly helped with his bulls and string of bucking stock and had since she was a young girl. After earning her associate's degree in business administration, she also assisted him with the office work during evenings and weekends. Monday through Friday, she worked as an administrator at the Roundup Emergency Care Clinic. Pushing papers was her forte, if not her passion.

Once, she'd aspired to work in management for a large corporation. Except she hadn't been able to get her foot in the door. Not like her ex-husband, whose career had soared while hers stagnated.

They'd originally planned to wait a few years before starting a family. With her career stuck in neutral, Flynn saw no reason to postpone having the children she'd always wanted. Her ex-husband adamantly refused, and Flynn was forced to let another dream go unfulfilled.

Her discontent increased when her older sister, Nora, a pharmacist, married a great guy and promptly bore the first of Flynn's two nephews. How was it her sister seemed to effortlessly attain everything Flynn wanted?

If her father retired, there'd be opportunities. She'd been considering them for weeks with great deliberation. More since she lost her head and slept with Ace.

His abrupt departure had hurt, but it also drove home the point that the time had come and gone for her to let the past go and move forward.

The idea of returning to school appealed to her the most, but it would be next to impossible without moving from Roundup.

A rumbling from the crowd caused Flynn's head to snap up. Midnight was being led into the ring. No, *dragged* into the ring, by two wranglers. With all four hooves digging into the muddy dirt, the horse lowered his hindquarters almost to the ground and resisted the tug from the two lead ropes connected to his halter. A third man, the livestock foreman hired by Wally Dunlap's heirs, followed behind. He held a buggy whip and flicked it in the air behind Midnight, the snapping sound intended to encourage the horse.

It didn't. Midnight bore down harder.

Flynn wanted to shout a protest. She wasn't alone. Ace sprang to his feet, an angry scowl on his face, his flyer crushed between his fingers.

Just when she thought he might leap across six bleacher rows and over the ring fence, the horse went suddenly still and straightened. The wranglers must have decided to quit while they were ahead because they abandoned their efforts and stood, the lead ropes stretched taut.

Midnight ignored them. Raising his head, he stared proudly and defiantly at the audience. His mane and forelock fluttered in the same chilly breeze that snuck up the back of Flynn's neck and caused her to shiver.

Or was the horse himself responsible for her reaction?

Up until this moment, she hadn't understood the fuss. Sure, Midnight was good-looking, with quality bloodlines and a proven history as a champion bucking horse and sire. But there were lots of stallions like him for sale these days.

Seeing Midnight in the ring, however, she glimpsed the greatness in him that had excited her father and Ace and everyone else at the auction.

"Isn't he something?"

"Are you sure about this, Dad?"

"I don't want Ace and Sarah to have him."

"Please don't turn this into a competition with them."

Her words fell on deaf ears. The auctioneer's singsong litany had started.

"What do you say? Let's start the bidding at twenty thousand dollars. Do I have twenty thousand?"

As if on cue, people inched forward in their seats, Flynn and her father included.

"Fifteen, do I hear fifteen?"

When the auctioneer dropped to five thousand dollars, the bidding took off. Her father didn't join in until the going price reached ten thousand dollars. Ace refrained, Flynn noticed, his attention riveted on the horse.

Her father's hand continually went up as he outbid everyone. When the price reached twenty-seven thousand dollars, only her father and one other man remained.

Flynn began to worry in earnest. Did her father have that kind of money?

"Twenty-seven, twenty-seven, someone give me twenty-eight thousand?" the auctioneer intoned.

"Twenty-seven, five."

Every head in the stands turned toward the sound of a new voice. It belonged to Ace.

"Dammit," Flynn's father groused beneath his breath and raised his hand again. "Twenty-eight."

"Twenty-nine." This from the other man.

With Ace's participation, the price was quickly driven up to thirty-five thousand dollars, her father making the last bid.

Flynn went from worrying to panicking. Surely he couldn't raise that much money. He was letting the excitement of the bidding cloud his judgment.

"Dad, don't be foolish."

"I want that horse."

"We'll buy another horse." A less expensive one.

"None of them are like Midnight."

Evidently Ace felt the same, for he shouted, "Thirty-six thousand dollars."

The other man promptly resigned with a discouraged head shake. "Too rich for my blood."

That left Ace and Flynn's father.

How was this possible? The two men she cared most for in the whole world were fighting over a stupid horse.

Wait a minute, she didn't care about Ace.

Right.

If someone ever invented a cure for unrequited love, she'd be the first in line to try it.

"Thirty-seven thousand," her father shouted.

The crowd clapped and cheered. Easy for them, Flynn thought, it wasn't their life's savings on the line.

"This is insane," she hissed. "You don't have thirty-seven thousand dollars."

"There's my line of credit with the bank."

"That's for running the business!"

"Buying a bucking horse is business."

"No, this is an absurd rivalry and refusing to let the Harts get one up on you. What's the matter with you? You don't act like this."

For a moment, time froze. Then his face fell, and he groaned miserably. "Oh, God. What's wrong with me?"

She reached for his hand and squeezed it between hers, relief leaving her weak.

"I don't know what came over me. It's just…" He groaned again.

"I have thirty-seven thousand dollars," the auctioneer boomed. "Do I have thirty-eight?"

Ace and his mother bent their heads together and conferred behind the shield of their hands.

"Going once."

Flynn went rigid. Why wasn't Ace bidding?

"Going twice."

Oh, no! What if the Harts dropped out?

Easy. Her father would have purchased a horse he really didn't need for a sum of money he couldn't possibly afford.

This couldn't be happening!

"Thirty-eight thousand," Ace shouted.

Flynn's heart started beating again.

When the auctioneer finally called, "Sold to number fifty-seven," a minute later, she let herself breathe.

The auction was over, and her father had spent no more than the price of gas for a round-trip.

Why, then, did he appear glum?

"Dad, you okay?" All around them the bleachers had started to empty, yet her father didn't rise.

"Yeah, sure."

"Is your indigestion bothering you again?"

"I'm fine." He promptly pushed to his feet and extended a hand to her. "Come on. Let's go home."

Flynn couldn't be more ready and happily dropped the subject of his health and listlessness. Maybe she'd phone her sister, Nora, tonight. See if she could convince their dad to open up about what was bothering him lately. Perhaps he was having a midlife crisis or had grown tired of being single all these years.

Grabbing two cups of coffee at the concession stand for the drive, she and her father strode across the area between the barn and the field that served as a parking lot. A line of people had formed in front of the converted motor home that was being used as a consignment office. The door to the motor home opened, and Ace and Sarah emerged. Ace went first, turning to assist his mother. They both wore happy smiles, Ace's devastatingly handsome.

Flynn ignored the quickening of her pulse. That smile had been her undoing once too often.

"Hold on a second." To her surprise, her father started toward the Harts.

"What is it?" She hurried after him.

Her question was answered when they met up with Ace and Sarah.

"Congratulations." Her father shook Sarah's hand, then Ace's. "You got yourself a fine stallion there."

Flynn sensed Ace studying her, and her gloved fingers curled into tight balls. She would not return his look, not give him the satisfaction of learning the extent to which he affected her.

"Thank you, Earl." Sarah beamed. "I have to confess, he was almost yours."

"The right person bought him. Just wanted to tell you and that there are no hard feelings."

"I appreciate it. Truly, I do. Are you still considering adding to your string? There should be some quality livestock at the Miles City Sale."

"Naw. I'm going to quit the business."

Flynn exhaled. This time he sounded serious.

"What will you do?" Sarah asked.

"Sell off my string, the ranch, everything. Move to Billings to live near Nora and her husband."

"Oh, Earl. That's a big step."

"What are you going to do?" Ace asked.

It took Flynn a moment for her to realize he was speaking to her.

She did look at him then, unable to stop herself.

"Attend Montana State University," she said with newfound determination. "Enroll in nursing school."

"I didn't realize you wanted to be a nurse."

"For a while now." She glanced at her father. "I've been talking to some of the nurses at the clinic, and I think I'd be good at it."

Not that she didn't enjoy her job at the clinic—parts of it, anyway. But she was capable of so much more than grunt work. She wanted to have an impact. Make a difference. Contribute in a more meaningful way.

"You'll be a wonderful nurse." Sarah gave Flynn a brief but affectionate hug. "Earl, you must be proud."

"I'm proud of her whatever she does."

Flynn's triumph dimmed when she met Ace's frown. Seriously? What did he have to be annoyed about?

"We're going to miss you," he said stiffly, and stuffed the sale papers he'd been holding into the front pocket of his jacket.

Your family, or you? Flynn wanted to ask, fairly certain she already knew the answer wasn't him.

FLYNN WAS LEAVING! Moving to Billings. And she wanted to be a nurse. Ace couldn't believe it.

Not that she wouldn't make a great nurse, he just didn't recall her ever mentioning it before.

Of course, the last time they were together, their talk had centered on their lovemaking and how incredible they made each other feel. Not any potential career changes.

"Heads-up!" Duke yelled.

The warning came in the nick of time. Ace jumped onto the bottom rung of the fence and out of the way a scant second before two of their newly purchased bucking mares trampled him. He remained clinging to the fence until the coast was clear, then hopped off.

"Three more to go," Uncle Joshua hollered from the pen. "Coming your way."

Ace's uncle lived on Thunder Ranch and was in charge of their remaining bulls and cattle. He'd moved to the ranch when his twin sons, Duke and Beau, were knee-high, as he was fond of saying. Before then, he'd spent many years working for Flynn's grandfather.

For supposed rivals, the Harts and the McKinleys were connected on many levels.

Ace's thoughts circled right back to Flynn.

She was moving.

As much as he hated her leaving, it probably was for the best. She deserved a man able to commit to her, not one dividing himself between his vet practice and managing his family's various businesses.

"Pay attention," Duke complained.

"Sorry," Ace grumbled. "Got a lot on my mind."

They herded the remaining three horses down the narrow aisle and into the waiting stock trailer. Their hooves created a tremendous clatter as they hopped inside to join the other two horses, who shifted to accommodate the newcomers. A few squealed, defending their small territory against their neighbor.

While some bucking horses were friendly enough around people, others weren't. Driving them down a narrow aisle and up into a trailer was often the easiest and most effective method of loading them.

"Midnight the only one left?" Ace had been so preoccupied with Flynn, he'd lost track of the horses they'd already loaded. He glanced over at the second trailer they'd brought and started counting.

"The wranglers are bringing him round now," Duke said.

Ace didn't wait. He disliked the manner in which the wranglers and livestock foreman had handled Midnight during the auction. Not that they'd hurt him, but they'd been unnecessarily heavy-handed.

While Duke and Uncle Joshua made sure the horses were secure for the trip, Ace trudged up the aisle to the pen holding Midnight. One wrangler held the horse's lead rope while the other manned the gate.

"Thanks for your help, guys," Ace told the wranglers. "I'll take it from here."

"Your horse." The wrangler at the gate stepped aside.

Ace went right up to Midnight and grabbed the lead rope from the second wrangler's outstretched hand. The rope went instantly slack. Well, well, Midnight was no longer fighting.

"Good boy," Ace crooned, stroking the horse's neck.

Midnight took a hesitant step toward the gate, then another.

"That's right." Ace walked along beside him, pleased Midnight was going to make this easy. He could use something going his way after his encounter with Flynn.

He and Midnight reached the gate. It was wide enough for only one of them to pass through at a time. Ace started to go first.

All at once, Midnight charged through the gate, shoving Ace aside and into the railing. He tried but couldn't hang on to the lead rope and it tore from his grasp.

Free at last, the horse broke into a gallop.

"Look out," Ace yelled as Midnight bolted down the aisle.

Wranglers scrambled out of the horse's path, diving for cover. Ace ran after him, slipping and sliding in the muddy ground and nearly losing his balance twice. Pain sliced through his back from his collision with the railing.

When Midnight reached the end of the aisle, he skidded to a halt and stared at the trailer, his flanks heaving, his high-arched tail swishing nervously. Thank goodness the opening was blocked by the trailer, or else the horse would have likely made for the hills.

He swung his large body around as Ace approached,

tossing his head angrily as if to say, "Drats, foiled again."

"Where exactly did you think you were going?" Ace stopped, bent, braced his hands on his knees and studied the horse, his lungs on fire.

Midnight pawed the ground, then turned back to face the trailer. A panel had been closed, separating the trailer into two compartments, the rear one empty. Ace could imagine the horse weighing his options.

"Make this easy, pal. Go in the trailer."

Duke and Uncle Joshua came over, their faces split by amused grins Ace didn't find the least bit funny. They'd exercised considerably more intelligence than him and remained on the opposite side of the fence railing, clear of harm's way.

"You should have seen yourself running after that horse." Uncle Joshua broke into laughter and elbowed Duke in the ribs. "Where's a video camera when you need one?"

Duke, usually more somber, laughed along with his dad.

"I just want to get this damn horse loaded," Ace grumbled.

Midnight snorted and pawed the ground again, his lead rope dangling in the mud.

"Need help?" the livestock foreman asked. He strolled toward Ace, the buggy whip gripped at his side.

"We're okay." In Ace's opinion, that livestock foreman and his whip were the reason Midnight bolted in the first place.

Raising his arms and waving them slowly, Ace clucked to Midnight. The two wranglers came up behind Ace, blocking any potential escape route.

Duke started toward the slim opening between the fence and the rear corner of the trailer. "You want me to grab his lead rope?"

"No, stay put," Ace ordered. "The last thing we need is someone getting hurt."

Someone else getting hurt, he thought, and rolled his sore shoulder.

Five minutes later, Midnight had yet to budge.

"Aren't you supposed to be a horse whisperer?" the livestock foreman asked, a slight jeer in his voice. "Can't you just whisper him into the trailer?"

If only it were that simple.

Clouds gathered in the sky overhead, and the temperature had dropped by several degrees. It was going to rain again. Possibly snow. They really needed to be on the road soon to avoid any dangerous weather conditions.

Midnight stared at the trailer holding his companions. He wanted to be with them. Horses were herd animals by nature and this was his herd. But he was also stubborn and unwilling to give an inch.

"All of you, leave," Ace said.

"What?" Uncle Joshua scoffed. "You crazy?"

"You heard me. Leave." Ace turned to the wranglers and livestock foreman. "And no one comes round until that horse is loaded."

"I'm not leaving," Uncle Joshua protested.

"Come on, Dad." Duke clapped his father's shoulder. "Ace knows best."

The men shrugged and grumbled and complained, but they also did as requested. Ace was pretty sure he heard the livestock foreman refer to him by a rather colorful name.

Walking casually down the aisle, Ace left Midnight alone. He waited at the pen, keeping an eye on the horse. Unless Midnight chose to jump the five-foot fence, an unlikely probability, his options were limited.

"Let's go, boy," he muttered to himself. "Into the trailer. Nobody's watching you."

Midnight lifted one front leg, held it poised in the air.

Ace mentally willed the horse forward. "Come on, you can do it."

He noticed a few stragglers and the cleanup crew observing with obvious interest. His mother, too. He didn't care, as long as they stayed away.

A horse inside the trailer whinnied. Another one clanged a hoof against the sidewall.

It was apparently the encouragement Midnight needed. Tentatively, he approached the rear of the trailer. Placing one front foot on the trailer floor, he waited. And waited. Finally he hoisted the front half of his body inside.

"Halfway there, pal," Ace murmured.

With a mighty grunt, Midnight hopped into the trailer, settling himself in the empty compartment as if it were just another day, just another trailer ride.

Ace held up a warning hand to his cousin and uncle when they would have climbed the fence. He let a full minute pass before he started down the aisle. When he reached the trailer, he swung the rear gate closed and latched it, the metallic clink making a very satisfying sound.

"Hallelujah!" Uncle Joshua exclaimed. "Let's get the heck out of here before the storm hits."

Ace checked Midnight one last time, chuckling to himself. He was going to like this horse.

CHAPTER THREE

ACE AND DUKE climbed into the cab of the truck hauling Midnight and the mares. His mother and uncle got into the cab of the other truck. They formed a small caravan as they slowly navigated the road from the auction grounds to Highway 12.

"You hungry?" Duke asked.

"Starving." Waiting out stubborn horses was hard work, as was an unplanned confrontation with an irate woman.

"I'll call Dad in a bit. Maybe we can eat at the truck stop we passed on the way here."

Ace removed his cowboy hat and set it on the seat between him and Duke. By prior agreement, they'd split the chore of driving. Ace had taken the first shift to the auction from Roundup, needing the distraction to combat his nervousness.

He wished he was driving now, he could use another distraction. When he wasn't contemplating Midnight's puzzling behavior, he was imagining Flynn packing boxes and cartons in preparation for moving. She'd been a fixture in his life for much of it, except during the time she was married.

He'd never liked her husband and was convinced the fool didn't deserve Flynn.

Ace didn't deserve her, either.

He recalled her face that morning three weeks ago and grimaced. Could he have treated her more cruelly? He'd told himself it was necessary, that to lead her on would be unfair. She'd form expectations, ones he couldn't meet.

The truth was he'd been running scared, that morning and every day since. Even before they'd gone to her house, before their first kiss outside the Number 1 Diner, something inside him had changed. He finally admitted to himself that Flynn was someone he could easily fall for, had, in all likelihood, fallen for years earlier and simply denied it.

"Some news about Flynn going to school to be a nurse." Duke glanced at the side mirrors before changing lanes.

"Who told you?"

"Your mom. She's worried."

"About Flynn? Why?"

"No, about you. She said you took it pretty hard."

"Why would I take it hard? I think it's a great idea." Ace shoved his fingers through his hair, wiping the sweat from his brow. "Want me to call your dad? The truck stop's coming up soon."

"Not for half an hour."

Ace didn't want to discuss Flynn. He hadn't told anyone about the night they'd spent together and wouldn't. Not even Duke. And they were more than cousins, they were good friends.

In some ways, Ace had a better relationship with Duke than he did with his own brothers. Colt was frequently off to some rodeo and Tuf had enlisted in the Marines. On the other hand, Ace and Dinah were close.

She was the little sister he ordered around, doted on, protected, and whose secrets he safeguarded.

His gut clenched at the reminder. Flynn and Dinah talked on a regular basis. Had she confided in Dinah about her and Ace? It was possible.

"I don't know why your mom's worried," Duke said thoughtfully. "For a while there we all thought you and Flynn were going to hook up."

"That was years ago." Duke was one of the few people who knew Ace and Flynn had dated.

"I'm talking last month." Duke slanted Ace a bemused smile. "We saw you and her leaving the Number 1."

Ace abruptly sat up, then slumped against the seat, afraid of giving himself away. "We?"

"Dad, Beau and I."

Both his cousins *and* his uncle?

"Royce, Harlan and Gracie were there, too."

Three of the Harts' ranch hands? Great. Ace and Flynn might as well have taken an ad out in the *Roundup Record Tribune*.

"I don't want to talk about it." Which was not the same as saying nothing happened, and Duke probably picked up on the subtle difference.

"Your business."

Duke respected Ace's wishes for the remainder of the drive to Thunder Ranch, avoiding the topic of Flynn and Ace even when his mother brought Flynn up over dinner at the truck stop.

Ace was never so glad to see the exit for home.

They drove the mile-long driveway into Thunder Ranch, past the main house with its rustic charm and fieldstone wall to the various outbuildings, one of them a newly constructed mare motel. Luckily they beat the snow, which started falling in earnest the minute they pulled up in front of the horse barn.

"It's too late and too cold." Ace reached behind the seat and retrieved his and Duke's yellow all-weather ponchos. "Let's just put the mares and geldings in the west paddock for tonight. We can move them tomorrow if there's a break in the weather."

"And Midnight?"

"The clinic."

Ace had constructed a pair of shaded corrals behind the horse barn, which also contained a small office he used for his vet practice. The corrals were for quarantining sick or injured animals while he treated them. It wasn't an ideal location for Midnight, but it would suffice until the construction of his stud quarters was completed.

Duke braked to a stop, letting Ace out long enough to dash through the snow and relay their plans to his uncle in the other truck.

"Meet you at the paddock with the rest of the horses once we've unloaded Midnight," he told his uncle.

"You going to need some help?"

"We can handle it."

Ace returned to the truck. Midnight, impatient to get out, had begun kicking the trailer wall. He was still creating a ruckus while Duke backed the trailer to the corral gate. If all went as intended, the horse would go right from the trailer to the corral without incident.

Turning on an overhead floodlight, Ace positioned himself at the trailer door. Duke reached through the open slats and unfastened Midnight's lead rope from where it was tied.

The horse stood perfectly still.

Ace wasn't fooled. When he sensed the moment was right, he opened the trailer door.

"Welcome home, boy."

The horse flicked his ears and cranked his big head around, calmly assessing his new surroundings.

"I think he'll be okay," Ace told Duke confidently after several uneventful seconds. "Now that we're away from the auction and that livestock foreman."

"Yeah, okay. If you say so."

Before Ace could reply, Midnight flung himself sideways out of the trailer, landing with a wet thud on the ground. Ace and Duke tripped over their feet attempting to escape danger. Midnight catapulted into the corral. Running and bucking—oh, man, could that horse buck—he circled the corral a few times before coming to a stop.

"Duke! Are you all right?" Ace slammed the corral gate shut, then ran to his cousin, who leaned awkwardly against the trailer wheel well.

"I'm fine." He cradled his left elbow close to his body.

"Here." Ace gripped his cousin's forearm and gently manipulated the affected joint. "Does that hurt?"

"Hell, yes."

"Hurt like you fractured it?"

"Naw. Nothing a little ice, aspirin and a cold beer won't fix."

"Sorry about that."

"Not your fault. Is Midnight okay?"

"Him? That horse is made of solid steel. You going to be able to work tomorrow?"

"Shoot, I'm tougher than that." Duke served part-time as one of Roundup's deputies under the recently elected sheriff—none other than Ace's sister, Dinah. "It's you I'm worried about."

"I didn't get hurt."

"I mean your investment." He hitched his chin at the corral. "You and your mom have a lot on the line."

They did. Ace believed in his mother's vision, which was that a secure future lay in their bucking stock contracting operation. To that end, she'd taken out a three-hundred thousand dollar loan, which he'd cosigned.

If they didn't succeed, Ace could potentially lose his vet practice.

He'd worked too hard, sacrificed too much, for that to happen.

"I'll drive the mares to the paddock," he said.

"Forget it. I'll meet Dad with the mares. You stay here and settle Midnight in."

"Are you positive?"

Duke's response was to head for the cab of the truck.

Ace shut the trailer door. After his cousin drove off, he retrieved two flakes of hay from the small stack he kept by the corral and tossed them in the feeder. Midnight started eating immediately, happy as a pig with his slop.

"I should have counted on you doing something crazy," Ace muttered, disappointed with himself. When it came to horses, his instincts were usually right on the mark.

Midnight stopped eating long enough to give Ace a you-just-met-your-match look.

Yeah, he had.

Most stallions were unpredictable to some degree,

as were many bucking horses. Midnight, as Ace was quickly realizing, verged on unmanageable.

What had happened to this fine animal in the past two years to so dramatically alter his personality?

Duke wasn't the only one worried. Ace couldn't help wondering if he and his mother had made a mistake, paid a small fortune in a stud horse they couldn't handle and didn't dare put with their mares on the chance he'd injure them.

FLYNN STARED AT the pregnancy test wand. Just how reliable were these things?

Pretty accurate, she knew from working at the emergency clinic.

She could always go to the clinic, have the doctor administer a second test in order to confirm, but why? Her body had been telling her for days what the test wand in her hand confirmed: Flynn was having a baby.

She'd become, she realized with a sigh, a statistic. One night of lovemaking, and she'd gotten pregnant. What were the odds?

Considerably greater than with a couple who actually practiced birth control.

Flynn was no idiot; heck, she worked in the medical profession and witnessed the results of unprotected sex on a weekly basis. She could offer excuses. More than once she'd forgotten to take her birth control pill and hadn't gotten pregnant. Her night with Ace had been spontaneous and they were caught unprepared. According to her cycle, it was a safe time of the month.

She moaned softly.

The fact was they'd both acted irresponsibly, and Flynn held the consequences in her hand.

No, carried them inside her. Setting the wand on the bathroom sink, she pressed a palm to her belly.

A baby! The timing couldn't be any worse and, my goodness, what would Ace say?

She slipped the wand into her robe pocket and inspected herself in the bathroom mirror, tilting her head to the side. She was going to be a mother in, she mentally counted, about eight months! Thanksgiving time.

Did she look any different?

What had her own mother thought when she realized she was carrying Flynn's older sister, Nora?

That a baby was the last thing she wanted?

Flynn considered calling Dinah, asking her friend to meet her after work. Flynn could use an ear to bend, a shoulder to lean on. But Dinah was Ace's sister and the two of them were thick as thieves. Flynn couldn't chance Ace finding out about the baby until she was ready to tell him. Until she'd decided on a course of action.

She'd have the baby, there was no question of that. With the possible exception of Ace, she hadn't wanted anything more. Ever. Her way of compensating for her mother's abandonment, she supposed, and Paul's. His refusal to even consider having children for years and years into the future had been the final, backbreaking straw in their shaky marriage, ending with him walking out on her.

A baby. She still couldn't believe it! The prospect petrified her. Wanting children didn't necessarily mean she was ready to be a mother. It also thrilled her. This was a dream come true.

Flynn stumbled from the bathroom, the news of her condition, more than the condition itself, making her light-headed. She usually awoke after her father, so it was no surprise to find him in the kitchen, drinking a cup of coffee, nibbling on a piece of toast and reviewing paperwork.

"Morning, sweetie pie." His tone lacked his usual enthusiasm and his smile its usual luster.

Who was she kidding? Her father's smile had been mostly lusterless for months.

How to tell him about the baby? She longed to share her news with someone who loved and understood her. Dinah was out of the question and Nora, the next logical choice, would be in the middle of dropping her sons off at day care on her way to work. Forget calling her mother. Flynn wasn't in the mood for a lecture.

She reached for the pot of coffee on the counter, then stopped. Returning the mug to the cupboard, she grabbed a juice glass instead. Caffeine wasn't good for the baby. Orange juice, however, very good.

"What are you looking at, Dad?"

"This is a listing agreement with the real estate agent I hired."

"Really?" She sat at the table. "When did you talk to him?"

"Her. And it was yesterday. We met while you were at work."

Well, he'd certainly moved quickly. He'd only just announced to the Harts on Saturday he was selling everything and getting out of the business. Today was Tuesday.

"Are you going to sign it?"

"Already did." He held up the agreement for her to see. "Just reviewing it and making notes."

"Wow." Flynn's throat inexplicably tightened. This

wasn't the first time she'd moved from Roundup. Why, then, were her emotions threatening to spill over?

Must be the baby and hormones.

"Sweetie pie, what's wrong?"

Flynn glanced up to find her dad studying her. "Nothing. Actually, everything's falling into place perfectly. You're selling the ranch, we're moving to Billings, I'm going to nursing school."

"Then why are you crying?"

She touched her cheek, stunned to find it damp.

What a mess. Everything wasn't perfect.

Having a baby was supposed to be exhilarating. Deeply satisfying. One of life's greatest joys. Flynn felt those things. She was also still in shock and uncertain. At this moment, those feelings overwhelmed the others.

"Dad," she blurted. "I have something to tell you. You're going to be surprised. A good surprise, I hope."

Please let him be happy for me.

He laid the listing agreement aside, his expression concerned. "You're not going back to school?"

She could do both, right? Go to school and have a baby?

"No. I am." She swallowed. This was much harder than she'd anticipated. "I'm... Wow." She gathered her wildly racing thoughts. "I'm pregnant."

He sat back, his eyes wide and unblinking. "That *is* a surprise."

"I only found out myself a few minutes ago when I took the home pregnancy test."

"How far along are you?" he stammered.

"A month or so."

Flynn's chest tightened, and her eyes stung. She

wished her father would stop sitting there, staring at her. "You're disappointed in me."

"God, no, Flynn." He sprang from his chair, hauled her to her feet and clasped her to him. "I love you, I could never be disappointed in you. It's just like you say, a surprise." He set her back from him, brushed her hair from her face in a familiar and tender gesture reminiscent of when she was a young girl. "I love being a grandfather. It's one of the reasons I want to move to Billings. And I know how much you've always hankered for kids of your own. I just figured…"

"That I'd be married."

"Something like that. I'm your old man." He shrugged apologetically. "Can't help wanting what I think is best for you."

Flynn hugged him fiercely, laid her head on his chest.

"I'm happy for you, sweetie pie."

"I'm happy, too. And a little nervous."

"Kids are a big step." He kissed the top of her head. "But you'll do fine. And you'll be a wonderful mother." He grew suddenly serious. "You are keeping the baby."

"Of course I am!"

"That's good." He patted her reassuringly. "Is Ace the dad?"

Now it was Flynn's turn to stare at her father in confusion. "H-how did you—"

"Because, there really hasn't been any other man for you."

If her father knew, then chances were Sarah Hart did, too. All those months trying to hide her and Ace's relationship from their parents had apparently been for nothing.

Flynn grimaced. What would Ace's mother, his

whole family, think of her when they found out about the baby?

"Do you love him?" her father asked.

Flynn involuntarily stiffened. Dinah Hart had been the only one to ask her that before. She'd noticed Flynn's crush on her older brother, a crush that had developed into much more when she and Ace dated.

Except Flynn had kept those feelings hidden and always would, not even telling Dinah.

"I— I'm… It's complicated."

Thankfully her father didn't pressure her for more. They returned to their chairs, and he clasped her hand across the table. "I take it you haven't told Ace yet."

"No."

"Are you going to?"

Flynn pushed her half-empty juice glass away. It suddenly didn't appeal to her anymore. "I wouldn't hide the baby from him. But I'm going to wait until I visit the obstetrician. Make sure everything's okay."

"Well, you could have picked a worse guy."

"Dad!"

"I meant that as a compliment. I've always liked Ace. It was John Hart I had a problem with. The man drank like a fish and practically ran his ranch into the ground before he died."

"That's harsh."

"Well, he did. But I have nothing other than respect for Sarah and Ace. He's ten times the man his father was. All them kids are, in their own way. But Ace most of all. He stepped up. Took over as head of the family. Runs the ranch with his mother. Hell of a vet, too. He'll make a good dad."

"I don't think Ace would agree with you about his

father. He and John may have butted heads, but Ace loved him. After John died, Ace took over because he thought it was what his father would have wanted."

In her mind, Flynn could hear Ace telling her those exact words ten years ago when he ended their brief dating relationship.

"Like I said, he's a better man than his father. He's trying to make something of that ranch, and not just for himself. Nothing he wouldn't sacrifice for his family. Nothing he wouldn't sacrifice for you and your baby, too."

"You're probably right."

"He'll insist on doing the right thing."

"I'm not getting married, if that's what you're implying." Flynn shocked herself with her vehemence.

"Why not?"

"Come on, Dad. I already have one disastrous marriage under my belt."

"You didn't love Paul."

Just how much had her father observed? She'd evidently underestimated him for years.

"I did love him." Not like she had—did—Ace. "In the beginning. We…" She hesitated, her voice thickening. These emotional highs and lows simply had to stop. "We drifted apart."

"He ignored you."

"Not always."

"Almost always." Her father snorted. "More interested in his job than you."

Paul's ambition was a quality Flynn had liked and admired when they first met. She hadn't foreseen that his ambition would one day consume him. After a few years, it became obvious he knew his coworkers more intimately than he did Flynn and shared more with them. She grew to resent that same ambition she'd once admired and the endless hours he put in at the office.

"He wasn't the only one at fault. I made my share of mistakes. I let him walk all over me instead of putting my foot down."

Her father snorted again, his way of saying his girls were perfect.

Flynn smiled despite her weepiness. He may think she had nothing to do with her failed marriage, but Flynn knew better. She'd made mistakes, the first one being rushing to the altar.

She'd met Paul in one of her classes at community college; they hit it off and got engaged shortly after graduating. Flynn had assumed their similar career goals—to advance, to climb the corporate ladder—would bind them. She hadn't anticipated their differences when it came to starting a family.

Flynn had asked him for a separation, hoping the shock would shake up Paul and force him to admit how much he loved her and wanted to stay married.

Only, what he'd said was, "Why bother with a separation? Let's just get a divorce." He'd packed up his belongings and left the next day.

"I'm not going to make any rash decisions," Flynn announced resolutely. "This baby is too important to me."

"Too bad about nursing school," her father said. "You'd have made a good nurse."

Flynn straightened. "I can still go to school. I'll start the enrollment process now. Take online classes until after the baby's born."

She was going to be a mother. A single mother. Now

more than ever she needed a decent job with security and benefits and potential for advancement.

"That's an awful lot to have going on at once. Especially if you're working, too."

She would need to keep working. She couldn't afford to pay for school otherwise.

Her temples began to throb. There was so much to think about.

"I'll start slow. One or two classes."

"Hmm," her father mumbled in a tone that implied maybe Flynn should reconsider. "What about Ace? He's going to want to be a dad to your child."

"And he can be. Visit as much as he wants. Billings is only an hour away from here."

Her father chuckled and raised his coffee mug in a toast. "Good luck with that."

"What?" Flynn made a face. "I'll be generous."

"We're talking about Ace Hart. The man isn't going to want you to go anywhere, not with his child. He's going to fight you tooth and nail and we both know it."

Flynn hated it when her father was right.

CHAPTER FOUR

ACE FISHED HIS keys from his jeans pocket as he headed out of the barn.

Flynn had called that morning requesting he meet her at the old fishing hole on Thunder Creek when they were both off work. He'd agreed without hesitation, assuming she was giving him the chance to make good on the apology he owed her.

Now that he was about to see her, doubts crept in.

There'd been an unusual nervous quality in her voice. He hadn't heard anything like it in ten years, not since he'd asked to meet her at the same fishing hole. His father had recently died, and Ace had informed Flynn it was over between them.

His thoughts returned to the auction five days ago. She hadn't been nervous then.

Could she have changed her mind about moving and going to nursing school?

Even if she had, she wouldn't insist on a private meeting in a secluded spot to inform him. There had to be another reason.

Like giving him the chewing out he richly deserved without any prying ears nearby.

He was about to start the engine when Gracie came running from the barn to his truck, one hand securing her hat to her head, the other one clutching a piece of paper. The single mother and only female ranch hand had worked for the Harts two years this coming May. She took a lot of flack from the men and repaid them by dishing out an equal amount, which earned her their respect. Ace liked her, too.

He lowered the driver's side window, letting in a blast of cold air. Thunder Creek probably wasn't the best meeting place.

"What's wrong?"

"The blood work on Midnight just came in from the lab," Gracie said in a huff when she reached the truck. "I thought you'd want to see it before you left."

Ace grabbed the sheet of paper and quickly scanned it, his heart hammering.

He hoped to discover a cause for Midnight's unruly disposition and aversion to people. In an attempt to eliminate any underlying medical reason, he'd put the horse through a battery of health tests, which only made him distrust Ace even more.

"Bad news?" Gracie had assisted Ace during the exams and had taken an interest in Midnight.

"No, good news." Actually, the results couldn't be any better. Like every other test Ace had conducted. "Everything's normal."

Which meant the horse's behavior problems were the result of his genetic makeup, social environment or handling.

His *recent* handling, Ace thought, distaste filling his mouth. Midnight had successfully competed in rodeos for years before Wally Dunlap became ill and turned over the management of his string to a hired foreman. The only reputation Midnight had earned before that was giving cowboys record-breaking rides and producing superior quality offspring.

What had happened to trigger such a dramatic change in him?

Ace was determined to find out.

"Thanks, Gracie." He handed the paper back to her. "Can you put that on my desk for me? I'm going to—" He paused. Gracie had been one of the people to see him and Flynn at the diner last month. "I'll be back later tonight."

"Sure thing, boss. Oh, and I forgot. Colt gave me a message for you. He left for the PRCA Championship Rodeo in Fargo and will be home on Monday."

Ace's fingers choked the steering wheel. He stopped squeezing only when he noticed Gracie's gaze cutting to his hands.

When was his brother going to grow up, quit playing and do something more around the ranch than the least amount of work he could get away with?

No, that would make things easier on Ace, and Colt was all about himself.

"See you in the morning." Ace started the engine. "Call me if there's a problem with Midnight."

Grace hurried off in the direction of the barn and Ace's office.

He drove away, his focus changing from his brother to Flynn and their meeting.

The road to the old fishing spot was bumpy and winding and overgrown. Piles of unmelted snow and soggy patches made the driving treacherous. Ace hoped Flynn had borrowed her father's truck and not brought her compact car.

She was already waiting for him when he arrived—

her father's pickup parked with its left front wheel resting on an incline. The roar of furiously rushing water filled his ears as he picked his way down the slope. Barren brush snagged his pant legs. Come summer, when the snow had long melted, the river would once again flow lazily and the woods be overgrown with thick, lush greenery.

Flynn sat near the bank on the trunk of an overturned pine tree, a recent casualty of their hard winter. She held her spine rigid, as if bracing for the worst. Did the prospect of seeing him fill her with that much dread?

For the thousandth time, he wished he could return to that morning weeks ago.

"Hi." He spoke softly so as not to startle her, though she'd surely heard his boots crushing twigs and scraping across rough ground.

She swiveled to face him, watching him descend the last few feet. "Hi." She smiled weakly. "Thanks for coming."

He lowered himself onto the tree trunk beside her, choosing it over the boulder which sat twelve feet away. Their thighs brushed momentarily before she scooted sideways to accommodate him, but not before a rush of heat shot through him.

"You okay?" he asked, curious if she felt the same heat.

"Fine." She held her clasped hands in her lap, their pale color matching her cheeks.

No heat rushing through her.

"Flynn, whatever you need. I'm here for you."

"This is difficult." She swallowed. Fidgeted. "I really hope you're not angry with me."

"There's nothing you can do to make me mad."

"You say that now."

"If anything, you should be mad at me. I'm really sorry for the way I bailed on you. There was no excuse for it." Not a good excuse, leastwise. Losing his nerve was a poor reason if Ace had ever heard one. "I can't tell you how much I regret it. The leaving. Not… the night. Us."

He needed to shut his mouth before he said something more stupid than he already had.

She exhaled a shallow, thready breath. "You're not making this easy."

"Just tell me. What's wrong?"

She stared at the river with its pockets of foaming white water.

Was she, like him, remembering all the times they'd come here when they were dating? They'd fish for hours without talking much. If the evenings were especially sultry and the stars out in abundance, they made love.

"I really wish things were different," he said, his fingers inching toward hers. "That I didn't have so much going on."

She stiffened. "Or, what? You'd ask me out?"

"Yeah, I would."

"I'm pregnant."

Ace's hand went still, then fell to his side. "Wow."

"It was an accident. I didn't plan it. You have to believe me."

"I do." Their night together had been as spontaneous as it was amazing. "We failed to use birth control. It's my fault more than yours."

Of all the times in Ace's life for him to slip up and be irresponsible.

Look what happened. Flynn was pregnant.

Ace concentrated on breathing, on forcing air into his collapsed lungs.

"I went to the doctor yesterday," she said. "She told me everything's fine. Progressing right on schedule."

"That's good."

"You're upset."

"I'm surprised is all. Give me a minute."

He'd always wanted children. It had been a frequent topic during their long-ago fishing trips. Just not yet. Later, when his vet practice was established and the new breeding business was running smoothly. When he didn't have a quarter-of-a-million-dollar loan hanging over his head.

"I realize the timing isn't great."

Flynn had been reading his mind.

"I'll support you and the baby in every way. Financially. Emotionally."

"I'm going to apply for a student grant. That should—"

"You're not still moving to Billings?"

"My plans haven't changed."

"Well, they need to change. This is my baby, too."

"I realize that family is important to you. How could I not?"

She was referring to when they broke up ten years ago.

"After my dad died, I didn't have any choice. I needed to finish school and help Mom run the ranch. There wasn't anybody else to do it."

"So you said. Countless times."

"Tuf joined the Marines. Dinah was trying to turn her life around. Colt decided he'd rather be on the road than at home. What was I supposed to do?"

"Exactly what you did."

"We were nearly broke, thanks to my dad."

A surge of anger from years earlier resurfaced, stifling Ace. How could his father have been so careless with the ranch?

Easy. Alcohol had clouded his judgment.

"You're right, your mom needed you." Flynn rubbed her temples. "I didn't mean to dredge up the past."

"I want to be an active father. Change diapers. Take the 3:00 a.m. feeding. Rock him or her to sleep." Ace wasn't sure where this spontaneous paternal drive came from, only that the baby mattered greatly. "I can't do those things if you're in Billings."

"Like you said, you have an awful lot on your plate right now."

"This is my child. You have to stay."

"Billings isn't far. You can visit. Often."

"I'm not driving an hour to see my child."

"Once Dad sells the ranch and moves, there's nothing keeping me here."

Was he nothing?

Apparently so.

"What about your job?"

"I'm enrolling in nursing school."

"Won't that be an awful lot on *your* plate? School and taking care of a baby?"

"I can manage. Between my dad and my sister and day care."

"Day care?" He scowled. "You'd let strangers take care of our child?"

"I'll find qualified day care. The university may have a facility."

"No."

She gaped at him, her jaw slack. "I beg your pardon?"

"I don't want you leaving our baby in day care. There has to be another solution."

"Like what? You watch him?"

"Why not? He could stay here with me during the week and you have him on the weekends. My mom will help." As if she wasn't as busy as Ace.

"No way!"

"You don't get to make all the decisions, Flynn."

Her mouth quivered. "Neither do you."

Ace paused, breathed deeply. He hated being harsh with her. "It's only late March. You won't be starting school until, what? The fall?"

"I was hoping to take some online classes this summer."

"You can do that from here."

"And Billings."

"Not until your dad's ranch sells, which gives us a little time to decide. Together."

She shrugged.

"Flynn." He took a chance, reached out and captured her hand. "We're having a baby. It's pretty incredible when you think about it."

She wiped at the tears spilling from her eyes.

"Don't cry." He'd always been a sucker for a woman's tears and ached to kiss her.

Better not. She'd probably club him up the side of the head.

A hug, that was the safer option.

He put an arm around her, pulled her close and stroked her back. "It's going to be okay. *We're* going to be okay."

She surprised him by returning the hug and burying her face in his jacket.

He cupped the back of her neck, threaded his fingers into the hair that had escaped her colorful stocking cap.

"There's another solution, you know," he murmured.

"What's that?"

"We get married."

She pushed away from him. "Ace, I can't."

"Won't you at least consider it?"

"No."

Her quick and adamant rejection stung.

Was the prospect of marrying him really that intolerable?

"ACE, I'M SORRY. That came out wrong." Flynn rose from the log and joined Ace at the creek bank where he stood watching the water rush past. "I wasn't expecting you to propose. It really was a sweet gesture."

"Sweet?" He looked crushed.

"Okay, that came out wrong, too."

"Flynn, I'm serious. I want to marry you."

"I know you're serious. And, honestly, that's what scares me."

"Because of your divorce?"

"Marriage is a big commitment. Hopefully, a lifetime commitment. Take it from me, marrying for the wrong reasons can lead to a lot of unhappiness."

"A child seems like a pretty good reason to me."

She softened her voice. "You only proposed because you don't want me to move."

"That hit below the belt."

"Maybe, but it's true."

"How do you know?"

"Let's be honest. You don't have feelings for me—"

"I do. Couldn't you tell from our night together?"

"All right, then, what kind of feelings?"

"I care about you," he replied, a tad too defensively.

What had she expected? A flowery declaration? "I made a promise to myself after my divorce. I'm not going to marry any man who doesn't love me."

"Your ex-husband didn't love you?"

"Not enough to make our marriage work. The same with my parents. You know my mom walked out on us when I was young. What you don't know is Paul did the same thing to me."

Ace remained silent for several seconds. Several very telling seconds. When he finally spoke, it was haltingly. "The other night, it wasn't just the sex. I haven't been that close to anyone before."

Looking away was impossible and, boy, did Flynn try. "For me, either."

They'd been intimate a few times when they dated in college. Here at this very spot, in fact. But Flynn had been completely inexperienced and Ace not much more. Ten years had brought about a lot of changes, for both of them.

Ace's skill as a lover had been matched only by his emotional intensity. He wasn't always as strong and confident and capable as he wanted people to think. Sometimes he let his guard down.

He had that night, allowing her to see a vulnerable side of him he mostly kept hidden.

And she'd fallen a little more in love.

"There isn't anyone else I'd want for the father of my baby," she admitted. "You'll be a good one, I'm sure of it."

"Then give us a chance."

"I told you—"

"Not to get married. I realize I'm rushing you. But to be the best parents we can. Raise our child together."

She did owe him that much. "You're right. We have time. I won't be moving for a while."

"I'm not going to change my mind. I want you and the baby living close to me."

Flynn should have heeded her father's advice more closely when he'd warned her about Ace's determination.

"Are you going to tell your family?" she asked.

"Soon. Once I figure out what I'm going to say." He smiled crookedly.

Flynn turned away from that charming smile to stare at the sun descending toward the distant mountaintops.

"What's wrong?" Ace touched her shoulder.

"I'm worried about what they'll think of me."

"Mom will be overjoyed. She doesn't understand how she could raise four kids to adulthood and none of them make her a grandmother yet."

"I can see your mom being happy."

"And she likes you."

"I like her, too." Flynn couldn't picture a better, kinder grandmother than Sarah Hart.

Then again, almost anyone would be a better grandmother than Flynn's own mother.

"Have you told your parents yet?" Ace asked.

"My dad."

"And?"

"He's pretty excited. He adores Nora's two sons."

"What about your mom?"

He would have to mention her mother.

Flynn sniffed. "I haven't spoken to her since last Christmas."

Her contact with her mother was infrequent and that suited her fine. For some reason, Nora had fewer painful memories of their childhood than Flynn and could talk to their mother without resentment rising up to choke her.

"Are you going to tell her?" Ace asked.

"Maybe. If I don't, Nora will."

Flynn's gaze returned to the sunset. "My mother wasn't what you'd call a good role model."

"You're not like her, Flynn."

"Am I that easy to read?"

"You forget, I know you."

Not like he thought he did or he'd see the love she carried around for him in her heart.

A painful lump in the back of her throat made speaking difficult. "I would never abandon my children for anyone or anything. Ever."

"Neither would I. You and our baby are stuck with me for the long haul."

She believed him. The Harts were close-knit, and Ace unerringly loyal.

That loyalty also scared her. He may not abandon her or their child, but he wouldn't give as much of himself as Flynn needed. The family business and his vet practice would come first. It had before, it would again.

She shivered as a breeze swept over them. "We should probably head home. I don't want to drive that road in the dark."

He helped her to climb the slope, held her hand until she found her footing.

"I'll call you tomorrow," he said at the top where their trucks were parked.

The words hung between them. If only he'd told her that a month ago, their conversation today might have gone differently. She'd still be pregnant, but she wouldn't have so many doubts about his motives.

"All right. Evening is better. I'm working the day shift at the clinic this week."

He walked her to her father's truck and opened the door. Before she could climb in, he circled her waist and drew her close. It was nice to be held by a pair of strong, muscular arms, and Flynn let herself melt into his embrace. For a moment, she could almost believe everything was going to be all right.

How could she be mad at him for proposing and for wanting her to stay in Roundup? He might have had an entirely different reaction to her announcement. Told her the baby was her problem and refused any responsibility whatsoever.

Ace no sooner released her than her sense of security faded, leaving Flynn feeling alone and more than a little scared about what lay ahead.

CHAPTER FIVE

ACE LIKED STARTING every morning with a plan. Today, he intended to make headway with Midnight, somehow, someway. If he couldn't discover what lay at the root of the horse's unmanageableness and resolve the issue, he'd settle for behavior modification.

He gave himself one month.

If, at the end of that time, Midnight didn't make measurable progress, Ace was going to recommend to his mother they sell him at the Miles City Bucking Horse Sale, take their losses and acquire a new stud.

Second on his list for the day was breaking the news to his family about Flynn's pregnancy.

He'd kept the news to himself for several days, wanting to process the ramifications first. He still hadn't decided between one big announcement at dinner or approaching each family member individually.

Their reactions didn't worry him, he honestly believed they'd be thrilled for him and Flynn. There would be questions, however. Probing ones. He might grow less tired answering them all at once.

Carrying his favorite saddle to the pens behind the barn, he hoisted it onto the fence railing. Midnight tracked Ace's every move, ears pricked forward, eyes alert. Ace made a second trip to the tack room, returning with a bucket of water, a sponge and a container of saddle soap. He also brought along a half-dozen carrots.

Setting the cleaning supplies on the ground, he opened the swinging panel in order to form a single large pen.

Midnight huffed and remained resolutely on his side, guarding his territory.

Ace set about cleaning his saddle, all the while maintaining a quiet conversation with the horse.

"I treated an old donkey at Angie Barrington's animal rescue this morning. The darn thing had the worst eye infection I've ever seen. He'll be lucky if he doesn't lose his sight."

Midnight wasn't interested. His attention had started to wander to the mares and yearlings in the distant pasture.

After a few more minutes, a few more scrubbings on the saddle and a few more casual observations about his morning rounds, Ace removed his jacket and hung it on a fence post. The weather wasn't quite warm enough to forego outerwear, but he'd make do. Picking up the carrots he'd brought, he shoved three in each of his back pockets.

Fifteen feet wasn't so far away Midnight couldn't smell a treat, and he instantly honed in on the carrots.

Ace resumed nonchalantly cleaning the saddle. He could practically hear the horse's nostrils quivering. At one point, Midnight advanced a step closer, his hooves scuffling on the hard ground. Ace didn't turn around, just kept cleaning the saddle. With any luck, Midnight would venture near enough to snatch the carrots from Ace's pockets.

He was prepared to wait, the entire afternoon if necessary. Of course he might have the cleanest saddle on the whole ranch.

After another ten minutes, Midnight had crept inch by inch to about ten feet away, his head bobbing with frustration. He wanted those carrots.

All at once, he emitted a loud squeal and scrambled to the far side of the pen, hind legs kicking.

Ace looked up and spotted his brother Colt ambling toward him.

Just when Ace was getting somewhere.

He flung the sponge into the bucket, creating a small splash.

"What's up?" Colt asked, completely indifferent to Ace's irritation.

"I was working with Midnight. Until you scared him."

"I did? Sorry."

"Dammit, Colt. I gave strict instructions. I wasn't to be disturbed."

"You need a hand?" Colt rested his forearms on the fence beside Ace's saddle, clearly not receiving the message to leave any more than he had Ace's original instructions.

"Are you kidding?"

The only reason Ace didn't get angrier with his brother was because of Midnight. The horse watched them warily from the farthest corner of the pen. A shouting match would only spook him and make him even more afraid of Ace.

That, and losing his cool with Colt would do no good. His brother was immune, wrapped up in his own world most of the time.

"I said I was sorry."

Ace exhaled, reined in his temper. "It's going slowly. I'm more and more convinced the livestock foreman mistreated Midnight and probably the other horses, as well."

Colt shook his head. "I don't get people like him."

It was one of the few things Ace and his brother had in common. Mostly they were a study in contradictions, appearance *and* personalitywise. Strangers might not even recognize them as being related. Ace had inherited their father's six-foot-plus height and dark looks. Colt, with his blond hair, green eyes and boyish, devil-may-care smile, resembled their mother and was often mistaken for being younger than his thirty-two years.

A few inches shorter than Ace, he was also leaner, giving him the kind of build better suited for competing in rodeos, which he did at every opportunity. There wasn't a championship buckle he didn't covet, an event at which he didn't excel. And yet, he never seemed satisfied.

There had been a time when Ace was the better bareback bronc rider, and he still participated once in a while for fun or to blow off steam. As long as it didn't interfere with work.

Another glaring difference between him and his brother. Ace put the ranch and family first. Colt, himself. He got away with doing less because, in Ace's opinion, their mother let him.

In truth, so did Ace. Love and loyalty were nothing if not complicated.

What infuriated him the most was Ace knew Colt to be capable of so much more. His brother had true skill with horses and cattle, too. The kind of skill Ace envied. If Colt would just take life and himself a little more seriously, he'd astound everyone with his accomplishments.

And, possibly, Ace could relinquish some of his responsibilities around the ranch. Particularly in light of the fact he was going to be a father.

"Thought I should let you know I'm leaving Thursday for the Crazy Eights Rodeo."

"Any chance you skip this one? We're examining the mares on Thursday. Prepping them for breeding season next month."

"Sorry, bro. I'm behind in steer wrestling and bull riding. I can't afford to miss one weekend if I expect to qualify for Nationals."

"December's a long way away."

"Every rodeo counts."

Ace was wasting his time, but he couldn't stop himself. "I need your help. Darrell's girls are on school break. He's taking the week off."

"I can do it Monday."

"That's my surgery day."

"Then Tuesday."

"Forget it." Ace didn't bother reciting his list for Tuesday. Nothing short of a catastrophe would stop Colt from going to the rodeo in Bozeman. "I'll just work Sunday."

Another day of rest spent toiling. Ace should be used to it by now. Instead, he was tired and cranky.

"I'll help you with the stock for the Western Frontier Pro Rodeo," Colt offered.

He'd help because he was competing in that one, too.

"I realize you've got a lot on your plate right now," Colt continued, "what with the new breeding business and all."

"Do you?"

"Sure."

Ace sensed his brother's guard rise like an invisible shield in front of him.

"Then why can't you stay home this one weekend?"

"I told you. I'm behind in two events."

"Is making all-around cowboy more important to you than this ranch?"

"Hey, I respect you and what you do. You could return the favor."

"What I do is work. Damn hard. I don't gallivant around the countryside, chasing dreams."

"You chase dreams." Colt's gaze traveled to Midnight. "They're just here."

"This family needs you, Colt."

"This family has you."

"And if they didn't?"

Colt grinned. "Not going to happen."

"It might. Things change."

"Yeah, like what? We strike oil?"

"I have my own family."

Colt laughed. "You need a woman for that, or hasn't anyone told you?"

"Flynn's pregnant. I'm the father."

"I…" Colt took a step back, caught his breath. "I had no idea you and she were dating."

"We're not."

"Then how—"

"Long story."

"You're smiling."

Ace had been doing that a lot since yesterday. "I'm excited about the baby."

"You are?"

"Hell, yes. Why wouldn't I be?"

"I don't know. Are you ready to be a dad?"

"I'll be ready by the time the baby's born. I like kids. I've always wanted to have my own."

It was another area he and Colt seemed to differ. Ace's brother had never expressed any interest in settling down, much less starting a family.

"Then I'm glad for you." Colt's flat voice sounded anything but glad.

"What's wrong?"

"How did Mom take the news?"

"I haven't told her yet. I will at dinner."

"Good luck with that."

"You think she won't be happy?"

"She and Dad always wanted us to be married before we had kids."

"Yeah, well, I'm not." He would be, if Flynn weren't so stubborn.

"I need to hit the road."

"Colt. Hey, come on, man. Stay. I'm going to be spending a lot of time with Flynn while we figure things out. I could really use you."

"Maybe if I win this weekend, some of the pressure will be off."

The pressure his brother was under didn't compare to Ace's. He could feel it building inside him, a band stretched tight on the verge of snapping. But he maintained his cool, willed himself to calm down. Colt wouldn't change, and Ace refused to be like their late father, whose favorite method of motivating his children had been to verbally berate them.

Or had Ace, as the oldest, been pushed harder than his siblings?

"Fine," he said tightly. "Remember to call Mom, let her know you arrived. She worries."

"Yeah. And congratulations again. Flynn's a terrific gal."

Colt left, his gait just shy of a dead run.

Ace remained at the fence, watching him. His brother was always in a hurry to leave the ranch behind, but this exit was particularly hasty.

Strange.

Hopefully when Ace told the rest of his family about Flynn and the baby, they'd react better.

Ace resumed his chore of cleaning the saddle, his concentration a shambles. He'd pretty much decided to quit for the day and tackle Midnight's behavior problems tomorrow, when he felt something behind him. Startled, he patted his back pockets.

Son of a gun!

He spun slowly around.

Midnight stood a few feet away, smugly crunching a carrot.

Ace grabbed another one and held it out to the horse.

He snorted and retreated a step, still chewing.

"That's okay," Ace said, his anger at his brother dissipating. "It's a start."

A *very good* start.

THE STOCK PENS at the Western Frontier Pro Rodeo were already half-full when Ace and Colt arrived and parked their truck and trailer. Behind them were two more Thunder Ranch rigs, one carrying bucking horses and the other a pair of their most promising bulls.

Beau and Duke, Ace's twin cousins, had come along to help with the livestock and compete with Colt and

Ace. It had been over a year since all four of them went up against each other at the same rodeo. Ace was looking forward to it.

His decision to enter bareback bronc riding was likely the only reason he and his brother hadn't argued since Colt's return from Bozeman last week. Ace had entered today not to mend their differences but to show up his brother. Beating Colt would feel good. It would also prove Ace still remembered how to have fun and wasn't, as his mother liked to call him, a stick in the mud.

She'd taken the news of Flynn's pregnancy well. More than well, she'd been thrilled. True to Colt's prediction, she expressed her desire to see Ace and Flynn married first, a natural reaction for most parents in Ace's opinion. But she'd been happy for Ace. So had Dinah, who'd rushed over after getting off duty to celebrate with them. The only damper to the evening had been Colt. Rather than join them, he'd found some reason to retreat to his room.

Ace, his cousins and the ranch crew had barely started unloading the livestock when Colt made a beeline away from the stock pens.

"Hey, where you going?" Ace hollered after him.

"The entry booth, to sign in."

"It can wait. The rodeo doesn't start for four more hours."

"I won't be long." Colt, jogging backward, raised his hand in a farewell gesture.

Ace took his frustration out on the toolbox mounted to the side of the trailer and the finicky padlock securing the lid.

"Beau and Duke have left to sign in, too." Harlan came up beside Ace. "You should go."

Ace spared the ranch hand a brief glance, then returned to searching for the pliers he swore were right on top when he'd last checked the toolbox. "There's still time."

"Royce and I can finish here and then transport the stock for tonight's events."

"I don't want to leave you two with all the work." Moving ornery bulls and horses was a lot to handle, even for two of the Harts' most experienced hands.

"Why not?" Harlan plucked the pliers out from under a socket set and held them out to Ace. "That's our job, what you pay us for."

The idea did appeal to him, and he could sure enough use a break.

It had been a tough week. Not a day went by he didn't put in ten or twelve hours, then fall into bed shortly after supper, exhausted. Making matters worse, Flynn had given him every excuse in the book not to see him. Yeah, they'd talked on the phone, but she refused to reconsider her plans of moving to Billings. Every call had ended on a terse note.

Ace wasn't having any better luck with Midnight. Other than persuading the horse to accept a few more treats, he'd made no real progress.

"Go on," Harlan encouraged. "This might be your last chance to compete for a while."

True. With the baby coming, Ace planned on spending most weekends at home, hopefully with Flynn. He didn't let himself think about spending his weekends driving back and forth to Billings to visit his child.

He slammed shut the lid to the toolbox, the knot

of tension between his shoulders throbbing. The long hours and constant demands were having an effect on him. Eight bone-crunching seconds on the back of a wildly bucking bronc might be just the ticket to alleviate his stress.

"I won't be long." Ace repeated his brother's words to Harlan, the irony not lost on him.

"Bring some cold drinks back with you. Royce and I are parched."

Ace cut across the lot, which was reasonably dry thanks to several days of fair weather. The nights were still chilly, however, and the bucking stock would be feeling frisky.

It was going to be a good rodeo.

Colt had already signed in and left the entry booth by the time Ace got there. He spotted his brother near the arena entrance, talking to an attractive barrel racer.

Figures.

"I reckon they'll let just about anybody enter," a familiar voice behind Ace said.

He turned and grabbed the outstretched hand of his buddy Austin Wright, shaking it briskly. "I guess I'm going to have some competition today."

"Looks like it." Austin's affable grin was the same one Ace remembered from when they were young.

"What are you doing here?" he asked. "Thought you were chained to that tack shop of yours."

"I break loose once in a while."

Ace and Austin had grown up together, attended the same schools, the same church and vied for the attention of the same girls. They'd been fierce competitors on the basketball court as well as in the rodeo arena and good friends the rest of the time. In the years since high school they'd grown apart, despite living in the same town. In part because of Ace's grueling schedule, in part because of Austin's family situation. A father serving time for cattle rustling in a ranching community was a lot to live down.

"Let's get together later tonight," Ace said.

"I'd like that. After I embarrass you in the arena."

"Feeling lucky today?"

"Against you? Always."

"Loser buys dinner?"

"You're on." They shook hands again to seal their bet. "I heard you expanded your string."

"We did." Ace moved forward in line. "Brought a few of the new head with us today. They're coming on strong."

"Wish I'd drawn one."

"I pulled a McKinley bronc."

"Isn't he selling off?"

"He has some contracts still to fulfill over the next couple months." Ace found himself grinning, like he did every time he thought of Flynn and the baby. "There's something else. I'm going to be a dad."

"No fooling!"

Ace summarized the story of him and Flynn, omitting the details of their one-night stand.

"That's great." Austin beamed. "I'm really happy for you."

Why couldn't Colt be happy for Ace, too?

He and Austin continued chatting until it was Ace's turn to sign in. After Austin finished and they said their goodbyes, Ace made a quick stop at the concession stand before heading back to the livestock pens. Just as he walked up, two McKinley rigs rumbled on by—Earl behind the wheel of the first truck, Flynn beside him in the passenger seat.

Flynn!

She hadn't mentioned coming this weekend.

He checked in with Harlan and delivered the cold drinks, all the while keeping an eye on the truck with Flynn. When it came to a stop, the side door opened and she scrambled out. She then jogged around to the rear of the trailer and began directing her father as he backed up to a row of empty pens.

Ace hastened over and waited until Earl was finished parking before addressing Flynn.

"Hey, what are you doing here?"

"Same as you. Bringing stock."

Ace was prepared to toss her over his shoulder and carry her off if she attempted to help unload the horses. Fortunately she didn't, leaving the task to her dad and his trio of ranch hands.

Ace hadn't seen Flynn's father since the auction and braced himself for a stern talking-to. It's what he'd do in the other man's shoes.

"Afternoon, Earl," he said with a nod, and waited.

Earl went about his business, ignoring Ace.

He glanced at Flynn.

She shrugged.

"Sir, about the baby—"

Earl straightened, walked calmly over to Ace and stuck a finger in his chest. "I like you. But if you hurt my little girl, mark my word, there will be hell to pay."

"I won't hurt her, I swear."

"Glad that's settled."

"Me, too."

Earl poked Ace in the chest again before leaving.

Flynn laughed under her breath.

Ace wasn't amused and wiped a hand across his damp brow. "Is that a good idea, you being here? What with the baby and all?"

"What do you mean?"

"Bucking stock aren't known for their manners."

"I'm not going to ride the horses." She laughed again.

Though, in Ace's opinion, the situation was serious, her gaiety was a welcome change from their recent strain.

"Just being near them is risky. They kick. Bite. Charge."

"I promise to be supercautious if you promise to be less obsessive."

"I care about you, Flynn." Much more than she realized.

Instead of becoming prickly, she smiled softly. "Thank you."

Grateful for whatever had caused the change in her, Ace let the cozy sensation her smile triggered wind through him.

If only it could be like this between them every day.

"Speaking of taking risks." She pointed to the entrant number he carried in his hand. "I should scold you for the same thing. What if you get hurt?"

"I'll withdraw," he said immediately.

"No." She laughed again. "I don't want you to change just because we're having a baby."

We? He liked her referring to them as a couple.

"Our child is more important to me than bronc riding."

"Rodeoing's a big part of your life. It's your business."

"But not competing. I won't be any good to either

of you if I'm injured and unable to make a living. This gives me the excuse I need to quit without embarrassing myself."

"Compete, Ace. You like it and, be honest, you miss it."

"Sometimes." He'd been at the peak of his rodeo career back in college when they'd dated. He gave it up after his father died, like he had Flynn.

What if he'd been wrong all those years ago on both counts?

Their attention was drawn to the McKinley horses, who fussed and squealed and nipped at each other as they settled into the pen.

Flynn knitted her brows as she scrutinized them. "Hmm."

"Something wrong?"

"It's Fancy Gal." She started toward the fence. Ace followed her, determined to intervene if a horse so much as looked sideways at her. "She's been acting out of sorts all morning."

"Which one is she?"

Flynn pointed to a stout dun mare standing at the far end of the pen. Ears pinned back, teeth bared and swinging her head from side to side, she sent an unmistakable warning to her pen mates: stay away.

"She's one of my favorites and is usually pretty docile outside the arena."

"Want me to examine her?"

Relief lit Flynn's features. "Would you? I don't want to be a bother. You have your own string to worry about."

"I don't mind."

"I'll get her."

"You're not going in that pen with all those horses."
Ace put a hand on her arm. "Your dad can do it."

She sighed. "All right."

Ace liked her when she was agreeable.

He was rather confident it wouldn't last.

CHAPTER SIX

PREGNANCY SUITED FLYNN. She'd woken up that morning on completely the *right* side of the bed. Not that her doubts about the future had vanished. Far from it. But she felt good. Happy. Optimistic.

Her exuberance, however, dimmed as her concern for Fancy Gal escalated. The mare was clearly distressed and in pain.

It didn't take long for her father to separate the mare from the rest of the string, bring her out and tie her to the side of the trailer.

Flynn hovered near Ace as he conducted his examination. She had her suspicions about what ailed the mare and was curious to see if she was right.

"We probably shouldn't have brought her today." She stroked Fancy Gal's nose. Away from her pen mates, the mare was gentle as a lamb and calmly tolerated Ace's poking and prodding. "She's nineteen. Too old for competing."

"Not really," he said. "If they're in good health, horses can be competed into their twenties. But if you want to retire her, she'd make a nice broodmare."

"I hope whoever buys her does exactly that."

Ace ran a hand along Fancy Gal's abdomen. "Besides irritability, what are her other symptoms?"

Flynn pointed to the mare's shuffling hooves. "She keeps shifting her weight."

"I checked her feet," her father added, coming over. "No stones or abscesses or any problems that I saw."

"You won't take offense if I also have a look?" Ace picked up the mare's front hoof, braced it between his knees and dug around the soft underside with a pen-knife.

"I'd think you were a sorry vet if you didn't." Her father carefully supervised Ace's every move. Fancy Gal was one of his favorite horses, too.

Ace repeated the process with the remaining hooves. "They look fine." He took a step back and considered the mare. "Any signs of colic?"

"Nope."

"Yes," Flynn interjected. Colic was her guess. "She's been biting her flanks."

Ace placed his ear against Fancy Gal's abdomen.

Flynn held the mare's head firmly in place. Fancy Gal might be a lamb but sick animals often spooked and behaved out of character.

Ace straightened, his mouth set in a firm line. "Sounds like a war zone in there. I don't think you should compete her today."

"Poor girl," Flynn cooed, and scratched Fancy Gal behind the ears.

"Have we caught it in time?" her father asked.

He had reason to be concerned. Several years ago they had almost lost a prize gelding to a sudden and aggressive case of colic.

"I think so," Ace said. "Can you arrange for a separate stall or pen? She shouldn't be with the other horses."

"I'll talk to the barn manager."

"I can walk her," Flynn offered when her father left.

When their gelding had colic, she and her father had taken turns walking him all through the night. It had probably saved the gelding's life.

Ace shook his head. "I'd feel better if you got one of the men to do it."

"Fancy Gal won't hurt me."

"Not intentionally."

"I appreciate your concern, but I'm going to walk her and—"

"And I'm not stopping you," he finished for her.

"Something like that." Flynn squared her shoulders.

Ace's glance traveled from Fancy Gal to Flynn. "I don't like it."

"You have to trust me."

He groaned as if giving in to her caused him pain. "I've got some bute paste in my truck. That should help her with the discomfort." He promptly returned, a tube clutched in his hand, and administered the bute paste.

Fancy Gal didn't like the taste or the texture. She worked her jaw and rolled her tongue until the medication had dissolved.

Afterward, Ace accompanied Flynn and Fancy Gal to the vacant pasture on the far side of the warm-up arena. She started to tell him to leave, that she was fine on her own, then reconsidered. She liked him walking beside her. She reconsidered again the third time his arm brushed hers.

At the end of their first circuit, Flynn told Ace, "You should probably go. Your event is the first one after the opening ceremony."

"If she worsens or shows any other symptoms, call me immediately. I don't care what I'm doing."

"We'll be fine."

He acted as if he hadn't heard her. "I'll stop by in an hour to check on her."

"You don't have to do that."

"Yes, I do. You were lucky today. She's in the early stages of colic. A few more hours, her chances of making a full recovery would be a lot less."

Whatever personal issues she had with Ace, she couldn't deny he was a good vet.

"I know it's a lot to ask, and you just acquired all those horses at the auction…"

"Tell me."

"Dad's selling all the livestock. I want Fancy Gal to go to a good home, one where she can live out the rest of her life." Flynn fiddled with the mare's lead rope. "She's really almost never sick. And she would make a wonderful broodmare. I can get you a copy of her registration papers—"

"You want me to buy her?"

"Yes."

When he didn't answer right away, Flynn's heart sank.

"It was a stupid idea."

"No, it isn't. I just don't like doing anything that will make your leaving easier."

She glanced away, hiding her disappointment.

He took her chin in his fingers and tilted her face to his. "But I'll buy her."

"Seriously? Because I don't want you doing this strictly for me."

"Of course I'm doing it for you. And she'd be a sound investment."

"Thank you, thank you!" Flynn threw herself at Ace

and squeezed him tightly around the waist with her one free arm.

"Before you get carried away, we should probably talk price."

"I'll make sure Dad gives you a smoking deal."

Flynn sighed contentedly. This hug was so much nicer than the stiff one they'd shared at the fishing hole when she'd told him about the baby.

"In that case, maybe we should buy more of your father's horses."

"Oh, Ace." She stood on her tiptoes and impulsively pressed her lips to his cheek. The familiar scent of him instantly assailed her, weakened her knees so that she was forced to lean on him.

He went still.

Uh-oh. Big mistake.

She was about to pull away when he bent his head and sought her lips.

The kiss, light, tender and achingly sweet, lasted only a few seconds before he abruptly withdrew.

Not again!

Why was he always doing this to her?

Flynn stepped away, only to spy her father at the edge of the pasture, his gaze riveted on her and Ace.

FLYNN GAVE FANCY GAL one last thorough inspection before permitting herself to relax. The mare was better, nosing around the corners of her pen for a tidbit of hay rather than exhibiting signs of distress.

True to his word, Ace had stopped by earlier and examined her, noting her progress and advising Flynn to continue walking the mare at intervals for the rest of the afternoon, possibly into the evening. He also brought some warm bran mash to settle Fancy Gal's stomach, though where he acquired it Flynn had no clue.

"I have my connections," was all he'd admit before returning to the arena.

She glanced at her watch, straining to hear the announcements coming from the direction of the arena. Ace's event, bareback bronc riding, would be starting soon. She was just locking up the truck when her father strode over. He hadn't mentioned seeing her and Ace kissing earlier, but she wouldn't put it past him.

What a mistake! Why did she continually lose her head with Ace?

Unfortunately, there was no going back now.

"Did I tell you Ace drew True Grit?" her father asked.

"Seriously? No, you didn't."

The gelding was one of her father's best bucking broncs—or worst, if you were the cowboy trying to ride him.

When her father began reciting the other bronc/cowboy matchups, Flynn cut him off.

"Ace hasn't been in a rodeo since last fall. True Grit's a lot of horse, even for someone who competes regularly."

"That's how rodeo works. It's the luck of the draw."

Bad luck, Flynn thought. "What if he gets injured?"

"He's a big boy."

"He's also the father of my child. Your grandchild."

Her father chuckled.

Flynn took off at a brisk walk.

He chased after her. "Where you going?"

"To tell Ace not to compete."

"What with the way you're acting, a person might

suspect you have more feelings for him than you're willing to admit."

"This has nothing to do with me or my feelings."

Her father's persistent chuckling grated on Flynn's nerves.

She seldom ventured behind the bucking chutes where the participants gathered to assess the horses and their competition and to while away the time while they waited—usually nervously—for their turn.

Ace was there, along with his brother, cousins and Austin Wright. The moment he saw her, he broke away and met her halfway.

"Is Fancy Gal all right?" he asked.

"She's great."

"Are *you* all right?"

"Ace, don't compete."

"What?"

"Dad told me you drew True Grit. You know his reputation and his ranking."

"I'll be fine."

"See," her dad said, catching up with Flynn. "I told you."

"Please, Ace."

A twinkle lit his eyes. It also warmed her heart.

She was such a sucker.

"Weren't you just saying I shouldn't change because we're having a baby?"

"Yes, but True Grit is—"

"It's okay." He reached out and stroked her cheek.

"Promise me." She closed her eyes and sighed softly.

"I tend to agree with my daughter," Earl said. "True Grit probably has more giddyup than you're used to."

"Dad!" Flynn's eyes flew open.

Ace let his hand drop and turned to appraise her father. "I might be a little rusty, but I'm pretty sure I can sit that horse for eight seconds."

"That boast has all the makings of a wager."

Now Flynn was really upset. "No betting!"

Ace grinned. "What do you have in mind?"

"Flynn mentioned you're interested in buying Fancy Gal and maybe a few more of my string. I've got another potential buyer lined up. Hoyt Cammeron."

"Yeah?" Ace visibly perked up.

"You last the full eight seconds on True Grit, and I'll sell you any of my string you want and throw in Fancy Gal for free. You eat dirt, I sell the string to Hoyt, including Fancy Gal if he wants her."

"You can't," Flynn objected.

"You're on." Ace stuck out his hand to her father.

"Ace, get over here," Colt hollered. "Beau's up next."

"See you at the stock pens when I'm done." Ace squeezed Flynn's arm, then nodded curtly at her father.

"I'll be there, too. With Hoyt," Flynn's father added.

She waited a mere second after Ace left before whirling on her father. "How could you, Dad? A bet? Really? And what's this with Hoyt? You told me you'd no more sell that man a broken-down pony than any of your string."

There was that chuckle again.

She groaned with frustration.

"Come on." He placed a hand on the small of her back and guided her toward the stands. "We'd better hurry before it's Ace's turn."

At her wit's end, Flynn went with her father to the crowded bleachers where they found two empty seats. Second to the last row, unfortunately. She couldn't remain still as one cowboy after the other went. Beau did well, his score landing him in the lead. His position lasted only until Austin Wright's turn. Austin had also drawn a McKinley horse and was the first competitor that day to successfully ride one.

Finally, after what felt like forever, Ace's name was called.

Flynn gnawed her lower lip as she watched him straddle the fence and sit True Grit. The horse, raring to go, shifted nervously in the narrow chute, bumping into the side panels and tossing his head.

Ace didn't hurry.

He was too far away for Flynn to see, but she imagined him testing the rigging and adjusting his grip on the handle until it satisfied him. He'd place his feet above the horse's shoulders, correctly marking the horse before entering the arena so as not to be disqualified before his ride even started. He'd listen to the advice of his brother and cousins and buddies who were clustered together and hanging on the fence.

In the end, he'd trust his instincts.

Suddenly, the chute gate flew open and True Grit exploded into the arena, front hooves solidly planted on the ground, his back ones reaching for the sky. Not the biggest horse there by any means, his claim to fame was his ability to bend himself into the shape of a twist tie while achieving incredible heights.

Today was no exception.

Rocking onto his hind legs, True Grit reared, standing almost completely vertical. Ace clung to the rigging, leaning so far back his head lay against the horse's rump and the toes of his boots touched the horse's ears. Even in that impossible position, Ace spurred the horse, urging him to buck higher, buck harder.

True Grit gave it his all, hitting the ground with his front feet and spinning in a full circle with such force, Ace was almost knocked off.

Flynn gasped and covered her mouth with her hand.

What was wrong with the timer? Surely eight seconds had passed. More like a full minute.

True Grit executed another gravity-defying buck, his goal to fling Ace over his head and into the stands. By some miracle, Ace hung on.

The buzzer went off. Instantly, Flynn was out of her seat. "He did it!"

Applause and cheers broke out from the crowd as the pickup men surrounded Ace, hauled him off the horse and deposited him—still in one piece, thank God— onto the ground. As Ace walked across the arena, he picked up his hat from where it had fallen and waved it at the crowd.

Flynn started toward the aisle.

Her father grabbed her wrist, waylaying her. "Where are you going?"

To congratulate Ace, but she didn't want to tell her father that. "Walk Fancy Gal."

"Don't you want to see Ace's score?"

It didn't matter to her, only that he'd finished. "Sure." She sat back down.

A few seconds later, Ace's score was blasted from the speakers while simultaneously appearing on the scoreboard.

"Eighty-three," her father muttered. "Not great, not bad."

"Pretty good for someone who only competes oc-casionally."

"I'm glad to see him get Fancy Gal and whatever other horses he wants."

"Not Hoyt Cammeron?"

"Hoyt was never interested."

"What!" Flynn stood, braced her hands on her hips and glared at her father. "Then why the bet with Ace?"

"It was for you."

"Me?"

"I wanted to see how bad he wants you. How hard he's willing to fight."

"This was about the horses," she insisted.

"No, it wasn't. And he knows it, too."

"You're crazy."

"Maybe so." Her father wore a smug smile. "But now we have an answer."

ACE REACHED FOR his ringing cell phone, groaning in agony as every muscle in his body rebelled. Gracie's number appeared on the display. "Yeah," he barked.

"You said to call you when Flynn McKinley arrived."

"Thanks. Have her meet me at the main paddock." He disconnected, let his phone drop onto the mattress and didn't move for a full two minutes.

Finally, when he'd mustered enough strength, he pushed to a sitting position with the agility of a ninety-year-old man and lowered his feet to the floor.

Two days since the Western Frontier Pro Rodeo, and he still hurt like a son of a bitch.

Lasting eight seconds in bareback bronc riding and winning his bet with Earl had been great. Finishing in seventh place and beating out his brother and cousins, even better. He didn't even mind buying a steak dinner for his friend Austin, who'd finished second.

Thank goodness Ace hadn't qualified for the finals on Sunday. He'd be a cripple. Colt, Beau and Duke had been left with overseeing the loading of the livestock for the long, *long* return trip home during which Ace had suffered their endless ribbing. Deserved ribbing.

What had made him think he could compete once or twice a year and not come away feeling as though he'd gone for a joyride inside a cement mixer?

Rising from the bed, he tucked his shirt into his pants, put on his boots and grabbed his hat off his dresser. Break time was officially over.

He hobbled through the adjacent sitting area and out a door that lead to an enclosed patio. Some years ago, when it became apparent Ace would be staying on the ranch and helping his mother, he'd remodeled two of the downstairs bedrooms into a master suite with a private outside entrance. That way he could come and go at all hours, one of the hazards of being a vet, without disturbing the rest of the household.

Plus, Ace liked his solitude—until lately, anyway.

Waking up next to Flynn had been nice, her smooth, warm curves snuggled next to him, her hand folded inside his even in sleep.

Then he'd realized what a mistake he'd made. Not sleeping with her, but letting her get close. Letting her glimpse the raw need he ruthlessly kept concealed behind a competent, take-charge exterior.

Ace wasn't weak like his father had been. He wouldn't use alcohol or berate others to compensate for his insecurities.

His Polaris sat parked beside the patio entrance in its

usual spot. The all-terrain vehicle was his usual mode of transportation around the ranch when not riding a horse.

There would be no riding horses for several more days if the ibuprofen he'd been swallowing like Halloween candy didn't kick in soon.

Starting the Polaris, he drove to the paddock, the same paddock where they'd put Wally Dunlap's mares after the auction. The drive took only a few minutes. A bumpy, excruciating, teeth-grinding few minutes.

He expected to find Earl or one of the McKinley hands with Flynn, only she'd come by herself.

"Thanks, Gracie," he told the ranch hand after crawling out of the Polaris.

She picked up on his cue. Striding toward the barn, she said, "See ya later, Flynn."

"Geez, Ace, are you all right?" Flynn gave him a concerned once-over, taking in his bent posture.

"It's nothing."

She covered her mouth and laughed.

"Not funny." He went to the back of the horse trailer and inspected the five mares and one gelding inside, Fancy Gal and True Grit among them.

"It is too funny." She came up behind him, trying not to smirk. "That'll teach you to bust broncs without getting into condition first."

It would. If he were smart, he'd quit rodeoing for good. He couldn't afford to be laid up.

Unless he and Flynn had a son. Then he'd teach their boy everything about horses and cattle and ranching and rodeoing. On second thought, he'd teach the same things to a daughter.

A fresh wave of determination surged inside him. There would be a new generation of Harts. Rebuilding their flagging business, securing the future, took on a whole new meaning. As did carrying on family traditions, instilling in his children a love and respect for the land and the animals that inhabited it.

Wait a minute. Children?

Who exactly was he planning on having more children with? Flynn had turned down his marriage proposal. She was also moving to Billings.

He unlatched the rear door on the trailer, suppressing a groan.

"Wait, I'll help." Flynn reached for the handle and instantly withdrew when their hands touched. "You, um, don't want to injure yourself any worse than you already have."

There'd been a time when she wouldn't have been jumpy around him.

Was that a good sign?

"Cut me some slack," he joked in an attempt to relieve the awkwardness. "I'm getting enough grief from everyone else as it is."

He opened the trailer door, wincing at the pain. Maybe he should have accepted her help.

Eventually, all six horses were unloaded and exploring the paddock. Ace and Flynn stood side by side at the fence, watching them.

"You picked the best from my dad's string," she observed.

"Yeah." Ace was pretty happy about his selection. Several of the horses were nothing special to look at, but they could buck, and that was what counted. "Fancy Gal have any more problems with colic?"

"None, and I've kept a close eye on her."

"How are *you* feeling?"

"Good. Fantastic, in fact."

"No nausea?"

"A little last night."

"When's your next doctor appointment?"

"May first."

"I'll go with you."

Flynn pushed off the fence. "There's no need."

"I want to."

She started back toward the truck.

Ace caught up with her, though it was with some difficulty. "What's the matter? You don't want me to go?"

"It's not that." She shoved her hands into her down vest pockets. "What's going to happen when I leave?"

"With your doctor appointments?"

She sighed. "The more attached you get, the harder it will be."

"I'm going to be attached to my kid."

"I was talking about me."

"We agreed we're going to try and get along. Do things together."

"Getting along doesn't include kissing."

She had him there. "Was it so awful?" he asked, attempting a wry grin. "You did participate."

Her defenses visibly shot up. "You're missing the point."

"I don't think I am." He waited until she'd shut the trailer door. "Don't go to Billings, Flynn. Marry me."

"I told you no, and I told you why. Nothing's changed."

"You have to admit, there were some pretty serious sparks between us."

"Sparks aren't enough." She gazed at him pointedly.

"Sometimes, love isn't enough. But it has to be there for a marriage to survive."

"Then don't marry me, but stay in Roundup. We need more time to figure this out."

Her expression fell, telegraphing her disappointment with his answer.

He scrambled to gain ground. "Our kid deserves to have both his parents raising him."

"Couples who live apart successfully raise children all the time. My parents did. Well, my dad did."

"And he ran a demanding business."

"But he always put me and my sister first. There wasn't a single dinner he missed." Her gaze fastened on him. "Can you make the same promise? Because I won't consider staying otherwise."

"I'm willing to change."

"How?"

"Once the business is operating profitably and the loan is paid down, I'll cut back on my hours."

"When will that be?"

"A year. Possibly a little longer." In reality, it would be more like three years.

"You haven't cut back in the last ten years," she said skeptically.

"Yeah, but now there's a baby on the way."

"Which is all the more reason for you to focus on your family's business. It's your livelihood. I can't support this baby on my own."

And he'd promised to take care of his child. He couldn't do that with only the income from his vet practice. Neither could he saddle his mother with the entire responsibility of managing the ranch and paying down the loan.

His determination returned tenfold. He'd do it all, work and be there for Flynn. Be a better man than his father.

"Give me a chance to prove myself."

"I am. That's what we're doing."

"If we were married, there—"

"I was married to Paul, and it didn't make a bit of difference. He still put his career above me." She headed for the cab of her truck. "There's no reason for me to think you'll be any different."

"I'm going to continue proposing until you say yes."

"That should be interesting," she said over her shoulder, "since I'm going to continue saying no until you propose for the right reasons."

"What's more important than our child?"

"You should be asking yourself, what's *just as* important as our child."

CHAPTER SEVEN

FLYNN STEPPED INTO the stark, utilitarian lobby of the Roundup Sheriff Station, a white plastic grocery bag clenched in her hand. She came here on occasion to visit Dinah and once when she was a senior in high school. Dinah, Flynn and a few of their friends had been questioned in the matter of a teenage prank that had involved drinking and several cans of spray paint.

Flynn had been innocent. Dinah, a little less innocent. Funny, her friend was now the sheriff and the one questioning delinquent teenagers.

A lot had changed since those days. Flynn would have never guessed she'd be married and divorced, living at home again and about to embark on single motherhood.

"Is Sheriff Hart in?" she asked the male deputy behind the counter.

"Your name?"

"Flynn McKinley."

She took a seat on a bench in the lobby to wait. Dinah appeared a few minutes later, a bright smile on her face, her khaki uniform neatly pressed.

Seeing her friend often gave Flynn a start. Dinah closely resembled Ace, though her eyes were hazel as opposed to brown. Even so, there was no mistaking their relation.

"Hey, what are you doing here?"

"I brought you a peace offering." Flynn held out the plastic bag.

Dinah peeked inside at the package of miniature Snickers bars and grinned wickedly. "Come on back." She led Flynn down the hall and to her office. "Not sure why you think you need to bring me a peace offering, but I won't complain."

Snickers bars were one of Dinah's guilty pleasures.

Behind the privacy of her closed door, Dinah gave Flynn the brief hug she wouldn't in front of the other deputies and clerical staff.

"What's up?"

"I wanted to apologize."

"Did you do anything requiring an apology?" Dinah sat behind her desk while Flynn settled in the chair across from her.

The package of candy was opened, and a handful of bars quickly distributed between them. The image of Dinah, all proper and official in her uniform and chomping on candy, brought a smile to Flynn's face.

"I should have told you about the baby," she said between bites. "Not waited until Ace did."

"No worries. I get it."

"I wasn't sure what I was going to do. Heck, I'm still not sure."

"Marry him," Dinah said matter-of-factly, catching Flynn off guard.

"Did Ace tell you he'd proposed?"

"He didn't have to. I know my brother." Dinah evaluated another Snickers bar before popping it in her mouth with a contented sigh. "When's the big day?"

And here Flynn had thought she'd be the one to break the news to her friend.

"There is no big day. I refused."

"Why? You love him."

"But he doesn't love me."

"Nonsense."

"Dinah, he doesn't."

"Ace holds his cards close to his chest. He's always been that way. Got worse after Dad died. He's afraid of being hurt."

It was hard for Flynn to imagine Ace as being afraid of anything. Then again, she'd seen his vulnerable side the night they'd made love and she'd conceived.

"I'm not sure I want to be married to a man who won't or can't express his emotions."

"Isn't that better than a man who tells you he loves you and doesn't mean it?"

She was referring to Paul.

"Selfishly, I'm asking you to give him a chance." Dinah made a pleading face. "There isn't anyone else I want for a sister-in-law."

"Me, either." Flynn didn't think there was anyone she'd rather have for a husband than Ace, but only if he returned her feelings.

"I love Colt and Tuf. They're great guys in their own way. But the truth is, if I were in a jam, Ace would be the first one I'd call. He'd come through for me. He will for you, too."

"Is it wrong to want a man who will sweep me off my feet?"

"Are you so sure he won't?"

"I thought he might. Once. Then he left. Ducked out of my bedroom like he'd done something wrong."

"Thank you, Dad." Dinah snorted and sat back in her chair.

"What does your dad have to do with this?"

"He had two sets of rules. One for us, one for him. He always put these unrealistic expectations on my brothers, Ace in particular. I wouldn't be surprised if Ace woke up the next morning thinking he'd wronged you. The guilt probably ate him alive."

"He had nothing to be guilty about."

"Try telling him that."

"Great." Flynn slumped in her chair. "He not only doesn't love me, he proposed to me out of guilt in addition to duty. Be still my foolish heart."

"Come on, that's not true."

"It is, according to what you just told me."

"Flynn, don't move to Billings. Not yet. Give Ace a little more time, he won't disappoint you. Once he gets the breeding business off the ground and the problems with Midnight resolved, he'll be able to think clearly, realize how he feels about you."

"Falling in love with someone isn't a decision you make. It's either there or it isn't."

"No, but letting yourself embrace that love *is* a decision."

Flynn wanted to talk to Dinah longer about Ace, except her desk phone rang.

"I've got to go," she said after hanging up, her formerly pleasant expression now grim. "Domestic dispute. A bad one."

"Thanks for seeing me."

"I miss you." Dinah hugged her again before walking out the door. "Let's have a girls' night out soon."

"Sounds good."

Dinah took off the moment they reached the lobby, shouting orders to the deputy behind the counter before disappearing through another door.

Flynn found herself a little in awe of her friend. Was this the same girl who'd giggled with her over teen magazines when they were twelve? The same woman who'd rebelled at seventeen and raised all kinds of hell?

Maybe Dinah was right and Flynn should give Ace another chance. Each of the Hart children bore scars thanks to their father's actions.

Was Flynn any different? Her own mother's abandonment had damaged her every bit as much as John Hart's betrayal did Ace.

No wonder her and Ace's relationship was such a mess.

"ARE YOU SURE about this?" Ace's mother asked, trepidation lending an unevenness to her voice.

"I don't think we have a choice," he answered. "We need to know one way or the other if we can use him, and we need to know before breeding season is in full swing."

Yesterday, Midnight had been moved from the pens at Ace's clinic to his permanent location in the stud quarters. His spacious stall opened out into a paddock. From there, he could see horses grazing in the near pastures and cattle in the far ones.

Gracie had been assigned the task of exercising Midnight an hour or more every day in the round pen. For some reason, he tolerated her better than Ace or any of the other ranch hands, allowing her to lead him to the pen and put him through his paces.

It was a development Ace found interesting and relevant. More than ever, he was convinced Midnight had been treated poorly at the hands of the livestock foreman and, as a result, distrusted people. Men in particular. Rehabilitating the horse, if he was indeed capable of being rehabilitated, would require time and patience and careful strategy.

A woman handler might provide the key.

Ace preferred not to isolate Midnight from his brethren. Horses were normally social animals. But until he could be handled without worry, they were better off safe than sorry.

There was, however, one exception.

Midnight was being put to the test for the first time.

Ace and his mother waited in the breeding shed for Gracie to retrieve Midnight from his quarters, connected to the breeding shed by a corridor. Ace had designed the facility himself as well as developing the stringent guidelines for their breeding program. An established routine and contained environment were both essential components of that program.

"How's Flynn?" His mother asked the question daily.

"Working too hard."

"At the clinic?"

"And for her dad. I wish she'd take it easier."

"Flynn's always been a go-getter. Has she had any luck enrolling in nursing school?"

"Not that she's mentioned."

After their disagreement last week, Ace and Flynn were back to communicating mostly by phone. He didn't pressure her, but she could only put him off so long. Her next doctor's appointment was in less than two weeks, and he would be there with her.

"Do you think she and Earl would come to Sunday brunch if I invited them?"

"You can ask." Ace liked the suggestion. Refusing his mother would be much harder than refusing him.

"She still resisting your charms?"

"Hard to believe, I know."

"Not that it's my business, but has it occurred to you that marrying her might not be the best idea?"

"What? I thought you were gung ho about all us kids being married first."

"That would be best, ideally. But I'm concerned if you somehow convince Flynn to marry you, you'll wind up alienating her."

"I've already promised her I'd try and cut back on work."

"I'm not talking about work. I'm talking about love. Flynn is a romantic. She isn't interested in marrying because it makes sense or is the right thing to do."

Ace was still digesting what his mother said when a loud banging came from the direction of Midnight's quarters.

"Everything okay?" Ace hollered.

"We're good." Gracie's confident reply carried down the corridor.

"Aidan," his mother said. "She needs help."

"Gracie knows what she's doing."

Like him, his mother was nervous.

He debated going to investigate, prepared to step in at the first sign of trouble. But he'd rather not agitate Midnight if at all possible. They had a lot riding on to-day's outcome.

After double-checking Miss Kitty's lead rope, he craned his head to peer down the corridor.

What was the holdup?

He absently patted the mare, a rangy bay that had once been part of Wally Dunlap's string. She flicked her ears, her only sign of anticipation. None of this was new to her, she'd already borne two foals by Midnight. She was also fully in heat and receptive.

All things considered, she made a perfect candidate.

It was Ace's hope Midnight would get the job done without a fuss and without caring who else was in the breeding area with him.

A clattering of hooves on the concrete floor accompanied a high-pitched squeal. Midnight and Gracie promptly burst into the breeding shed, a whirlwind of raw energy.

"Easy now." She gripped the stud chain firmly in both hands, but the horse was clearly in the driver's seat.

The instant Midnight spied Miss Kitty, he dialed into her. Prancing, snorting, his nostrils flaring, he showed off for her.

She did what came naturally, what her instincts dictated, and raised her tail.

Midnight went into a frenzy.

"Whoa, boy!" Gracie tugged, barely hung on.

Ace didn't think, he reacted. "Mom, get back!" He pushed his mother aside, then grabbed the stud chain from Gracie's hands.

Midnight tossed his head and ripped the chain from Ace's grasp. He had only one thing on his mind: Miss Kitty.

"Watch out!" Ace motioned for Gracie to stay back. It was too dangerous intervening at this point. Better to let nature take its course and hope for the best.

It was over within a minute. Midnight abandoned Miss Kitty, his interest waned.

When Ace reached for the stud chain, the horse did an about-face. Huffing, he raced back down the corridor to his quarters.

Gracie started after him.

"Leave him," Ace ordered, angry at himself more than the horse. "He can't go anywhere." He turned to his mother. "You all right?"

She stepped forward, several shades paler than normal. "Well, that didn't go as planned."

Ace went over to inspect Miss Kitty, unhappy with what he saw. She'd suffered minor lacerations on her back and flanks, the result of Midnight's steel shoes. Luckily for all of them, she was familiar with Midnight and the breeding process. A different mare, and the results could have been disastrous.

"I think maybe we should sell him." Ace's mother watched over his shoulder as he cleansed and treated Miss Kitty's wounds.

"You could be right."

Gracie looked ready to cry.

"None of this is your fault," he assured her.

She sniffed. "I'll go shut his stall door."

Ace packed up his medical case, silently berating himself. He'd rushed. Midnight wasn't ready.

"None of this is your fault, either." His mother patted his arm.

"Yeah? I'm the one who insisted on buying him."

"And I supported you."

Gracie returned, relief evident on her face.

"How is he?"

"Sweet as a lamb. All in a day's work to him."

Ace wasn't fooled. The good horse act wouldn't last.

He untied Miss Kitty's lead rope and handed it to Gracie. "Take her to my clinic."

"Wait, Gracie, I'll walk with you," his mother said.

"I have some contracts in my office to sign and ship." She glanced over her shoulder at Ace. "You coming?"

He shook his head. "I'll catch up with you later."

He traveled the connecting corridor to Midnight's stall, observing the horse for several long moments. Midnight observed Ace in return, the same intelligent look in his eyes Ace had witnessed that day at the auction.

"You're going to have to do better next time," he said, realizing he wasn't ready to sell the horse.

Midnight lowered his head to the stall floor and blew lustily, shooting a cloud of the dry bedding into the air.

Stallions were typically a handful, but they could be taught manners. Midnight needed to learn some, or relearn them in his case.

"What happened to you after Wally got sick?"

Midnight snorted and stared inquisitively at Ace, all traces of fight and flightiness gone.

Was being bred to Miss Kitty or something else responsible for the difference?

An idea came to Ace. He jumped into his Polaris and drove to his office at the clinic. There, he made a phone call to Wally Dunlap's son, glad to reach the man on his first attempt, and identified himself as the new owner of Midnight.

"Can you tell me something about him?" he asked.

"Like what?"

"His history. Any problems. His care and routine."

"I'll try. I wasn't very involved in Dad's business."

"Did your father pasture Midnight with other horses or in separate quarters?"

"Both, I think. He had a system. Might have had to

do with the season. Sometimes Midnight was in the pasture with other horses, sometimes by himself."

"Were the horses mares?"

"Could have been. Though, honestly, I don't remember Midnight being all that aggressive with geldings or other stallions, unless there was a mare in heat. Even then, he was able to be restrained. Dad couldn't have competed him in rodeos otherwise."

What Wally's son said was true.

"About the livestock foreman you hired, did he keep to your dad's system?"

"No. He said he preferred to house studs away from the other horses."

Ace asked the man a number of additional questions before thanking him and disconnecting.

He found his mother in her office on the opposite side of the barn.

"You going to be home for dinner tonight?" She closed the ledger she'd been reading and shut off her computer. "I'm making chili and corn bread."

"That's an offer I can't refuse."

"It'll be ready in a couple hours. How's Miss Kitty?"

"No worse for the wear." He sat in her visitor chair. "I spoke to Wally Dunlap's son just now."

"You called him?"

"I wanted information. I'm thinking of putting Midnight in the pasture with a few mares."

She drew back in surprise. "Is that wise?"

"According to Wally's son, Midnight got along with other horses and was regularly put to pasture with them." Ace summarized his phone conversation. "I think it's worth a try."

"When are you going to test your theory?"

"This afternoon. He's as calm as I've ever seen him."

"And if he hurts the mares like he did Miss Kitty?"

"We'll have him on a twenty-four-hour watch."

"You can't stay up all night."

"Gracie, Harlan and Royce will help. We'll take turns."

His mother smiled. "I'm glad you're not giving up on him. Or yourself."

"I still believe Midnight's the right horse for us to build our breeding business."

"That kind of tenacity will win over Flynn."

"You think?"

Her smile widened. "I'm counting on it."

So was Ace.

"HE'S A BRAND-NEW HORSE!" Gracie grinned exuberantly.

"I wouldn't go that far." Ace downplayed his excitement, which exceeded Gracie's. He didn't want to get ahead of himself only to be disappointed.

They'd pastured Midnight with the mares nearly a full twenty-four hours ago and, so far, it was going well. *Really* well.

"You have to admit," Gracie insisted, "beauty soothes the savage beast."

"Midnight clearly likes the ladies."

He reminded Ace more of a besotted puppy than a beast, following the mares around and pleading for their attention. What had happened to the fiery stallion from yesterday?

Ace had carefully selected the six mares he'd put with Midnight. All but one were from Wally Dunlap's string. At the last minute, Ace decided to include Fancy Gal. She possessed a solid, dependable temperament he hoped would rub off on Midnight.

One of the mares gave Midnight a little warning kick.

"I bet she won't be so standoffish next week," Gracie observed.

Probably not. Mares' cycles often accelerated when they were in the vicinity of a stallion.

"We need to diligently monitor them," Ace said. "If Midnight shows the least sign of aggression, I want him moved straightaway."

"I'm betting that won't happen."

Ace tended to agree. Right now, Midnight looked ready to roll over and have his tummy scratched.

"You came up with a good idea, boss."

"I don't know about that. Pasture breeding works fine for our mares. Any potential clients will want their mares hand bred."

Or inseminated artificially, but Ace was determined to worry about one obstacle at a time. Today, that was modifying Midnight's behavior enough to ensure a decent crop of foals next spring. Breeding season in Montana lasted only until the end of June. They either saw immediate progress or made the difficult decision to sell Midnight while there was still time to acquire another stud.

A few of the more friendly mares meandered over to the fence for the homemade horse treats Ace had gotten from Angie Barrington's horse rescue. He and Gracie willingly obliged them.

"Have you decided which of the livestock to take to the Torrington Rodeo?"

"True Grit, definitely, and I'd like to try Razorback. He's showing a lot of potential."

For the next several minutes, Ace and Gracie talked shop.

"I'd better see how that mechanic's coming along," Gracie said. "He promised to have the tractor repaired before the evening feeding." She sped off in one of the ranch's numerous ATVs.

The horses, startled by the noise, galloped away, stopping just as abruptly at the fence to nibble on lush green grass. All except for Midnight. He'd set his sights on Fancy Gal, perhaps because she was new.

"You like 'em a little older, huh?" Ace chuckled to himself as the stallion put on a show, prancing in circles around the mare, giving her affectionate nuzzles and nips on the neck and rump.

She took it all in stride, mostly ignoring him—which only encouraged him to try harder.

"She's a tough one, boy. You might pick a different mare."

There was no accounting for love, and Midnight had been hit hard. He continued courting Fancy Gal, to no avail.

Ace was about to leave when Fancy Gal suddenly displayed a change of heart. Nickering softly, she returned Midnight's nuzzles.

"Well, I'll be damned."

The old girl wasn't so tough after all.

When Ace finally left several minutes later, the two horses were standing side by side, head to tail, Midnight resting his chin on Fancy Gal's hindquarters while she grazed unconcerned.

"Maybe I am a genius." Pleased with himself, Ace climbed into the Polaris, feeling almost as good about Midnight as he did about the prospect of becoming a father.

His mood promptly dimmed. If only Flynn were as easy to sway as Fancy Gal.

He could use a little of Midnight's luck when it came to the fairer sex.

Luck or persistence? Midnight was one determined fellow, and it had paid off.

Ace parked the Polaris outside his clinic, pushed back his cowboy hat and scratched his head.

All kidding aside, he could be on to something. The more Ace thought about it, the more convinced he became. He'd been wrong to jump the gun and propose to Flynn. Twice. She was understandably cautious after her unhappy marriage and painful divorce.

She was also understandably cautious after the way Ace had treated her. Any woman in her right mind would be.

What he needed to do was take a page from Midnight's book and woo Flynn. Patiently and persistently. Practice that tenacity his mother had mentioned.

Removing his cell phone from his belt, he dialed Flynn's number. She answered on the fourth ring. Had she been considering not taking his call?

"Hey, it's Ace. Did I catch you at work?" He'd forgotten evenings were the best time to reach her.

"It's all right, I'm on break."

He noted the hint of reservation in her voice but didn't let it deter him.

"I was wondering, are you free tomorrow evening?"

"What's up?"

"Pizza and wings at the Brick Oven." The restaurant was one of her favorites. "Unless you'd like to eat somewhere else?" A long pause followed. "Flynn? You still there?"

"Are you asking me on a date?"

"I am."

"Is there something you want to discuss?"

"No, I just want to take you out to eat."

"We're not, um, romantically involved."

They could be, if she gave them a chance.

"It's dinner. Between two people who happen to be having a baby and working toward establishing a healthy, solid relationship."

"I don't know…"

"Come on. You have to admit, things have been tense between us lately. Enjoying a casual meal on neutral territory will do us good."

Another longer pause followed. "O…kay."

Ace was glad she couldn't see the huge smile he wore. "What time are you off work?"

"Six."

"Is seven too early?"

"Seven's fine. But we can't have pizza. Spicy food doesn't sit well with me these days."

"Where'd you like to go?"

"It's beef Stroganoff night at the Number 1 Diner."

The place where it all started. Interesting that she would choose it.

"Great. And I promise, nothing but food's on the menu."

No kissing, no sneaking into her bedroom, no incredible, mind-bending sex.

"I'm going to hold you to that," she warned.

"See you tomorrow."

He disconnected, his good mood restored. He had a dinner date with Flynn, and Midnight was settling in with his harem of mares.

Ace's day couldn't get any better.

CHAPTER EIGHT

THE SMELL OF impending rain struck Flynn the moment she stepped from Ace's truck. She'd remembered a coat but forgotten an umbrella. Getting wet, however, was the least of her worries.

She and Ace were having dinner.

Not that they hadn't eaten together before—when they'd dated, of course, and on occasions when she'd joined the Harts for birthdays and holidays.

Then there had been the night of their indiscretion. Hard to believe that was almost two months ago.

"It's crowded," Ace commented as they strolled across the parking lot to the diner's front entrance.

"The beef Stroganoff special is always popular."

The potpie special was also popular, which is what the restaurant had been serving the night Ace went home with her.

How in the world had that even happened?

She'd been on a date. Correction, was supposed to have been on a date. The guy had called at the last second, after she'd arrived at the diner to meet him, and canceled. Something about his clothes dryer malfunctioning. Seriously? She'd tried to convince herself she didn't care. He wasn't anyone important, she'd only agreed to go out with him because a mutual friend had set them up.

Rather than leave, Flynn had stayed and ordered dinner. To spite him, she supposed, and because she was hungry.

Ace had dropped by the diner on his way home from treating a yearling filly with a severe respiratory infection.

"Two tonight?" The hostess's question startled Flynn, returning her to the present. "Follow me." The woman grabbed two menus and escorted Flynn and Ace to a table that couldn't possibly be any more out in the open.

She cringed inside as Ace pulled out her chair. Discreetly scanning the room, she counted three familiar faces, nodding in response to their smiles of recognition. It could be worse. At least none of the Hart ranch hands were there.

Why had she suggested this place? She'd have been better off with pizza and wings and a case of heartburn.

She fingered the edge of the menu as she studied it, which was ridiculous since she knew the offerings by heart.

"Evening, folks." Their waitress, all of eighteen and cute as a button, flashed them a dimpled smile. "Can I get you something to drink?"

Ace waited for Flynn to order first.

"Umm…" Iced tea was out of the question, unfortunately. "Lemonade," she said with a sigh.

"Same for me."

"I thought you didn't like lemonade that much."

"Neither do you."

"I'd have iced tea if caffeine wasn't bad for the baby. No reason you can't."

"Lemonade's fine."

He was being sweet again, like at Thunder Creek

when he'd proposed. She'd tell him that, except the last time hadn't gone well.

He'd also been sweet two months ago when he'd spotted her sitting alone at a table not far from this one, come over and asked her what was wrong. Funny, Flynn thought she'd been doing an admirable job hiding her disappointment about being stood up. But Ace had always been good at reading people, her more than most.

He'd sat and told her the other guy's loss was his gain, bought her dinner and regaled her with amusing stories of their errant childhood. By dinner's end, Flynn was having so much fun she couldn't even remember the guy's name.

Later, outside, she and Ace had kissed. Spontaneously. Lightly, at first. Then, in the span of a single softly issued moan, everything changed.

She was the one who'd suggested they go to her place. Her father was having a night out with his cronies and wouldn't be home until late. Ace had followed her in his truck. Flynn was convinced during the fifteen-minute drive that one or both of them would come to their senses. It didn't happen.

If anything, the clandestine nature of their rendezvous added to the excitement. He'd parked his truck behind the barn, then met her at the kitchen door.

They couldn't stumble down the hall to her bedroom fast enough.

"How's work going?" Ace's voice penetrated Flynn's thoughts.

She blinked and set her menu down, acutely aware of the flush creeping up her neck and cheeks. She had to stop dwelling on that night. His touch. The tangled sheets strewn across his naked body.

"Fine. We've been busy this week. The flu seems to be going around."

"You need to be careful you don't get sick."

"I'll be okay. I don't have too much patient contact."

"As much as I hate the idea of you moving, I'd almost rather you were going to school than exposed to sick people all day."

"There are probably just as many sick people on campus."

"Sorry if I'm coming on too strong."

"You're…not."

Turning away from his charmingly crooked smile was a lot harder tonight than it had been at Thunder Creek. There, the dim restaurant lighting wasn't softening his features, reminding her of the younger Ace she'd fallen head over heels for.

They managed to make pleasant small talk for the remainder of the meal. Ace didn't bring up the baby again, her moving to Billings or school. The closest he came was when he asked, "Has your dad had any offers on the ranch?"

"No, and he's disappointed. A few people have come by, but they were more curious than anything else. The real estate agent keeps telling Dad it's a difficult market these days."

"I think more people are trying to sell their ranches than buy one."

"Or they're looking for a bargain. Dad's pretty set on his price."

"Did my mom call him about Sunday brunch at the house?"

"She did. I think it's set for next weekend."

The waitress appeared and removed their plates.

"Can I interest you two in dessert? We have fresh-baked red velvet cake and key lime pie."

"No, thanks. But don't let me stop you," Flynn added when Ace practically drooled at the mention of key lime pie.

"Do you mind?"

"Go on. And I'll have a coffee. Decaffeinated, please."

A rat-tat-tat sound started. Flynn and Ace simultaneously glanced at the ceiling.

"Guess the rain's finally started," the waitress said, and scurried off to bring their pie and coffee.

"I was hoping we might escape more foul weather," Ace said. "I'm tired of mucking through soggy fields and getting my truck stuck in a wash."

"It has been an awfully wet spring."

Ace demolished his pie in four bites.

Flynn had no idea where he put it. There wasn't an ounce of fat on him, while she ruthlessly watched every crumb of food she ate in order to maintain her size six figure.

Size *pregnant*, soon.

She should probably enjoy Ace's appreciative glances while they lasted.

He supported her elbow as they left the restaurant. Considerate, without being pushy.

"You want my hat?" he offered.

They waited outside the front door, assessing the pouring rain.

"I won't melt," she said with a laugh.

"You wait here while I get the truck."

He'd no sooner uttered the words when they heard a loud metallic crunch in the darkness to their right.

"What's that?" Flynn asked, peering through the downpour at the headlights of a compact SUV.

Ace was already in motion, sprinting in the direction of the disabled vehicle.

She followed, holding the flaps of her coat closed around her as she jogged between puddles. Reaching the SUV, she found Ace bent over the open driver's side window.

"Are you sure you're okay?" He had to practically shout in order to be heard above the rain.

"I'm fine. Just embarrassed," came a disembodied female voice.

The door opened and Sierra Byrne stepped out.

Flynn immediately recognized the owner of the diner. She and Sierra had taken exercise classes together off and on through the years.

"Hey, Sierra. Can I help?"

Within seconds, the rain had soaked the young woman. Flynn could feel the dampness penetrating her own coat and ignored the discomfort.

"It's just a fender bender," Sierra insisted. "I mean, I hope it's a fender bender."

They all three inspected the rear of her car, which sat a few inches from the parked minivan she'd hit. Between the darkness and the rain, it was impossible to discern the damage.

"Do you have a flashlight?" Ace asked Sierra.

"No."

"I do. In my truck." He was off before Sierra could stop him.

Flynn put her arm around Sierra's waist. "You want us to take you to the clinic?"

"Really, I'm okay."

"You're shivering."

"I'm mad at myself. I can't believe I missed seeing that van."

"It was an accident."

Sierra's gaze went to Ace. "I'm glad to see you with Ace. I always thought you two would make a perfect couple."

Flynn felt her flush return, though how that was possible in the midst of a downpour, she wasn't sure. "We're not together. Not like that."

"Too bad."

"We're having a baby."

Where had that come from? Flynn had decided to keep the news to herself, Ace and their families until she'd reached her second trimester and figured out her plans.

"You are?" Sierra's face brightened. "I'm so excited for you. Congratulations."

They were hugging when Ace returned.

"Forget about me," Sierra chided him. "You two go on and celebrate. Flynn told me about the baby," she added when Ace looked confused.

He grinned broadly, like a proud papa. "Thanks. But I'm here, and I have my flashlight, so we might as well take a look." He aimed the beam at Sierra's SUV first, then the van. "Doesn't appear too bad. A couple small dings in the bumpers is all. Easily fixed."

"Darn it." Sierra pouted. "Guess I'd better get back inside and find the owner. Give him my insurance information."

"Want us to go with you?"

"Honestly." She gave him and Flynn a small push. "Get out of here. You're soaked."

They were, and Flynn's teeth were starting to chatter.

Ace hurried her along to his truck with a parting "Be careful" to Sierra.

Opening his passenger side door, he helped her in, then raced to his side. The rain continued to fall in torrents, making a thunderous noise as it pummeled the truck.

Ace started the engine and turned on the heater. "Better?" he asked when the air finally blew warm.

"A little." Flynn's teeth had yet to cease chattering.

"Take off your wet coat." He was already shrugging out of his jacket. When he finished, he helped her with a sleeve that stubbornly clung to her clothing.

She laid the sopping coat across her lap, which only added to her misery.

"That's not helping." Ace deposited the coat in the back alongside his jacket. He'd yet to put the truck in reverse. "I'd offer you a blanket, but the only one I have is a saddle blanket and it's covered in horse hair."

"I'll be all right." She would, if she could just get warm.

She reached for the seat belt buckle. It slipped from her stiff fingers and was sucked up by the roller.

He bent toward her.

She assumed he was going to buckle her in. Instead, he flipped up the console separating them, put an arm around her shoulders and drew her across the seat to nestle beside him.

Flynn might have protested if not for the sudden warmth flooding her.

"How's that?"

"Good."

They stayed where they were, the rain continuing its

assault. They stayed even when the heater had raised the temperature in the truck cab to a lovely, toasty level.

"I think I'm okay now," Flynn said, breaking the silence, which had actually been nice and companionable, and attempting to return to her side of the seat.

Ace didn't release her.

She looked up at him, about to ask if something was the matter.

His dark gaze swept over her face and sent every thought in her mind fleeing, save one.

I'm in big trouble.

A tiny sigh escaped her as he lowered his mouth to hers.

She should push him away, tell him no. This kind of recklessness was exactly what had landed them in the pickle they were today.

Except she didn't push him away. Not when his lips brushed hers, not when his hand reached up to tenderly cradle her cheek, not when he pressed her into the seat and deepened the kiss.

The roar outside filled her ears as Ace's heated kiss filled her senses. Raised her awareness. Sent her spinning. They were no strangers to intimacy, but this, oh, this was different. There was an emotional connection unlike any she'd experienced before. They were linked, by the child she carried, the history they shared, the feelings they had for one another.

Wrapping her arms around his neck, she returned his kiss with matching fervor, wrenching a low, desperate groan from him. It wasn't enough. She placed her right palm over his heart, needing to feel it beat, faster and stronger as their kiss intensified.

Imagine a lifetime of this, a small voice inside her murmured.

She'd have it if she accepted Ace's proposal.

The next instant, sanity returned. Incredible kisses were no reason to get married.

Ace evidently sensed the change and released her. She drew back slowly. His hoarse, unsteady breathing echoed inside the truck cab. She, on the other hand, couldn't draw in air fast enough to feed her starving lungs.

"I'll take you home," he murmured.

"That's probably a good idea." There would be no repeats of past mistakes tonight.

They didn't speak much during the drive. Flynn preferred silence, she wasn't ready to discuss the kiss. She'd rather cherish it for a while longer than analyze their actions or apologize for them. She'd be doing plenty of that later on her own.

Halfway to her father's ranch, Ace's hand reached across the seat for hers. He didn't let go of her until he pulled up in front of the house.

Before she could open her door, he raised her hand to his lips and kissed it.

She sat in stunned silence, staring at him in the murky darkness. Had he really just kissed her hand? Ace Hart?

"Good night, Flynn."

Wordlessly, she got out of his truck and stood in the rain, watching his truck's disappearing headlights.

In all the years they'd known each other, in all the time they'd dated, he'd never been so romantic.

An exquisite shudder coursed through her.

She wasn't just in big trouble, she was heading for disaster.

"MORE COFFEE, HONEY?"

"Please." Ace held out his mug for a refill, taking another large bite of his breakfast burrito while his mother poured.

"Not so fast," she warned. "You'll give yourself an upset stomach."

He slowed his rate from supersonic to just plain hurried. "I promised Angie I'd stop at the animal shelter this morning after the livestock were loaded. One of her rescue ponies has laminitis."

"Colt and Joshua can oversee the loading."

Colt might if their mother asked him. His brother seemed dead set on avoiding Ace lately, ever since he'd learned about the baby.

"We'll see," Ace mumbled, washing down his burrito with a swallow of coffee.

They were sending a dozen horses and two bulls to the Torrington Rodeo. The rodeo promoters, a husband and wife team, were new clients. Ace's mother was eager to please them, as she'd received bad news earlier in the week when a different contract was canceled during the option period with no real explanation. Their second one.

Normally Ace would accompany the livestock to the rodeo. With the stakes being so high, they didn't need anything to go wrong. But he wanted to stay home to supervise the pasture breeding with Midnight. After nearly a week they were ready to switch out some of the mares.

Colt and Uncle Joshua and the crew Ace had personally selected to travel with them to Torrington were more than up to the task. The rodeo promoters would be happy with the Harts' livestock and their service.

"Gotta run, Mom."

"Wait." She paused from clearing the table. "Do you have a few minutes to talk?"

"If it's about Midnight, he's doing great. Still enamored with that mare of Flynn's. He'll pay attention to the other ones, only as long as he needs to, then he's right back to mooning after Fancy Gal."

"I'm glad the breeding's going well, but it's actually Flynn I wanted to discuss."

Ace sat back down in his chair, finished the last bite of his burrito. When his mother affected *that* tone, he wasn't going anywhere.

"What about Flynn?"

"Have you two made any definite plans yet?"

"No."

"But you're seeing each other."

"Twice in the last week."

Their second outing, to the frozen yogurt shop and public library, hadn't ended the same as their dinner date. Namely, no kiss. Just a hug. Ace would have preferred more. Flynn's keep-away signals had discouraged him from trying.

A shame. Their kiss outside the diner was all he could think about, next to the night they'd spent in her bed.

How could they have dated all those years ago and not kissed or made love with the intensity they did now? What change was responsible?

If he concentrated, he could feel the sensation of her silky skin beneath his fingertips, smell the scent of her floral body wash, taste her lush mouth.

"What did you say?" he asked, realizing he hadn't heard his mother.

"Is Flynn still set on moving to Billings?"

"Yes."

"I wish she wasn't."

"Me, too. I'm working on changing her mind."

"What if I talked to her?"

"I don't know about that. She might think you're interfering. Dig in her heels."

"I suppose." His mother sighed, stared at the window. "I hate the idea of my first grandchild being so far away."

"Tell me about it."

She pressed a hand to her chest and sniffed. "I'm sure it's much worse for you. That was a thoughtless thing to say."

"What's wrong, Mom? You seem sad today."

"It's your brother Tuf."

"Have you heard from him again?"

"No, and that's the problem. One brief phone call to tell me he's been discharged, that he's okay, he'll be in touch soon and not to worry. Nothing about where he is or what he's doing." Her voice hitched. "How am I not supposed to worry?"

"I know." Ace had been so consumed with his own problems, he hadn't noticed the strain in his mother's face and the sorrow in her eyes. "Tuf's a marine. Former marine, anyway. He's capable of taking care of himself."

"You're right. But he's still my little boy. My baby. Why won't he come home?"

Ace was also concerned. It wasn't like Tuf to alienate himself. He'd always kept in regular contact with them up until shortly before his release. Ace was also angry at Tuf—for putting their mother through unnecessary upset and for shirking his responsibilities. Ace had been understanding as long as Tuf was in the Marines, but he was a civilian now. It was long past time for him to come home and take his place in the family business.

One responsibility-challenged brother was bad enough. Ace didn't need two.

"Have you tried calling someone in the Marines?" he asked.

"Even if I could figure out where to start, I'm not sure they'd tell me anything. They're probably not allowed."

"Maybe we should hire someone to track him down."

"Like a private detective?" His mother shook her head. "That's expensive. And Tuf wouldn't like it."

"I don't like what he's doing to us." Ace stood, then bent and kissed his mother on the cheek.

"I'm sorry to pester you and add to your load," she said.

"Don't give it a second thought."

That was what family did, be there for each other. Dinah, Uncle Joshua and his cousins understood. Colt and Tuf just assumed Ace would pick up the slack.

He headed out the kitchen door, started his Polaris and drove to the main barn. Once there, he immersed himself in the job of loading the livestock. It proved useful in fending off his thoughts. Between Flynn, her moving, the baby, the canceled contracts, his mother and his brothers, he had a lot of fending off to do.

Colt wasn't anywhere to be found. So much for his mother's assurance that he'd help them. Gracie and Royce were there along with Uncle Joshua. Oddly enough, Harlan was AWOL, too. The young ranch hand was as dependable as they came.

"Anyone hear from Harlan this morning?" Ace asked.

"No, and that's strange," Gracie answered from inside one of the trailers. She was hosing it out before the horses were loaded.

Ace dialed Harlan's number on his cell phone. He was in no mood for slackers and ready to tear Harlan a new one for being late.

"Hello," a breathy female voice answered, taking Ace momentarily aback.

Then he remembered who he was dealing with and what a ladies' man Harlan was. "Is Harlan there? I need to speak to him."

"He can't come to the phone."

"This is his boss, Aidan Hart. What's wrong?" Ace didn't care that Harlan was typically a good employee. If he was nursing a hangover and lolling around in bed with a woman, Ace was firing him.

"He's asleep."

"Asleep!" At eight in the morning? "Wake him up now. Please," Ace added through gritted teeth.

"I would, but the doctor said not to."

"The doctor?"

"At the emergency room last night. The poor baby has some kind of food poisoning. I don't know what he ate. We were at the Open Range Saloon. He took me dancing." She giggled. "We got these nachos off the happy-hour menu—"

"Is Harlan okay?" Ace didn't care about the dancing and what caused the food poisoning.

"The doctor said he'll be fine. Just needs to rest. The medicine makes him groggy. Guess I should have tried to call you. I had an awful time getting him from the truck into bed. That's not how it usually is." She giggled again.

"Thanks for letting me know. I'll send someone by later to check on him." Ace disconnected, feeling guilty for condemning Harlan before learning the facts. "Where's Colt?" he asked out loud.

The same answer came back as the first time Ace asked the question. No one had any idea.

He dialed his brother's cell phone, relief surging through him when Colt promptly answered.

"Where are you?"

"About halfway to Torrington."

"What! Why aren't you here? We're loading the stock."

"I told you I was going early."

"No, you didn't," Ace snapped.

"I could've sworn."

"Dammit to hell, Colt."

"I'll me—you th—help wi—"

Whatever his brother said was garbled as their reception went from poor to nonexistent.

Ace shoved his phone in his pocket, barely restraining himself from pitching it into the side of the trailer. His energy was better spent readying the horses for transport.

"Something wrong?" Uncle Joshua asked.

"Colt took off early for Torrington. Didn't tell anybody."

"We'll be okay."

"No, we won't. Harlan's sick. Food poisoning. He's on medication."

"That'll leave us one driver short."

"No, it won't. I'll go." He'd stop at Angie's rescue shelter on the way to treat the pony's laminitis.

There were days he'd give his right arm for a veterinarian assistant.

"What about Midnight and the mares?" Uncle Joshua asked.

"Gracie will have to be in charge." She couldn't fill in for Colt, not with two sons at home to watch.

Ace groaned. Taking three days off to attend the rodeo was going to wreak havoc with his schedule— his date with Flynn in particular. But what choice did he have? Hopefully she'd understand.

Just when they were making progress...

Ace cursed his brothers under his breath. How pitiful was it when he could rely more on an employee than family members?

When he next saw Colt and Tuf, he was going to give the both of them a much-needed lesson in priorities.

CHAPTER NINE

FLYNN REREAD THE printed email from the University of Montana, then set it down beside her, a sound of discontent escaping her lips.

Her father discovered her several minutes later, still sitting on the front porch swing and rocking idly.

"You're mighty glum," he observed.

"Transferring to the university isn't going to be as easy as I thought. And apparently I should have applied to nursing school last spring. There aren't any current openings."

"Can you still take classes even if you aren't in nursing school?" He sat on the sturdier of the two wicker chairs, easing himself into it with a weary groan.

"Sure. Once I complete the transfer process. Seems there's a problem with that, too. My transcripts are incomplete. I have to contact Billings Community College."

"You'll get it done."

"Yeah, but I'm frustrated. I really wanted to start with an online class or two this summer."

"Well, we may be stuck here a while longer."

"Why? What's happening?"

"Nothing's happening. That's the problem. Haven't had but one serious buyer look at the place, and it's been on the market a while now." He rolled his head from side to side, wincing as he did.

"Hurt yourself?"

"Naw, just sore. Think I might have overdone it."

He'd spent the majority of the day performing minor repairs from the list the real estate agent had given him. According to her, a little fixing up, a little cleaning up, a little sprucing up would improve her father's chances of selling.

"Not many people in the market for a ranch, I guess." Flynn recalled her conversation with Ace on the topic.

"I came down on my price."

And he'd probably have to come down a lot more. "Give it time, Dad."

He smiled. "I could tell you the same thing about school."

"You're right." She smiled back at him. "Are you that anxious to move?"

"Some days, yes. Some days, no. Lived here my whole life. Your grandfather built this entire place board by board."

Flynn felt the same. She'd wake up in the morning, excited about school and her return to Billings. By afternoon, she dreaded leaving Roundup.

And, if she were honest with herself, leaving Ace, too.

It was different before. When she'd headed off to college eleven years ago, she'd been moving toward something. A bright new future. Endless possibilities. Now, despite the excitement of continuing her education and expecting a baby, it seemed as if she was running away, and she couldn't explain why.

"Aren't you and Ace going out tonight?"

Two dates and already her father assumed she and Ace were an item.

"Not anymore. He left yesterday for the rodeo in Torrington. One of their hands contracted food poisoning. Ace stepped in."

"Don't take it so hard."

"I'm not."

"Really? Because you remind me of that Christmas you were seven and Nora told you there was no Santa Claus."

It was true. She'd been surprised at the depth of her disappointment when Ace had called to cancel. Her annoyance, now that was no surprise. Fair or not, thanks to her ex-husband, Flynn had a low tolerance for men married to their jobs.

"Cut him some slack," her father said. "He didn't stand you up for no good reason. They had a contract to fulfill."

"I'm not mad at him, Dad."

"You think he should have sent someone else in his place."

Kind of, yes. The Harts employed a lot of hands. "I have no idea." She pushed the email aside.

"Ace wants to be with you. He wouldn't have gone to Torrington if he had any other choice."

"That's just it. I want a man who has other choices. Who doesn't live, eat, breathe work."

"It's a date, Flynn. You'll go out with him again this week."

"What if it was more than a date? What if I went into labor or the baby was sick? Would he still run off to some rodeo because an employee called in sick?"

"You can depend on him when it really matters."

Flynn conceded she was probably making a bigger deal out of the canceled date than she should. Blame raging hormones. The tone in Ace's voice had been reminiscent of Paul's, and it struck an old, inharmonious chord in her.

"Maybe you should stay in Roundup. Get an apartment."

"Why wouldn't I move when you do?"

"Ace, for one. And the baby."

"I'm going to college, Dad. There are other nursing schools in Billings." Not affiliated with the university but as good.

"Are you certain being a nurse is what you want?"

"Absolutely." Or was she simply talking herself into it?

He inclined his head at the letter. "Wouldn't hurt anything if you waited until after the baby was born. Give yourself time to enroll in nursing school and straighten out that transcript problem."

"Those are small glitches."

"But you love Ace."

She did. Their dates, under the guise of doing what was best for the baby, were wonderful. Fun and heady. They were also difficult. She'd come home feeling like she was standing on the edge of a precipice, swaying in the ever-changing wind.

He liked her. Desired her. Respected and possibly adored her. He didn't, however, love her in return. And it hurt.

"How I feel about Ace is irrelevant. What matters is how he feels about me."

"He asked you to marry him."

"He did it for the baby."

"That's the excuse he gave you. Ace isn't a man of

fancy-schmancy words or romantic gestures. He'll show you he loves rather than tell you."

She thought of last week when he'd kissed her hand before she got out of his truck.

"If he loved me, he'd have sent someone else to the Torrington Rodeo."

"Ace isn't Paul. He's not using work as an excuse to avoid you."

Flynn's eyes stung. The wounds she'd believed healed clearly weren't.

At that moment, her phone beeped. "It's a text from Ace." She pressed the button and displayed the message.

How are you? Been thinking of you a lot.

Not fancy-schmancy words by any stretch of the imagination, but they melted her heart.

"From the look on your face, it must be a dandy message."

"He's just asking how I am."

And thinking about her.

Could it be? Were his feelings for her stronger than she'd realized?

Been thinking of you, too, she texted back.

OKAY, FLYNN ADMITTED IT, Ace was trying. He'd apologized for postponing their date, brought flowers when he picked her up—tulips, a dozen—and was taking her to a chick flick.

Of the thirty or forty people in line to purchase tickets, she estimated he was one of maybe six guys. The only cowboy. And he didn't seem to mind, either her choice of movie or standing out from the crowd.

She didn't mind him standing out, either, or the envious glances being cast her way.

"The movie's had some good reviews," he commented as they stepped ahead.

"You read them?"

"I checked online."

"Preparing yourself for the worst?"

"Not at all." He grinned, a mildly heart-fluttering grin. "I'm glad to be here with you. I don't care what movie we see."

Neither did she.

If he were a little less the perfect date, she'd be better able to resist him.

All the other couples in line were openly affectionate, either holding hands, arms wrapped snugly around each other or standing with their heads bent in whispered conversations. Ace and Flynn didn't touch, they hadn't since he'd kissed her hand.

"Maybe next time we can see an action movie." He dug out his wallet in preparation for purchasing tickets.

"You know, we don't always have to go on dates. We can just hang out. Talk. Go hiking. Horseback riding."

"You're not getting on a horse while you're pregnant."

She laughed, having made the last remark only to get a rise out of him. "Fishing, then."

"I like going on dates with you."

She liked it, too. More than she should.

They were two customers away from the ticket window when Ace's cell phone rang.

Flynn's heart plummeted.

"I'll send this to my voice mail—" He read the caller ID, said, "Sorry," and answered with a brusque, "Ace Hart." After listening for several seconds, he asked,

"How bad is she? Can she walk?" Another pause. "That's normal. She's probably in shock. How cold is it in the garage?... Okay, if you can reach her, cover her with a blanket or coat but don't disturb her."

"Is everything all right?" Flynn mouthed. They were almost to the window.

He gave her an apologetic head shake. "I'll be there as quick as I can. No, it's all right. Don't worry." He disconnected. "Flynn, there's been an emergency."

"I could tell."

They stepped out of line and started toward the parking lot. There would be no movie tonight.

Why was she surprised?

"It's a client of mine. The Andersons. Their son Curt ran over their family dog. The kid's sixteen and just got his license."

"Is the dog all right?"

"They don't know. She can't walk and is hiding under an old table in the garage. She's also bleeding at the mouth."

Flynn's frustration fled upon hearing about the dog's condition. "How's their son?"

"Pretty shaken up but otherwise fine."

"I didn't think you treated dogs."

"I don't, but the Andersons are also friends. You might have heard of them, they raise alpacas."

"I've seen the farm on the outskirts of town."

"It's quite an interesting operation."

They reached Ace's truck.

"Be sure and phone me later," Flynn said. "Let me know how the dog is."

"Actually..."

"What?"

"I hate to have to tell you this, but there's no time to drop you off first."

"You're taking me with you?"

"The Andersons live on the opposite side of town. I hope you don't mind."

"Um…no."

"This could take a while."

"Don't worry about me."

In the three years Flynn and Paul were married, countless last-minute work emergencies had cropped up. Not once did he suggest she accompany him.

"Will it be all right if I go with you?" she asked. "I don't want to get in the way."

"You'll be fine."

Ten minutes into the drive, Ace called the Andersons and received an update on the dog's condition. It remained unchanged. When they pulled into the alpaca farm, Mrs. Anderson was waiting for them in the driveway, wringing her hands.

"Thank you for coming, Ace." Her voice wobbled. "We didn't know what to do or who to call."

"No problem."

"Lovey's over here."

She hurried them to the garage. Flynn blinked at the bright florescent lights.

"Hello, Ace," Mr. Anderson said.

The two men shook hands, and Ace introduced Flynn.

A pale-faced teenage boy—he had to be their son Curt—sat cross-legged in front of an old dining room set. Someone had moved the chairs to the side, creating a pathway to the dog.

She lay beneath an old raincoat, only her nose and

muzzle showing. Even at a distance, Flynn could see dark blood caked on the side of the dog's mouth.

The son sprang out of the way. Ace knelt in front of the dog and carefully removed the raincoat.

"Hey, girl."

The dog trembled violently and gazed at him with a woeful expression.

He carefully opened her mouth and pushed her lips aside.

Lovey whimpered and jerked her head from his grasp.

Talking soothingly, he continued the exam, palpating her sides and belly. She tolerated this considerably better, though she panted laboriously.

"I don't detect any internal injuries."

"No?" Mrs. Anderson asked. She waited beside Flynn, her hands still clenched in front of her.

"Then how come she's bleeding?" Curt asked.

Ace peeled back Lovey's lip to show them. "She's cut the inside of her mouth on her teeth, probably happened on impact with the car. It doesn't look bad."

"Thank God." Mrs. Anderson went visibly weak.

"Why can't she walk?" Mr. Anderson asked.

"Let's see what we can find."

With profound gentleness, Ace lifted the dog out from beneath the table and set her on her feet—her three feet. She held her right front paw out in front of her at a painful angle.

Flynn could see now that Lovey was a yellow Lab, with possibly a little German shepherd thrown in for good measure. She demonstrated how she'd earned her name by giving Ace's face a thorough washing.

He chuckled, trying to evade her tongue. "I like you, too, girl."

When he pressed down on her paw, she whined and tried to retreat beneath the shelter of the table.

"Want me to hold her?" Mr. Anderson offered.

"No. She's in mild shock. I don't want to cause her unnecessary distress."

Flynn was impressed with both the compassion Ace showed Lovey and his kind treatment of the Andersons. She'd been fortunate to work with several nurses and doctors at the emergency clinic who possessed the same admirable bedside manner. They were one of the reasons for her wanting to become a nurse.

She hadn't really thought about how a veterinarian interacted with his patients' owners. Most of the vets her father had used over the years were nice but efficient. Not nearly as tenderhearted as Ace.

He'd been every bit as gentle and compassionate with Fancy Gal as with Lovey. It was obvious to anyone he loved his job, his patients and helping to make their owners' lives better.

She longed for the same things herself.

Perhaps they weren't so different after all.

"Flynn. Would you mind bringing me my medical case?" He passed her his keys. "It's in the compartment on the driver's side. Black box with a handle. The small silver key opens the lock. I also need a bottle of antiseptic wash. It's on the bottom shelf, white label. Make sure there's enough gauze and a roll of elastic cohesive bandage in the case. If not, grab a few more."

Flynn hurried to the truck. Opening the side compartment, she quickly located the items Ace needed.

Mrs. Anderson returned at the same time as Flynn. Apparently she'd been dispatched to fetch a pan of warm water.

Using a bulb syringe procured from his medical case, Ace flushed out Lovey's mouth with the antiseptic wash and cleaned the blood from her muzzle.

"What about her foot?" Mrs. Anderson asked.

"My guess is she's broken two or three toes." He showed the Andersons the raised bumps on Lovey's paw. "I'm going to bind the paw to stabilize and protect it and give her an injection for pain—she'll be in a lot of it from the broken toes and the blow she sustained. She should be okay until Monday morning when you can take her to your regular vet. But I wouldn't recommend waiting any longer."

"She ran out in front of me as I was pulling in the driveway," Curt lamented. "I didn't see her. There was just this awful thud." He cringed.

"Go easy on yourself." His mother squeezed his arm. "What's important is that she's going to be fine."

Ace finished binding the paw. Lovey was visibly relieved when he snipped the tape and released her. She barely noticed the injection he administered.

"Keep her quiet and warm for the next couple days. Make sure she has water available but don't be alarmed if she doesn't drink or eat much. It's normal. Call me if there's any change for the worse."

All three of the Andersons walked Ace and Flynn to his truck where she helped him load the supplies.

"What do I owe you?" Mr. Anderson asked Ace.

"I'll just add the charges on the bill for my regular visit next week."

Mrs. Anderson hugged him warmly. "Thank you again."

"I'll see you Wednesday," Ace said as he and Flynn

opened the truck doors. "Let me know what your vet says about Lovey."

When they were back on the road, Ace asked, "You want to try and catch the late show?"

Flynn shrugged. "If you don't mind, I'd rather not."

His features fell ever so slightly. "I'm really sorry about ruining the evening."

"You didn't ruin it at all. I enjoyed going with you to the Andersons'."

"Don't ever take up poker. You haven't the face for it."

"It's true. I really did have fun." She gazed at him earnestly. "What you did for the Andersons, that was nice."

"They're good people."

"You are, too, Ace. A good person and a good vet. I can tell by the way you treated Lovey and Fancy Gal. I never thought being a vet was all that cool until tonight."

He grinned. "If I knew you were interested in my vet practice, I'd show you my clinic rather than take you home."

"Let's go!"

"I was joking."

"I'm not."

"It's getting late." He checked the digital clock on the dashboard.

"Not that late. Come on," she insisted. "I've never seen your clinic."

"Okay." Ace's smile remained in place until they arrived at Thunder Ranch.

He flipped on the lights at the entrance to the main horse barn. The occupants stirred at the disturbance, milling in their stalls and nickering.

"My office is this way." He patted a curious head here and there as they walked down the aisle and past the tack room. Opening a door, he turned on a second light and waited for Flynn to enter first.

She didn't recall what this room had been before its current incarnation. A storage area, perhaps? No more than ten feet by eight feet, it contained a desk, a computer straight out of the stone age, a printer/scanner/fax machine almost as old, shelves filled with numerous medical volumes and reference books, a small refrigerator in the corner with a microwave on top and a four-drawer lateral file.

"This is nice," Flynn observed.

"You really gotta watch that poker face."

"Quit it!"

"It's small." He shrugged. "I don't need much. Not yet."

"Does that computer actually work?"

"I could probably use a new one."

She indicated a door beside the cabinet. "Where does that lead?"

"I'll show you." They went outside. Ace flipped on a third light switch, illuminating two covered pens. A young calf stood in one of them, his huge eyes woefully sad. "This is my hospital ward."

"What's wrong with him?" Flynn went over to the calf, who investigated her fingers with his sticky tongue.

"He's an orphan. His mama died a few days ago."

"Oh, no! What happened?"

"Rattlesnakes. She inadvertently wandered into a nest of them."

"Poor thing." Flynn scratched the calf between the ears. "What are you going to do with him?"

"Try and put him with another cow and calf, see if the cow will accept him. If not, I guess I'll be hand-raising him."

The calf brayed mournfully.

"What's wrong?" Flynn asked.

"He's hungry. He's always hungry."

"Can we feed him?"

"Sure."

They went back into Ace's office where he prepared the calf's formula, pouring the mixture into a huge baby bottle.

The calf brayed louder than before the second they appeared with the bottle.

"Slow down!" Flynn giggled as the calf sucked lust-ily, emptying the contents in a matter of minutes.

"You're hired," Ace told her when they were done. "But you'll have to come back tomorrow."

"Maybe I will." Flynn realized she was serious. Back inside the office, she asked, "What kind of software do you use for your practice?"

"'Fraid I don't have a very sophisticated system. Spreadsheets, mostly, and those are pretty basic."

"How do you keep track of your patients' histories?"

"A manila file folder." He rested a hand on top of the lateral file.

"Honestly? Ace, you need to update your system. And buy a new computer," she added emphatically.

"I know. I haven't had the time."

"I could help." The words popped out of her mouth before she could stop them, not that she wanted to.

"You would?"

"It's what I do at the clinic. I can't imagine there's much difference."

"You haven't seen my system."

"Let me take a look at it sometime this week. You may not need to make as many changes as you think."

"I'd really appreciate it. And I'll pay you."

"You will not!"

"I can't ask you—"

"You're not asking, I'm offering. And it's something I like doing."

"What about nursing school? Will helping me get in the way?"

"It shouldn't. As it is, I've hit a bit of a roadblock."

"A bad one?"

"Nothing I can't resolve. Helping you will give me something to think about other than how long the process is taking."

"I won't say no. I can use an expert."

Pleasure bubbled up inside her.

Soon after that, Ace took Flynn home. The hug and peck on the lips he gave her at the door felt right and natural. Before going inside, she reminded him of her upcoming doctor's appointment.

Her father was still up when she strolled into the kitchen, humming softly.

"You're home early. Have a good time?"

"I did. A really good time." She fixed herself a glass of iced water and told him about her evening with Ace.

"Sounds like fun."

"It was."

The most fun she'd had with Ace in…possibly ever.

What did that say about their evolving relationship?

CHAPTER TEN

"You didn't tell me how the calf was doing."

"Fine." Ace wiped his sweaty palms on the legs of his jeans.

"Did you find a cow to accept him?"

He stared at the door leading to the exam rooms. "Um, yeah. Finally."

"What's wrong?" Flynn asked.

"Nothing."

"You seem kind of on edge today."

"Do I?" He leaned forward in the visitor's chair, feeling his shirt sticking to his back.

"Are you anxious about the ultrasound?"

"A little." He and Flynn had finished with her exam and were waiting for their turn in the imaging room.

"The doctor said everything appears normal and right on schedule."

"I heard her."

"Then why are you sweating like a pig?"

"I'm excited."

"Talk about a lousy poker face."

"I'm not anxious."

"Are you afraid of doctors? Because you've been like this since we arrived. I thought you were going to pass out during my exam."

"Don't be ridiculous."

"You're a vet. How can a vet be afraid of doctors?"

He exhaled. "I guess I know too much."

"What happened? Did you have a traumatic experience as a child?"

"I broke my arm when I was seven. It didn't heal correctly, so the orthopedic surgeon had to rebreak it."

"That's not so terrible."

"Without anesthesia or painkillers!"

"You poor kid." She patted his hand. "I'll be with you the whole time. I won't let the mean, evil doctor near you."

"I'm supposed to be the one supporting and comforting you," he said glumly, irritated at himself.

"Is your broken arm why you became a vet?"

"Actually, it was old Doc Pilchard's fault. Remember him? He'd come out to the ranch, let me help him treat the horses and cattle. I'd keep the IV bag raised while he removed an abscessed tooth or reattached a torn ligament."

Next to his dad teaching him to ride and bust broncs, Doc Pilchard's visits to the ranch were some of Ace's fondest childhood memories. The old vet had retired after a lengthy and respectable career, beloved by all.

That was Ace's ambition. He would not end his life like his father, tainting everyone and everything important to him.

"And yet," Flynn said, "you quake at the prospect of being in the room during an ultrasound. There aren't any needles involved, or has no one told you?"

"I hear the gel they use is cold."

"You'll be fine." She squeezed his fingers, her tone soothing rather than ridiculing or patronizing.

When she would have withdrawn her hand, he held fast. After a few seconds, she relaxed. So did Ace.

A man wearing a lab coat and looking barely old enough to be out of high school stepped into the waiting area and called her name. He escorted them down a chilly hallway to an even chillier room.

"Undress down to your underwear and put on the gown, open in the front," he said, and shut the door behind him.

There was no curtain or privacy screen behind which to change. Ace sat on the only chair in the room and glanced away while Flynn removed her clothes and donned the gown. When she finished she sat on the edge of the exam table, holding the gown closed.

"Cold?" Ace asked.

"A bit. What about you?"

"Great."

"Don't tell me all that shaking is from nerves."

Luckily the imaging technician returned, relieving Ace of having to respond.

"Lie back," he instructed Flynn, and went about preparing for the ultrasound.

Before long he was gliding the probe over Flynn's still flat belly. He stopped, pointed to a blurry image on the monitor beside her.

"There. See?"

The image became clearer as he held the probe in place.

"Yes!" Flynn radiated delight.

Ace saw only a white-and-gray swirl.

No, wait! There was a shadowy oblong shape in the center of the screen and within it, a small spot pulsated.

"That's your baby's heart." The tech smiled.

The shape slowly took form. A head. Body. The beginnings of arms and legs.

"Look here." The tech moved the probe, and a small ghostlike face suddenly appeared amid the swirl.

Flynn said something. Ace couldn't hear her over the roaring in his ears.

This tiny human being was his child. Alive and thriving. Soon he'd be holding his son or daughter in his arms, picking a name, showing him or her off to his family, walking ten feet off the ground.

"It's too early to determine the sex," the doctor said.

"I don't care," Ace blurted, unable to tear his gaze away from the monitor.

"So, you won't mind if I hope for a boy?" Flynn asked.

He reached for her hand and gripped it tightly. "Boy, girl, one of each, it doesn't matter."

"One of each!" Flynn stared at the monitor. "There is only one baby, right?"

The tech moved the probe. "Just one. The right size for nine weeks and the right stage of development. Congratulations."

Flynn sighed happily.

"Baby's first pictures," the tech said, pressing buttons on the ultrasound machine. A moment later an image slid out, the thin paper curling. Then another, and another. "Here you are." He handed the images to Flynn.

Ace leaned in close for a better look. They were the most amazing pictures he'd ever seen.

He and Flynn were still staring when the tech left and the doctor returned. She recited a list of instructions to which Flynn nodded and mumbled a reply. When they were alone again, Ace laid his palm lovingly on Flynn's stomach.

"It's real, isn't it? We're having a baby."

She covered his hand with hers, her eyes misting. "Yes, we are."

"I won't let you down. I'll be a good father." He'd be a good husband, too, if she'd accept his proposal.

Nodding and swallowing, she gave Ace the images and sat up.

"Can we get copies of these on the way home?" he asked.

"Sure."

This time Ace didn't have to glance away while Flynn dressed, he was still transfixed by the images. How could something this tiny grow into a baby? Into a full grown person?

"Would you be upset if we had a girl?" he asked.

Flynn finished dressing and came over. "All I want is a healthy baby."

"I'll be better during the next doctor appointment."

"You don't have to come every time."

He stood. "Yes, I do. I promised I'd be here for you."

"As long as you don't faint in the delivery room."

"Thanks for the vote of confidence."

"Want me to take those?" She held out her hand.

Ace was hesitant to relinquish the images. He did, and she slipped them into her oversize purse.

When she started toward the door, he reached for her. "Flynn, wait."

"What is it?" She gazed at him, her expression curious.

"I meant what I said. I love our baby and can't wait to be a dad."

Her vivid blue eyes dimmed. "Ace…"

"Don't bring up that you're moving. That nothing's changed. Not today."

"All right, I won't," she answered quietly.

Ace watched her closely as she stopped at the front desk and set her next appointment, waited for the elevator, walked across the parking lot.

He was determined as ever not to give up, on her or them.

Now that he'd seen his child's face, watched its speck of a heart beating wildly, he had more reason than ever to fight for Flynn and the life they could have if she'd just give them a chance.

FLYNN SAT ON the corner of her bed, staring at her copies of the ultrasound images. She and Ace had visited the one-hour photo shop on the way home from the doctor's office and got copies made—for him, his mother and Flynn's sister.

Ace was so excited, like a kid with his first puppy. He'd described the images to the store clerk, a middle-aged man who listened with surprising patience. The man had gone on to tell her and Ace about his own experiences with his wife during her pregnancies.

Flynn had to admit, Ace was cute and his reaction touching.

It made hurting him all the worse.

And she would hurt him, terribly, when she moved. There had to be some way she could minimize the blow.

Yeah, right. All the pictures in the world couldn't replace being with your child.

"Anybody home?" Her father's greeting echoed through the house a scant second after Flynn heard the kitchen door open and close. He'd been gone the entire morning, meeting with a potential buyer for their remaining bucking stock.

"Hey, Dad," Flynn called, taking the ultrasound images with her to show him.

He was in the kitchen, fixing himself a plate of left-over lasagna. "Aren't you working today?"

"Evening shift. I go in at four." She held out the images. "I went to the doctor today. Ace came with me."

Her father tilted the various sheets toward the overhead light to see better. "Well, well. This is…what is this? A baby?"

"Here." She pointed to the head.

He uttered, "Ah!" in that tone people used when they pretended to understand what the other person was talking about.

"The picture's a little fuzzy."

"No, I can see." He grinned but, like frequently of late, it faltered. "My newest grandchild."

"Ace says he wants a girl. I'd like a boy."

"One of you is going to get your wish." Her father sat down at the table with his reheated lunch.

"How'd your meeting go?" she asked.

"He's interested. We have to agree on a price."

His lackluster smile faded completely.

Flynn's concern escalated. "Are you really ready to retire? You can still change your mind."

"I'm tired of running rodeo stock, of maintaining this place. It's a demanding life. One fit for someone younger than me."

"I agree it's hard. What else are you going to do?" Her father was only fifty-seven. Hardly old enough to don a cardigan sweater, plunk down in a rocking chair on her sister's front porch and while away the hours.

"Play with my new grandchild."

"Much as I know you'd both enjoy that, it's not enough to keep you busy."

"I'll probably look for a job." He pushed aside his half-eaten lunch. "There has to be something in Billings I can do. Hardware store or one of those home improvement warehouse stores. I'm pretty handy when it comes to tools and remodeling."

Funny, she hadn't thought about it before. Both she and her father were about to embark on career and lifestyle changes, hers infinitely more exciting.

"Any more nibbles on the ranch?" she asked.

"A couple's supposed to come by this weekend."

"You don't sound too enthused."

"The real estate agent already told me they can't afford to pay what I'm asking."

"Then why are you bothering with showing them the ranch?"

"No harm in it. And we can always negotiate on the price if they're serious." He scraped his plate clean and loaded it into the dishwasher along with his fork.

Flynn noticed the slump of his shoulders, heard the dejection in his voice. "You okay, Dad?"

"I'm tired is all. Didn't sleep good last night."

She suspected his weariness stemmed from more than insomnia. The selling of the ranch, the getting out of the business started by her grandfather, the economic recession, were having an effect on him and his frame of mind. She was no expert on depression, but she'd recently begun suspecting her father might be suffering from it.

Convincing him to see a doctor or counselor would be next to impossible. He'd insist he was fine and dandy and didn't need any headshrinker.

"You know," she said in a cheerful voice, "there is something you could do in Billings."

"What's that?"

"Date."

At least she got a chuckle out of him.

"Can't imagine any woman interested in going out with me."

"Why not? You're handsome. In good shape. Have all your hair—mostly—and all your teeth."

This time his chuckle rang with genuine mirth.

"It's not that far-fetched, Dad."

"Just where would I meet these women interested in a man with all his own hair and teeth?"

"An online dating website?"

That earned her a belly laugh.

"Why not? Lots of people do it. I read somewhere that a third of couples in long-term relationships these days met online."

"I think I'll leave the dating to you and Ace."

She went to the fridge and raided it. Carrying an armful of fresh vegetables to the counter, she started separating and washing them. "I'm fixing myself a salad to take to work. Want one for later?"

"You're ignoring me."

"I'm not. Ace and I aren't dating."

"What would you call it? And, yes, I will have a salad for later if you're offering."

Flynn broke off a large chunk from the head of lettuce. "We're trying to get along so that when the baby comes we'll have a strong and healthy relationship."

"Since when is going to dinner and the movies and helping him with his vet practice necessary for *getting along?*"

Since when was kissing in the rain necessary?

What would her father say if he knew about that?

"He's going to be brokenhearted when you leave," her father said, giving voice to her earlier thoughts.

She stopped chopping lettuce. "You're right. Maybe I should quit seeing him. Seeing him as much, anyway. I'd hate giving him false hopes."

"He's courting you, you know."

"What? No!"

"Trying to win you over."

"Where did you get such a crazy idea?"

"It's obvious."

She began slicing the tomatoes, rather forcefully.

Ace courting her? Oh, God, he was. She'd been blind not to see it.

"You gonna dice those tomatoes or pulverize them?"

"Huh?" She looked down at the mess on the cutting board.

This courting thing couldn't continue. She had to put an end to it.

The problem was, she liked spending time with Ace, liked helping in his office, liked going on patient calls with him. If she were to examine her own motives, they would probably fall considerably short of innocent.

"He might not be the only one brokenhearted when you leave."

Was her father a mind reader?

More reason than ever to quit seeing Ace so much.

"Want some chicken in your salad?"

"Flynn, honey, I think you should reconsider moving. And Ace's proposal."

She set the knife down.

"You could do considerably worse than him."

"That's no reason to get married, Dad."

"You have a good job here."

"I have a job I like but pays mediocre and has zero potential for advancement. Not unless I return to college and earn my bachelor's degree."

"You have friends here."

"I'll have you and Nora in Billings."

"What are you afraid of?"

"Nothing." *I'm afraid of being married to a man who doesn't love me as much as I love him.*

"Being a single parent isn't easy. Believe me." Her father returned to the table, dropped tiredly into a chair. "As little trouble as you and Nora gave me, I had a lot of rough years after your mom left."

"Why did she leave?" Flynn had asked that question before, of both her parents, though not for a very long time. Her dad's answer always came across as rehearsed and censored. As if he was afraid she couldn't handle the truth.

Her mother's answer, however, was painfully honest. She hadn't been ready for marriage or a family.

Did not being ready make it okay to discard your children like an old pair of shoes that went out of fashion?

Ace may be a little bossy and pushy, but at least he'd stepped up and assumed responsibility.

"I'd say she fell out of love," her father replied, "except I'm not sure she ever was in love to begin with. Not with me."

"Are you saying there was another man?" Flynn abhorred the idea of her mother being unfaithful. It would, however, explain a lot.

"You should ask her why she left."

The answer must be yes.

"If you're worried about affecting my relationship with her, don't be." Flynn put both salads in plastic storage containers and placed them in the refrigerator. "There isn't much of a relationship to affect."

"I'd change that if I could. Your mother has her faults, but she's always loved—"

"If you're going to say she always loved me and Nora, save your breath. It's not true."

"She loves you the best she knows how."

Big deal.

"I'm thankful to Mom," Flynn said. "She's taught me a lot. About what kind of parent not to be, about what kind of marriage not to have."

"The success of a marriage doesn't depend entirely on one person. I made mistakes, too."

"Like letting her go?"

"I'm sorry to say this, but I don't think that was a mistake. For any of us."

"Oh, Dad." Flynn went over and hugged him, then sat down beside him. What courage it must have taken for him to admit that.

"I didn't make it easy for her to love me. She always wanted more than Roundup could offer. I wasn't about to leave the ranch or my parents or my hometown."

"Why did you two get married?" Flynn knew from the date of her parents' wedding and her sister's birthday, it hadn't been a necessity.

"I pleaded with her. Made promises. Tried the best I could to sweep her off her feet."

"Kind of like Ace is doing with me."

"He's trying to show you the good life you and he can have. I bought your mother's affections with exorbitant gifts and trips I couldn't afford. She said yes, thinking it would be like that always. And, of course, it wasn't."

He turned away. Not before Flynn caught the sorrow in his eyes.

More than twenty years had passed and her mother's abandonment still haunted him.

"You loved her."

"I did, even if I wasn't quite sure of the commitment involved."

"Exactly my point, Dad. Ace doesn't love me. I couldn't bear ending up like you and Mom. And I certainly don't want to repeat my own mistake with Paul. Having two people walk out on me is more than enough, thank you."

"Just because he hasn't said the words? Ace isn't demonstrative."

"I need to hear them. I'm not going through my life, always doubting my husband's feelings for me."

"I'm sorry." Her father patted her cheek. "I never realized how much your mom and I messed you up. I'd say being with her was a mistake, but then I wouldn't have you and Nora. Nothing is more important to me than my daughters."

"I feel exactly the same about my baby."

"Tell that to Ace."

"I can't." Flynn rose. "You should have seen his face during the ultrasound. He said he loved our baby. Not me, our baby. And the look on his face… Ace *is* demonstrative. And the man I marry will look at me like I'm the sun and the moon, and he'll tell me every day how much I mean to him. I won't settle for less."

CHAPTER ELEVEN

ACE HAD YET to meet a horse that didn't love grain. He'd barely closed the pasture gate behind him when the mares started the long walk toward him, recognizing the buckets he carried and anticipating the treat contained within. He dumped the cracked corn into the feed trough, the swishing sound it made prompting several of the mares to break into a trot.

Fancy Gal might love Midnight, but she wasn't adverse to leaving him in the dust for a few mouthfuls of corn.

Ace took a moment to examine the mares, circling them as they ate. To his vast relief, none showed any signs of injury as a result of breeding with Midnight. The stallion was behaving himself.

Speaking of which... Midnight stomped his front hoof in protest at being ignored. His harem paid him no heed.

"Haven't you learned by now how fickle females can be?" Ace asked.

Midnight snorted and tossed his head.

He wanted some corn, too, but wouldn't venture near Ace. Not without incentive—which Ace removed from his shirt pocket.

The carrot gleamed brightly in the afternoon sunlight.

"You got ahold of the mares?" Ace said to Gracie.

She'd followed him into the pasture, slipping halters on the five mares while they polished off the corn.

"We're good to go."

And they did go, back toward the gate. Gracie resembled the Pied Piper, only she led horses instead of mice, first three and then two. She was met by Royce, who helped her tie the mares to the fence railing outside the pasture.

There would be no distractions for Midnight.

"It's just you and me, boy." Ace held out the carrot. There were several more in his shirt pocket. "No need to be shy."

Eventually the horse approached, his steps plodding. Indeed, the condition of his hooves was one reason Ace had committed himself to making progress today. Midnight needed his old shoes removed and his overgrown hooves trimmed.

If Ace didn't tame the horse soon, he'd have no choice but to tranquilize and restrain Midnight. That wouldn't be pleasant for any of them, including the farrier.

Ace snapped the carrot in half, holding the two pieces at arm's length.

Midnight's ears pricked forward.

"Come on, boy, carrots are your favorite."

Ace had tried a variety of treats. Midnight liked them all, but he was fondest of carrots.

Head hanging in defeat, he covered the last few feet, arched his neck and moved his lips in a grabbing motion.

"Not yet." Ace withdrew the carrot. "You have to come closer."

Midnight jerked back, indignation blazing in his black eyes. It didn't last. He quickly succumbed to temptation and took another step forward.

Ace contained his excitement. This was the closest Midnight had voluntarily ventured to anyone except Gracie.

When the horse was finally within touching distance, Ace rewarded him with the carrot half. While he was occupied eating, Ace tentatively stroked the side of Midnight's large head.

The horse reacted as if prodded with a hot poker and promptly bolted.

Ace stood statue still. Eventually Midnight calmed and approached again, not taking nearly as long. When Ace gave him the other carrot half, he tolerated a light petting on the neck, his hide twitching, his eyes saucer wide.

"That's it. Good boy."

Slowly, Ace removed another carrot from his shirt pocket. Midnight immediately swiped it up. He was too busy savoring the tidbit to notice Ace's hand move to his shoulder and chest.

Excitement coiled inside Ace, threatened to explode. He hadn't been able to touch Midnight since the auction.

"I'll buy a whole truckload of carrots if that's what it takes."

He fed Midnight the last one, assuming the horse would desert him the second he realized no more treats were forthcoming.

Only he didn't.

He stayed and let Ace continue to pet him with slow, easy strokes. After a few minutes, Ace stopped, only to have the horse bump his arm.

Ace's pulse jumped. Now, *this* was progress.

"You want more?" Ace took a chance and scratched Midnight's nose. "You're not such a tough guy after all," he said when the horse blew lustily.

Unfortunately, the moment came to an abrupt end. Ace's mother neared the fence. The second Midnight spied her, he twisted away and galloped to the other side of the pasture, bucking and kicking.

The mares, still tethered, started fussing. They were rodeo horses, after all, and wanted in on the fun.

"Cut 'em loose," Ace told Gracie and Royce.

Within minutes the tiny herd was frolicking in the pasture, Midnight and Fancy Gal reunited and running side by side.

Ace returned to the gate, shutting it behind him.

"Aidan!" his mother gushed. "I saw you and Midnight. That was impressive! Congratulations."

"I'd hoped to be further along by now." He had, but that didn't diminish his pride at his accomplishments.

"At this rate, you'll get there in no time."

"What brings you here?"

"I have some thoughts on the cattle drive tomorrow."

The month of May marked the official start of horse breeding season at Thunder Ranch. It was also when the recently born calves were vaccinated, dewormed, examined and, if necessary, treated. Tomorrow the ranch hands, headed by Uncle Joshua, would be riding the Harts' remaining unleased range, rounding up the cattle and driving them to the holding pens in the south hundred acres. It was a monumental job that would take, at minimum, two full days to complete. The entire family would be on board to assist.

After some last-minute conferring with Ace and his mother, Gracie and Royce headed off to prepare for the morning.

"You going to be home for dinner tonight, or do you have plans with Flynn?"

Ace and his mother began strolling toward the barn. "Not tonight."

Ace would have liked nothing better, but she'd flatly refused his invitation.

"Aren't things going well with you two?"

His scowl must have given him away. "They were. At least, I thought they were. Something's changed the last couple of days."

"Be patient with her. It's paying off with Midnight."

"What if her father sells the ranch? He's had a few interested buyers looking at the place. And he's finalized a deal for his remaining livestock."

Flynn hadn't mentioned the deal to Ace, she didn't need to. Rodeo contracting was a small world and news traveled fast.

"Even if he sold the ranch tomorrow, you'd still have a month or two before the escrow closed."

They reached the barn. Ace held open the door to his office for his mother. Inside, he cranked on a small window air-conditioning unit to clear out the stuffiness. Spring in Montana had arrived, and the days were growing warmer and warmer.

"That's better." She waved a hand as if to fan herself.

He plunked down at his desk, his mother in the chair opposite him. For the first time that day, he noticed her face. It was drawn and paler than usual and there were dark circles beneath her eyes. She also moved as if she carried a heavy sack strapped to her back.

"You doing okay, Mom?"

"Nothing a glass of cold water and a few minutes with my feet up won't cure."

"You look more than tired."

Ever since Tuf's cryptic phone call, she'd had nights

when she paced the halls rather than slept. Ace had lost count how often he awoke to the sound of her footsteps padding down the stairs or banging cabinets in the kitchen as she fixed herself a cup of tea.

"How are you sleeping?"

"Okay for the most part."

She was exaggerating and they both knew it.

"Are you worried about Tuf?"

"I worry about all my children."

"Why me?"

"You work too hard. You've taken this new business to heart, which is wonderful. But it's not your responsibility entirely. You need to delegate."

"To who? Colt? When he's not working he's off rodeoing. And most of the hands are putting in overtime as it is."

"Then cut back. You're going to be a father soon."

"Which is why I'm working my tail off. Babies aren't free."

"You have to find a way to balance work and a personal life. Would it really be so terrible if we didn't put Midnight out to stud?"

Ace was aghast. "That's the whole reason we bought him. He has to earn his keep. As it is, we're not taking in the stud fees we'd planned."

"We'll have at least twenty foals next spring from our mares."

"That's a drop in the bucket compared to what we could be doing." Ace felt his blood pressure elevate and forced himself to relax. "You've seen the numbers, what our projected revenue could be. We have to establish Midnight as a proven breeder. Rehabilitate him enough to hand breed him to clients' mares."

"You're right, of course." She slumped in her chair.

"I apologize, Mom. I didn't mean to lecture." Ace smiled.

His mother didn't. "You're passionate about the business. I admire and appreciate that."

"What about Colt has you concerned, other than his chronic aversion to responsibility?"

His mother sighed. "Don't be too hard on him."

Ace didn't think he was hard enough.

"Something's bothering him lately."

"He's been gone more than usual." Ace recalled his brother's strange reaction to the news Flynn was expecting. Could there be a connection?

"I can't help thinking he's wrestling with something big."

"I wish he'd wrestle with it at home. We really could use him." Ace could use him.

"Please don't lose faith. Colt's not that different from you."

"Are you joking? We couldn't be more different!"

"Not when it comes to being disappointed and hurt by your father. Tuf and Dinah, too, for that matter. We've each of us responded in our own way to his drinking. You take on too much responsibility as a result. Colt takes on too little. Tuf left altogether."

"I should have realized Dad had a problem. That he was making bad financial decisions."

"You were away at college and vet school."

"I came home every month."

"I didn't notice, either. We choose to see what we want when it comes to the people we love."

Like his brothers?

His mother's observation sat like a lead ball in Ace's

stomach. "Colt needs to grow up. Pull his weight around here."

"Maybe we just need to figure out what motivates him. Flynn, too."

"I'd give anything for the answer to that. She's warm one day, cold the next."

"Being pregnant isn't easy."

"This is more than being pregnant."

He hadn't asked her to marry him again or to reconsider moving. Both topics were guaranteed to trigger a negative reaction.

"Everything was great until after the ultrasound."

"What did you say to her?"

"Nothing I haven't before. That I'd be there for her and the baby."

"Hmm." Now that they were on a different subject than his father and brothers, his mother looked better. Less stressed. "Since you can't pinpoint what went wrong, pinpoint what went right."

Ace raised his brows. "How do you mean?"

"What were you doing when she seemed to be having the best time?"

Ace didn't have to think twice. "When we went to the Andersons and treated their dog. She said she really enjoyed seeing me at work and helping me."

His mother's eyes sparked. "Ask her to go with you on another call."

"I don't have anything scheduled until next Tuesday, and I'm tied up for the next two days vaccinating the calves."

"There you go."

"What? Are you suggesting I ask her to help with the vaccinating?"

"Why not?"

"She's pregnant. It's grueling work. Hot and dirty."

"Just to watch, then."

He opened his mouth to protest, then reconsidered. "She does like animals. No." He shook his head. "It's a crazy idea."

"Sometimes the craziest ideas are the best. What have you got to lose? Unless you want to wait until next Tuesday."

He definitely didn't want that.

With a philosophical shrug, he pulled out his cell phone and called Flynn. After saying hello and asking how she was feeling, he mentioned the calves. "I know it's late notice, but I was wondering if you'd like to come to the ranch the day after tomorrow and…help me. We'd have to get an early start."

"I'd love to!"

"You would?"

"What time should I be there?"

He almost fell off his chair. "Um, seven. Wear old clothes."

His mother smiled smugly at him from across the desk.

"Okay. I'll see you then." He disconnected, still not quite believing what had just happened.

"See?" His mother nodded approvingly. "You just needed to find the right motivation."

Now, if only he could find the right motivation to convince Flynn to remain in Roundup and marry him.

UP UNTIL TODAY, Flynn had experienced very little morning sickness. Then again, she hadn't been tossed around the front seat of Ace's pickup truck like a sneaker in a clothes dryer.

"Can you drive a tiny bit slower?"

He glanced her way. "You want to stop for a rest?"

"No, no." She refused to reveal how truly nauseated she felt. He might turn around and take her home, and she was determined to help him vaccinate the calves.

"I'll be okay once we get there." Which would hopefully be soon.

The day was spectacularly gorgeous. A vivid blue sky lay suspended above rolling green hills. In the distance, elk grazed. Beyond them the mountains rose up, their still snowcapped tips buried in the clouds.

Flynn had been cooped up all week. When she wasn't at the clinic or helping her dad finalize the company books, she was on the phone with Billings Community College and the University of Montana resolving her transcript problem or online researching prenatal care. She'd resisted going into town in order to avoid Ace, his family and their mutual friends.

It was one thing for her and Ace to spend time together for the sake of their child. Quite another to be romantically involved. People looked at her, at *them,* with the same knowing glances her father frequently cast in her direction.

That wasn't all. Flynn had begun to secretly hope for more from Ace—an admission, a confession, an indication—and that was dangerous. Might as well tape a break-me sign over her heart.

Which left her to wonder where exactly accompanying him to vaccinate the calves fit.

Not a date, that was for sure.

She was assisting him with his job, like when she'd updated his spreadsheets and reorganized his files last week.

The novelty of that still amazed her. Work had never been anything she and her ex-husband shared, other than discussing their respective days over dinner.

Some of the nurses at the clinic complained that they could *never* work alongside their spouses or partners, the strain would surely end their relationships.

The few times that Flynn had helped Ace went smoothly. Enjoyably. No strain whatsoever.

That might change, however, after spending six or seven straight hours with him. Like today.

"I'm surprised you agreed to come along," he said.

"It's just too beautiful to stay indoors." She winced as they went over another bump on the road and pressed a hand to her roiling stomach. "Plus, I needed a break."

"Been busy?"

She nodded, then instantly regretted it, the motion causing her nausea to escalate. "I finally got accepted into the University of Montana."

"Good for you!"

"Even though I can't enroll in nursing school until the spring, I was happy. Then, I started applying for a student loan."

"Uh-oh."

"They're drowning me in paperwork. I no sooner submit one piece of information and they want another. They actually asked for my dad's last tax return. My dad's! Because I live with him. Isn't that an invasion of privacy or something?"

"Hang in there." His tone was genuinely supportive and sympathetic. "It'll be worth it."

She smiled weakly. To be honest, the lengthy process

was wearing her down, and she'd lost most of her initial enthusiasm. For nursing school, not broadening her horizons or finding a more rewarding career. She'd even gone so far as to check into related professions, including respiratory therapy and physical therapy.

Maybe being pregnant had something to do with her waning interest. She couldn't recall ever being so tired.

Ace, and leaving him when she moved, certainly wasn't the reason. Absolutely not. Impossible.

"Sit tight," he said, "we're almost there."

There was the south end of Thunder Ranch and the cattle operation. Barns, pens, trailers and chutes came into view. A dozen trucks and just as many cowboys on horseback had already arrived.

"Busy place." Flynn peered out the window, the low, long braying of cattle growing louder as they approached.

"There's a lot more to vaccinating calves than you think."

"Practically all my life living here, and I've never participated in a cattle roundup."

"Sorry to disappoint you, but the cattle were mostly rounded up yesterday. The men are going after a few strays today."

"Too bad."

"Next time you can go along."

Much as she'd have liked to attribute the nervous tingling in her tummy to morning sickness, Flynn couldn't. It was pure Ace and that disarming smile of his.

"I don't suppose it's the same as in those old Westerns on TV. Head 'em up, move 'em out and all that," she joked.

"Not exactly. We use trucks."

A shame. She could easily imagine Ace on horseback, herding the cattle to... She squinted. A large corral, from what she could tell.

"It used to take a full week to vaccinate and deworm all the calves when we were running five thousand head." He parked the truck beside a similar one bearing the Thunder Ranch bucking horse logo. "We'll probably finish in a day and a half."

"How do you feel about that?" She opened the door and hopped out, meeting Ace at the side of the truck.

"About finishing in a couple of days?"

"About only running a few hundred cattle instead of thousands. I mean, you grew up raising cattle. That was your family's livelihood. Their heritage."

"It's been a change."

He opened the side compartment on his truck and removed a large plastic case, along with a smaller cardboard box which he handed to her.

"But not a bad one," he continued. "I like practicing veterinarian medicine."

"More than breeding horses?"

They walked toward a group of pens where a half-dozen ranch hands, including Beau and Duke, were sorting the calves, checking their ear tags and noting the numbers on a clipboard. The mamas weren't happy at being separated from their babies and made their objections known with loud vocal protests.

"For me, horse breeding goes hand in hand with veterinarian medicine. Especially once we incorporate artificial insemination into our program."

The plastic tote obviously wasn't as heavy as it appeared, for Ace carried it with ease.

"You think you'll get to that point? Where you're shipping semen across the country?"

"I can't settle for anything less. Not if we're going to be successful and make money. That loan we took out won't pay itself down."

Flynn liked chatting with Ace about the ranch and his practice and their breeding program. It was a side of him unfamiliar to her. They'd both been focused on school when they dated and residing in Billings. They'd go home on weekends. Separately. John Hart and Flynn's father were at the height of their rivalry then.

"What about you?" Ace asked. "Your life is changing, too. Returning to school is a huge step."

He didn't mention moving. Neither did she.

"School and a baby, too."

His expression turned serious. "Be careful you don't overextend yourself."

"We've already talked about this," she insisted. "I'm starting out a part-time student. Two classes tops."

He set the plastic case down. "I meant today. Vaccinating the calves."

"Oh. Sorry." She bit her lower lip. "I'll take frequent rest breaks, I promise."

"Stay away from the pens and chutes. Cattle can be just as unpredictable as bucking horses and just as dangerous."

As they set up their station, Ace was greeted by his uncle Joshua who updated him on their progress so far.

"What exactly does vaccinating and deworming the calves involve?" Flynn asked when he was finished.

"We drive the calves one at a time from the pen down that narrow chute and into the headgate."

"Headgate?"

"Over there." He pointed to a large metal contraption

that stood at least five and a half feet tall and appeared to be operated by a series of levers.

She grimaced and rubbed her throat. "Looks uncomfortable."

"Actually, it's not uncomfortable at all. The calves will raise a fuss for sure, but it is the safest, gentlest and most effective way to restrain them while giving them injections."

Flynn was fascinated. "Can I help?"

He laughed. "You're not running calves down the chute."

Protesting would get her nowhere. "There must be something I can do."

"How handy are you with a syringe?"

"I want to be a nurse, remember?"

"Good." He opened the lid of the plastic box, revealing a supply of syringes and bottles of clear liquid. "Let me show you how. I need about a hundred of them filled."

She picked up a syringe, eyed the needle beneath the protective cap. "It's huge! Those poor calves."

"It won't hurt. Not any more than when you get a flu shot."

"Hmm." Flynn remained unconvinced.

"Squeamish?"

"Please, don't insult me." Her queasy stomach betrayed her by choosing that moment to lurch.

"I can get Gracie to help me."

"Not on your life." Flynn squared her shoulders and stuck out her chin. "Show me what I need to do."

CHAPTER TWELVE

"Flynn," Joshua Adams called, attempting to hold a calf steady while reading the ear tag. "Do you have this one?" He recited the number.

She ran down the list on her clipboard, flipped pages and checked off the calf. "Got it."

Having filled all the syringes, she'd been given the task of logging each calf as it was sent down the chute to the headgate.

According to her check marks, they were better than halfway done. A lot of calves and a lot of hard work. Flynn was sweating profusely, and she hadn't labored a fraction as hard as Ace, his uncle, cousins and the ranch hands.

She was also having a thoroughly grand time.

The physically intensive labor was made easier by a friendly camaraderie among the participants. More than once she found herself the brunt of a good-natured jest, and she laughed along with everyone else.

Her attention was diverted as the next calf trotted down the chute, bawling at the top of its lungs. Gracie closed the headgate and before the calf quite knew what was happening, Ace had administered the injection and dewormer.

"Hold on, little fellow." Gracie scratched the calf on the forehead. "Almost done."

Ace conducted a quick exam. "Wait a second," he said when Gracie would have released the lever and freed the calf.

Ace knelt down.

Flynn understood the purpose of restraining the calf when it suddenly kicked out with a hind leg. Luckily, the potential blow missed Ace by a good two feet.

"Flynn," he called. "Bring me the Biozide Gel."

She grabbed the jar from his medical case and brought it to him. Over the course of a few hours she'd learned the names of almost every item in his case.

"Is he hurt?"

"Nothing much." Ace applied the gel to a small nick on the calf's chest. "Probably got into a tussle with one of his buddies."

"Boys will be boys." Gracie winked at Flynn. "Have two of them myself. Twelve and fourteen."

Flynn imagined her son, a miniature version of Ace, roughhousing with his friends on the Harts' large front lawn or swimming in their backyard pool. Probably the way Ace had roughhoused and swam with his brothers when he was young.

Then she imagined her son in an apartment in Billings—which was probably where she'd be living because she couldn't afford much more on her income, not while she attended school.

Those play sessions at the Harts' would be during the weekends when Ace had their son.

Unless they had a girl, like Ace wanted, then it would be tea parties.

Nah. With Ace for a father, she'd probably be tough as any boy.

"Lunch is here," one of the hands hollered, rubbing his hands together in anticipation.

"Finally," Gracie exclaimed, releasing the calf so that it could be returned to its mother. "I'm starving."

Flynn was, too. Her nausea had disappeared not long after starting work. So, she now noticed, had her fatigue.

The truck carrying their lunches pulled up and Sarah Hart emerged.

"Come and get it!"

Four hungry men beat her to the rear of the truck and began unloading the ice chests.

"You ready?" Ace asked Flynn.

"More than ready." She helped him close up the medical case.

Lunch consisted of sandwiches, fat dill pickles, individual bags of potato chips, cold drinks and homemade brownies for dessert.

Flynn sat on the lowered tailgate of Ace's truck, removed her ball cap and ate like a starved animal, licking the brownie crumbs off her fingers when she was done.

"Finished already?" Ace joined her, the other half of his sandwich still in his hand, his bag of chips unopened.

"Lightweight," she muttered.

"Do you mind?" He nodded at the tailgate.

In reply, she scooted over.

"I guess you're eating for two." The truck rocked unsteadily as he made himself comfortable.

"That's my story, and I'm sticking to it."

"Want my brownie?"

"No, thanks." She'd already had two. "I'm glad you invited me today."

"I should have warned you how labor-intensive it was going to be."

"Doesn't bother me."

"You taking it easy?"

"I feel fantastic. Lately I've been getting tired and can hardly keep my eyes open. Today I'm the Energizer Bunny."

"Wait till tonight. Then you'll be tired."

"If I'd known how much fun your job is, I'd have come with you sooner."

"You're welcome to tag along anytime." The look he sent her implied his invitation included more than work.

Emboldened, she asked, "What if I took you up on that offer?"

"Nothing would make me happier. You're a good assistant. And those spreadsheets you did for me, they're a whole lot better than what I came up with."

His praise sent a ribbon of warmth winding through her.

She inclined her head at Ace's mother and uncle. "Whatever they're talking about must be serious."

Ace looked over. "Numbers, I imagine," he said, finishing his sandwich.

"Numbers?"

"How many cows are pregnant, what's the anticipated herd size next year, how many calves to sell off, how many acres of alfalfa should we plant, what the current price of seed is. Want me to continue, or have I sufficiently bored you?"

Flynn whistled. "There's a lot to this ranching business." The only cattle her father had owned were a few calves for roping practice.

"Which is why we have to keep up our strength." Ace held out his brownie.

She caved. "All right, but just half."

He broke the brownie in two, giving her the larger portion.

They sat for a moment in silence, enjoying the sunshine and listening to the conversations around them.

"What do you like best about your job?" Flynn eventually asked.

"Not the paperwork, that's for sure."

"Me, either, though I'm actually pretty good at it."

"Not the headaches and the infinite little details that seem to pile up, either."

"Kind of like me and school."

Ace glanced around. "On the other hand, I love days like this, being outside with the animals. Solving problems, overcoming challenges. That's what keeps me interested."

"Challenges like Midnight?"

"When I figure out what makes that horse tick, I'm throwing a party." He took a sip of his soda. "What about you? What do you like best about your job?"

"Helping people," she answered without hesitation. "I don't have as much direct patient contact as the nurses and doctors, but when their experience is a little better, a little easier because of me, they're grateful. For the most part. It's what makes me want to go to work every day."

"We should all be so lucky to feel passionate about our jobs."

"It's the same for you. Like when you helped the Andersons with Lovey."

"I suppose."

She bumped elbows with him. "Stop being such a guy and admit it."

He laughed. "Okay, you got me. I like helping people. And animals. Even fluffy little kittens."

She lifted her gaze to him and said softly, "I bet you do like kittens."

"Babies, too."

Her heart flip-flopped.

This wasn't good. If she expected to protect herself from the temptations Ace Hart presented, she couldn't go all mushy inside just because he said "baby" in that silky voice of his.

She was strong, she could resist.

And she might have succeeded if he hadn't reached up and brushed a lock of flyaway hair from her face. The sensation of his fingers brushing her skin sent shivers coursing through her.

Steady, girl.

He leaned in, and her willpower flew out the window.

Kiss me.

Someone passed close to the truck, saving Flynn from making a fool of herself.

"Looks like lunch is over." She leaped to her feet.

People were up from their makeshift seats and starting back to work.

Ace didn't mention their close encounter, and neither did Flynn. For the next two hours they continued working in tandem, their established routine like a well-oiled machine.

Fortunately, Flynn barely had a spare second to recall their almost PDA. When she did, her pulse skipped erratically and her mind wandered.

"Flynn?"

"Sorry." Heat infused her cheeks. How long had Ace been talking to her before she heard him?

"We're done."

"We are?"

"That was the last calf for today. We'll finish with the strays tomorrow."

She glanced at the clipboard and then her watch. "It's only three o'clock."

"We've been at it since seven. Aren't you ready to call it a day?"

Not exactly. "Yeah, sure."

She helped him pack up and carry the supplies to his truck.

He closed the side compartment on his truck, stood, waited and finally said, "We could go out, if you want."

Alarm bells went off in her head. Hadn't she been avoiding him all week so as not to encourage him?

"Go where?" she asked.

A gleam lit his mesmerizing dark eyes. "Fishing."

Fishing! At Thunder Creek. Like they used to do when they were dating.

The alarm bells clanged louder.

"I don't know. I'm filthy." She plucked at the front of her shirt.

"We have time if you want to take a quick shower. The fish won't start biting till dusk."

Every logical and rational brain cell in her head screamed at her to tell him no. To go fishing with Ace was asking for trouble. Too many memories, good and bad.

She opened her mouth and what came out was: "Sure. Why not?"

ACE DROVE HOME after dropping Flynn off. They agreed he'd return for her in a half hour, which didn't give him much time.

The first thing he did when he walked into the kitchen was throw together some food to take, pilfering items from the refrigerator without much thought. The same with the pantry. Cheese, cold cuts, crackers, olives, strawberries, granola bars, anything that looked the least bit edible.

Okay, maybe not granola bars. Cookies instead. She'd liked the brownies at lunch. When he finished packing the food he grabbed some bottled water.

Kind of a mishmash dinner, but it would suffice.

Next he hit the bathroom where he washed up, then changed into a clean shirt and jeans. Last, he headed to the garage and retrieved the fishing gear. Good, he still had a few jars of bait and his lures weren't a tangled mess.

Before leaving he stopped quickly to check on Midnight. Fancy Gal, the stallion's constant companion, came over to the fence for a petting along with the other mares.

To Ace's amazement and delight, Midnight came, too. Willingly. Almost eagerly. Without Ace using a carrot to bribe him.

"Nothing like having the love of a good woman to make us complacent, is there, boy?"

Ace envied the horse. He wanted to know that same feeling with Flynn.

It could happen. She'd agreed to go fishing.

She wasn't waiting for him when he pulled up in front of the house. Instead, Earl stood at the top of the porch steps, rocking on his heels and wearing an unreadable expression. Ace hadn't seen or spoken to Flynn's father since the Western Frontier Pro Rodeo when Fancy Gal had colic. When Earl had seen Ace and Flynn kissing.

She'd mentioned once that Earl was happy about the baby. He might be less happy that Ace was the father.

He got out of the truck, his nerves on edge. Despite being almost thirty, Flynn was still her father's little girl and the love of his life.

"Howdy, Earl."

"Ace. Good to see you. Flynn will be right out."

They met at the foot of the porch steps and shook hands. Ace breathed a sigh of relief. "How've you been?"

If he thought to engage Earl in small talk, he was very wrong.

"You be careful with my Flynn."

"I will. I'll watch her every step, make sure she doesn't slip and fall."

"I'm not talking about the creek."

Of course not. "I won't hurt her. You can count on it."

"You did before."

"She told you?"

"She didn't have to."

Ace wouldn't make the mistake of underestimating Earl again.

His attention was distracted by the appearance of three individuals from around the corner of the house. From their dress and manner, he identified them as a real estate agent and her clients.

The woman gave Ace a polite smile, then spoke to Earl. "Thank you for letting us see the place on such short notice."

"No problem."

"We'll be in touch."

They would be in touch. If the clients' excited glow was any indication, they liked what they saw.

Ace was glad for Earl. Not so glad for himself.

He waited by the porch swing, just beyond hearing distance, trying not to think about Flynn moving and failing miserably. After a round of handshakes, the real estate agent and her clients left.

Earl's smile was much too tickled pink for Ace's liking.

"That went well," Ace said, rejoining Earl.

His reply was a satisfied grunt, not that Ace expected details.

Thirty to sixty days for an escrow to close. He couldn't afford to waste one second.

Flynn stepped through the front door. "Sorry I'm late." Her glance traveled from her father to Ace. "Everything okay?"

"They seemed taken with the place." Earl went to her and kissed her cheek. "And they're already prequalified for a home loan."

"Did they make an offer?"

"The Realtor said she'd be calling later today and then she winked at me."

It was even worse than Ace first thought.

"Dad, that's great!"

Earl grunted again, with even more satisfaction. "Don't be late, you two. That road isn't easy to drive in the dark."

Ace couldn't talk, his throat had gone dry.

He helped Flynn into the truck. She'd changed her

clothes and carried a canvas tote which he stowed behind the seat.

"I brought some snacks along," she said when they were underway.

"Me, too," he mumbled.

"Then I guess we won't starve."

He tried to laugh but couldn't muster more than a weak chuckle. "Your dad was pretty happy."

"About what?"

"The ranch selling."

"I'm not going to celebrate until everyone's signed on the dotted line."

Maybe not, but her eyes glinted with undeniable optimism.

A stilted silence descended on them for the remainder of the drive.

Ace mentally kicked himself for not kissing her at lunch. No way in hell would he let a second opportunity pass without taking advantage of it.

At the creek, they unloaded the food and fishing gear. Ace insisted on carrying everything except the tackle box and blanket. Even then, he held Flynn's arm as they descended the slope to the bank.

She stayed behind and laid out the blanket on the only relatively flat spot in the area while he made two more trips back and forth to the truck.

She was stripping off her shirt when he returned with the lawn chairs. Beneath the shirt, she wore a bikini top.

Ace froze. "What's going on?" he croaked.

She bent and rolled up the legs of her denim Capri pants. "It's so warm out, I thought I'd get a little sun while we fished."

Fished? He blinked. For a moment, he'd forgotten where they were and what they were doing.

She promptly reminded him. "Come on, slowpoke."

It wasn't the sight of her skimpy top that immobilized him, but the gentle curve of her belly poking out above the waistband of her pants.

Flynn was noticeably pregnant and she'd never looked sexier.

CHAPTER THIRTEEN

FISHING POLE IN HAND, Flynn stepped gingerly off the bank and into the brisk water. Her toes curled inside her sneakers, which sank into the soft creek bed.

"Where you going?" Ace asked, his voice unsteady.

Was it the creek or Flynn unbalancing him?

"The pool."

Unless flooding this past spring had drastically altered the topography of the creek bank, there was a large pool just around the bend and several boulders providing perfect seating.

"Wait for me."

Ace's gaze on her bare back sent a series of tiny tremors racing along her spine.

She waded deeper into the creek, using the cool water to extinguish her burning thoughts.

He'd seen her in a bathing suit before. Countless times. Seen her entirely naked more than once. Here, in fact, when they'd gone skinny-dipping. Why today did the sight of a little skin cause him to stare at her with hungry eyes?

Flynn wasn't the siren type. She didn't attempt to charm men with her feminine wiles. She might have given it a try if they panted after her like Ace was apparently doing.

It was so unlike him, so unlike her, she almost burst into laughter.

"Don't dawdle." She glanced behind her, and the laugh she'd been holding back died.

Ace had removed his shirt, too.

His muscled chest and arms gleamed in the bright sunlight, as did his dark brown hair. The contrast was quite…appealing.

A memory surfaced, almost painful in its intensity. She'd run her hands along those same muscles, felt them bunch beneath her fingertips as he'd hovered over her, nibbled her neck, slid a knee between her legs to part them.

Her sneaker abruptly slipped on a moss-covered rock, and she teetered for a moment before regaining her balance.

"Be careful," he warned. "The current's pretty strong."

He entered the creek, creating a small splash. Along with his fishing pole, he carried the tackle box.

She eyed it pointedly. "You think I'm going to lose my hook?"

"It's happened before." Ace had nearly drowned once trying to unsnag her hook that had become caught in an underwater trap. "Today I'm cutting the line."

This was much better, thought Flynn. She hadn't liked the somber mood on the drive over.

He was going to have to get used to the idea of her father selling the ranch. Possibly soon if the potential buyers today made an offer.

She was going to have to get used to the idea, too.

A month ago she wouldn't have been torn. She'd have left Roundup without a second's hesitation.

Since then, her relationship with Ace had changed. The question was, into what?

She loved him. The miserable, hopeless kind of love. Not head over heels. That had been back in college, before Ace broke her heart. He wasn't now and never had been anywhere approaching the edge of that mysterious and magical realm she resided in, much less crossed over into it.

And she was tired of being stuck in there alone.

Appreciative glances and tiny tremors were all well and good, but Flynn wanted spontaneous declarations, can't-wait-until-he-calls flutters and secretive glances across the dinner table that no one else understood.

She wanted him to love her. Love her beyond reason.

The farther along the creek they traveled, the faster the water rushed by them. Flynn shivered as it swirled past her knees.

"Cold?"

"No." She turned, her eyes instantly drawn to Ace's wet jeans clinging to his thighs. "Maybe a little."

What a lie! Chilled was the last thing she felt.

"We can go back," he said.

"Wimp," she teased, hoping to distract herself as much as him. "The bend is right there."

"You sure you're okay?"

"I'm fine."

"I promised your dad I'd watch out for you."

The genuine anxiety in his voice caused her to look at herself through his eyes, a pregnant woman traipsing along a creek. She conceded his concern wasn't overblown.

She also conceded she might be trying to prove

something—to Ace and herself. Exert her independence.

Suddenly, her interest in fishing diminished.

Not enough for her to suggest returning, however.

The creek abruptly widened, the water becoming warmer and more sluggish as they entered the pool.

"If there are any fish in here," Ace commented, "we've scared them away."

"They'll come back."

The boulders were where they'd always been since Flynn and Ace started coming here, jutting up from the ground like giant mushrooms. She parked herself on the first one, pulling her sodden sneakers out of the water.

Ace sat down so quickly, he wobbled. "Whoa!"

"You'd think a man as good as you are at riding broncs could sit a boulder."

"Different skill set required." He set the tackle box down on a wide, flat rock. "Need me to bait your hook?"

"Sir, you insult me." Truthfully, Flynn had always been the better and more avid fisherman.

Soon their bobbers were dancing merrily on the water's glittering surface and conversation flowed easily.

"Did you see today when that mama cow butted Harlan right in the..." Flynn cut her gaze to her lap. "I never heard a grown man yelp so loud."

"Or so high," Ace added with a grin.

"And your poor cousin Beau. I swear, he stepped in every cow patty there was."

"It was like his boots had built-in homing devices."

They shared a few more chuckles. After a while, the sun's soothing rays gave Flynn a case of the lazies.

"I guess the fish aren't biting today," Ace murmured.

"There's no rush."

Sometimes doing nothing together could be just as enjoyable as doing something.

"Tell me a secret." She flashed him a mischievous grin.

"Forget it."

"Come on. I'll go first."

It was a game they'd played in their dating days. Sharing secrets. Mostly funny ones. Occasionally sad. Now and then a little shocking.

As far as Flynn knew, neither of them had revealed their secrets to a single soul.

They'd trusted each other in those days.

She needed to trust him again.

Without waiting for him to answer, she blurted, "I cheated on an advanced calculus midterm. Bought the answers from some kid."

Ace's jaw went slack. "You're kidding!"

"I was sick the week before the test. Bronchitis. I studied. Tried to. My brain was mush. Math was always hard for me. I couldn't afford less than a C in the class."

"Miss Goody Two-shoes Flynn cheated on a test." He shook his head in dismay, but one corner of his mouth tilted in a grin.

"Only that one time. I was desperate. I worked my tail off the rest of the semester to make up for it."

After a moment, Ace admitted, "I got drunk after my dad's funeral."

"Sorry, Ace, but that's no secret. We could tell."

"I was drunk for two straight days."

She sat back. "Really?"

"And hungover for four."

"Ow!"

"The worst part is, I repeated it after you and I broke up."

Now, that *was* a secret.

"I still thought about you every day," she confessed. *And every night.* "Even when I was married."

"I've only dated three women since you."

"That's no secret, either." She swung her fishing pole back and forth, watching the line slice through the water. "Dinah told me."

"They all dumped me. For the same reason."

"Which was?"

"I think the exact quote went, 'I'm tired of being with a guy who's hung up on his old girlfriend.'"

Flynn's hand froze. "Is it true?"

"You know it is."

That was the problem, she knew no such thing. "Why did you leave me that morning?"

He stared at the distant mountains, his reply, if he was even going to give her one, trapped in his throat.

Don't shut me out now. Not like before.

"The simple answer is I got scared." He spoke slowly. Reservedly. "The complicated answer is…more complicated."

"Let's stick to simple, then," she gently urged. "Scared of what?"

He turned his head to look at her. "You."

"What did I do that was scary?" Flynn hadn't been clingy or needy or demanding. Not anything that typically scared off men. Now or then.

"You took my breath away."

"I don't understand."

"That's the complicated part. Us, being together, it was unexpected. I wasn't ready."

"For what?"

"The feelings I had for you. *Have* for you. It's different this time."

Flynn noticed she was gripping the fishing pole like a lifeline and relaxed her grip. "Different how?"

"Stronger."

"Doesn't sound like a reason to rush off. Sounds more like a reason to stay."

"The timing sucked. My mom and I were signing the loan documents that morning, finalizing our expansion plans. I'd just taken on another new client the Andersons recommended. We were entering contract negotiations with two new rodeo promoters. It wasn't fair to start something I couldn't finish."

"You seriously thought rushing off and not so much as sending me a one-line text wouldn't hurt?" Flynn's eyes stung with unshed tears. She blinked them away before Ace saw.

"Not as much."

"As what? Dating for a few weeks and then dumping me?" She reeled in her line.

"Yes."

"Because you did it before?"

"Breaking up with you was one of the hardest things I've ever done."

"Hmm. So, by leaving that morning you were sparing yourself difficulty. Not me."

"You're twisting this around." He reeled in his line, too. Yanked it in was a better description.

"I think I'm calling it exactly right."

Fishing, playing secrets, both had been bad ideas. She slid off the boulder and into the creek, the cool water giving her a jolt.

"Flynn, wait."

"What are we doing? What's changed that you're suddenly not too busy to have me in your life? Ah, yes, the baby." She cut him off before he could answer. "You have time for him or her but not me."

Pole in hand, she trudged forward, the current impeding her progress.

"Don't go," he said.

"Why is it okay for you to always take off and not me?"

He came after her, water sloshing, tackle box swinging. "I was wrong."

"Which time?"

"I should have called you. Explained."

"News flash, Ace." Anger propelled her forward. "That would have made it only infinitesimally better."

They reached the bank where they'd left the blanket and their gear. The slope looked higher than Flynn remembered, and she hesitated.

"Let me go first."

"I can do it." She raised a foot, teetered unsteadily.

Ace grabbed her by the arm. "Quit being so stubborn."

"Fine." She moved to the side and watched as he effortlessly scaled the bank. "Show off," she grumbled under her breath.

Situated on solid ground, he reached out a hand to her.

She accepted it grudgingly. The next second, she was hoisted onto the bank. Ace circled her waist with one strong arm, though it was completely unnecessary.

"You can let go."

He didn't and instead increased his hold on her.

"Ace—"

"Here's another secret." He lowered his head and brushed his lips across hers. "I left that morning because I realized how easy it would be to fall for you. That I probably already had years ago and kept denying it."

Quite a line for a man who typically held his cards close to his chest.

Flynn's resolve melted. He may not love her to distraction, but he obviously had genuine feelings for her. Or, perhaps he did love her and simply refused to admit it.

Either way, he was making it hard to resist him.

He pressed his hand to her belly, splayed his fingers wide. "We're going to be a family. Nothing or no one will come between me and you and our child."

In that moment, Flynn let herself believe him. He was here, with her, taking time away from work. Fishing, of all things, because that was what she'd wanted.

He kissed her then, vanquishing all coherent thoughts and leaving only sensation. A thrumming pulse. A quickening in her middle. Tingling nerve endings.

She ceased fighting it and gave in to her body's electric response.

BEFORE FLYNN QUITE realized what was happening, Ace swooped her up in his arms and carried her to the blanket. Setting her on her feet, he resumed kissing her, his tongue demanding and receiving an eager and willing response from her.

It had been like this before when they made love. She'd lost her head, surrendered to the wildly sensual feelings he aroused in her with just a kiss. A caress. A murmured word. A low groan.

She'd made a mistake.

Not the baby. Heavens, no. That was wonderful. Incredible. But the hurt in the wake of his leaving… She couldn't cope a third time. Despite his recent efforts, nothing about his work and commitments had changed. Ace's ability to devote himself to her depended entirely on his job demands, which were numerous.

He must have sensed her reservations, for he tore his mouth away from hers and gazed intently at her. "We don't have to do this if you're not ready."

Seemed kind of silly for her to refuse him when she was carrying his child.

"I'm not going to run out on you afterward," he said, a rough edge to his voice. "I swear."

She didn't think he would. Not today. Not if he wanted to see her again before the baby was born.

Nonetheless, doubts lingered.

"I slept with you before because I thought there was a chance for us," she said. "A possible future."

"There is. More than ever."

"You left me. Twice. It isn't easy for me to lay open my heart to you a third time."

"I want to marry you, Flynn. Be the kind of husband you deserve."

Do you love me? She almost blurted the question out loud.

What would his response be if she did?

"I'm afraid."

"Of what?" He stroked her cheek with the pad of his thumb.

They had stood there before, in the same spot, Ace

kissing her senseless. He was very hard to resist, and Flynn was no longer sure she wanted to.

"This, us…matters to me," she said.

"Me, too."

"I wouldn't be here with you, wouldn't have invited you into my bed, if I didn't care greatly for you."

It was the closest she'd come to admitting she loved him.

He gathered her into his arms. "I won't hurt you."

"You can't make that promise. Who knows what will happen?"

"I won't hurt you intentionally."

People seldom did. Tell *that* to the pain when she was curled on her bed, crying herself sick.

Here was Flynn's chance to say no. To tell Ace his track record stank and she refused to set herself up for another big disappointment.

But then he pressed those incredible hands into the small of her bare back, and what came out of her mouth was a tiny moan of acquiescence.

Ace gently lowered her onto the blanket. She barely noticed the rough ground beneath them, her attention was focused entirely on them. His smoldering dark eyes, the sharp inhalation of her breath, the small currents of desire zinging through them both as he struggled to restrain his need.

They'd never come together when he didn't thrill her, and today was no exception.

He settled beside her, his hand roaming her body. Every now and then he paused to explore further, trace the slope of her waist, the curve of her hip. She arched, sighed, quaked when his fingers strayed to a particularly sensitive spot.

Sliding on top of her, he kissed her mouth, her neck, the soft mounds of her breasts spilling out of her bikini top. Inch by tantalizing inch, he worked his way down to her rounded tummy.

With one swift jerk, he unfastened the top of her pants, exposing more skin and the edge of her sheer panties.

"You are so beautiful," he whispered, his breath warm against her skin. "So perfect."

She wriggled when he kissed her navel, then writhed when he traced the outline with his tongue.

Abruptly, he moved up her body, his lips stopping every few seconds for a taste of her. Reaching her bikini top, he tugged the flimsy fabric aside, then closed his mouth around her nipple.

Pregnancy had made Flynn's breasts more sensitive. She raised off the blanket as fire shot through her. Ace helped her out of her bathing suit top, not waiting for her to lie back down before covering her breasts with his hands. She pulled his head down, silently urging him to take her in his mouth again.

He didn't stop there. Sliding his hand into the opening of her jeans, he breached her panties and found her damp center. She shifted her hips in response, willing him to soothe the burning ache inside her.

Thankfully, Ace had always been attuned to her during their lovemaking and very accommodating.

When she could stand no more, when her need demanded satisfaction, she rolled him over onto his back and straddled his middle.

"Hey, what's this?" he asked, his initial shock quickly replaced by a wicked grin.

"Why should you get all the fun?"

She ran her open palms over the muscled planes of his chest, combed her fingers through the patch of crinkly chest hair, stroked the smooth expanse of his taut stomach.

Talk about perfection.

He reached for her breasts, but she caught his hands and returned them to his sides.

"Not yet."

He groaned with frustration.

She squirmed down his body, eliciting more groans, until she reached his thighs. Once there, she unsnapped his jeans, exposing him as he had her.

He was ready for her, his arousal unmistakable.

She teased him through the fabric of his briefs, and he ground out her name on a ragged breath. Just as her fingers closed around him, he grasped her shoulders and pulled her down on top of him. The next second, he rolled them over so that they faced each other.

Smiling seductively, she slid her jeans off.

Ace pinned her beneath him and entered her. Slowly. Deeply. Flynn cried out from the pure joy of it. Each thrust took her to a new place, a new level of awareness.

Soon, however, she craved more.

Curling her arms around his neck, she brought his ear to her mouth.

"Harder," she whispered. "Faster."

"I don't want to hurt the baby."

"You won't."

"Sweetheart, I—"

She lifted her hips to meet his. "You *won't*."

Still, he held back, until Flynn reached a hand between their joined bodies. Then he lost control, which had been her plan all along.

Her climax hit her with sudden and exquisite force, leaving her shaken and weak and utterly sated. Ace cupped her face between his hands. When she would have closed her eyes, he demanded, "Look at me."

She complied. With their gazes locked and her mind crying out her love for him, his body shuddered in release. Flynn held him, willing the moment to last and last.

Stroking his back, she clung to him, the setting sun warming them with the last of its rays. Soon, before she was quite ready, he rolled off and snuggled her close.

He brushed at her hair. Flynn hated to think what it looked like and laughed with embarrassment.

"I like it when you do that," he said, and nuzzled her ear.

"Laugh?"

"Yeah, your eyes light up."

She tried to hide her face in his neck. He wouldn't let her and continued to stare at her with such unabashed emotion, she forgot about her embarrassment.

"That was wonderful." She skimmed her finger along the stubble on his jaw.

"Marry me, Flynn."

Like that, her complacent mood evaporated.

"We can be good parents to our child without a marriage license hanging on the wall."

"I don't want you to move."

"That's not a good enough reason." She sat up, silently scolding herself for not anticipating this. "It's no reason at all."

"You owe it to our child to give us a chance."

She saw in his eyes her refusal had struck a nerve. Rising to her feet, she tugged on her clothes. If he'd told her he loved her and then proposed, her reaction would be entirely different.

"We've been through this before."

He also stood and dressed. "Just because your mother walked out on you and your family doesn't mean the same thing will happen to us."

This time he'd struck a nerve with her.

Why did he have to go and ruin everything by proposing and then bringing up her mother?

"I don't think we should date anymore."

"Come on, Flynn."

"It feels like you're trying to ease your guilty conscience. Not…"

"Not what?"

"Nothing."

If he couldn't proclaim his love for her after what they'd just shared, she was wasting her time.

"What do I have to do to prove myself?"

"I don't know." She started shoving items in her tote bag.

"There has to be something."

She said the first idiotic thing that popped into her head. "Call me a hundred times between tonight and tomorrow."

"That's all?"

"It's a safe bet. You won't have the time."

"Tell you what." He thrust his arms into his shirt-sleeves. "I call you a hundred times by eight o'clock tomorrow morning, you agree to spend the entire weekend with me, from Friday night to Sunday evening."

"I'm scheduled for a half shift on Saturday."

"Then, any time you're not at the clinic."

"But you have to work."

"Maybe I won't."

"This I have to see." Flynn was confident she'd be spending the weekend alone.

She reached for a corner of the blanket, intending to fold it. Suddenly, a muffled trilling came from inside the tote bag. Her cell phone.

She dug it out, checked the display and gaped at Ace, who held his cell phone to his ear.

"You've got to be kidding." She hit the End button, rejecting the call.

He grinned. "One down, ninety-nine to go."

CHAPTER FOURTEEN

THERE WERE DAYS when Flynn felt like a child on a sugar high and could barely sit still. Others, her eyelids drooped and her feet dragged and she stared greedily at people drinking caffeine-infused beverages like a dog waiting for a treat.

Fortunately, today was the sugar-high kind of day. If not, she wouldn't be able to handle her and Ace's upcoming hike along Bent Arrow Bute.

She'd actually wanted to go horseback riding, her favorite pastime for beautiful Saturday mornings. Ace naturally nixed the idea, and they'd compromised on hiking.

He'd loaded their backpacks. His was the heavier one and contained most of their supplies, which, for a day hike, weren't many. Judging by the weight of her backpack, she was carrying a bag of roasted almonds and a travel-size package of wet wipes.

The trail Ace had chosen was for novices. Another compromise. Flynn told herself not to argue. It was important to him that he do things for her, watch over her, even though she felt completely capable. What really mattered was they were spending the entire weekend together. No interruptions except for her half shift at the clinic this afternoon.

He'd won the bet, called her a hundred times before

eight in the morning. She'd shut her phone off at ten and woke up eight hours later to fifty-seven missed calls. Had he slept at all?

As a result, they were hiking this morning and having dinner this evening. Pizza and wings. She'd caved. Tomorrow they were watching NASCAR races on television and grilling burgers.

Flynn smiled to herself. She'd won the bet, too.

They were nearing the trailhead where their hike would commence when Ace's cell phone rang.

"Hey, Uncle Josh. What's up?" His expression changed from happy-go-lucky to concerned. "Where are you?" After a brief exchange of information, Ace pulled over and put the truck in park. "Send Beau and the rig with the bulls ahead. I'll make some calls. See what I can line up. I'll get back to you shortly."

"What's wrong?" Flynn asked when he'd disconnected.

"One of the trucks broke down on the way to an amateur rodeo in Bozeman. Uncle Josh thinks the alternator has gone bad. They're stuck on the side of the highway about twenty-five miles outside of Roundup."

"Oh, no!"

"Uncle Josh called for roadside assistance. The service station is backed up and can't guarantee a repair truck there for at least three or four hours."

"Why so long?"

"They didn't say."

"Will your uncle make the rodeo in time?"

"That's the problem. I'm going to see who's available to meet with them and swap out trucks. That way, Uncle Josh and Colt can get back on the road. Whoever I get a hold of can wait for the repair truck."

Flynn listened as Ace placed call after call to various ranch hands. Everyone was either unable to break away, out riding the range, not answering his call for whatever reason or, like Colt, on route to the rodeo with their uncle Joshua.

Swearing ripely, Ace tossed his cell phone onto the seat.

Flynn sensed his next remark and braced herself for a rush of disappointment.

"I'm sorry." His tone was contrite. "I'm going to have to rescue them. If I leave now, I can be there in an hour. Less if I drive fast."

"Isn't there someone else you can call? What about your cousins?"

"Duke's on duty today and Beau is with Uncle Josh."

"No other employees?"

"It's the weekend. A lot of them are off."

"Would they be willing to work this once?"

"It's not right for me to ask them just so I can take the day off."

"Why not? You put in more hours than they do."

"It's my ranch, my responsibility, not theirs."

"You deserve a day off, too."

"Not if it endangers our livestock. Those horses can't wait on the side of the road long and be in any shape for the rodeo. It's a one-night event. Tonight. No time for them to recuperate if they're stressed."

Flynn sighed, annoyed at herself as much as anything. "I understand. I'm not intentionally being petty."

"And I know you're disappointed."

Better than half of the dates they went on were cut short or interrupted by some emergency call.

"You can come with me," he suggested, raising his eyebrows.

"I have to be at the clinic by two. That's cutting it kind of close."

"Can you trade shifts with someone?"

"I doubt I'd find someone this late."

There were some women who'd leap at the chance to be stuck in a vehicle with a handsome, sexy cowboy for hours on end.

Not Flynn. It wasn't that their hiking excursion had been canceled or that she'd miss her shift at the clinic. Rather, it was that Ace had gotten to the point where he assumed she'd go with him and relieve him from the difficult position of having to choose between her and work.

She was feeling taken for granted.

Not unlike when she'd been married.

Of course, someone had to help Ace's uncle. Those poor horses couldn't remain in that trailer. And the Harts had a contract with the rodeo promoter that needed to be fulfilled.

But couldn't Ace at least contact one or two of those men off work and ask if they'd be willing to drive the truck?

"It's okay, just take me home," she said.

He stroked her arm. "I'll make it up to you at dinner tonight."

"Call first. I'm sort of tired."

"Hey, now, a bet's a bet," he added with a mischievous grin.

"Yeah, it is," she answered pointedly.

"Flynn, I don't—"

"It's all right. Really."

Ace started the truck, his jaw muscles clenched tightly. He thought she was being churlish, she could tell.

She considered changing her mind. He couldn't help that the alternator on his uncle's truck went bad.

If only he'd tried a little bit harder to keep his promise, she might feel differently, might have gone with him.

She still could.

"This isn't by choice, you know."

"Enough with the apologizing," she bit out more sharply than necessary, and immediately regretted her outburst. "Work comes first."

And it would be the same after the baby was born.

Flynn watched the passing landscape. Maybe she shouldn't be so hard on Ace. In truth, if it had been a veterinary emergency interrupting their date, she probably would have gone with him and not minded at all.

What did that say about her?

"Let's skip grilling hamburgers tomorrow and drive into Billings for dinner. Dress up and go some place fancy."

He was trying to make amends. She should let him.

Except part of her wondered if this was how it would always be. Him having an emergency, her feeling hurt and disappointed. Him apologizing and scrambling to appease her.

The pattern was a familiar one, too similar to what she went through with Paul.

What if, like her ex-husband had done, Ace stopped trying after a while?

Not going to happen, not if Flynn could help it. They had a child to consider, a child she was determined would be first on both of their priority lists. To insure that, she'd have to put forth as much effort as Ace.

"Sure, we can go out to dinner tomorrow. That'll be nice."

He smiled, visibly relaxed. "Good."

"On one condition."

"Not another hundred phone calls."

"You don't cancel. For any reason. If something comes up, I don't care what it is, you'll either have to be creative, more determined than you were today or have a contingency plan in place."

"You're serious."

She shrugged. "If you're not up to the challenge…"

"I'm up to it," he scoffed. "Rest assured."

When Flynn walked in the kitchen door a short time later, her father was talking on the phone. He sent her a what-are-you-doing-home look.

"Long story," she mouthed, and headed to her bedroom where she changed out of her too-tight hiking shorts and into the roomiest pajama pants she could find. Pretty quick, she'd have to go shopping for maternity clothes. The prospect raised her spirits.

A knock sounded on her door. "You decent?"

"Come on in, Dad."

He wore an enormous grin.

"Did that couple finally make an offer?" She grabbed a ball cap off the bookcase and plunked it on her head, pulling her hair through the hole in the back.

"No, the real estate agent called yesterday, said they weren't interested unless I dropped the price some more. A lot more."

"Then why are you smiling?"

"That was the asset manager from the Missoula Cattle Company."

Her interest piqued. "The same company leasing the Harts' land?"

"Yep. They want to lease my land, too."

"All six hundred acres?"

"Except for the house. They said I can keep it and the barns and a few acres. They'll even pay for new fences."

She stared at him, his words yet to fully register. "We're not moving?"

"I am. You can stay here if you change your mind about school. Or, come with me. In that case, I'll probably rent the house out. With the money the Missoula Cattle Company is willing to pay for leasing rights, I don't have to worry about selling."

"How long is the lease for?"

"Three years, with an option for three more." He practically danced with excitement. "It's an incredible deal."

"When do they want to take over?"

"Soon as I meet with them and sign the contract. This coming week. Though I was thinking I should probably have an attorney review the contract first. Just to be on the safe side."

"Good idea." Flynn sat on the bed, her legs suddenly unable to support her.

The day had arrived. They were leaving Roundup!

Or, she could stay here in the house. Close to Ace.

Choices. Options. She was once again faced with them and not a lot of time to decide.

"I'm going to call your sister."

"Sure," Flynn muttered at her father's retreating back.

After several moments of staring into space, she popped off the bed, went to her desk and fired up her laptop computer, logging on to the internet.

She decided to take the same advice she'd given Ace and promptly set about developing her own contingency plan, starting with a job search.

"Yeah, I see you." Ace squinted through the windshield at a tiny white truck and trailer about a half mile up the road. "Be there in a second."

He hung up with Colt, wondering how long this ordeal would last and wishing like heck Flynn had come with him. Why had she said no?

During the first half hour of his lonely drive, he decided she was angry that yet another of their dates was interrupted. During the second half of the drive, he considered the situation from her point of view.

Had he really tried as hard as he could to get someone else to rescue the stranded truck?

The more he thought about it, the more he realized the answer was no. Had Flynn not been with him, he would have gotten on the road immediately. Attempting to find someone else, making calls, had been strictly for her benefit.

What he'd wanted was for her to go with him like before.

That she hadn't readily agreed confused him. Frustrated him. Irritated him.

Like before.

His own words hit home.

Why should she be the one to always compromise?

Regardless of what happened, he couldn't let anything go wrong at dinner tomorrow night. Flynn was right about another thing. He needed a contingency plan. Someone he could count on in a pinch.

As he pulled up behind the stranded truck and trailer, Colt stepped into view and greeted him with a wave.

No reason his brother shouldn't help him.

Unhooking a trailer filled with horses wasn't an easy feat. The livestock had to be unloaded in order to lighten the trailer. Vehicles slowed as they passed the orange safety cones Uncle Joshua set out, their occupants gawking at the sight of ten horses tied to the outside of a trailer.

Ace was grateful the rig hauling the bulls hadn't been the one to break down. Then they might have surely caused an accident.

Once the trailer was unhooked, they were faced with the task of rolling the nonrunning truck ahead and out of the way. Between the two of them, Ace and Colt were able to push the truck while Uncle Joshua steered. They all three were sweating profusely by the time they'd hooked the trailer up to Ace's truck and finished reloading the last horse.

Colt slipped in behind the wheel, Uncle Joshua in the passenger seat. All things considered, it could have gone much worse.

Ace called the service station and received an update on their estimated arrival.

Colt rolled down his window. "How long?"

"Two to three hours," Ace grumbled.

That was the problem with living in a small town and no sizable metropolis nearby. Few resources. Fortunately, he'd brought a few files along and could tackle some work while he waited.

He stepped up to the driver's side window. "Before you leave, I have a favor to ask."

"What's up?" Colt accepted the cold soda Uncle Joshua procured from their travel ice chest. "We really need to get on the road if we're going to make it before the rodeo starts."

"I'm taking Flynn into Billings for a special dinner tomorrow night. Someplace nice."

Colt flashed Ace his trademark jaunty grin. "If you're looking for the name of a good restaurant—"

"I can manage the date. What I need is for you to stick nearby and cover for me in case something comes up."

"Can't. Already made plans. I'll be out of town."

"You're leaving on a Sunday afternoon?"

"Something came up. I'll be back Tuesday."

"Two days? Why didn't you tell me?"

"I didn't know for sure I was going until an hour ago. I was waiting on a phone call. Can't you change your date with Flynn?"

"I already promised her." And Ace refused to ask Flynn to move their dinner to Tuesday. Not for an excuse as flimsy as Colt received some phone call and was disappearing for two days.

"Where are you going?"

"I have business."

"What kind of business?"

"Personal," he said, his voice low and terse.

Colt had been acting stranger and stranger in recent weeks, and Ace was getting tired of it.

"This leaving all the time has to stop."

"You're not my keeper."

"And you're not just an employee. You're a member of the family. We all depend on the livestock contracting business to support us. You can't continue taking off whenever the mood strikes."

"You're taking off tomorrow night."

"Sunday. Not Monday. You have an obligation, a responsibility."

Colt's features shut down. "Don't lecture me."

"Someone needs to."

"I'm not staying home just to babysit while you go on a date."

Ace's anger erupted. "Why the hell not? I stay home every time you take off for some rodeo."

"This is important."

"So's my dinner with Flynn. We're having a baby."

An odd emotion flickered across Colt's face, and he shoved the transmission into drive. "Uncle Joshua can help you."

Up until then, their uncle had remained out of the conversation. "Whatever you need, Ace."

Colt eased the truck and trailer slowly forward, effectively putting an end to the conversation.

"We're talking when you get home," Ace hollered after them, doubting Colt heard.

Where was a punching bag when you needed one?

Between Flynn, the truck breaking down and his disagreement with his brother, Ace was feeling perfectly dandy.

Three hours sitting on the side of the road in a truck with no air-conditioning and nothing but a few work files and his own thoughts for company didn't improve matters. Neither did the mechanic, who took almost an hour to complete a simple repair. Ace practically had steam pouring out of his ears when the man finally finished.

Nothing sounded better than the truck's engine roaring to life.

"This here replacement battery will get you home but not much further," the mechanic advised. "You're going to need to bring the truck in for a new alternator."

"Appreciate the help." Ace presented his credit card for the total of the bill.

"Sorry it took so long. We're short one man today."

Ace knew the feeling.

His tension ebbed only slightly as he drove home, his truck eating up the miles. He checked the dash clock. Barring any unforeseen complications, he'd reach Thunder Ranch by four. He could throw on some fresh clothes, see to a few chores and be at Flynn's by six.

Not too late for supper and a stroll around the center of town.

She'd told him to call first.

He grabbed his phone off the seat, only to have it ring in his hand. A number he didn't recognize appeared on the display.

Ace didn't answer. If the call was important, the person would leave a message. They didn't.

Good. Turns out practicing restraint wasn't that tough.

He changed his mind about calling Flynn, not taking a chance she'd say no, and decided instead to simply show up. Even if he only got to stay a few minutes, he'd let her know she was the one person he wanted to see most at the end of a long and arduous day.

Anticipation had him putting pedal to the metal.

His mother knocked on his bedroom door as he was changing. "There's some leftover pot roast I can heat up if you're hungry."

He opened the door, tucking in his shirt. "Maybe later. I'm heading over to Flynn's. I won't be late."

"All right."

"You feeling okay, Mom? You look beat." It seemed he was asking her that same question a lot lately.

"I spent most of the day on the monthly financials.

Not my strong suit, and it wore me out." She rubbed her chest beneath her collarbone.

"Mine, either, or I'd help you."

"You do enough already."

"So do you. How are the financials looking, by the way?"

She shrugged. "We're getting by."

"It'd be better if we had those stud fees coming in."

"Have you tried another hand breeding?"

"Later this week. I'm waiting for a mare to come into heat."

"I'm sure it'll go well. Midnight's making great progress." She stood on tiptoes and kissed Ace's cheek. "Tell Flynn hello for me and invite her over. I'd love to see her."

"There was a young couple looking at her dad's place the other day. They seemed pretty interested."

"Then you'd better hurry and win her over."

He thought of dinner tomorrow. "I'm working on it. Trust me."

Ace parked behind Flynn's house and jogged to the kitchen door, knocking briskly. She must have been standing right there, for a second later she tugged the tiny curtain aside and peeked out at him.

The door promptly swung wide. "Hey."

"I know I should have called first."

"Come on in." She stepped back. "I'm assuming the vehicle swapping went okay."

"More or less. I have to drop the truck off at the shop on Monday for a new alternator."

He gave her a hug, noticing she wore an oversize T-shirt and leggings. Definitely lounge wear and not strolling-around-the-center-of-town wear. The faint sounds of canned laughter floated in from the family room.

"You watching TV?"

"Actually, I've been in my room on the computer. Just came out to the kitchen to start dinner when I heard you knock." As if suddenly reminded, she went to a simmering pot on the stove and stirred the contents.

"I wasn't planning on staying." Ace's hope for an evening together were dashed when she said nothing about joining her and her father. "Just came by to say hi and make sure you were all right." Make sure *they* were all right. "And to apologize for earlier."

"Again?" She crossed her arms over her waist, which emphasized the small mound of her belly. "This is becoming a habit."

She wasn't entirely kidding, he could tell.

Did he apologize to her that much?

Did he screw up that much?

"You were right, I should have tried to reach a few more people today before giving up. I have this tendency to think I'm the only one who can resolve a problem."

"You don't say?"

Her sparkling smile encouraged him. He covered the distance separating them in two strides.

"I missed you."

Without giving her a chance to respond, he took her in his arms, covered her mouth with his and proceeded to show her just how big a fool he'd been.

She returned his kiss with a burst of passion that surprised him as much as it excited him. If not for her father in the family room, Ace would have swept her into his arms and stolen her away to her bedroom.

Instead, he released her. Reluctantly. Waited for his pounding heart to slow. "Maybe I should stay."

She smiled coyly, letting Ace know how much she liked unbalancing him.

He stumbled to the kitchen table and dropped into a chair. A half-dozen papers were fanned out in front of him. The headings jumped off the pages, striking him like tiny darts.

Employment Application.

He picked up the closest one. It was for a hospital in Billings. His heart resumed pounding, but for a different reason. "What's this?"

Flynn glanced over from the stove, let out a small sigh. "I was going to tell you tomorrow at dinner."

"You're applying for jobs? In Billings?"

"Dad got an offer from the same cattle company leasing your land. If he takes it, and he thinks he will, we're going to be moving in a couple weeks."

Not thirty to sixty days.

The paper in Ace's hand dropped to the table. "You can't."

"Can't move?"

"I thought…you and I—"

"Nothing's changed."

"It has." They'd made love at Thunder Creek.

"Yes, all right. We're getting along. Which is what we wanted. We'll still get along when I live in Billings."

"I want to marry you."

"Do you love me?"

The question stunned him. "Of course," he stuttered.

Pain flared in her eyes.

He tried again, more convincingly. "I love you, Flynn. I do."

She nodded, compressed her lips together. "Didn't mean to drag it out of you."

"Dammit, I'm trying."

"You are. But loving someone, well, it shouldn't be something you have to struggle at. I know. I've been in love with you for a long time."

She had? She *had!*

"Then marry me and stay here."

"You're asking me to give up a lot."

"For us. For the baby."

"What are you going to give up? What sacrifice are you going to make?"

"Once the breeding business takes off, it'll be different. I'll have more time."

"In two or three years. You said so yourself."

He didn't respond, his previous joy deflating.

"As you can see, I have employment applications to complete," she said dismissively. "I'm sure you're tired after all the driving you did today."

Once again, Ace had handled the situation badly.

He got up. One look at her stoic features told him this was a discussion better left for another day.

"I'll see you tomorrow. For dinner."

"We don't have to go."

Yes, they did.

"I promised you. Uncle Joshua will be back from the rodeo and will cover for me. We won't have any interruptions."

"Fine."

She didn't need to tell him this was his last shot. Her tone said it all.

CHAPTER FIFTEEN

A UNIFORMED YOUNG man stepped out from behind a podium as Ace pulled up alongside the curb.

"Valet parking?" Flynn asked, mildly amused.

"We have a car tonight, I figured, why not."

They did indeed have a car. A Mustang. Convertible. It belonged to Harlan, one of the Harts' ranch hands. Ace had borrowed it. She didn't think she'd ever seen him drive anything but a truck or a tractor or that Polaris of his.

He looked good behind the wheel—and in the charcoal-gray suit he'd worn. No cowboy hat and no boots, either. Another first.

She'd give credit where it was due. Ace had gone all out tonight to make the evening special for her. Car, clothes, swanky restaurant.

The one and only downside to the evening was her slinky maroon cocktail dress. It pinched uncomfortably in the middle.

Ace didn't appear to notice. He'd whistled appreciatively when he first saw her, his eyes eating her up like that key lime pie he favored.

She caught their reflection in the restaurant's glass entry doors and thought they made a striking couple, her poofy tummy aside.

Ace gave the hostess his name and after a short wait,

during which they exchanged small talk with a couple celebrating a recent promotion, they were escorted to a booth by a window overlooking a lighted garden.

In the center of the table was a vase with a trio of red roses, around which had been tied a large silver bow. At first, Flynn assumed the arrangement was part of the restaurant's decor. Then she noticed the small envelope with her name on it.

"Are these from you?" she asked, already removing the card.

Ace didn't answer

"Three down, ninety-seven more to go," she read out loud, and smiled at the reference to the hundred-phone-call bet they'd made, flattered and touched. "Thank you."

"You're welcome."

"People are looking at us." She lifted the vase and brought the roses to her nose, inhaling their heady scent.

"They're looking at you, trying to figure out how a lug like me scored a date with such a beautiful lady."

She set the roses down. If anything, people were looking at Ace, an appealing combination of rugged handsomeness and polished sophistication. She wouldn't mind seeing him in a suit more often.

He might have better luck getting her to stay in Roundup and accept his proposal.

As yet, they hadn't discussed her seeking a job, nursing school, the lease for her father's land or her admission that she'd been in love with him for years. They would, eventually.

For the moment, Flynn enjoyed the roses and their easy conversation and the lovely view of the garden.

A waiter appeared. She and Ace placed their drink

orders, a virgin margarita for her, and asked for more time to peruse the menu.

"Did you wind up watching the NASCAR races this afternoon?" she asked.

"For about an hour."

"Good." At least he'd gotten a little break from work. "What about you?"

Flynn set her menu aside. Their reprieve from difficult conversation was apparently at an end. "I filled out employment applications, paper and online."

"How did that go?"

She could tell he strove to keep his voice neutral. "There really aren't a whole lot of opportunities out there. Not ones any better than what I have now, either paywise or interestingwise. I'd still rather go to school."

"Then do it."

"I have to work. Part-time, at least. Have to support myself while I take classes." And the baby. She didn't expect Ace to pay for everything.

She gave him credit for not mentioning she could come live with him and he'd support her.

"Interviewing for a job won't be easy," she continued. "I know employers aren't supposed to discriminate, but the second they realize I'm pregnant, they'll probably choose another applicant."

Ace turned a page on his menu.

"No comment?" Flynn wondered if he was secretly glad of the obstacle she faced.

He gazed out the window. "It's staying light out a lot later these days."

Smart man.

The waiter returned with their drinks and took their orders.

"Are you still planning on being a nurse or just working?"

"I'm not sure."

The decision that was so simple six weeks ago had become complicated. Ace, the baby, Flynn's father retiring and leasing the ranch, all meddled with her thinking.

"You'd rather remain in the business admin side of the medical field?" Ace asked.

"Oh, no. I still want to do something more meaningful, more hands-on. Like you."

"Vaccinating calves and examining pregnant mares isn't what I'd call meaningful."

"Removing a malignant tumor from a child's beloved pony and giving him a few more years with his owner is. Curing my favorite horse of colic is. So is saving a family's pet dog."

"Lovey's life wasn't in danger."

"The Andersons didn't know that until you arrived." She sipped her drink. "That's the kind of rewarding work I want to do."

"Then go to veterinarian school."

She laughed. "I couldn't."

"Why not? You're smart. You love animals."

"I'm not cut out for surgery, no pun intended. I like assisting you. That part's fun. And interesting. And challenging."

"Then study to be a vet tech."

She started to protest, only to stop when chills ran up her arms. That wasn't such a bad idea. In fact, the more she thought about it, the more it appealed to her. She did love animals. She did like helping Ace. And working with people.

A vet tech. That was a degree she could probably obtain at community college. Far less difficult than getting into nursing school.

She could return to Billings Community College.

Roundup had a small community college, too, with online classes. She'd checked once.

Their dinner rolls arrived. Flynn was about to question Ace about the requirements for becoming a vet tech when his cell phone rang.

She tensed. Oh, no! Not again.

He removed the phone from his jacket pocket and glanced at the caller ID. "It's Uncle Joshua." He hit the Disconnect button.

"You're not answering it?" She was amazed.

"He's filling in for me tonight." Ace set the phone on vibrate and laid it beside his plate. "Whatever problem he has, he can resolve it without me."

Wow. This was a pleasant change of pace.

"How long does it usually take to become a vet tech?"

"Depends on the school." Ace had barely started to explain when his phone went off again. He studied the display a moment longer than before, then disconnected.

"Uncle Joshua again?"

"Yes." This time, Ace slipped the phone in his shirt pocket, his facial muscles taut.

"If you want to call him, go ahead."

"I promised, no interruptions tonight." He grabbed a dinner roll and buttered it, his movements stilted.

His phone vibrated again, humming like an angry hornet.

"I'm going to turn this off." He whipped the phone out of his pocket, only to pause. "It's Dinah."

The few bites Flynn had taken of her roll turned to lead in her stomach. Something was wrong. "You'd better get it."

Ace clearly felt the same way, for he answered his phone with a brusque, "Hey, sis." As he listened, his face drained of color. "I'll be right there."

"What's the matter?" Flynn asked when he started to rise.

"It's Mom. She's been taken to the hospital. They think she's had a heart attack."

FLYNN WALKED THE empty barn. All her father's horses were gone. The bulls, too. A rodeo stock contractor from Idaho had purchased the remaining few head, picking them up this morning.

This morning had also been when her father had received a lease agreement from the Missoula Cattle Company via email and made an appointment with a local attorney to review it.

The wheels were in motion. In a few weeks, her father would be moving to Billings. He couldn't wait. She, on the other hand, was still undecided about what to do.

One minute, remaining in Roundup with Ace, attending Roundup Community College, felt right. The next minute, she was convinced staying would simply delay the inevitable.

Why hadn't he called?

She'd taken a cab home from the hospital about two o'clock last night. By then, Sarah was in stable condition and resting comfortably, her family by her bedside—Ace, Dinah, Joshua, Beau, Duke and Colt, who'd arrived at the hospital about one o'clock. Tuf had yet to be located, though the family continued trying.

She hoped for Sarah's sake they reached him soon. Constantly worrying about his whereabouts had no doubt contributed to her heart attack.

Maybe Flynn shouldn't have left the hospital. Ace had insisted she go home, telling her there was no point in hanging around. His mother was, according to the doctor, out of danger and ready to be moved to a regular room. One of them should get some sleep.

Flynn left only after Ace agreed to call her bright and early. She'd slept very little, rising soon after dawn, her eyes gritty, her worry for all the Harts a throbbing ache in her chest.

A glance at her phone confirmed that she hadn't missed a call from Ace in the fifteen minutes since she last checked her phone.

Where was he?

Maybe Sarah was better, and he'd gone home to get some sleep.

What if she was worse?

I won't leave Roundup, Flynn thought. Ace might need her. At least until Sarah was well. The cattle company didn't want the house. Flynn could research vet tech degrees, finish packing, decide her future course once and for all.

Give Ace more time to convince her to marry him.

More time to fall in love with her. *Really* fall in love, not just say the words because she'd put him on the spot.

What about the hundred phone calls? The roses? The afternoon at Thunder Creek making love?

If those weren't an indication he had strong feelings for her, what was?

Three little words. Until he spoke them straight from the heart, Flynn wouldn't be entirely sure if what he felt for her was enough to last a lifetime. Enough to guarantee he wouldn't abandon her like her ex-husband and mother had done.

Like Ace had done ten years ago.

The echo of footsteps had her whirling toward the barn entrance, her pulse thrumming.

"Ace!"

He stood in the shadows, an inky silhouette against a dim backdrop. Still, she instantly recognized him.

She ran toward him, threw her arms around his neck. "How's your mom?"

"Better. They're going to keep her a day or two for observation. Run some more tests."

He squeezed her tight as if this was what he'd been waiting for all day, all night. Flynn forgot her worry, forgot how tired she was and hugged him back.

"That's not too bad for a heart attack," she said into his rumpled dress shirt.

"She didn't have one. Not technically." They drew apart and walked hand in hand out of the barn into the sunlight. "She has angina."

"I...don't know what that is."

"It's a sign of trouble. Sort of like a pre-heart attack. Definitely her body giving her a warning. She may require a stent. We'll know more later today."

"How's she handling the news?"

"All right. The cardiac surgeon is very optimistic that with the right treatment and adequate rest she'll be fine."

"Will she be on medication?"

"Yeah. The doctor said it might take a few weeks to find the right combination. He warned her, warned *all* of us, that unless she makes some serious lifestyle changes, she could have another episode."

"Changes like diet?"

"Lots of food restrictions, apparently. Mom will not

be happy. Exercise, too. The right kind. And here's the hardest part. Reduce her stress levels."

"Oh, Ace." Flynn hugged him again. "She's going to be all right. That's the important part."

"She has to be careful the rest of her life or else the angina can develop into a serious heart condition."

"Your mother's very conscientious. Plus, she has her family to watch out for her."

Ace let go of Flynn's hand, his features clouding.

She knew instantly something else was wrong. "What is it?"

"The doctor was adamant. Mom has to drastically minimize her stress."

"Maybe if you can find Tuf, get him to come home, she won't worry as much."

"That's definitely the first item on my list, but not the only one."

It was coming. Another breakup. He had the same distant look in his eyes, the same tightness in his voice, the same stiff posture from ten years ago.

No! her mind screamed, so loud it surprised her when her voice came out calm and even. "You have to take over for her."

"I don't have a choice. I'm the only one who can do it."

Just like when his father died. Ace, the ever loyal son. Except when it came to Flynn.

"But you're not the only one," she said.

"Who else is there? Tuf is gone. Dinah has her job as sheriff, which is pretty much 24/7. Colt is undependable. At least he has been up till now."

"Talk to him. He may step up if you ask him."

"He didn't when Dad died."

"What about your practice?"

"I'll have to refer some of my customers to another vet."

"But you've worked so hard."

"My family's entire future is at stake. If we don't make a success of the contracting and breeding business, don't pay down the loan, I won't have a practice to worry about."

"What about us?" Flynn asked in that same calm, steady voice.

"Please be patient with me. I'll be there as much as I can for you and the baby, but I probably won't have time to go out like we've been doing. Not for a while."

"I don't care about going out. That was never important to me. I like being with you. Working with you. Hanging out with you."

"Let me see how it goes." He rubbed his temples and exhaled wearily. "We have to determine the extent of Mom's care before I make any decisions. And her workload. Where we stand with our current stock contracts, the financials, the alfalfa crop."

It seemed to Flynn the choice of whether to stay or go had been made for her.

She glanced away to hide her hurt and disappointment. "Call me if you need anything. I'll be packing over the next few days."

"You're moving?" He looked stunned, as if they hadn't had this same conversation a dozen times already.

"Don't you think it's for the best?" She cleared her throat. It didn't dislodge the burning lump stuck there. "I don't want to add to your problems."

"You're not a problem."

"We can talk when you're not so tired."

"I don't want you to move."

"You just said you didn't think you'd have time for me. Which I completely understand."

"Give me a couple weeks."

"What difference would it make? Your responsibilities don't come with an expiration date."

"I have a responsibility to you and the baby, too."

"The difference is we can get along without you. The same isn't true for your mother."

"I'm going to be an involved father."

"When are you going to fit me and the baby in your schedule? A week from Tuesday?"

"I can't support a baby, can't do right by him or her, if the business fails."

"He or she will need more from you than a weekly child support check." Flynn needed more, too.

"Why does it have to be all or nothing with you? Why do I have to choose between my work and my family and you?"

"Because love and marriage and raising a child is a full-time commitment. I won't settle for less."

"I'm not Paul."

"No, you're not. He didn't have a family depending on him like you. On the other hand, he didn't have a baby on the way, either."

"That's not fair."

"Our child deserves the best from *both* his parents. Problem is you're only capable of giving a limited amount."

"For now," he insisted.

"Fine. You can give what you're able to just as easily in Billings as here. Easier, in fact. Sleep on it. You'll see the rationale when you're not so exhausted."

She started to walk away.

He didn't follow. "You're being selfish."

"Me!" That stopped her in her tracks.

"You can't expect a man not to have other responsibilities besides you."

"I have other responsibilities, too. Yet, I don't let them consume me to the exclusion of everything else. The entire fate of the Harts doesn't rest entirely on your shoulders, Ace. It never has, not even when your dad died. You've just convinced yourself it does."

"Who would run things if I didn't?"

"You've never given anyone else a chance." Her voice rose. "I don't know why I missed seeing it before, but you know what? You use your work and your family as an excuse not to fall in love. Not to commit."

"That's ridiculous."

"Is it? Just think. Whenever you're in danger of getting close to me, I'm not talking about marriage but emotionally close, you suddenly have more responsibilities. Another iron in the fire. Sorry, Flynn, can't be with you because I'm too busy."

She was allowing her anger to get the best of her. Reining it in, however, wasn't possible.

"There can't be any future for us," she said. "Not until you stop being afraid."

"Maybe your expectations are unrealistic."

Finally! Something he said made sense.

"Maybe they are. Or maybe yours are. We'll probably never find out. I'll call you before my doctor's appointment next week. In case you want to go with me."

This time when she walked away, he didn't call her back.

CHAPTER SIXTEEN

ACE ABSENTLY PATTED Midnight's neck, then caught himself as Fancy Gal nudged his arm, demanding her share of attention.

The stallion was standing next to him, allowing Ace to touch him! And without Ace having to coax him with a carrot.

Another day, a different time, Ace would have broken into an ear-to-ear grin and congratulated himself on his success. All his efforts, his endless hours, had finally paid off.

Except he wasn't much in the mood for grinning and hadn't been since Flynn left him to stew alone in her father's barn.

They'd spoken in the eight days following their argument. On the phone, not in person. About her next doctor's appointment. About how she was feeling. About his mother's prognosis and adjustment now that she was home from the hospital. About Flynn's decision to obtain her vet tech degree and how that was proceeding—much more swiftly than nursing school.

What they didn't talk about was their situation. If Ace tried to bring up anything remotely personal, she promptly ended their conversation. As a result, he'd stuck strictly to safe topics and kept his frustrations to himself.

He wasn't a content man. He was, in fact, miserable and fairly certain he'd made the worst mistake anyone could by not going after her.

All he'd wanted was to marry Flynn and provide for her and their child. Instead, he'd hurt her. Alienated her. Convinced her to doubt his feelings for her rather than to rely on them.

Ace shut the lid on his medical case, untied Fancy Gal's lead rope and removed her halter. He'd spent the last two hours making the rounds of the ranch, examining the first two rotations of mares that had been pastured with Midnight. Seven of them, including Fancy Gal, were pregnant.

Yet more reason to celebrate. Not exactly the auspicious start to their breeding business Ace and his mother had originally planned for, but, assuming more mares were bred, they'd be guaranteed a sizable crop of foals next spring.

Ace would feel better if their mare motel was filled to capacity with customers' horses and Midnight relied on to hand breed with them.

No, not even that would make him feel better.

Why hadn't he told Flynn he loved her when he had the chance? In such a way she would have believed him.

Ace gave Midnight and Fancy Gal a final pat on their rumps, rewarding them for standing quietly during his examination of Fancy Gal.

"Congratulations you two, you're going to be parents. Well, buddy, in your case, a parent many times over." Midnight nosed Ace's empty shirt pocket. "Consider yourself lucky your girl here's not the jealous type."

When the stallion's search failed to produce a treat, he snorted angrily.

"Sorry, fresh out of carrots." Ace scratched the horse's nose, wishing he could marvel at this advancement. "Eventually I'm going to have to separate you two. When she's closer to foaling."

Midnight abruptly meandered off.

"Hey," Ace called after him. "Don't be mad. I understand how you feel. I'm in the same boat. My girl's having a baby, and I can't be with her."

Whose fault was that?

"Talking to horses now?"

Ace pivoted at the sound of his brother's voice. That explained Midnight's sudden departure. The horse still didn't like anyone except Gracie and, apparently, Ace.

"What are you doing here?" A thought galvanized him. "Is Mom okay?"

"She's fine," Colt said agreeably. "Supervising the woman you hired to help with the laundry and housework. Complaining up a storm that you're a dictator who won't even allow her on the computer."

"Let her complain." Ace grabbed his medical case and met up with Colt on the other side of the gate. "I'll take that as a sign she's feeling better."

They headed toward Ace's truck, which he'd parked nearby. Now that he was finished checking the mares, he had several appointments, appointments he should have gotten to yesterday but had run out of daylight.

"She's worried about you," Colt said.

"Don't know why. I'm not the one who nearly had a heart attack."

"You might be, at the rate you're going."

Rather than answer, Ace loaded his medical case in the side compartment on his truck.

"Come on, you're a wreck. Have you looked in the mirror lately?"

Ace had. That morning. A stranger stared back at him—one with a four-day growth of beard, dark circles beneath his eyes and a rather unflattering grayish complexion.

"I don't have time for this," he grumbled.

Before he could jump into his truck, Colt grabbed his arm. "Hey, wait a minute."

"I'm running late."

"Talk to me."

"Aren't you leaving for Utah today?"

"I canceled."

"What about qualifying for the NFR? I thought you were behind in steer wrestling and bull riding."

"It won't hurt me to take some time off."

Ace wished his brother had said that weeks ago. Years ago.

"I thought maybe we could go out for a beer tonight."

"A beer?" Ace couldn't remember going out for a beer with his brother for…ages.

They weren't close. Not like they should be. Not like when they were younger.

All of them, including their mother, were casualties of John Hart's life and his death. The man had left a legacy, just not the one he'd intended.

"I'm not good company," Ace said, sliding in behind the steering wheel.

"I know you've been down since Flynn dumped you."

The bluntness of Colt's remark stung.

"And you wonder why I don't want to go out with you."

"I can help you."

"With what?"

"Whatever you need. You're working too hard."

"Mom put you up to this?"

"She and I might have talked."

"That's what I figured."

"She's right. You need a break before you kill yourself."

"I like working. It keeps me out of trouble."

"Keeps you from hurting, too. It was the same when Dad died. The busier you are, the less you have to think. Feel."

"I don't need you to psychoanalyze me, too."

"Too? Who else has been doing it?"

"No one." Flynn's comments from the other day were still eating at Ace, and he'd be damned if he was going to discuss them. Especially with Colt.

"Was it by chance—"

"You'll shut up if you know what's good for you."

"Why won't you let me help you?" his brother demanded.

"The truth? I've counted on you before, and you've let me down. Let the family down. It's just simpler if I, if I—" Ace stopped in midsentence, momentarily struck dumb.

"What? Simpler if you do it yourself? Is that what you were going to say?"

It had been.

Up until this second, Ace hadn't noticed the similarities between his relationship with Flynn and his relationship with his brother. Now, it stared him in the face. His beard-stubbled, gray face.

He'd disappointed Flynn, and she didn't trust him. Just like he didn't trust Colt.

Ace sure didn't like what he was learning about himself lately.

Maybe if he gave his brother another chance, Flynn would do the same for him. Did karma work like that?

It was worth a try, he supposed. And he did need help. Even if Colt relieved him of only one or two tasks, it would lighten his load. Enable Ace to hit the sack earlier—so he'd have even more time to stare at the ceiling instead of sleeping.

He grabbed a pad of paper and pen off the seat beside him. Scratching out several notes, he ripped the sheet of paper from the pad and handed it to Colt.

"Take care of these for me."

Colt scanned the list, his brow crinkling. "Research prices on breeding mounts? Wait. Is this what I think it is?"

"The season will be over soon. We have to do something with Midnight the rest of the year. I'm thinking artificial insemination. In order to do that, we're going to have to train him to use a mount and to collect the—"

"I get it. You don't have to draw me a picture."

"Mom was going to call the grain distributers this week and get prices. You can do it for her."

Colt gave Ace a smart salute. "See you when you get home, boss."

Ace started to tell his brother not to flake. Instead, he clamped his mouth shut, hearing their father's voice inside his head saying those exact words. *Shouting* those exact words. At him.

He wouldn't treat Colt the same way he'd been treated.

Whatever it took, he'd be a better parent to his son or daughter than John Hart ever was. He wouldn't put his family in financial jeopardy and expect them to fend for themselves. He wouldn't drink in solitude rather than spend time with his wife and baby. He'd be there always. Responsible. Dependable. Loyal.

Weren't those the same qualities that had driven Flynn away?

ACE LEFT THE RANCH and headed for his first appointment at the local riding stables. Angie's animal rescue shelter was his last scheduled stop for the day. He didn't leave there until well after 6:00 p.m. On the way home, an idea occurred to him and quickly took shape.

Ignoring his debilitating exhaustion, he went straight to the family room upon returning home, looking for his mother. She was resting on the couch, the TV blaring, a bored expression on her face. It beat the heck out of the pale, taut expression she'd worn the days following her angina episode, made worse by their inability to locate Tuf.

When his youngest brother finally did come home, he'd have a lot of explaining to do—after which, Ace was going to kick Tuf's ass all the way to the center of town.

"What have you been up to while I was gone?" he asked, striding into the room.

"Aidan! You're home." His mother pushed to a sitting position, picked up the remote control and silenced the TV. "I've been up to nothing at all, thanks to you, Mr. Warden." Her smile turned to a mock frown. "You're going to have to grant me parole soon."

"That's just what I had in mind."

She brightened. "At last!"

"I was at the animal shelter this afternoon. They're really understaffed. I was thinking you could volunteer there a couple mornings a week or something."

"Volunteer?"

"Sure." He sat on the couch next to her. "It would get you out of the house. Give you a chance to be physically active without overextending yourself. And I think working with the puppies and kittens will be good for you. Mentally and emotionally."

"I can't possibly. Once I get back to work—"

"When you get back, it'll be on a part-time basis."

"Only temporarily."

"We'll see."

"Aidan." She said his name in that way mothers tended to do.

"Come on. Angie can use the help."

"It's not right. You're doing the job of two people." She pointed at the TV. "And I'm watching game shows."

"Colt is helping me."

"He is?"

"I'm waiting to see how that goes."

"I bet he'll surprise you."

"I hope he does."

His mother pursed her mouth thoughtfully. "What if I get attached to the animals?"

"Adopt one."

"I haven't wanted another dog since old Buster passed away last year."

"People who own pets live longer. It's a proven fact."

"So do people who are happy."

He intentionally took her remark the wrong way. "All the more reason to get a dog."

"Okay, okay. You've convinced me. When do I start?"

"As soon as the doctor clears you."

"How are you doing?" She studied him critically. "You look terrible. Are you sleeping? Eating enough?"

"Yes and yes." Just not much, which he was sure his mother had already figured out. "I'm going to hit the shower, then the office. Pay some bills. Place some orders online."

"What about dinner?"

He rubbed the back of his neck where the muscles ached. "I'll grab a sandwich after I clean up. Take it with me to the office."

"It's not my place to tell you how to run your life, but I'm going to anyway."

"Mom, not now."

"You have to make some changes."

"I am. I gave Colt a list."

"That's fine. It's also not enough. You have to delegate," she continued. "You can't go on, carrying the entire burden of this family. Doing my job and yours. You have a life of your own, a baby on the way."

"Everyone else has their own life, too."

"They can do more. I've asked them already," she said proudly, "since I'm sure you won't."

"Right, Colt."

"And Joshua and Dinah. Beau and Duke, too."

"Mom—"

"They want to help. That's what family does for each other."

"I can handle things."

"Stop, Aidan. This isn't a criticism. Far from it. You do an amazing job. I couldn't possibly have run this ranch all these years without you. But Flynn needs you. Your child needs you. More than we do."

"What about your angina?"

"I'm going to be fine. All I need is a little rest." She squeezed his hand, brought it to her cheek. "We're going to get through this, like we always have. Together."

The doorbell rang, and Ace rose.

"It's all right." She pulled on his wrist. "Lisa Marie will answer the door. Probably the UPS man. He's always late."

Lisa Marie? Oh, yeah. The woman he'd hired to help with the housework.

He really was tired.

"Shower and eat," his mother told him. "A real meal, not a sandwich. Then call Flynn."

"She won't talk to me. Not about what's important."

"Then maybe you should go there. Refuse to leave until she listens. This constant working, it isn't good for you. Take it from me. Too much responsibility is what drove your father to drink. To push you kids too hard. Turn his back on the ranch. Turn his back on me."

Was that true?

His father had definitely changed the last few years of his life.

"I don't want you to end up like him," his mother said softly. "Flynn is a wonderful girl, and you're going to have a beautiful baby. My first grandchild." Her eyes misted. "It would devastate me if I couldn't see the baby because you and Flynn weren't on speaking terms."

"I screwed up with her." Ace scrubbed his face, the beard feeling strange scratching his palms. "Really screwed up."

"Then apologize."

"I have."

"Apologize again. However many times as it takes."

"I love her, you know. I think I always have."

"I do know. I could see it."

"I was afraid to tell her how I felt. I always thought there was no way this incredible woman could possibly return my feelings."

"She does. I could see that, too."

He took off his hat, wiped his eyes and nose with his shirt sleeve. "There isn't anything I wouldn't do for her."

"Tell her." His mother's glance cut briefly to the entryway. "It's not too late."

"She's leaving next week."

"But she's here now."

"And refusing to see me."

"No." His mother tilted her head toward the entryway. "I mean, she's here now. Right here."

Ace turned and stared at Flynn, the shock of seeing her sending a jolt tearing through him.

She stood in the entryway, her father beside her. He held a card and a large, leafy floral arrangement.

How much of what Ace had said to his mother had she heard?

Judging by the startled look in her eyes, most of it.

"Well, don't sit there like a bump on a log," his mother whispered. "Here's your chance."

Who was he to disobey his mother?

FLYNN'S HEART SOARED. She pressed a hand to her chest in a feeble attempt to contain it.

Ace loved her! He wasn't just saying what he thought she wanted to hear or what might convince her to marry him. And he'd loved her for a long time.

Why hadn't he told her before? What a difference it would have made in their lives.

"You going to just stand here?" her father asked. "Or are you going to put him out of his misery?"

"I… I…"

Ace approached her. Her heart might be soaring but, for the first time, his was right there on his sleeve for all to see.

"Flynn. You're here."

"To visit your mother."

She'd imagined running into him, imagined what she'd say. But that had been before she overheard him tell his mother he loved her.

They stood facing each other, Flynn acutely aware of their parents' curious stares.

Her father must have grown tired of waiting, for he stepped around her. "Sarah, it's good to see you." He held out the plant and card. "How are you doing?"

"I'm well." She stood and accepted the gift. "Thank you, Earl."

"Doesn't appear as if these two are going to settle their differences on their own. Not without a little help from us."

She smiled. "What were you thinking?"

"Have you had your dinner yet?"

"I was waiting for Aidan."

"What do you say we grab a bite somewhere? My treat. If we take my truck, Flynn can't leave. That ought to force 'em to talk to each other."

"I admire a man with a plan."

"No, don't! There's something I want to say first." Flynn swallowed, gathered her courage, which she'd never needed more. "I've been selfish. I didn't realize until now that this baby isn't mine alone or even mine and Ace's alone." She turned to him, then to his mother. "If I move, I won't just be taking him away from his father, but from his grandmother and uncles and aunt, too."

"He'll also have family in Billings," Sarah said gently. "Your sister and, before long, your father, too."

"That's exactly my point. Dad will have my sister and her sons." Flynn touched Sarah's arm fondly. "If I move, you won't have any grandchildren nearby."

"Oh, Flynn." Sarah's hand fluttered to her throat.

"I don't understand." Ace's rough and gravelly voice didn't sound at all like him. "Are you staying in Roundup?"

"Yes, I am."

She took his hands in hers, marveled again at how they could be both strong and gentle. Grip the rigging on a wildly bucking bronc or tenderly bandage a dog's injured foot. Twist a wrench to loosen a frozen lug nut or explore her body with shiver-inducing caresses.

Soon, his hands would hold their baby.

"If you do stay," Ace said, "it has to be for me. Us. Not for my mother or any guilt you might have."

"I could live with guilt." Flynn sought his gaze and held it steady. "What I can't do is live without you."

"I love you, Flynn."

This time she not only heard the words, she felt them deep inside her, echoing until they matched the rhythm of her heartbeat.

"I love you, too."

Suddenly he was holding her, and they sealed their declarations with a kiss that would have lasted longer if not for Flynn's father clearing his throat. Loudly.

"If you meant what you said earlier about doing anything for me…"

"I did. I'll work less, cut back on my vet practice—"

"The working less part is okay." She touched his cheek with its dark, scratchy stubble. Later she'd tell him how sexy he looked. "But don't cut back on your vet practice. I have a better idea. Let me help you. I'll run the office and assist you on calls. In between, I'll go to school."

He smiled broadly. "Deal."

"You haven't heard my list of demands yet."

His brows rose. "Demands?"

"For starters, you're going to have to do something about that ancient piece of junk you call a computer. And your filing system." She rolled her eyes.

"Is that all? Because I have my own demands."

Did he now?

"What are they?"

"Date night once a week, including after the baby's born. And Sundays are family day. No work unless there's an extreme emergency, and I mean extreme. At least one Sunday every month we visit your family in Billings."

"I think we can manage that." She blinked the tears from her eyes.

Sarah, too.

"There's one more piece of business we have to get out of the way," Ace announced.

"Business?"

He turned to her father. "Earl, I intend to marry your daughter. I'd like your blessing."

Sarah gasped with delight and clapped her hands together.

"Well." Flynn's father rubbed his chin as if considering his answer. "That's really up to my daughter. I'm not sure she'll have you after what you've put her through over the years."

Sarah punched him lightly in the arm. "Earl."

"Well, he's not the easiest man to get along with."

"And you are?"

He shrugged.

"Answer him," Sarah insisted.

"You going to do right by her?" he asked Ace. "Take care of her? Because if you don't, I'll—"

"Dad!" Flynn laughed. "Enough."

She sobered when Ace drew her into his arms.

"I'll take care of her. Count on it." He spoke as if they were the only two people in the room. In the world. "You're everything to me, Flynn. Every time I see you, every time I kiss you, it's like falling in love all over again."

Her knees wobbled. If he'd proposed to her like that before, she'd have said yes.

"Say you'll marry me." He bent and brushed his lips across hers in the lightest, tenderest of kisses. "I'll ask you a hundred times, a thousand times, if that's what it takes."

"Yes. Yes, yes, *yes!*"

"Did you hear?" Sarah grabbed Flynn's father by the arm. "She accepted!"

"I heard, I heard." He pretended to scowl. The glimmer in his eyes gave him away.

Flynn paid them little attention. She was too preoccupied kissing her fiancé and letting him sweep her off her feet—literally.

Ace had scooped her into his arms and was twirling her in circles. The room was spinning when he finally put her down. Then he kissed her again, deeply and fully, and she realized it was Ace and their love, not the twirling, that made her dizzy.

"I can't wait to spend the rest of our lives together," she whispered in his ear.

"And here I thought you accepted my proposal in order to guarantee yourself a job when you finish school."

"What!" She squirmed.

He didn't release her, pinning her to him until she stopped protesting.

"Come on, Sarah," Flynn's father said. "Let's get out of here and have that dinner. I'm starving."

"We'll come with you," Ace said.

"Stay," Sarah said. "You have plans to make."

"I want to celebrate," Ace insisted. "And I can't think of a better place than the Number 1 Diner. Call the rest of the family. Tell them to meet us there. We'll make an announcement."

The place where it had all started just three short months ago.

That seemed entirely appropriate, Flynn thought as she and Ace walked arm in arm out the door and into their future.

EPILOGUE

"Mom, don't overdo it," Ace warned. "Slow down already."

"Stop fussing." His mother waved him away. "It's your wedding day. You should be thinking about your bride. Not me."

"My wife," he corrected, liking the sound of it. "And I am thinking about her."

His glance strayed to Flynn, who was huddled with Nora and Dinah. Her sister and brand-new sister-in-law were fawning over the diamond ring Ace had recently purchased and Flynn's dress, which had belonged to Ace's mother and was hastily altered to fit Flynn.

"She's beautiful," his mother said, linking her arm through his. "I'm glad you both finally came to your senses."

"She is beautiful." With Flynn for a mother, their baby—Ace was still hoping for a girl—couldn't be anything but gorgeous.

"Are you ready to cut the cake?"

"Almost." Ace wanted to spend just a few more minutes enjoying the reception from where he stood.

His mother and sister had done an amazing job, pulling the wedding together in just ten days. Though dark clouds gathered overhead, the weather had thankfully cooperated, and the ceremony went off without a hitch.

Ace and Flynn had chosen not to wait and opted for a simple civil ceremony in the Harts' spacious front yard. Red checkered cloths covered the tables, enough to accommodate the hundred and fifty guests in attendance. Paper flowers taped to the backs of chairs fluttered in the breeze. Children clambered on and over the bales of straw that had been arranged in a semicircle to create a makeshift altar.

Most of the guests were complaining of overeating. Blame the barbecue beef and chicken and the best coleslaw anyone had ever tasted. Flynn's father's secret recipe.

The day was almost perfect, and would be if not for the two empty chairs at the wedding party table.

Both Ace's brothers were absent. They still hadn't been able to locate Tuf. Neither had he called them. And Colt... Ace didn't know what to think.

His brother had promised to be at the wedding, was supposed to serve as Ace's best man. Only Colt hadn't come home last night, wasn't answering his cell phone and wasn't returning the countless messages Ace had left. Finally, an hour before the ceremony, Ace had asked his cousin Duke to stand in for him.

Colt had been stepping up the past week, lending Ace a hand with the work around the ranch. But now this. He'd evidently returned to his old ways.

Ace was angry and disappointed and frustrated. Mostly, he was hurt and sad. Today was his wedding day, the only one he intended to have, and his brothers had missed it.

"Hey, you two." Flynn strolled over to join Ace and his mother.

He couldn't immediately speak, his breath having

left his lungs in a soft rush. She had that effect on him, and he hoped it lasted forever.

Thoughts of his brothers fled. This was their day, his and Flynn's. They would enjoy every moment of it and let nothing interfere.

"Flynn," his mother said, "I was just asking Ace. Are you ready to cut the cake?"

"Thank you, Sarah, for everything you've done." Flynn hugged her. "I hope you'll let me return the favor."

"You already have. You're giving me my first grand-child."

"Would you like to come with Ace and I to the doctor's office next month? We're having another ultra-sound."

His mother's face positively glowed, and she grasped Flynn to her. "I would like that very much."

Flynn's father came over. He placed an affectionate hand on Sarah's shoulder. "Did I miss something?"

"I'm just being a sentimental fool."

"I think you're rather charming."

Ace almost did a double take. Was Earl flirting with his mother? A quick check with Flynn assured him she'd noticed something, too.

Well, his mother could do worse, if she was indeed interested in Earl. And Earl couldn't do any better than Ace's mother.

"When are you leaving?" Earl asked.

"Around six."

Ace and Flynn were spending four days at a luxury inn in Billings. He'd wanted to take her on a longer, more exciting honeymoon, but that would have to wait a while. Flynn had yet to finalize her schedule for school, which would start this fall, and Ace still had to move.

They were going to live in Earl's house. He'd generously offered to rent it to them at a reasonable rate. Eventually, when the loan Ace and his mother had taken out was paid off and Earl's land lease with the cattle company was at an end, Ace intended to buy the entire ranch from his father-in-law.

In the months to come he'd move up his vet practice to Earl's barn. For now, Ace was leaving it here, close to Midnight, the mares and the bucking stock.

Suddenly, thunder rumbled ominously overhead.

"Uh-oh." His mother peered at the sky with its ever darkening clouds. "We'd better hurry with the cake."

More photographs were snapped as Ace and Flynn stuffed cake into each other's mouths. The guests had barely finished eating when the skies opened up and let loose with a magnificent downpour.

People scrambled and scurried in a dozen different directions, carrying leftover food inside, collecting trash before it blew away and removing tablecloths and serving dishes.

Ace grabbed Flynn's hand and started running.

"Where are we going?" she gasped.

"To the barn."

"What about our guests? The gifts."

"Later."

Clothes soaked and their breath coming in bursts, they ducked into the barn and stood just inside the entrance, watching the rain come down and listening to it strike the roof with a mighty force.

Like the night Ace had kissed her in his truck outside the diner.

Flynn must have been remembering as well, for she grabbed the lapels of his Western-cut suit jacket and pulled him toward her. "Did I tell you how handsome you look today?"

"Did I tell you how much I love you?"

"Yes." She snuggled against him. "But you can say it again. I won't complain."

"I am without a doubt the luckiest guy in the world."

Wrapping her and their unborn child in his embrace, he kissed her. Their second one as husband and wife.

"Two down." He nuzzled her ear. "And a million or more to go."

* * * * *

We hope you enjoyed reading

DUSTY: WILD COWBOY

and

AIDAN: LOYAL COWBOY

by *New York Times* bestselling author
CATHY McDAVID

Both were originally **Harlequin®** series stories!

Discover more heartfelt tales of love, family, small towns and cowboys from the **Harlequin Western Romance** series. These contemporary romance stories are of everyday women finding love, becoming part of a family or community—or maybe starting a family of her own.

 HARLEQUIN®

Western Romance

Romance—the Western way!

Look for four *new* romances every month
from **Harlequin Western Romance**!

Available wherever books are sold.

www.Harlequin.com

HOTRCMDBPA0517

"You want to have my baby," Nick Monroe repeated slowly, leading the two saddled horses out of the stables.

Sage Lockhart slid a booted foot into the stirrup and swung herself up. She'd figured the Monroe Ranch was the perfect place to have this discussion. Not only was it Nick's ancestral home, but with Nick the only one living there now, it was completely private.

She drew her flat-brimmed hat straight across her brow. "An unexpected request, I know."

Yet, she realized as she studied him, noting that the color of his eyes was the same deep blue as the big Texas sky above, he didn't look all that shocked.

For he better than anyone knew how much she wanted a child. They'd grown quite close ever since she'd returned to Texas, to claim her inheritance from her late father and help her mother weather a scandal that had rocked the Lockhart family to the core.

She drew a deep, bolstering breath. "The idea of a complete stranger fathering my child is becoming increasingly unappealing." When they reached their favorite picnic spot, she swung herself out of the saddle and watched as Nick tied their horses to a tree.

Nick grinned, as if pleased to hear she was a one-man woman, at least in this respect.

He looked at her from beneath the brim of his hat. "Which is why you're asking me?" he countered in the rough, sexy tone she'd fallen in love with the first second she had heard it. "Because you know me?"

Sage locked eyes with him, not sure whether he was teasing her or not. One thing she knew for sure: there hadn't been a time since they'd first met that she *hadn't* wanted him.

"Or because," he continued flirtatiously, as he unscrewed the lid on his thermos, "you have a hankering for my DNA?"

Aware the only appetite she had now was not for food, she quipped, "How about both?"

Don't miss WANTED: TEXAS DADDY
by Cathy Gillen Thacker, available June 2017 wherever
Harlequin® Western Romance
books and ebooks are sold.

www.Harlequin.com

HARLEQUIN

Western Romance

ROMANCE—THE WESTERN WAY!

Save **$1.00**

on the purchase of ANY

Harlequin® Western Romance

book.

Redeemable at participating Walmart outlets.

Save $1.00

on the purchase of any Harlequin® Western Romance book.

Coupon valid until August 31, 2017.
Redeemable at participating Walmart outlets.
Limit one coupon per customer.

52614806

Canadian Retailers: Harlequin Enterprises Limited will pay the face value of this coupon plus 10.25¢ if submitted by customer for this product only. Any other use constitutes fraud. Coupon is nonassignable. Void if taxed, prohibited or restricted by law. Consumer must pay any government taxes. Void if copied. Inmar Promotional Services ("IPS") customers submit coupons and proof of sales to Harlequin Enterprises Limited, P.O. Box 3000, Saint John, NB E2L 4L3, Canada. Non-IPS retailer—for reimbursement submit coupons and proof of sales directly to Harlequin Enterprises Limited, Retail Marketing Department, 225 Duncan Mill Rd., Don Mills, ON M3B 3K9, Canada.

U.S. Retailers: Harlequin Enterprises Limited will pay the face value of this coupon plus 8¢ if submitted by customer for this product only. Any other use constitutes fraud. Coupon is nonassignable. Void if taxed, prohibited or restricted by law. Consumer must pay any government taxes. Void if copied. For reimbursement submit coupons and proof of sales directly to Harlequin Enterprises Limited, P.O. Box 880478, El Paso, TX 88588-0478, U.S.A. Cash value 1/100 cents.

5 65373 00076 2 (8100)0 12278

® and ™ are trademarks owned and used by the trademark owner and/or its licensee.

© 2017 Harlequin Enterprises Limited

HWRHOTRCOUP0517R